HITLER VERSUS ME

HITLER VERSUS ME

The Return of Bartholomew Bandy

Donald Jack

Canadian Cataloguing in Publication Data

Jack, Donald, 1924–
  Hitler versus me : the return of Bartholomew Bandy

(The Bandy papers ; v. 8)
ISBN 0-7710-4377-5

I. Title. II. Series: Jack, Donald, 1924–   . The Bandy papers ; v. 8.

PS8519.A3H57 1996   C813'.54   C96-930599-0   PR9199.3.J33H57 1996

Typesetting by M&S, Toronto
Printed and bound in Canada

The publishers acknowledge the support of the Canada Council and the Ontario Arts Council for their publishing program.

A Douglas Gibson Book

McClelland & Stewart Inc.
The Canadian Publishers
481 University Avenue
Toronto, Ontario
M5G 2E9

1 2 3 4 5   00 99 98 97 96

To Douglas M. Gibson, who was responsible for starting
The Bandy Papers, and so deserves everything he gets.

CONTENTS

PART 1

Looking a Bit Chilly

FOR ME THE WAR really started the morning that we made a wrong turn over Trenton, Ontario. We were on a cross-country navigation exercise from Camp Borden, the service training school sixty miles north of Toronto, droning along in an Avro Anson, high above a patchwork of grey woodland and white fields bordered by wiggly black snake fences.

My student, Bernard Greaves, was droning, too. "You're not a very good instructor, are you, sir?" he was saying.

"Whatjamean, not a very good instructor?"

"Falling asleep at the controls that way."

I turned to squint through the window at the flat white country-side. The snow, saturated with sun, reflected painfully into my haggard early-morning optics.

"You're supposed to be flying the aircraft," I said.

"As my instructor, you're still supposed to stay awake, you know," said Bernard in his posh public-school voice. He was among the first batch of English entrants to take service training in Canada.

"Well, I had a hard night," I mumbled.

"Yes, I heard you and the CO singing 'There Is a Tavern in the Town.' You'd obviously found it."

"Anyway, I wasn't asleep just now," I said. "I was consulting the instructor's manual." And indeed, the little red book was open on my lap . . . face down.

"And that's another thing," Bernard said, altering course slightly, "you never get the patter right. Not like Mr. Bruin. He learned every word in the patter book, just the way you instructors are supposed to. He always got it right. He knew exactly what to say. You always knew exactly where you were with Mr. Bruin, before he was killed."

"I'll have you know I was instructing before you were born," I said, glaring almost as hard as I was shivering.

The young whippersnapper merely emitted a sound like a bicycle valve. Nineteen years old, he had a baby face complete with rosy cheeks and moist, red, petulant lips. God knows how he had managed to earn the white flash in his blue-grey cap – he did not look like a pilot. Pilots were supposed to have firm jaws and dry lips. They were certainly not supposed to toss their heads irritably whenever I was around, the way Bernard did. In my opinion that was not an aircrew sort of mannerism.

But then, of course, he was the son of Air Vice-Marshal Greaves, chief of the RAF's Fighter Command. Which was why I also tended to indulge the boy, for Greaves was an old friend of mine.

I drew the leather flying coat closer around my shuddering thorax. God, it was cold. Panefully cold – the Avro Anson had more windows than a greenhouse, and every one of them leaked frigid air. And I was bored silly, this February of 1940. "Anyway," I continued, "I told them I wasn't cut out to be an instructor. I told them I only wanted to get over there and fight. But would they listen? Desperate need for instructors, that's all they could say. Much more valuable to the war effort as an instructor. I mean, it's such a waste of a precious resource – me. In case you don't know it, Bernard, I've had a great deal of fighting experience – even in wartime."

Bernard issued another bicycle-valve effect. "And that's another thing," he shouted over the soporific baritone of the engines. "You're always saying ridiculous things like that. Even in wartime, indeed.

"And that was long, long ago," he continued, with a quite unnecessary duplication of painful words. "You're much too old, now, for fighting. Why, you must be even older than my poor old pater up there in the far north."

"I am not. He's years older than me. I'm only forty-five."

"You look at least fifty-five. You have a face like the Nile Delta."

I glared again at Greaves – a priggish, repetitive youth if ever there was one. Impertinent, too. I would have given him a good telling off, had he not been so well-connected.

"And I hope," the brat added, "you don't think you're fooling me with that wig."

"Wig? Wig? What're you talking about?" I enquired, with a light laugh. "Wig?"

"You may fool the others, but not me. I saw it once, lying dead on your pillow."

"You did not."

"Yes, I did. That time I burst in to wake you up and tell you you were late for my lesson."

"Nonsense," I said. However, just in case he was right, I added sycophantically, "You – er – haven't mentioned this misunderstanding about the state of my scalp to anyone else, have you, Bernard?"

I was a bit sensitive about my bald acreage, you see. And I must say I was pretty relieved when Bernard replied testily that he had better things to do than gossip about my skimpy follicles, and that my secret was safe with him.

In fact, my very existence seemed to be a secret. When I walked into the Canadian recruiting centre at the Waldorf Astoria in New York last September, I had been received with cries of welcome, and excessive but nonetheless thoroughly well-deserved praise and flattery. The civilized and splendidly well-informed Canadians down there had identified me right away as one of the great aviators of the century. They had signed me up as a flight lieutenant, with the understanding that I would be zooming through the European cumulus in a Spitfire on the way to becoming an air marshal before you could say Adolf Shickelgruber. At least, that was my understanding.

But since then I'd become steadily more anonymous, and worse, unpromoted. Worst of all, I had been made an instructor. An instructor! And with a third-class rating, too. And that was what I had been doing for months – bloody instructing. The odd weekend pass to the fleshpots of Toronto was the highlight of my life. Toronto! That was how bad things were. And I was losing hope that I would ever reach a front-line squadron, no matter how badly I did the job.

At this point some of Bernard's words began to register. By holding my forehead steady and closing my eyes, I managed to review the conversation and isolate the important words. "Uh," I said, "what did you mean about pater being in the far north?"

"What?"

"You said something about your father being up in the far north."

"Did I? Yes, well, he is."

"Far north of where?"

"Canada, of course."

I sat up, forgetting to shiver. "Your father is over here?"

"He was going to come and see me at Camp Borden, but something came up," Bernard said peevishly.

"Whereabouts exactly is he?"

"I told you – in the far north – Ottawa."

I gaped. "The chief of Fighter Command is in Ottawa?!"

"He's staying with your prime minister. Didn't I mention it?" Bernard said, too innocently. "I only heard yesterday."

I sat back, staring through the windscreen. Lake Ontario was now in view, and soon we would be intersecting the shoreline. The lake was frozen surprisingly far from the shore, the ice partly decorated with snow. The wind had patterned the snow into graceful designs swirling over the grey ice.

Bernard aligned the nose of the aircraft with a straight stretch of Highway 2 as it reached the first scattered houses and farms of Trenton. Soon we would be over the air base, which was where we were to turn for the flight back to Camp Borden.

I reached over for the map on which Bernard had plotted the

course, folded it neatly, and stuck it in my pocket. "Turn about ten degrees to port, will you, Bernard?" I said.

"What?"

I put my hands on the co-pilot's control column and did it for him.

"Time to go home, is it?" Bernard asked.

"Actually, Bernard," I said in my famous whine, "I'm so impressed with your work that I've decided to give you some VFR practice. I want you to see if you can reach a certain destination by visual means alone."

"What destination?"

"Oh, I don't know. Let's say . . . Ottawa?"

"Oh, no!" Bernard said; and grabbing his own stick, he turned the wheel until we were pointing back at Camp Borden.

"Whatjamean, oh no?" I said, firmly grasping the dual control and forcing us eastward again. "It's not much more than an hour's flight."

"I know what you're up to," he shouted, wrenching again. "Well, I'm not getting into trouble for your sake!" he cried, forcing the plane into a steep bank in an effort to head homeward.

I turned the banking turn to my own advantage, forcing the aircraft eastward again. "We have to go to Ottawa!" I shouted. "It's vital!"

"I'm not going!" he hauled.

"Be reasonable, dammit!" I wrenched.

"We're due back at Camp Borden for lunch, and that's where I'm going to be!" Bernard screamed, yanking, twisting, and dragging at the controls until the Anson was flung about as if caught in a thunderhead. The struggle continued for quite a while, Bernard even embracing the stick with both arms, hoping no doubt to bring his shoulder muscles into play as well as his hands and arms – and even his legs, for he was now jamming on the left rudder as if he thought that would help. But I was embracing my steering wheel as well, grunting and straining in an effort to prevent him from turning tail in the face of a little risk, challenge, and private enterprise. Meanwhile, the lumbering Anson continued to clodhop all over the sky, losing quite a bit of altitude in the process.

"Let go, you cad," Bernard screamed. He actually said that, and not in any satirical sense. He seemed quite genuinely indignant. "I'm not going hundreds of miles off course just so you can further your rotten career," he cried. "Let go the stick, I'm flying this plane, not you, you rotten . . . !"

But I was stronger than him, and as the sun was suddenly blotted out by a newly arrived weather front, he finally gave up. Adopting a mulish expression, he announced that he would not be responsible for the consequences of such a flagrant dereliction of duty and that he was not going to fly the aircraft any longer. Whereupon he folded his arms and sulked the rest of the way.

As if in keeping with Bernard's mood, the weather rapidly deteriorated from then on. The brilliant sun had long since disappeared by the time we landed at Uplands, and I got another reminder of what a Canadian winter could be like. Various winds, which had rendezvoused in Winnipeg and been despatched across a thousand miles of frozen terrain, were all converging on Uplands aerodrome as I stepped out of the Anson; winds which had collected all sorts of sharp materials en route – sleet, freezing rain, pieces of ice honed on an arctic grinding wheel, icicles whittled to a needle point, aqueous daggers and crystallized bayonets, discarded razorblades, shards of glass, and so forth. I felt the effect keenly; my Civil War adventures in Spain had left my blood as thin as mess oxtail soup.

Bernard refused to speak to me until after I had phoned the CO at Camp Borden to explain that we had taken a wrong turn. Even then he only spoke because he had to. "What did he say?" he demanded.

Actually the CO had said very little. I had been out with him the previous evening, and he was not keen on listening to my loud voice. "Well, good luck with the air marshal," he husked. "But try and get back sometime this week, okay, Bart?"

Frankly I think he was hoping I would succeed in getting to Europe. Though friendly enough, he was not overly enthusiastic about having a middle-aged instructor on the staff. It lowered the tone, somehow. Instructors were supposed to be young, keen, dedicated. I looked like Old Father Time's grumpy tutor.

"Well, what did he say?" Bernard repeated.

"Who, the CO? Oh, I don't think he'll be too hard on you, Bernard."

Agitatedly he removed his leather helmet and smoothed his Brylcreamed locks. "Why should he be hard on me at all?" he squeaked. "It wasn't my fault!"

"Actually I said it was. I said you had an urgent appointment in Ottawa at the VD clinic."

"*What?*"

"Don't worry, the CO was quite understanding. Well, *fairly* understanding."

Bernard was still looking a bit pale as I negotiated a ride into town with a flight sergeant from the admin office. "You didn't *really* say that, did you?" he bleated.

By the time the car drew up outside the aerodrome admin office he was shouting at me again. But I couldn't hear him, as I was busily adjusting my earmuffs.

Rather rudely, he lifted up one of the muffs and hollered in my ear, "You're hoping to barge in on my father, aren't you? And browbeat him into getting you operational."

"Browbeat? I never browbeat."

"Well, you can do it without me! I'll wait here until you get back from town."

"Don't you want to see your old man?"

"Not with you! And don't worry, when I get back I'll tell them the truth. And I'll tell them I never want to fly with you again!"

I couldn't understand his turning down the opportunity to see his father after all these months. I mean, *I* was looking forward to seeing Cyril Greaves, and I wasn't even related to him.

Gaining admission to the prime minister's residence was to prove the least of my problems. It was quite easily accomplished by an old friend of mine, Jim Boyce. You will, I am sure, remember Boyce, the WWI naval flyer, political campaign manager, and opportunist lecher. It was my good fortune as well as his that he had once again been taken aboard the Department of External Affairs. He had served in the Department twice previously and been thrown out on each occasion, the first time for seducing the wife of his department head, and the second time when his new department head discovered that he had seduced the wife of his old department head.

Now the exigencies of war had brought him back again, to do a job he was well suited to, that of carousing with newsmen, otherwise known as briefing the press. Other duties included delivering "Summaries" to the prime minister's staff. What they were summaries of I didn't ask. All I was interested in was his regular access to the official residence.

Over an early lunch at the press club I managed to allay his suspicions as to my motives. "You're sure it's just this air marshal guy you want to meet?" he asked. "Nothing to do with the PM? I mean, if you're going to bugger the chief all over again . . ."

"I assure you most sincerely," said I sincerely, "that I just want to see my old friend Cyril Greaves. He's definitely staying at Laurier House, the PM's place, is he?"

"Yes, I checked. Anyway, the PM isn't home. He's busy borrowing money in New York at the moment," Boyce said, watching me carefully to gauge whether my reaction was to be one of relief or disappointment.

It was relief, genuine relief. I had locked hornswoggles several times with Mr. Mackenzie King in the past, and I saw no advantage whatsoever in reminding him that I was still available for misunderstandings and other contretemps.

"In that case I think I can get you a billet there beside your old comrade-in-arms. I assume you're staying overnight? The town's pretty full and it's tough to get a hotel room. But listen" – he treated me to a manly leer – "I happen to know the housekeeper at Laurier House, and since the PM's out of town I'm sure I can fix it for an old friend of the air marshal."

"You'll get me a room in the residence? That's great. Thank you, Jim."

"Why not?" Boyce said cheerfully. "It'll give us a chance to catch up. You can tell me all about how you mistakenly joined the wrong side in the Spanish Civil War."

Suddenly his face turned mournful. He reached across the table-cloth and held my wrist briefly. Lowering his voice in the already hushed dining room, he said, "I heard what happened to Sigridur, Bart. I'm very sorry."

I nodded and looked at him gratefully; and also a little curiously. At the age of fifty, Boyce was even more homely than he'd been in his flaming youth. He really was the ugliest man west of the Richibucto, the Miramichi, and the Kouchibouguac. Like me, he'd lost much of his hair, but the fool had done nothing about it, so his pate was shamelessly nude from the middle of his forehead to an unseemly bump at the back of his head. His large brown eyes were as stupid-looking as ever, quite bovine in their dull, melting curiosity, though the brain behind them was, of course, far from inactive. To round off the picture of an Ottawa Valley Cyrano, he had a lumpy nose that overhung a set of Prussian-blue jowls, the whole backed by a complexion that looked as if it needed a good scrubbing with Snibbo, the country's favourite toilet cleaner.

Yet he had often made me feel quite jealous; for despite being a physiognomical eyesore he had always been astonishingly success-ful with the ladies. I think it was because he could make like a Franklin stove whenever he met a pretty woman, radiating enough warmth and sympathy to melt the stoutest chastity belt. I could testify that on one occasion at a cocktail party in Ottawa's Château Laurier, he talked an MP's wife into inviting him to her room upstairs only two minutes after meeting her for the first time. *Two minutes.*

We drove along Laurier Avenue until we reached the massive yellow brick house where the PM hung his hat. He had lived there for so long – actually since Lady Laurier gave it to him in 1921 – that most Canadians had forgotten that Laurier House was actually a private residence. Now, outside it, a red-nosed Mountie stood on

guard. He clumped his frozen feet and waved us through with nary
a glance at Boyce's ID card.

It was perhaps just as well that we hadn't had to stop the car
at the gates. It might not have been able to move off again, for the
driveway was glassy with packed snow. As it was, Boyce's big 1939
Chrysler shimmied like your sister Kate as it whined up the short
driveway between the six-foot banks of snow.

The parking lot at the side of the great rambling house with its
tall mansard roof had been only partially cleared. There were just
two spaces available. One was signposted for the Prime Minister, the
other was occupied by an anonymous black Ford. An aircraftsman
wearing a leather jerkin over his blue battledress sat in the driver's
seat. He had the engine running, presumably to keep him warm in
the below-zero temperature.

Cheekily, Boyce parked in the PM's slot – "What the hell – he
isn't due back for two or three days." As we walked round to the
front door, our boots squeaking in the snow, I couldn't help noticing that a sort of runway had been created in the deep snow in the
side garden. There was about a hundred feet of cleared space three
or four feet wide, with patches of yellow grass showing through
here and there.

"That's the chief's walkway, when he's in residence," Boyce
explained.

"Walkway?"

"The PM likes to take Little Pat for a walk even in the depths of
winter, so he has the gardeners clear that channel in the snow
where he can talk to his mother."

"Ah," I said as if I knew all about it. "To Little Pat."

He snorted something that sounded like "Pat the dog." I looked
around, in vain. "Are you telling me to pat a dog?"

"No, no," he said angrily. "Pat *is* a dog."

This was just as baffling.

"That's not like you, Jim," I said reproachfully, "calling the Prime
Minister's old mother a dog. I mean, she may not look . . ."

He interrupted me with a wave of his hand.

"I didn't call her a dog. Anyway, she's dead."

"Little Pat is dead?"

"No, his *mother* is dead."

"He takes his dead mother for a walk? What does he do, drag her behind as he trudges up and down his walkway?"

"Oh, Christ," Boyce said, "I'd forgotten what you were like. Let's start again. He takes his dog for a walk out there, and while he's doing so he talks to his dead mother. That is, he confers with her as if she were still alive."

"Ah."

"I thought you'd know that," Boyce said impatiently. "Everyone knows that. It's his most closely guarded secret." And before I could get any further clarification he had entered the house without knocking.

A positive retinue of people drifted into the hall as we removed our coats. First there was a pooch, which presumably was Little Pat, though nobody thought of introducing us. I was cautious at first, for I didn't get on well with animals. So I regarded this one, a yappy-looking Scottish terrier, quite warily as it waddled over. However, after an apathetic sniff, it retreated and sat down near the stairs, looking a bit fed up.

Next there was a butler, a portly chap bulging out of a cutaway coat, who seemed to be on good terms with Boyce, followed almost immediately by someone who was not. This was a short, sturdy-looking man with horn-rimmed glasses and wearing a plain black suit. He greeted Boyce with a mere two degrees of cranial declination. "You might at least remove your galoshes before you come in," he said to Boyce in a margarine voice: rather soft and oily.

"That's very true," said Boyce, as thoughtfully as if the other had made an observation of some profundity. Waiting until I was balanced on one leg, trying to remove my flying boots, Boyce introduced me. "Mr. Slatter, this is Flight Lieutenant Bandy, he'll be staying overnight. Bart, this is Mr. Hinckley Slatter. He's Pensions and Disabled."

Wearing one boot I hopped forward and took Mr. Slatter's hand and pressed it tenderly. "I'm so sorry to hear that," I said. "Hunting accident, was it?"

"What?"

"Mauled by a polar bear, were you? Trampled by a moose?" And, when Mr. Slatter continued to look blank: "Or perhaps you've been disabled since birth?"

"I mean he's with Disabilities," Boyce said. "Disabilities, Pensions, Redundancies, and National Security."

"Security?"

"I am presently acting as chief of security here," Mr. Slatter announced huffily. "Eyes and ears," he said, tapping his temple knowingly. "On wartime alert night and day."

"Yeah, him and the Mountie on the gate," Boyce said, and as Slatter gave him a disdainful look, he turned happily to the butler. "How's things, Arnie?" he said breezily. "Is *le grand fromage* around?"

"Sir?"

"The visitor. Air Marshal Whosit?"

"Ah. He's in his room, Mr. Boyce."

"Fine. Could you tell the visitor that he has a visitor. He'll know him – Bartholomew Bandy."

As the butler proceeded upstairs, a pleasant-looking lady in a black dress entered the hall, and was introduced as the housekeeper. My good luck became clear as Boyce put an arm round her and squeezed her close, murmuring sweet somethings in her lughole, his hand perilously close to her starboard bust cup. Mr. Slatter stood there blinking and scowling. "I suppose we could prepare a room at the back for the flight lieutenant," he said coldly, "but it's most irregular. Still, if you swear it's a matter of national importance . . ."

"Sure is," Boyce said, winking at me, as I got down to wrestling once again with my second boot.

At which point the big cheese himself came lurching down the staircase. He was wearing a hat that blazed with gold braid, and was followed by the butler and an LAC. The airman was struggling with three large suitcases.

I came ostentatiously to attention in my stocking feet, boot in hand, and beamed all over my face at the sight of Air Vice-Marshal Cyril Greaves. The sight was not exactly beauty unadorned. In fact, old Greaves looked even odder and more lugubrious than I remembered him, with his artificial lower teeth – the originals had been extracted in a crash-landing – and his even more artificial-looking upper teeth, which were genuine.

He nodded distractedly in my direction – "Be with you in a moment, Bandy" – before turning to Mr. Slatter, and murmuring at him. I certainly didn't mind waiting a minute or two for my old friend Cyril, who would do anything for me. He had known and admired me from the moment in 1918 when I fell out of his aircraft. (He thought I had gallantly done it on purpose to test an experimental parachute. And I had been shamelessly exploiting his high opinion of me ever since.)

Mr. Slatter, looking important, wheeled on the butler and ordered him to fetch the air vice-marshal's coat. Whereupon the butler nodded imperiously at the housekeeper. And she, dragging herself away from Boyce, went to fetch the coat, which was three feet away.

As for the LAC, he was busily trying to open the front door with his foot so as not to let go of the luggage. He finally managed it and staggered out, admitting waves of icy air into the mansion.

I dropped the boot, saluted the air vice-marshal, strode softly forward, and shook his hand so vigorously that his hat fell off and rolled importantly across the floor. I was expecting him to flatter me unmercifully when he said, "I'm terribly sorry, Bart, but I can't stop now. Got a train to catch." And, reperching the hat on his rapidly greying hair, he dived into his epauletted greatcoat. "Been recalled."

"What?" I said, staring at Cyril's strange teeth, which stuck out from below his great, bushy, mournful moustache.

"Summoned back to London. Can't stop," he said, already halfway to the door, which Mr. Slatter, with an oily smile, hastened to open for him.

"You're leaving?"

"Sorry, Bandy," he said, reverting for a moment to his usual humble posture in my presence. Lowering his voice, he murmured regretfully, "I know what you want, Bart, but I suspect I'm not going to be fighter chief much longer. Can't help you. Sorry." And he turned and, uttering a hurried goodbye to the others, swept out of the door.

Feeling like death painted on a wall, as they say in Iceland – in Icelandic, of course – I prepared to turn in for the night. I had switched off the light and drawn back the bedroom curtains so the false dawn would help wake me in the morning for an angry flight back to Camp Borden. I was just turning away from the window when I glimpsed a dark shape moving cautiously through the snow in the garden.

For a moment I thought it was a grizzly bear, but then recognized it as a bulky man wearing a fur coat and cap. He was making his way along the back wall of the house where the snow was only knee-deep.

Well, it was no business of mine. It wasn't my house. Why should I care if Mackenzie bloody King got burglarized? Let that pompous fellow from Security and Disabilities handle it, why should I stumble about out there in the freezing compartment that was Ottawa, doing his damn job for him.

Anyway, it was a guard, probably, making his rounds . . . a furtive guard, sidling close to the back wall of the mansion. . . .

I tell you, it had nothing to do with me! So I closed the curtains to blot out the sight. Then I opened them. Then I closed them again, lost my balance, and knocked over a fine example of a ribbon-backed Chippendale. Or maybe it was a Hepplewhite. I started to get dressed, now as annoyed at myself as I had been all evening with Cyril Greaves, the swine.

Annoyed? I had been seething with indignation all evening over Cyril's refusal to use his influence on my behalf. Dammit, Cyril was supposed to think the world of me. For twenty years he had been unable to deny me anything, such was his respect for my abilities and his awe at my derring-do. Like the time I was sent on a mission to the British protectorate of Iraq, and, reaching Egypt, found myself unable to carry on to Baghdad. It was Cyril Greaves, then chief of staff to the AOC, Middle East, who had come to my rescue, laying down the red carpet, providing me with special transport and with every RAF facility he could lay his big, hairy hands on.

Now, just when I needed him most, he had allowed his position as Chief of Fighter Command to be undermined by his enemies, and had thus utterly failed me. To help him pull himself together I had even accompanied him to the cathedral-like railway station opposite the Château Laurier, reasoning with him all the way. "Darn it, Cyril, you got to get me out of instructing and into Spitfires," I kept saying in reasonable tones. "I mean, all you have to do is pull rank on some Air Ministry scribe or Pharisee. And do it quickly, Cyril – please? You know, while your reputation is still intact and you still have some influence left," I wheedled.

I was still cajoling in this fashion when the train to Halifax via Montreal pulled out of the station. I nearly broke a leg jumping down onto the platform. To recover, I had been forced to detour through two or three taverns on my way back to the residence, where, to avoid any unjust accusations of being under the weather, I had lurched straight to bed, fortunately without meeting a soul, even though the house seemed sort of crowded, somehow; you know, bustling, as if an important development had . . . developed.

Now, two or three hours later, I was downstairs again, and since Eskimo carvings had not yet made it to the south I was bearing a candlestick as a handy weapon; complete with candle, as a matter of fact, as it would not come unstuck.

When I finally got my flying boots on again and reached the solid oak front door I found it unlocked. *Tsk-tsk*, I thought, deploring the almost total lack of domestic security that the Prime Minister was receiving . . . except, of course, that he wasn't here, was he, he was busy putting the country in hock to the Yanks.

All the same, this failure even to lock the front door was carrying trust in the good intentions, honesty, apathy, etc., of your typical Canadian citizen a bit far, not to mention the danger from filthy foreign spies. I don't mention that particular danger, because everybody knew that Canada was much too nice to have foreign enemies.

I was still *tsk*ing as I drew my flying coat from the cupboard, noisily fought off the wire coathanger, and thrust myself into the leather folds. I then stole silently into the night, brandishing the candlestick.

The icy air hit me an almost physical blow. God, I'd forgotten how cold Ottawa could be in winter. Nevertheless, I forced myself to wait until my eyes adjusted to the night; though a quarter moon was providing quite a bit of illumination.

As the shadowy figure had been heading for the left side of the house I proceeded to creep in that direction; or rather to flounder, for the snow was much deeper along that side, wind-moulded into swirling silvery banks that sparkled in the moonlight.

As I approached the corner of the mansion I became aware of a murmuring voice. Surprised – surely burglars or assassins weren't supposed to talk to themselves, at least not on duty – I peered round the corner – and there was the intruder.

Bundled up in a fur coat and cap, he was walking along the above-mentioned trench – the channel specially snow-ploughed for the PM's nocturnal perambulations.

The nerve of the guy – strolling along the Prime Minister's special walkway in the PM's very own garden, sauntering along the channel as if he owned all the snow in sight. I felt quite indignant on behalf of our Prime Minister. I mean, Lady Laurier hadn't made him a gift of Sir Wilfrid's old home so that anyone who felt like it could wander through the yard.

Admittedly I didn't much care for William Lyon Mackenzie King. He had behaved in a very mean way toward me in the past over the misunderstanding with my plane and his place at Kingsmere when I hadn't actually hit him with the plane, for heaven's sake. All the same, I felt that the cheek of this intruder could not go unpinched. I'd subdue him and then call for RCMP assistance, perhaps with a brief line or two from "Rose Marie."

Accordingly, high-stepping it through the snow like a nervous Colt (or Smith and Wesson), I moved forward with the candlestick at the ready. My arm was raised and I was just about to clobber the fur-clad interloper on his fur-clad head when I heard him say, "I wish you were here to help me decide on this conscription problem, Mother."

I froze, literally and metaphorically. It was not just the words. It was the voice. A distinctly unmellifluous voice, all too well remembered from crackling radio broadcasts and several catastrophic personal encounters in the past.

And I had very nearly created another with the candlestick, concussing Canada's Prime Minister.

Slowly, heart whacking against hard-breathing ribs, I looked back to see if it was possible to retreat, using the same holes in the snow that had brought me this far, but I didn't see how I was going to manage it without attracting his attention. I suppose he had failed to hear my flounderings until now because he had been talking to himself and moving away along his channel. But any moment now he would be turning back, and it was too late to fall into step behind him like the back half of a pantomime horse. I sank slowly into the thigh-deep snow at the side of the walkway until only my toupee was showing. And once again I heard him talking to his mother. Just the way Jim Boyce had described it. Our Prime Minister really did talk to his dead mother, asking her advice, confiding, conferring, concocting. He was doing it right now, soliciting her opinion on the vexed issue of whether or not to introduce conscription so as to provide a more reliable supply of recruits for the war. It was an issue that was already beginning to strain relations between French Canadians and the rest of the country, and Mr. King had been struggling to find an answer that would not endanger his political support in Quebec.

Only now he was saying some very strange things to his deceased mom. For after discussing conscription with her at some length as he perambulated up and down under the quarter moon, I distinctly heard him say, "No, I must be firm about this, you know. Just because I used to let you into my bed doesn't mean I have to keep on doing it. Yes, I know you always liked sleeping with me, but . . . and after all, you have a nice, comfy place of your own, you know."

Mackenzie King slept with his mother? Or vice versa? My face grew so hot with embarrassment that the snow began to sizzle around it and melt into my flying boots. Good God. Good God. I knew his political alliances had made for strange bedfellows and that politics in Ottawa were always being described as incestuous, but this . . . A Prime Minister who actually . . . I could hardly bring himself to complete the thought.

"Besides," I heard him say, "you've got fleas."

Fleas?

Slowly I rose out of the snow in order to obtain a proper view of his walkway, which revealed that he had a dog with him. The same Scotch terrier that had so apathetically sniffed me in the hall earlier this evening.

It was waddling behind the PM as he paced back and forth. Though even as I watched, it gave up and plopped its haunches onto the scraped ground, and gazed – kind of resentfully, it seemed to me – at its master as he turned back once more.

"Come along, Pat," said the PM. "I want to ask your advice about whether we should ever consider a raid on the French coast." But the little dog continued to sit there and stare after him.

So it appeared that our Prime Minister talked to his dog. Oh, well, why not? If he chatted intimately to his dead mother, why not to his pooch? Why not to the heaps of stone he kept putting together to create a garden of architectural ruins up there at his place in Kingsmere? Why not to this very candlestick in my hand? Why not to –

"*Who's there?*"

I started as Mr. King's fearful voice rang through the crystalline air. He had seen me at last. I crunched to my feet and spoke up quickly to allay his fears. Never the most courageous of men, he was already starting to retreat along his little ravine, darting appealing glances at his dog and making encouraging gestures with his hand in the hope that it would go for my throat.

"Ah, good evening, Prime Minister," I cried as I floundered forward, making reassuring noises to the effect that I was merely his guest, the chap his staff had so generously offered to put up for the night until he could get back to his nationally important work at Camp Borden.

"Oh, yes," he said, nodding, still a little nervously, but now gesturing to Little Pat to hold back from a ferocious attack. "We try to do our best for our servicemen. You're an aviator, I gather?"

What a relief. He hadn't recognized me yet, although he was looking at me keenly. To postpone the moment for as long as possible I kept my face in shadow, and tried to disguise the voice that had long ago caused him to burst most of the tiny blood vessels in his pudgy face.

"I suppose you – ah – heard me talking to myself," he said, starting to walk again. "Just a little habit of mine."

"Nothing wrong with that, sir," I said heartily, falling into step beside him. "Do it myself all the time. Though I couldn't help overhearing a little of what you were saying, sir, about conscription," I continued, trying to sound thoroughly sycophantic and managing it very well. "That sure is a thorny problem, isn't it, sir?"

"You're a volunteer, I suppose?" he asked.

At which point opportunism reared its ugly head, suitably disguised as patriotism. As we strolled over the scraped yellow grass and shiny patches of packed snow I said, "Yes, sir. And darned anxious to get into the fray, sir, to defend democracy against the forces of evil and corruption, sir."

Hold it, Bandy. Beginning to employ an English accent. Often did that when nervous.

Also, it might be better not to mention corruption. It was the corruption of his government that I had challenged back in the Twenties, and that had led to his driving me out of the country. "At the moment, though," I continued, "I feel I'm wasted at Camp Borden, you know, as an instructor. It's just that I've proved myself in combat many times, sir, and feel I could contribute far more to Canada and the war effort in a front-line squadron, sir. Now if you could just see your way to dropping a line to the Minister of Militia and Defence – "

"Haven't I met you before, Lieutenant?" he interrupted, pausing to squint at me. "You sound rather familiar."

"Oh, no, sir," quoth I, dropping my voice an octave or two. "I wouldn't dream of being familiar with you, sir."

"H'm. Incidentally, how do you feel about that subject — conscription?" he asked abruptly.

"Ah. Ah." I made a show of giving the subject a great deal of thought and even cogitation. "Well, sir, it seems to me that when the first flush of enthusiasm for overseas adventure dies down in the bosoms of our splendid Canadian youth to be replaced by rather more normal considerations of self-interest and self-preservation, conscription will become necessary if we are to fulfil our obligations to our allies, and thus guarantee Canada a principal role in the postwar era so as to obtain valuable and substantial commercial advantages over our competitors."

What the Archangel Gabriel was I talking about? I still had no idea, even after I had concluded with the words, "On the other hand, of course, as Prime Minister for — er — so many years, you are well aware that there are political considerations to be . . . uh, considered."

"Yes," King grunted gloomily.

"But I'm sure something can be worked out," I said heartily. "It may not be necessary. Conscription if necessary, you know, but not necessarily conscription?"

Mr. King dribbled to a halt and stared at his dog, who was still sitting there at the end of the channel looked bored stiff.

"Conscription if Necessary, but Not Necessarily Conscription," the PM mused, adding some capital letters. "That's very interesting, Mr. . . . ?"

"Bandy," I supplied before I could stop myself.

He stared up at me from beneath bushy eyebrows. His eyes widened. Then he nodded slowly: "Yes . . ." he muttered. "Of course. Bandy."

I didn't say anything but contented myself with twisting myself despairingly into the shape of a gibbet.

To my astonishment I heard him mutter, "Yes, well, that's all in the past, isn't it? I won't even ask what you're doing with my

candlestick, or even the candle stuck in it. Perhaps you're a Roman
Catholic – like so many of my fine Liberal supporters. Still, all we're
interested in now is defeating the common enemy, isn't that so,
Bandy?"

Daring to hope I said, "And . . . and if you could send me to
Europe I could help do that, sir."

"If that's what you really want, Bandy, to be sent to Europe, I
don't see why not. For old time's sake," he added, causing my jaw
to fall and shatter on the ground into a thousand fragments of
canine teeth, incisors, premolars, bicuspids, and the jawbone of an
ass. Calling Little Pat to heel he set off for the house, looking surprisingly cheerful.

Floundering back to the house afterwards, I fell over the man I'd
observed slinking along the back wall of the house. Like me, he had
crept close to the PM's walkway, and had been listening from a
similar hole burrowed in the snow.

I'd been so distracted by the discovery that the Prime Minister
had returned to the house during my absence that I'd thought no
more about the figure glimpsed from the bedroom window. I guess
that subconsciously I'd assumed that the furry PM and the mysterious furry figure were one and the same.

The crouching man uttered a Slav epithet, and lurched away. I
made a grab for him, but succeeded only in wrenching a handful
of fur from his coat (which must have been in scurvy shape to have
lost so much fur so readily) and then he was gone. There was no
sign of the Mountie supposedly on guard. My God, did the Force
have no sense of tradition?

It wasn't until I was in the house showing them the handful of
fur that it occurred to me that the man had sworn in Russian.

I described him as best I could to Mr. Slatter, but he knew all
about him. "Oh, him," he said, polishing his glasses. "He's from the
Soviet Embassy. He's always hanging around. We checked up on
him once, but the Embassy explained that if their man really
was hanging around various Canadian institutions, it was merely a

manifestation of their Soviet admiration for all things Canadian.
They also said their man was a bit eccentric – he was from the
Cypher section, I seem to recall.

"Perfectly harmless," Mr. Slatter concluded, resuming his horn-
rims and spreading his arms. "I mean, what possible interest could
they have in our Canadian affairs, eh?"

STILL CHILLY

ONE OF THE CANADIAN pilots had been for a walk along the Bournemouth promenade. His hands and face returned to the hotel in shades of purple and turkeycock.

"Jeez, is it always this cold in March?" said he in shuddering tones.

"Cold?" I scoffed. "If you think this is cold, just wait 'til summer."

There was a small fire in the lounge: numerous lumps of wet coal and a glow worm. I was huddled closest to it on the pretence of protecting the fire from the fierce draughts and helping it to draw.

"First time I was in England," I informed the restless throng, "I was sent to Salisbury Plain. It was so cold that lumberjacks shot themselves in droves. And that was in August."

"And there isn't a damn thing to do here," another pilot observed, "except stand around in pubs in damp battledress, steaming like fish."

It was certainly true that Bournemouth in wartime was a trifle deficient in entertainment value. The beaches were deserted, the arcades boarded up, the pier closed off, and even the sea seemed listless. Meanwhile the seaside landladies had been recruited into the knitting corps, on behalf of the British army that was sheltering in the lee of the unbreachable French defences known as the Maginot Line. The inactivity in the town was matched by the torpidity of the war. Militarily, hardly anything was happening except for the deadly pamphlets that the RAF was hurling at the cowering enemy.

"Do you think there'll ever be any real fighting?" Merv asked.

"It's becoming increasingly evident that the Germans are real-izing that their situation is hopeless," I pronounced. "They will soon sue for peace, don't you worry."

"You mean we'll never get into action, sir?"

The respectful "sirs" which dotted these queries were certainly a nice change from young Greaves's impertinences. Unfortunately they were a tribute to my advanced age, as well as to the depth of my knowledge, perception, and experience.

"No need to address me as 'sir,' lads," I said with a democratic nod or two. "I'm not one to pull rank. I'm just a flight lieutenant – though of course that will soon change, as soon as they realize who they're dealing with."

Altogether there were eleven newly qualified pilots in our group, none of them more than twenty years old. With my time-beaten face and mature manner, I was a distinct oddity, not just because I seemed pretty old to be a pilot but because of various rumours about my past.

When one of them began to ask questions on that very subject, my chequered history, I thought it was about time to demonstrate some leadership qualities, so they'd know the sort of person they were dealing with. I sprang to my feet and speaking firmly and authoritatively said, "See here, boys, something must be done immediately about this danged fire, especially as this is inspection morning, and we want to impress the billeting officer with our famed Canadian know-how and improvisational ability. Now, I happen to have considerable experience in overcoming the natural tendency of British fireplaces to discourage heat of any kind. The first thing you have to do, gentlemen, is to help it to draw. This is accomplished by holding a sheet of newspaper across the opening of the fireplace – here," I said, pointing to the fireplace in case they hadn't noticed it. "Whereupon the amplified draught from the chimney does the rest. So, George, go and fetch said sheet of news-paper and bring it to me immediately."

"You already have it, sir," said George Goodwin, a cherry-cheeked youth.

"What?"

"There was only one newspaper this morning and I saw you stuffing it under your shirt and down your pants, to keep warm."

"Ah. Ah," I said, nodding. "Right. Right. Well, then we'll have to use something else," I said; and, glaring around authoritatively to ensure their fullest attention, I left the room.

In a hurry to get back to the "guest lounge" while I still had the men's attention and, may I say it in all modesty, their respect, I rummaged quickly through the cupboard under the stairs and found a large rag. I returned with it, and immediately demonstrated how it should be done by holding the rag over the fireplace opening and blotting out the miserable view of hissing coals.

After a minute or two it worked beautifully. A roaring sound arose as the draught from the chimney increased tenfold, and a red glow showed through the rag. At the same time I continued to chat in an easy social fashion to the young pilots.

"You're not really serious about flying Spits, are you, sir?" George Goodwin asked.

"'Course. Just because I'm approaching middle age – "

"Approaching? He's overshot it," someone mumbled.

"I heard that!" I said, as one of the lads kept pointing at the fireplace and trying to say something.

"Surely your reflexes must be shot to hell, by now."

"They are not. They're as good as they ever were."

"You mean you always were kind of slow, sir?"

"Listen here, George, I'll put you on charge for dumb insolence if there's any more of that," I said stoutly.

"But sir," another pilot officer chipped in, "George's insolence wasn't dumb at all – I heard it quite plainly. Didn't you hear it, Roge?"

"Yes, I distinctly heard George being insolent. He wasn't being dumb at all."

"I guess the flight lieutenant is getting deaf in his old age. You're a bit hard of hearing, aren't you, sir?" another of the little swines asked, bellowing into my earhole.

They all laughed like drains and I realized that I, who used to discomfit, was now the discomfitee. Could it possibly be that I was growing pompous in my old – in my maturity?

To make matters worse, I was now coughing like an old man; you know, a bit rheumy and hacking. But then I realized there was a cause other than decrepitude for the respiratory uproar. The rag over the fireplace was smoking something chronic. I had failed to notice how oily it was. It was certainly oleaginous enough to be sending out billows of madder brown smoke which had already filled the lounge and was wafting out into the lobby and dining room. It was so dense that the pilots were having difficulty in finding an exit. They were beating at the dark clouds and smut with waving arms, now coughing and retching in an elderly fashion themselves.

By now the cloth was smouldering so badly that I could not possibly run outside with it and in the process pollute the entire ground floor of the hotel. Unfortunately, the alternative, of dropping the rag into the fireplace so as to consume it on the now thoroughly excited coals, was worse. Bursting into flames, the rag poured more smoke than ever into the lounge, except now it was a dense black colour that reduced visibility to the length of your traditional horsewhip.

But the restricted visibility was not quite enough to conceal a view of the billeting officer and his important guest from London. Seeing the clouds of smoke issuing from the lounge, they had unwisely rushed in to investigate, and were now retching, wheezing, and staggering about as helplessly as the rest of us, and as desperately attempting to find the exit through the petroleum-based peasouper.

It was bad enough having to explain to the billeting officer. What made it particularly embarrassing was that his companion was a senior official from Canada House in London. This was none other than my old acquaintance Lester Bowles Pearson, who was supposed to spread goodwill and peace wherever his profession as a diplomat took him.

Peace, indeed! I'd never met such an unpeaceful person as "Mike" Pearson. Every time we met he ended up in a red-faced rage. We had known each other since we were fellow students at the University of Toronto, him in arts, me in medicine, and he had flung a rock at me during some OTC manoeuvres in the Don Valley. We had encountered each other on many occasions since, and each time he had ended up spitting and lisping in a fury, usually over my latest promotion, which, in his unvarying opinion, was invariably unjustified.

Like me, Pearson was a former member of the Royal Flying Corps in WWI, and on this occasion he had travelled down from London to see how his Second World War successors were coping with the frightful rigours of your typical Bournemouth hotel. I didn't see him until he and the rest of the pilots had gained the relative clarity of the outer lobby. (I say the rest of the pilots, though in fact one of them was reported as missing and was never seen again – though some people suspected that a young lady named Myrtle McWhirter had something to do with his disappearance.)

However, we were talking about the distinguished visitor, Lester Bowles Pearson. As we emerged from the reeking clag into the lobby, coughing and choking together, he saw me clearly for the first time. Clutching at his bow tie he uttered a strangled gargle, which was somehow made all the more frightful by his intrinsic lisp. "Oh, no! Thith ith impothible!" he cried, "ith Bandy again!" And though bent double with hacking, and busy ejaculating puffs of smoke, he yet managed to point a quivering finger at me and shout, "I'm abtholutely thertain you had thomething to do with thith!"

Poor old Pearson. I knew that he had some secret ambitions about leaving diplomacy for the world of politics, but of course the bow tie and the lisp made the whole idea ludicrous.

In Ottawa, before locking himself in the toilet of the train to Halifax and the warship home, Air Vice-Marshal Greaves had promised to see me if I ever did manage to get to England. But as the days drifted by and April arrived in a volley of showers, no calls came from the Air Ministry. I phoned, I wrote letters and reminders. I hung 'round his office. But somehow, whenever I was there in person, he wasn't.

Otherwise I mooched with the pooch around Bournemouth. The pooch was a portly black mongrel of an unknown brand, though there were nudges and winks of cocker spaniel in its past. It must have had an owner, for it was well looked after. It had tagged along the very first time I walked the promenade, and had taken to waiting outside the hotel for me nearly every morning, though it was neither allowed to enter the hotel nor seemed to wish to do so.

I was suspicious, at first. "It's planning something," I told young George Goodwin. But it seemed so perfectly contented merely to accompany me on my walks that I was quite tickled. "It's the first dog that's ever taken to me," I said to George, wonderingly. Once or twice when it followed me to Bournemouth station and gazed up at me with its appealing hazel eyes, I even took it up to London for the day. Yet whenever we returned to the seafront hotel it would say ta-ta with a warm glance and waddle off, presumably back to its owner.

There was not much to do or even to see during our perambulations along the sparkling barbed wire that guarded the beach from seaborne assault. Fading posters advertising jolly holidays in Poole, Weymouth, Exmouth, flapped in the saline wind. I went into a sweetshop to buy some candy, but didn't have the requisite coupons and so came out empty-mouthed. I bought a newspaper, all of four pages long because of the newsprint rationing, and read it in a teashop that I swear was chillier than the ocean promenade. I read that the Prime Minister, Mr. Neville Chamberlain, had made a speech to the effect that Hitler had missed the bus. The Allied strategy was strangling the German economy. The Royal Navy had done much to halt the delivery of desperately needed ores from Scandinavia. Soon, supplies of vital raw materials by land would be stopped. It was only a matter of time before Germany collapsed from lack of iron filings and knackwurst.

Thus Mr. Chamberlain was confirming everything I had told the young pilots, and my respect and admiration for his rectitude, acumen, and leadership went up numerous notches. But the report also dismayed me. I'm afraid that I wanted the war to get serious, for personal reasons. I had been hoping for equipment that would enable me to do something towards balancing the Spanish account, and the Spitfire seemed to be just the right sort of equipment to do it in. So it wasn't just me trying to recapture my youth with all its excitements and adventures. There was also the minor consideration that while the First World War was a totally pointless waste of lives, the Second, though a direct descendant of the First, was undoubtedly a just war. Besides, even if I was getting into it partly for the adventure, what was wrong with that?

The call finally came. The gloom lifted. And on the glorious morning of April ninth, I tootled up the Strand and arrived at the Air Ministry with a good many minutes to spare before the interview that would finally, I trusted, see me onto the strength of a front-line fighter squadron.

I had all the relevant records with me, valid and up-to-date, the sea air had freshened up my face and deducted a decade or two of folds and wrinkles, and I was wearing my best uniform, though without the twenty or so medals I was entitled to wear – the authorization had gotten lost, somehow, between Ottawa and London. I was also wearing my best hairpiece, firmly pinned down against such contretemps as occurred on the Bournemouth prom when a particularly strong gust had revolved it 180 degrees, with the result that the artificial parting had started from the back of my neck while a fringe had appeared in front, nestling on my nose.

Luckily, only the screaming seagulls had observed this, and I had since acquired from an expert in London a harmless glue that would firmly affix the toupee to my ever-widening tonsure.

At the Air Ministry I was asked to wait in the corridor outside the offices of Fighter Command as there was no room to move in Greaves's crowded anteroom. This put me in the way of the corridor traffic, of which there was a surprising amount. At first I felt like a bollard, with waves of traffic flowing on either side. Then I felt like somebody going up a down elevator, buffeted by elbows and clipped by the little cardboard boxes that everybody was carrying. The boxes were supposed to contain gas masks, but as no gas had appeared over the past seven months most of the containers now held hankies, choccy bars, corn plasters, and French letters.

I had to keep shifting aside to make room for officers of various ranks, wireless operators bearing message forms, Waaf corporals in wrinkled blue stockings, despatch riders in oily uniforms and silly helmets, and civilians in suits so identically pinstriped as to make their owners seem just as much in uniform as their military brethren and sistren. In addition there were numerous self-important guards, guides, and commissionaires escorting supplicants – invariably to the wrong departments, judging by the expressions of dissatisfaction from the visitors as they went past again, going the other way.

Some disturbing news was being discussed in the corridors. Something about a German invasion force having been spotted in a Norwegian fiord, or something. Whatever the nature of the crisis, it had certainly created an air of tension around the place. It seemed to permeate the whole building.

The sensation was real enough in the fighter chief's quarters. The staff in there, comprising three junior officers and a Waaf with a less-than-regulation-length skirt – it was actually exposing her fat knees – were huddled together in a taut group when they were not busy answering shrilling telephones and warding off various pests and importunates.

"Hey, listen, fellows," one stalwart visitor said in a strange whining accent that was presumed to be Canadian, as there was a Canada flash on the sleeve of his smart, flight lieutenant's uniform, "I had an appointment for ten o'clock, and it's now twenty to eleven."

"You'll be lucky to see him at all, old boy. This is not a good day."

"What gives, anyway?" enquired the tall, distinguished-looking Canadian with the face of a Derby winner surmounted by a fine head of hair; but the staff was too busy turning away yet another batch of lobbyists even to answer.

By eleven o'clock I was getting a bit cheesed off with being buffeted and postponed. After all, I was considerably in Greaves's debt. That alone should have made me welcome, and given me priority over the hordes of senior officers who were being allowed in and out of his office without let or hindrance. I mean, where was his sense of gratitude, for having been allowed to help me so often in the past. I was never one to take things lying down, unless there was a woman involved, and so I seized the opportunity as soon as it arose. It arose at eleven fifteen when a large and obviously very important politician in morning coat and striped trousers came beefing along the corridor, sending bespectacled warrant officers and dainty Waafs flying in all directions.

Even I, resistant to aggressive personalities, was aware of him the moment he appeared. It was the way he was barging through the mob like a corvette through flotsam and jetsam. Even his face barged: a hard, masterful face with disturbing blue eyes above which sat a pair of eyebrows like Colorado beetles.

Not wishing to be run over I edged back, my heels clacking against a glass case of interesting war trophies – pieces of shrapnel, fading identity cards, fossilized field rations, and the like. I expected the civvy to sweep past. Instead, he burrowed straight into Air Vice-Marshal Greaves's suite of offices, parting all before him like Moses in the Red Sea.

"Who's that?" one of the waiting officers asked in an awed whisper.

"Drummond."

"What?"

"Sir Amyas Drummond. Minister of something or other. Or deputy minister, is it?"

"That's right!" came an excited whisper from the rear. "It's Drummond. The one who refused to admit those German Jews when he was with the Home Office. You remember?"

"They say he's a closet uglyist," said a bespectacled admin officer.

I turned and looked at him. "I read something about that in the papers, but I thought it was some kind of joke," I said, preparing to look sophisticatedly amused if he confirmed that it was an example of English humour.

Apparently it wasn't. "Oh, no," said the admin type, who looked as if he would know all about things like Existentialism, Positivism,

Dadaism, Schismism, and the like. "I seem to remember Havelock Ellis mentioning Uglyism in his *Psychology of Sex.*"

At the mention of sex there was a stir of interest. "Uglyism is something to do with sex, is it?" someone asked.

"Of course, though it's a sexual inversion rather than perversion."

"And Drummond has it?"

"I believe so, though he hasn't come out yet, of course."

"What is it anyway?"

"Uglyism is the phenomenon of being drawn to unprepossessing persons of the opposite sex," he explained, polishing his glasses in an erudite way, "through a deep-seated conviction that you don't deserve a good-looking partner."

He launched into the subject with rising enthusiasm, but I was too busy gate-crashing to hear any more. Drummond had been towing several aides and assistants behind him as he bulled his way up our passage. His retinue was now pushing and shoving its way into Cyril's office in its eagerness to keep up with its master.

I joined the entourage, shoving into Cyril's inner sanctum with alacrity and the other minions.

Inside the office another scrum formed, for the space was already taken up with half a dozen air force officers. Until the arrival of the minister they had been meeting confidentially around Cyril's desk. Their serious expressions rapidly turned into a variety of consternations as they caught sight of Sir Amyas Drummond, and there was a confused scraping of chairs as they all jumped to their feet.

As I sidled in, one of Drummond's people kept looking at me. Finally he edged up and said hesitantly, "I say."

"Eh?"

"You're not with the minister's party, are you?"

"If he's having a party, I sure am," quoth I, and before he could sort it out I had edged still deeper into the claque. I had intended alerting Cyril to my presence right away, but there were so many people between me and his desk that to attract his attention I would have needed to jump up and down, waving a shirt attached to a broom handle.

Even then, Greaves probably wouldn't have noticed. His attention was riveted much too apprehensively onto the burly newcomer. The moment Sir Amyas had appeared, Greaves had scrambled to his feet and started to babble. A minute later he was still gibbering.

I shook my head, greatly disappointed in Cyril. His old trouble. He had always tended to be overawed by authority, even the little I sometimes aspired to. In his modesty and lack of pomposity and self-esteem he had always been overly respectful toward his seniors.

"Oh, come on, Cyril," I kept thinking now, "the man's only a lousy politician, after all, not King George, Mark VI, for God's sake."

Yet in spite of my mute rooting he continued to babble like a gramophone record played too fast, until finally the minister interrupted. He did so in a voice that, normally quite deep and well modulated, was now grating and contemptuous, the aural equivalent of a bastard file.

"Greaves," Drummond said, kicking aside an air force officer or two and standing foursquare, or even fivesquare, in front of the desk, leaning forward with his great fists on its top. "Do you mind explaining why you are still here?"

"Sir?"

"Why you are still occupying this office, when I made it clear that the new chief of Fighter Command was to take over without delay?"

I started, and my heart immediately sank without trace. New chief of Fighter Command? Oh, my land – it sounded as if I'd lost my only contact in the RAF hierarchy.

Greaves's face was red with embarrassment. Trying not to look at his air force chums, he replied haltingly, "There was a question as to whether you – whether there was authority to – to act in what might be described as – well, rather an arbitrary fashion, sir. Someone in the legal department intimated that – "

"You are questioning my authority as Parliamentary Under-Secretary of State for Air, are you?" Sir Amyas enquired, in a decidedly dangerous sort of voice.

"No, sir," Greaves said, so hurriedly and so miserably that I winced. "It's just that – as I say, we – "

"The failure to provide proper air cover for the Norwegian operation was the last straw, Greaves, and that's all there is to it. I want you out of this office immediately. I've had quite enough of your dithering and procrastination."

"Sir, we were simply not consulted in time, you know that. We were – "

"I know only that you have proved yourself utterly incompetent in this vital post," Drummond said, raising his voice; and, disregarding the shame he was causing Cyril by dressing him down in the presence of his own staff, not to mention the stripe-trousered brigade, he continued to lambaste poor old Greaves in a well-modulated bellow for a good five minutes.

Having known Greaves for twenty years I supposed that the deputy minister had some justification for his criticisms. Cyril had never been a particularly dynamic leader, though he had managed well enough in the interwar years through his gentle methods and hesitant encouragements. So far, his shortcomings in the top-gear school of leadership had gone unnoticed, given the peacetime malaise and the generally lackadaisical conduct of the war so far. It was his bad luck that the war now looked like hotting up at last.

All the same, he did not deserve the pasting he was getting from the politician; or at least he didn't deserve to have it done in public. For not only was the deputy minister humiliating him in front of his friends and colleagues, but in front of hosts of visitors and supplicants and others clustered outside the office as well, who could hear everything that was being said.

Looking at Greaves's crimson face as he stood there and took the abuse, it all struck me as being decidedly ungentlemanly. And I definitely felt like intervening in some way. On the other hand I certainly didn't want to make an enemy of this ministry fellow. I needed all the help I could get, especially as it now appeared that Cyril's influence was on the wane.

After all, I didn't owe Cyril Greaves a thing. I'd only known him since 1918. I mean, what had he ever done for me, apart from one

or two minor favours. He was only a casual friend, really. I mean.
It wasn't my fault that he had cocked up the Norwegian campaign,
or whatever it was he had done, or failed to do. I couldn't help it if
he was as "incompetent, spineless, ineffective, and totally out of his
depth" as was now being said about him.

So the best I could offer in the way of support was maybe to
cause some distraction or other, like breaking wind or into song.
Which was what I intended doing, as I found myself threading
my way through the crush of colleagues and inquisitors. I certainly
wasn't going to queer my pitch by sticking my neck out, even
assuming it was possible to stick one's neck out over a queer pitch.
So all I said, as I reached the front line, so to speak, was, "Why, if
it isn't old Cyril Greaves. Hello, there, sir. Really good to see you
again, Cyril."

At the sound of my voice Cyril started violently, swung round
and stared at me wildly, as if I were something really strange and
unexpected. His mouth opened but no words dribbled forth.

"We're old friends, you know," I continued, addressing the
nearest officer, a wing commander with a moustache like two
bottle cleaners. "Proud to know him, too. One of the best officers
in the air force, what?" Realizing that I was adopting a clipped
English accent, I made a face. The wing commander immediately
fell back.

Quickly rectifying the accent, I added, "Yeah, and served his
country with distinction in the past, as I guess you know, eh?
Right?" I asked the wingco; and, more sharply when he failed to
answer: "*Right?*"

"Yes. Yes, that's right, sir," he said; and only then noticed the mere
two rings on my sleeve.

A grating voice sounded in my starboard earhole. "Who is this?"
it enquired. "Who the devil gave you the right to interrupt in this
fashion?"

Cool as hot broth I turned to the politician, and found that he
was even bigger and more threatening close up. "Oh, sorry, sir," I
said. "I thought you'd finished. I couldn't hear too well from the
back of the room. But I gathered you were praising Mr. Greaves

for his lifetime of devoted service to the country and to the Royal
Air Force."

"I was doing nothing of the sort. Who the hell is this man?" the
deputy minister asked, whirling back to Greaves.

"Oh, sorry," I went on. "I was sure you must have been thinking him for all the fine work he's done over a long and distinguished
career – squadron commander on the Western Front and all that,
defending his country against its enemies for a quarter century,
serving in foreign parts for most of his life, saving the Empire
through punitive actions against tribesmen, pig-sticking in far-
flung corners of said Empire, sacrificing all the comforts of the
domestic hearth in order to keep his country safe from its enemies
and appeasers – "

By now the minister was wearing an expression suggesting that
I had asked him if he wouldn't mind wiping my bottom. Now his
voice had gone Dangerously Quiet. "What is your name?" he
asked, into the frightened hush. "Let's have your particulars right
now. Right now."

I'm afraid I prevaricated somewhat, and this seemed to enrage
Drummond all the more. Maybe it was my voice, or possibly my
face which had been likened to that of a superior sort of yak, but
the big man was now thoroughly upset. "How dare you adopt that
manner with me," he roared; and again turned to Cyril Greaves,
who was busily staring at me as if I had recently emerged from a
pumpkin. "Is this a member of your staff?"

"No, sir, this is . . . a friend."

"And a colonial upstart to boot."

"Surely you wouldn't boot a fellow just because he's a colonial?"
I said recklessly, though with a sinking heart at my own foolishness
in getting involved to this extent.

"And one," the deputy minister grated, ignoring the quip, "who
obviously doesn't know his place."

"24 Sittingbourne Place," I said, trying again.

"What?"

"You said I didn't know my place. Well, I do – it's the Spartan

Hotel in Sittingbourne Place. I have just one room with a bathroom down the hall. It's a bit, well, spartan, but you're welcome to visit any time, Mr. Drummond."

"Sir, sir!"

"No need to call me, sir, Mr. Drummond. I'm only a flight looie."

"I'm trying to get it into your stupid skull that I'm a Sir not a mister – Sir Amyas Drummond!"

"Actually, so am I."

A member of Drummond's entourage – I learned later that he had been fired that morning and had nothing much to lose, put in, "You're Sir Amyas Drummond as well? That could be dashed confusing."

"What I meant was that I'm also a Sir. But knighthoods go to too many undeserving people these days, so I don't use mine."

Apart from his laboured bull-like breathing, Drummond had quietened down by then, but he was white with rage. His eye sockets had gone all swollen and his staring blue eyes were cauldrons of liquified spite.

"Your name, please," he said into the quivering hush.

I knew by then that I had gone too far, quipwise, and there was nothing for it but to grovel. So I owned up to my name, and, coiling myself into a humble posture, added that of course I wasn't referring to him as being undeserving.

It was all much too late. He had turned to address a bespectacled squadron leader, and stabbed at him with a thick forefinger. "I want this man charged with – with some charge or other – insolence, for a start!" he said.

The squadron leader looked petrified. It was Cyril who broke the silence. "Insolence?" he asked. He was still pale as pathology, with eyes rimmed red. "Insolence? I don't think there is such a charge in King's Regulations, sir."

"What?"

"Of course, there's dumb insolence – we might be able to use that," Cyril said.

"Well, then, use that!"

"Except he hasn't been dumb, has he? If anything, he's been rather too talkative."

"Then charge him for being too talkative! But do something about his, his disgraceful manner toward me!"

"That'll be difficult too, sir. Usually he has very nice manners, when he's with well-mannered people. He's respectful towards men of the cloth, and even a few churchmen – always offers his seat to old lady in wheelchairs, things like that."

The deputy to the Secretary of State for Air suddenly went all quiet, and in yet another of his Dangerous Voices, said, "Are you trying to be funny, Greaves? If so I must tell you that you're about to find yourself in very deep trouble."

"You mean there's anything worse than the way you've treated me just now?" Cyril asked. "The way I've just been sacked in the most humiliating way possible?" he finished, shakily, but managing to meet Drummond's ferocious stare without flinch or falter.

One of my nails was a bit ragged. I took out my nail clippers and tidied it up. The click of the clippers sounded awfully loud in the silence.

ME AND MY DOG

AS THE MAGGOT DAYS burrowed deeper into April, everybody except me sensed that doom was approaching at maximum revs. Personally, I was preoccupied with going squadronwards, though even I noticed little signs here and there that the war was stirring from its hibernation. It was starting to growl and to look for somebody to eat – preferably the Prime Minister, in the opinion of some people. Neville Chamberlain was still announcing that everything would be all right on the night, and the French in the Maginot Line seemed to agree with him, but the growling sounds were growing louder. Take the way the Jerries had managed to conquer Denmark and Norway in about twenty-five minutes. That didn't seem too reassuring, somehow, not least when suggestions of operational bungling by the navy and air force began to pollute the atmosphere.

I don't know. It was starting to undermine my faith in good old Chamberlain.

Then came the month of May. "My God," someone cried, bursting into my London club in a most ill-bred fashion, causing a dozen newspapers to be lowered in glowering disapproval, "have you heard? The Germans have invaded Holland, Belgium, and France!"

"Gee, that's awful. But listen," I said, "did you speak to your friend in the Air Ministry about my application? Nobody there will talk to me any longer. In fact, they won't even let me in the building."

The Jerries were beginning to overrun various countries at an

unheard-of rate. When they drove their tanks around the Maginot
Line instead of behaving like gentlemen and attacking it head on,
it caused a great deal of indignation among the members of my club
who had not been told that the Maginot Line was an enormous
concrete fraud and could all too easily be driven around.

Still, Great Britain did not stand idly by and take these Teutonic
treacheries lying down. We promptly occupied Iceland and the
Faroe Islands. Though to be fair, we soon balanced this by aban-
doning the British Channel Islands complete with entire herds of
photogenic dairy cows.

Yet despite the danger, nobody would take me seriously as a
combatant. Just because the old joints creaked a bit, and I was
getting set in my ways and turning into a dog owner, they seemed
to think I was a hopeless prospect as a fighter pilot. If only they
could see things from the correct perspective: that I was a tremen-
dous asset, I said asset. Just to pick out thirty or forty examples of
my stunning career: after establishing myself as one of the top air
aces of the First World War, I was sent to Russia as part of the Allied
Intervention in their civil war, and I led a ragtag and bobtail mob
of White Russians to one of the most notable victories of the war,
the capture of the armoured train at Emtsa. I returned home with
the acting temporary rank of major-general (much to the chagrin
of the Canadian government, who found themselves paying me
most of their defence budget in the form of a senior officer's
pension). I then progressed to film acting (I still have the *New York
Times* review in my wallet), followed by aircraft manufacturing in
Gallop, Ontario, and if the latter enterprise was not entirely successful, this was only because I was busy with my charitable work
during those Prohibition times, i.e., engaged in supplying thirsty
Americans with fine Canadian whisky by air. This dangerous and
illegal activity led inevitably to my becoming a Member of
Parliament, where once again, defying the gravity of probability, I
slid up the ladder of success, becoming defence minister for several
hours before being hounded out of the country by Mackenzie King,
who, as we have learned, had now forgiven me for allowing myself
to be victimized by him. By the mid-twenties I was commander of

a Maharajah's air force, which, incidentally, was larger than the entire RAF presence in India at the time. After that I . . . well, you get the picture. I was one of the greatest leaders and aviators of all time. Ask anyone who owed me money. I had thousands of flying hours in my log books, and over the years had been awarded over twenty medals, orders, crosses, stars, and sashes, for gallantry and skilled lobbying. The gongs included no less than the Jhamjhar Order of Merit, the Jhamjhar Cross of Honour 3rd class, and the Jhamjhar Short Service Medal (though owing to some bureaucratic bungling, authorization to wear the various gongs had not yet come through from Ottawa, so that my tunic remained as fallow as that of the newest sprog pilot). Yet the new chief of Fighter Command still refused to see either sense or me. Even the most sympathetic member of his staff, a substantive flight lieutenant named Ralph who was no spring chicken himself, remained impervious to my record, my qualifications, my importunities, or my five-quid note.

"Look, old chap," he said, "I want to spare your feelings. So all I'm going to say is that nobody will ever take you on as an operational pilot because you're all washed up. I know it may sound terribly unreasonable to you, but they don't allow pensioners to fly fighters. Face it, man, you're obsolete."

"Anyway, you'll put in a good word for me with your new boss, will you, Ralph?"

"Oh, for heaven's sake!"

"All you have to do, Ralph, is phone my name through to any squadron that needs replacements and let them know I'm coming."

"I keep telling you, they wouldn't touch you with a lamplighter's pole. Incidentally, my name's pronounced Rafe."

"It could be worth another fiver, you know."

"I wouldn't dream of taking your money."

"You mean you'll get me to a squadron for free? That's darn good of you, Ralph."

"Rafe! And I told you, it's impossible. Can't you get it through your head? Nobody will ever take you on as a fighter pilot. You've simply had your day, why can't you be content with that?"

"You could easily sneak my name onto the roster or at least get me to an OTU, Ralph."

"Jesu joy of love's desiring, are you deaf?"

"Oh, sorry. I should have said Rafe. So – you'll put in a good word, eh, Rafe?"

But he wouldn't.

Then one day I read some splendid news in the papers. Winston Churchill had replaced Neville Chamberpot as prime minister.

Of course, in my opinion, this was no improvement at all, as Neville had been an outstanding PM. He had bought time for us so we could summon enough nerve to oppose old Hitler. Whereas old Churchill was an utter failure. Why, he couldn't even stick to his own political party, but had actually crossed over to the Opposition at one time, the dirty dog. But the point was that he was a new contact for me. I knew Churchill – old Winston. I'd met him several times – as recently as 1927 when he congratulated me on saving India. If anyone could get me into the fight, he could.

Why, he was even quoting his old friend Bandy. Just a few days previously in a radio broadcast he had promised the nation nothing but blood, tears, toil, and sweat, not necessarily in that order.

Well, I coined that phrase, most of it, anyway, as described in the second volume of my memoirs! In 1918, Winston had asked for my opinion concerning the situation on the Western Front. "A time of tears, sweat, and toil," I had replied portentously.

Mr. Churchill had immediately developed a faraway look. Now, twenty-two years later, he had refocussed on my immortal quotation – though I noticed he'd added the word "blood" to the phrase, without so much as a by-your-leave, either. Still, I wouldn't charge him for the extra word – provided he came through.

Unfortunately I couldn't get near him. From 10 Downing Street I met nothing but obstruction. "Do you seriously expect the Prime Minister to give you his personal attention when the fate of democracy hangs in the balance?" said this tinny voice on the phone.

"Why, what's happening?"

"What's happening? My God, man, where are you from – Lapland?"

"Gallop, actually. Though to be precise my birthplace was Beamington, Ontario, a town of sunbaked, frost-cracked brick, splintering timber, and brown grass, set astride a dirt road leading to Ott – "

"Mr. Bandy."

"Flight Lieutenant, actually. Though I don't expect to stay a flight looie for long."

"I don't expect you to, either. But Good Lord, man, don't you know what's happening? That the Germans have overwhelmed Belgium and Holland, and are threatening France – and our army over there is in danger of being annihilated – and you haven't heard?"

"Well, I don't have a radio. Or 'wireless,' as you call it. Anyway, I guess Mr. Churchill is pretty busy, is he, now that he's finally made prime minister?"

"You could say that, yes."

"All the same, I'm sure he'll see me," I wheedled. "Winston and I have known each other for twenty years, you know – on and off."

But they wouldn't put me through to the great man's secretary, even.

All this time I was also trying to persuade the Canadian government to fight in my corner. To that end, I had made many telephone calls and visits to Canada House on Trafalgar Square in an attempt to see Vincent Massey, the High Commissioner. On my first visit I very nearly succeeded; in fact I was on my way to his office upstairs when there was a commotion, a sort of sudden panic among his staff; whereupon a thin young fellow named Ritchie led me downstairs again, babbling excuses. After that I couldn't even get past the vestibule. I don't know. It was almost as if the distinguished Mr. Massey had been put on his guard, or had heard a peal of warning bells, or something. But that was an absurd suspicion. Why, I'd never even met Mr. Massey before, though he was dean at my old university and wore the same university tie – not the black one I was wearing now, of course, but the coloured one I'd worn once at the University of Toronto Convocation back in . . . whenever it was.

But devotion to duty finally paid off and wore them down, and one day I received an invitation to lunch with Mr. Massey at his club. Accordingly, on the appointed day, I marched through the spring sunshine with purposeful gait and singing heart, and reached White's on St. James Street a good half hour ahead of schedule. Once again I had Plato with me. Plato was the name of the dog that had taken a fancy to me. I learned this when, one day, having nothing better to do and curious as to where he spent the night, I followed him home. Home turned out to be a ghastly museum off the seafront masquerading as a tourist attraction. It featured grubby costumes draped over historical figures like Henry VIII and Jenkins, of War of Jenkins' Ear fame, glass cases filled with forgotten memorabilia, a variety of old posters, a vast stuffed rat with two-inch crimson teeth, and a knight in armour. The owner, who had a mildewed voice and a Local Defence Volunteer armband, informed me that I was just in time to see the exhibition before it closed for the duration. He himself was moving to Hackney. He had intended returning Plato to the pound, but if I was interested he was prepared to sell me the little mongrel. I replied that I wasn't the least interested, and turned to go. Unfortunately I caught Plato's eye. He was looking at me in so forlorn a fashion that I hesitated. It was a fatal hesitation. "He's so quiet you have to order him to bark, you know," said the owner, and demonstrated by barking himself. "Bark!" he called to the dog. Obediently Plato uttered a single, rather hoarse bark – and then looked at me as if to say, How can you resist such a talented member of the canine family? I couldn't, though I was thoroughly annoyed at myself – what the hell was I going to do with a dog? – and even more annoyed when I had to fork out two pounds ten and six.

Plato seemed to know right away that he had changed owners, and though he ended up as a squadron mascot rather than as my personal pooch, I did not subsequently regret the purchase. With those grey whiskers and appealing brown eyes he was a lovely old thing.

As we reached Mr. Massey's club, I was busily rehearsing a few flattering remarks that I might direct to the distinguished diplomat, like telling him how well his brother, Raymond Massey, was doing in the filums. I was also hoping to demonstrate my old doggy's talent, but that was not to be.

By now I was quite familiar with the world of London clubs, but even I was impressed by White's, the most prestigious of the lot. It glowed with history and tradition, and reeked of aristocratic glamour. In fact, later I applied for membership, but some swine blackballed me. The swine.

The commissionaire in his bottle-green outfit proved as uppity as the selection committee. Though I explained that Canada's number-one citizen was treating me to char and a wad at noon, he refused to let me kick the old heels in the bar until the High Commissioner's arrival. "And you certainly can't take that dog in there, sir," he said. It cost me half a crown to leave Plato leashed up in the cloakroom, while I had to wait in the hall.

There I proceeded to admire their fine staircase, which was lined with portraits of famous former members, and to listen to the foul language from the billiard room.

Then, a stroke of luck. Big, handsome, uniformed Randolph Churchill came treading very very carefully down the grand staircase, holding a headache in place with both hands.

Better still, he recognized me straight away. "Oh, God, are you back again?" he whispered, before lurching onward toward the bar, followed by his companion, a short, plump Royal Marine officer, who looked even more dishevelled than Randolph.

Seizing the opportunity to be sponsored by a member, I followed them into the bar. After opening a second bottle of champagne, the Prime Minister's son became slightly more communicative, whereupon I learned that he had been out on the tiles the previous evening with someone named Evelyn Waugh. This, presumably, was one of his many aristocratic lady friends – which I didn't think was very nice, for he had only been married for a few months to a nice, innocent girl from the shires named Pamela.

I'd first met Randolph while visiting his dad some years previously. He was a pretty unwelcoming young man, as I remember. Subsequently I'd heard him described as a noisy, arrogant bully, with only one redeeming feature: his love for and steadfast support of his

old man, during the time that Churchill was in the political wilder-
ness, scorned by one and all.

Glass in hand and slowly recovering, Randolph looked me over
as disdainfully as his painful, gritted eyes would permit. I, of course,
was in the RAF blue uniform, which was adorned with wings and
Canada flash, but with only two rings on the sleeves and not a single
helping of fruit salad on my manly breast.

"You've come down in the world, haven't you?" said Randolph.

He was no more welcoming when I told him that it was my
ambition to get to a squadron in France while there was still time.

"Say, maybe you could get me an appointment with your old
man," I suggested.

"You're too old to fight," he said rudely.

"I am not."

"'Course you are. Anyway, why should I help? Just because you
did the Empire a service way back there at the turn of the century,
or whenever it was. Doesn't make us chums, you know."

"Who's this?" asked his companion, an obese, scruffy gent in a
uniform so ill-fitting that it looked as if he were leaving room in
there for a servant or two.

"Bandy," Randolph explained. "Chap who saved India."

"Saved India? What on earth for?"

"Wants to meet my father. Wants to get into a fighter squadron."

"Taking pensioners now, are they? Situation must be worse than
I thought."

Randolph refilled his glass with champagne, then wiggled the
bottle. "Evelyn?" he enquired.

As he filled his friend's glass, I looked around for Evelyn, but I
couldn't see her anywhere. Meanwhile, Randolph, sipping at his
champagne, was asking, "Didn't you earn a title or something, over
the India business?"

"M'm."

For the first time his companion looked at me with a faint
glimmer of respect in his piggy eyes. "You have a title?" he asked.

"KCSI," I said in a bored fashion, adding nonchalantly, "never use
it, though. We don't go in for that sort of thing in Canada."

Randolph's pudgy friend was aghast. "You earned a knighthood and you don't use it?" he cried, but then winced at the volume of his own voice. "God, what wouldn't I give," he added in a whisper.

Suddenly expansive, Randolph turned to me. "Tell you what I'll do, though, Bandy," he said, holding his glass up to the light to inspect the bubbles. "I have quite a bit of influence nowadays. So, since my father has mentioned you once or twice not unfavourably, I'll see what I can do to get you into an active service unit."

"Would you? Thanks very much, Randolph."

"How would an anti-aircraft battery suit?"

"Huh?"

"You'd be in command of the battery, of course," he went on encouragingly. "And I could fix it to get you based in Hyde Park. That would put you right in the thick of things."

"Protecting the heart of Empire and all that," I said.

"Right. You'd be in range of the Ritz, all the best parties, night-clubs, gambling, and so forth," he said, dreamily contemplating the revelry that was in store for me.

But then, as if realizing that if given the job I might detract from his own share of the urban debauchery, he added peevishly, "Though I don't know why I'm going to all this trouble. You mean nothing to me personally." He peered morosely into the champagne bottle, then shook it. "Evelyn?" he asked, wiggling the bottle before replenishing his friend's glass.

Regarding the PM's son with some concern, I drew confidentially close and said, "I wonder if perhaps you've been imbibing too much lately, Randy."

"What?"

"Hallucinations, old man. Evelyn's not really here, you know."

"Damn well is."

"You haven't by any chance been encountering pink elephants as well, have you?"

"What?"

Ever so gently I informed him that he was seeing things. There was no Evelyn here.

"What are you talking about? He's right there."

"No, Randy," I said. "Face it, man: there's nobody here but us chickens." I touched his arm sympathetically. "Have you thought of seeking help for your condition, Randy?" I asked.

"What the hell do you mean – I don't have a condition! And don't call me Randy, Bandy!" He pointed at his companion. "*That's* Evelyn!" he bawled. Heads were turning around us.

"Well, I never," I said, turning to Randy's Marine buddy. "That's really your name?"

"Evelyn Waugh," said the Marine officer in a bored, contemptuous voice, and turned his back on me.

"Would that be Miss or Mrs.?" I enquired.

"Oh, God, what's the matter with the fellow?" Churchill asked despairingly. Then, bawling again: "He's a man, dammit!"

"Yes, yes, I see that," I said. "He just likes going around with women's names, that's all." I turned back to Waugh. "And do you wear dresses – like at work?"

"Of course I don't wear dresses at work!" the chap snapped.

"Just at home, eh?"

"I don't wear dresses at home, either!"

"So when do you wear them?"

"I don't wear anything at all, either at work or at home!" He was shouting now.

"But you'll catch cold if you don't wear something, Mr. Waugh," I expostulated. "Even a dress is better than nothing."

Waugh started to reply, sounding even more upset than Churchill; until after the first "Dammit . . ." he became aware how many members of the club had drifted into the bar and were listening attentively.

"Waugh? Isn't he the fellow who's up for membership?" one of them asked in an upper-class English murmur, i.e., capable of being heard over the roar of a Grand National crowd.

"M'm. Churchill's putting him up."

"But that other chap says he wears dresses."

"He denies it, of course."

"Well, he would, wouldn't he."

"Where there's smoke, there's . . . ?"

"Exactly."

"I don't think we should, you know . . . ?"

"No. They say that Waugh is hell."

At that point I told Randolph and his friend that perhaps I had better make tracks as I had an appointment for lunch in a few minutes. "I'm dining with the High Commissioner for Canada, as a matter of fact," I informed them offhandedly, to underline the fact that I was not just a common or garden acquaintance but someone who hobnobbed with people like commissioners.

Unfortunately it didn't underline properly. "You're dining with the commissionaire?" Randolph said. "Well, tell him from me that if he ever allows you in the bloody club again, I'll slit his guts and stretch his intestines across the room for a clothesline!"

As for Evelyn Waugh, when I heard later from a Colonel Laycock that on one occasion he was obliged to set a guard on Waugh's sleeping quarters to protect him *from his own men*, I wasn't the least surprised.

When I walked into the splendid red-walled dining room, or coffee-room as the members have been calling it for a couple of hundred years, the familiar features of Vincent Massey were nowhere to be seen. But there were other familiar features available, the plump, usually benign ones belonging to one of Mr. Massey's underlings: Lester "Mike" Pearson.

Puzzled, I walked over to his corner table. "Where's Vince?" I demanded.

Pearson looked at me as if he'd have liked to slit my guts as well. "I'm thubthtituting for him," he muttered. "We drew lots to thee which one of uth had to go."

"And you won, eh? Good show," I said, sitting and flapping my napkin. "But I'd have preferred a person with some influence, Mike. Not," I added tactfully, "that you're insignificant, but I'm sure you appreciate – "

"Look here, Bandy," he said, "let'th get one thing thtraight. If you're going to be ath unbearable here ath you've been at Canada Houth, I'm leaving forthwith."

"Unbearable? Me?"

"You're eathily the motht awful man I have ever met in my entire life," lisped he. "Eathily."

"Huh."

"That Bournemouth bithineth was typical, typical. I thtill have a bad cough," he said, and, indeed, illustrated his remarks with a bronchitic ejaculation. "And if you're going to thit there looking hurt, that'll be another reathon for me to leave pronto.

"Now," he continued, scrutinizing the menu, "I'll thee what I can do to get you to a Canadian thquadron – "

"Thank you very much, Mike," I said.

"It won't be eathy – too many people know all about you. But I'll thee what I can do."

In fact, nothing was to come of his efforts, but that didn't stop him from asking a favour in return. "If it'th all right with you, Bandy," he said, "we're being joined by a friend of mine, any moment now. He'th director of a military hothpital over here but he'th been recalled to head a rethearch team in Ottawa – in connection with air warfare, ath a matter of fact."

"But there was another thing I wanted to discuss with you, Mike. About my gongs."

"Gongth?"

"Yes. Where are my gongs? When is Ottawa sending the authorization so I can wear all my medals and things?"

"We're working on it," he muttered. "But about my friend. He's thailing from Liverpool tomorrow, and – ah! Here he ith now," Pearson said, rising and looking extremely respectful.

I watched a bit resentfully as the newcomer threaded his way somewhat clumsily through the dining tables with their pristine linen and glittering glassware surmounted by red faces. As he and Pearson exchanged pleasantries I tried to remember where I'd seen him before. And just as Pearson was about to introduce him, I said, "Well, I'll be hornswoggled. Fred Banting!"

"You know each other?" Pearson asked, his jaw dropping so far that his bow tie disappeared from sight.

"Bandy and I were at medical school together. And I'd know that face anywhere, despite the ravages of time," cried Sir Frederick Banting, Nobel laureate and discoverer of insulin.

We shook hands and beamed at each other. "Well, I'll be darned," I kept saying, as a disconcerted Pearson searched the menu for the cheapest lunch he could find.

"I'll be darned," Banting kept saying as well.

I looked at the knighted doctor with an admiration mixed with the rather unflattering memories I had of him, when he and I first entered the U of T medical school. I remembered that in his youth he had never looked youthful. With his long face and his large nose and the studious crease in his brow, he was neither pleasing in appearance nor interestingly ugly. Nor was he now. Though tall and husky, he looked as nondescript as ever in his crumpled civilian suit. He was the most unlikely Nobel prize-winner imaginable. In the years I'd studied and dissected along-side him, I don't remember him ever saying anything amusing, perceptive, unexpected, or profound. We had considered him a poler and a grind, and believed that by the time he graduated he would be well on the way to obscurity.

So when his great achievement became known, that he had succeeded in isolating the anti-diabetic hormone after only a few weeks' work at the University of Toronto, when a host of brilliant physiologists had failed to do so after a quarter century of endeav-our, we were astounded and humbled. His success was all the more astonishing in that he had accomplished it with poverty-stricken resources compared with the rich backing lavished on diabetic research in other universities around the world. In particular he was grudgingly allowed only a very limited number of the dogs needed for his experiments. But despite all the difficulties, through the essential vivisection of dogs, he had achieved one of the greatest medical triumphs in history.

I wanted to talk about it, but the most he would say was that it was his ignorance that had made it possible. "If I'd known anything about it, I'd never have had the nerve to start," he said, smiling through his discomfort. From the moment we sat down his eyes had started to water and turn red.

He was more interested in his surroundings. "So this is White's," he said, sneezing. "Say, do you know who I saw in the bar?" he said, naïvely open-mouthed. "Winston Churchill's son, Randolph. What d'you think of that, eh?"

"Gosh. But tell me about Professor McCleod."

But Banting was busy strangling. One violent blare after another issued from his redoubtable beezer, his sneezes rending the crimson dining room and the matching diners.

Recovering somewhat, he gasped, "Tell me, Bart, what did you do after you left medical school after shooting the Professor of Surgery in the back?"

Pearson looked up. "It was an accident," I told him stoutly.

"Thure."

"Well," I began expansively, turning back to Banting, "to bring you up to date, Fred. You will, of course, be aware that I soon became one of the greatest aviators of all time." But the rest was drowned out by another bugle call from his quivering conk, and by further gasps and wheezes and olfactory detonations, which racked Fred's ungainly frame from his tufty hair to his size-eleven boots.

Wiping his streaming eyes he gasped, "I seem to be having an attack of some, of some, *atchooo*!!"

"Ith there thomething we can get you, Thir Frederick?" a concerned Pearson asked.

Sounding like a spare tire being inflated he gasped, "I don't know what could be cause – cause – causing – *kerchew, kerblah, keretishow, ker* – oh, bloody hell!"

"Possibly an allergic reaction," I said, trying to sound terrifically knowledgeable.

To my surprise, Fred agreed, between bursts of sneezing, vapours of sinus material, and floods of tears. "Have either of you been in contact with a duh?"

"A duh?"

"A duh – duh – duh – CHOO! A dog? Lately?"

"No," said Pearson. "How about you, Bandy?"

"I get it whenever I'm anywhere within a hundred yards of any type of bow-WOW!!" said Fred, exploding again, his face drenched in wet misery.

"Bandy?" Pearson asking, looking at me hard.

"Well, actually . . ." I said.

"You see," Sir Frederick Banting said during a lull in the storm, "I'm allergic to dogs."

OPERATION GELDING

GLORY BE. ONE DAY my intense lobbying efforts finally paid off. I was offered the post of liaison officer on Salisbury Plain.

Not even a flying job. I was to be shipped into an army base to liaise with the brown jobs for a series of trials of experimental air weapons. As far as I could make out, the job involved little more than communicating from the ground with the pilots who would be doing the real work aloft.

"They need a new liaison officer," said the postings officer at Lincoln's Inn Fields, which was where the RCAF had established its headquarters. "The last one was killed by one of the experimental weapons."

"Sorry – don't want the job."

"We can't have you hanging around here any longer," the postings officer said. "There's a war on, you know."

"And I'm trying to get into it."

"Once and for all," he said exasperatedly, "get it through your head that there's no place for middle-aged gentlemen in front-line squadrons. We know you're a man of experience, Bandy, but Canada's trying to create a youthful, vibrant air force. We just can't have our cockpits filled with has-beens, specially one who resembles a pantomime horse. It doesn't present the right image, somehow."

"Pantomime horse?"

"A horse with a very strange head of hair, if you don't mind my saying so."

"Strange head of hair?"

"That wouldn't be a wig, would it?"

"A wig?" I laughed. "How can you say that about a fine head of hair like this?" I said, running my hand – very carefully – through said fine head of hair.

"That would certainly be another thing we couldn't have, Bandy – pilots who wear hairpieces. Imagine the shame you'd bring on the Royal Canadian Air Force if it ever got about that we had to resort to hairpieces to win the war."

"Can we get back to the subject, please?" I said loftily. "This job on Salisbury Plain – do you seriously expect me to even contemplate turning into a ground crew?"

"You got just half an hour to contemplate it, Flight Lieutenant. I'm sorry, but the fact is, we're getting pretty close to posting you back to Training Command – or getting rid of you altogether."

But then his expression softened, which reduced his face to the consistency of Carrara marble. Perching on his desk in front of me he wheedled, "Look, Bart, we all know you did pretty good in the first war and other assorted wars. Why not settle for past glories, eh? Face it, man, there's no way you'll ever be fit to fly a sophisticated modern fighter like the Spit. Your reflexes are bound to be shot long ago."

"My reflexes are as good as ever."

"All right, let's see how fast you can catch that bluebottle."

"What bluebottle?"

"See? Your eyesight is no good either."

"I beg your pardon?"

"Poor devil's deaf as well," the senior officer murmured to an invisible audience of physicians and nursing assistants. Then, more loudly to me: "I-said-your-eyesight is – "

"I heard, I heard," I said, loudly, like someone with defective hearing.

I composed myself, and said, "Sir, in Spain, fighter tactics didn't seem to have changed all that much over the past twenty – " But the postings officer was already halfway to the teletype to send me back to Avro Ansons.

Worse, the Ansons would probably be based in a place called
Gauntlet, which would probably be in Saskatchewan, miles from
the nearest tavern. "All right, all right," I called out, "I'll take the
liaison job." After all, as long as I was in Europe there was still a
chance of paying back the Nazis for shooting down that civil air-
liner in Spain. The one in which Sigridur was killed.

For a while, as Plato and I adapted to life on Salisbury Plain (still as
miserable as I remembered it from infantry training back there in
1916), I continued to believe that I would manage to reach the aerial
front, sometime, somehow, even if it meant undergoing plastic
surgery to transform me into Young Dick Daring of the Mounted.
But as the weeks passed I began to hay me doots, as they say in
Newcastle or somewhere up north. Maybe there really wasn't any
room for a chap as wonderful as me.

It was particularly frustrating because I felt pretty certain that
they would soon need every pilot who could turn and bank without
skidding. In France, it was said that the front-line Fairey Battles were
going down like pheasants on the glorious twelfth. Even the eight-
gun Hurricanes were taking a beating from the enemy pilots, many
of whom had gained useful experience in Spain. The RAF would
surely be desperate for fighter pilots as the position at the front grew
worse. And by Jove, it was growing worse. By the end of May,
Belgium and Holland had surrendered, France looked like going the
same way, and the British armies had been surrounded at a place
called Dunkirk.

"What do you think of their chances, Mr. Bandy?" people asked
respectfully. Presumably they had noticed the maturity on my face.
I was certain that the entire British Expeditionary Force was
doomed, but I had a sore throat at the time and was unable to speak
and enlighten the public to this effect. Fortunately, as it turned out;
a quarter of a million soldiers managed to escape from Dunkirk in
a vast flotilla of small boats and naval vessels.

The escape from Dunkirk seemed almost miraculous, and the
British, quick to rename defeat and call it a triumph of logistical

modification, marvelled over their cups of tea, and felt quite proud of themselves. Somehow, ordinary people were not fearful, but seemed almost exhilarated by the crisis. Features normally cast in moulds of pessimism brightened into mere despondency. Workers formerly noted for their skill in doing as little as possible for their little-as-possible pay began to work like demons to build warships and warplanes, and to replace lost tanks and guns. Knitting needles speeded up to a frightful rate, threatening to enmesh the entire army in yarn, and signposts throughout the country were pulled down or painted over so as to cause as much inconvenience as possible to those who had enough petrol coupons for their cars. Inmates of Strangeways Prison sang patriotic songs. So what if the army had lost almost all its equipment, the Air Force had been defeated in France, and the Navy had suffered ruinous losses off Norway and in the Channel? The country had been in a spot of trouble before, it would survive to have a spot of trouble in the future.

"Damn good job they abandoned this harebrained scheme to build a Channel tunnel," an old colonel said, "back in '72, what?"

I, too, was contributing valiantly to the cause. My job was to stand on a rickety platform and talk to a Lysander pilot through a headset clamped to my top-secret hairpiece.

This was on Salisbury Plain where they were testing the latest Secret Weapon, codenamed Gelding. It comprised a long cable suspended from an aircraft. At the end of the cable there was a clever scissors/cleaver arrangement which was designed to cut enemy telegraph and/or telephone cables.

In theory the pilot was supposed to come in low with his wire dangling. As the weapon swept over a line of telephone cables the butcher's scissors/cleaver at the end of the wire were supposed to snap shut and sever whatever was in the way.

During the first trial the pilot kept missing the line of cross-country poles that had been set up specially for the occasion. Understandably nervous of being stopped dead in the air, he came in too high. When he finally got down to the appropriate height, the contraption actually functioned. The cleaver swished across the sagging cables between two of the poles, the scissors action engaged and snapped shut, and some of the telephone wires parted and snaked to the ground.

The official demonstration of the weapon took place early in June, a month later.

It was a glorious day. In fact, it had actually been warm and sunny for weeks on end. Plainly, something had gone terribly wrong with the British weather. The latest news showed that something had gone terribly wrong with the war as well. The French government had abandoned Paris and fled to Tours.

As we waited for the officials to arrive in the camp, I fell into conversation with a chap named Walter. This was an army lieutenant who was mad keen on Salisbury Plain, not as an armed forces proving ground so much as an ecological site. His glasses kept slipping down his nose as he excitedly told me all about its numerous ancient monuments, its Bronze Age burial mounds, and the remains of its Romano-British villages.

"Gosh, yes," I kept saying.

"And its many enigmatic earth works."

"Wow."

"But most interesting of all, Bandy, is the remarkable wildlife."

"Wow, yes."

"Since joining the army I have spent most of my time studying the rich ecology of the Plain."

"Yes, wow."

"The quail and the stone curlew, Bandy, and the hen-harriers."

"Gosh, wow, yes."

"And the juniper groves. And the extremely interesting hobby."

"Yes, it's a fine hobby you've got there, Walter."

"I was referring to the hobby, the bird."

"Ah."

"Not to mention the entomological aspect, the marsh fritillary butterfly, the bee hawk moth, the – "

"Oh, Christ."

"I'm sorry if I'm boring you, Bandy. There are so few chaps who find – "

"No, no, Walter – I was referring to the wildlife that's just arrived," I said, indicating a large khaki Humber that was sweeping grandly into camp.

There were two passengers in the Humber, which was being driven by a lady in ATS uniform. One of two males was a civilian, who remained so carefully anonymous throughout the visit that I took him to be someone from one of the MIs – MI5, 6, 9, 13 1/2, etc. The other occupant was the Parliamentary Under-Secretary of State for Air.

Under the pretence of brushing the dandruff off his shoulders, I hid behind Walter.

Since that confrontation in the Air Ministry, I had done a little research on Sir Amyas Drummond in hopes of finding a way to ameliorate his oppugnancy, i.e., suck up to him. The first cutting I consulted, surreptitiously torn from someone's magazine, had characterized Drummond as a member of a well-known aristocratic family. This produced the first satisfying sneer. He didn't look at all aristocratic to me. Nevertheless, he was of medium-length lineage. As every schoolboy knew, the Drummonds were the ones who had so skilfully promoted the cause of Charles II. The family had done notable service to the Crown during the prince's flight following his defeat at the end of the Civil War when his father had lost his head. The Drummonds, it was said, had concealed the King for weeks on end in as many different houses, barns, and trees as possible in order to gain the loyalty of the various owners of the houses, barns, and trees. The householders and landowners could later boast – when it was safe to do so – that they had helped the sovereign to escape, and saved his life. It tended to bind them to the royal cause, and encouraged them to contribute money.

Otherwise the Drummonds were just another undistinguished family of aristocrats, spending their lives killing the birds and animals that got in the way of their Purdeys and foxhounds, acting as figureheads on boards of directors, and living off capital.

Sir Amyas himself was the most ambitious member of the family. Educated at Eton and Oxford, he was elected president of the Oxford Union and thus doomed to enter politics. Before then,

however, at the age of twenty-four, he obtained a commission in a
Guards regiment, and was despatched to the Middle East. He was
said to have fought bravely at Gallipoli in 1916, before being
wounded and taken prisoner by the Turks.

This dragged from yours truly a jot or two of sympathy despite
my every effort to sustain disdain; for I understood that the incompetent Gallipoli campaign – for which his beloved master Churchill
carried the can, incidentally – was the worst ordeal of the entire
war. And, my God, that was saying something. Certainly, on his
return from captivity, Lieutenant Drummond had taken a while to
recover from the experience. Home once more at the baronial hall
he had lain fallow for so long that the family must have seriously
considered planting him with corn.

In late 1926 he was elected to the House of Commons on the
strength of his fine record during the General Strike of that year –
he had driven a London omnibus for three days. In Parliament he
displayed a certain talent as a vigorous and effective administrator
in the increasingly important posts he came to occupy. He also
developed a pro-German reputation. His family traditionally had
connections with and many friends among the Prussian aristocracy,
and he made many visits to that country.

In the Thirties he was among the most ardent supporters of
Chamberlain and his umbrella. In fact, until as recently as April
of this year, he was among the many enthusiastic supporters of
Chamberlain's appeasement policy.

After Chamberlain was ordered to in-the-name-of-God-Go!
and Churchill took over, some sources expressed surprise that
Churchill had retained the Germanophile Sir Amyas Drummond
in the government. One crude commentator explained that it was
because he kept Churchill's boots so nice and clean – with his
tongue. But a soberer assessment was that Drummond was needed
as a ruthlessly efficient administrator.

Here on Salisbury Plain, I was still skulking behind Walter. He was
starting to get annoyed about it and asked irritably what I was
playing at.

"It's that frock who's just driven up, Walter. I don't want him to see me."

"The civilian? Yes, he's a cold-looking fish."

"No, the other one. Drummond."

"Oh, yes, we got a signal about him. He's come ahead of the official party. To make sure that everything's in order for the great man."

"What great man?" I whispered, cautiously watching the Parliamentary Under-Secretary. He hadn't seen me so far. Having bulged out of the car, he had now taken the arm of his ATS driver – a woman with, I couldn't help noticing, a fine healthy figure – and was leading her toward a group of hospitality tents.

"What great man?" I repeated.

"The Former Naval Person," Walter answered, looking mysterious.

"Gosh. You don't mean . . . ?"

"That's right," Walter whispered.

"The King?"

"No, no," Walter said. "You know."

I gazed at him blankly. He leaned closer and whispered, "The PM!"

My heart leaped. Not only did it leap, it somersaulted, did handstands, and sang two choruses of "Land of Hope and Glory" accompanied by the Black Dyke Mills Band directed by Albert Ramsbottom.

At last. I was to meet my friend Winston.

In the meantime I was keeping out of Drummond's way. Which was not easy as he was all over the place, inspecting things and asking questions. Judging by his expression he did not seem to think much of the preparations for the PM's visit, nor of the site, a temporary arrangement of canvas structures and hastily flung-up Nissen huts.

It was in one of the canvas structures that I was skulking when I met Drummond's thirty-five-year-old driver, Miss Guinevere Plumley. Which was awkward, for the structure in question was a toilet.

It was an army field version. Within its flapping fabric walls
there was a long tin urinal, the gutter blocked by Woodbine cigarette butts. There was also an open row of six toilet seats. These
were poised over a deep trench smelling of carbolic and other
things. The facilities also included a tin sink complete with a
dripping faucet that clung perilously to the end of a bent pipe.
The only available towel looked as if it had been trampled by a
Serengeti hippo.

Fortunately I was not actually blocking one of the holes when
this formidable-looking woman burst through the canvas opening.
I was washing my hands as best I could, considering the way the
discoloured water was ejaculating so fiercely through the faucet. So
my trousers were decent when she parted the canvas curtain and
pushed inside, wincing, urgently knock-kneed.

"Oh gorsh, sorry," she gasped, in a voice like a horn passage from
Wagner. "Can't stand on ceremony – there's no women's lavatory
for miles – stupid army." And hitching up her khaki skirt she
plonked herself on the end toilet seat in the row.

I stood feebly shaking rusty water from my hands, trying not to
look at her khaki panties, which were modestly covering her knees,
or her regulation suspenders, khaki, one pair, women for the use
of. There was a pause during which a look of bliss spread over her
face, while I carefully inspected the handle of the faucet, and then
the urinal drain. (That was how I knew that the debris blocking it
was composed of Woodbine butts and not examples of your superior brand of cigarettes, such as Capstan Full Strength, Balkan
Sobranie, or Senior Service.)

"Perhaps we'd better introduce ourselves," said the lady, making
standing-up and dress-adjusting noises. "I'm Guinevere Plumley."
As she came toward me and the faucet she wrenched at her
uniform. "Let me see, what am I?" she said, searching her khaki
attire for badges of rank. Finding neither stripes nor pips she said,
"I suppose I must be a private. How d'you do?"

I started forward with my hand out; but then thought better of
it. "How d'you do?" I replied. "I'm Bartholomew Bandy."

"I suppose you'd like me to salute you, eh?"

"There's probably a regulation against saluting in toilets."

"Oh. Jolly good. I'm with the Minister."

"Drummond, yes, I saw you arrive."

"Actually I'm hiding from him. He fancies me."

"Good heavens."

"You needn't sound so incredulous," boomed she, busily washing her hands and flinging droplets of water all over the place.

In fact, I was amply justified in sounding incredulous. Miss Plumley – there was no way one could think of her as Private Plumley – was an utterly splendid sight. Her figure as far north as her creamy thrapple was breathtaking, starting with a pair of gams that went on and on as far as the eye could see – and the eye had seen. The limbs had been turned with exquisite care on the genetic lathe. Next the eye was more than willingly led to a bottom designed by the gods with the help of their celestial geometry set, its curvature doubly evident even under the disapproving tunic, and firmly bonded to modest hips. Inevitably these cinched into a remarkably narrow waist considering the weight of superstructure it had to bear, a bosom perfectly counterpoised to the bottom and just as inadequately discipled by khaki cloth.

It was only when you reached the summit that the fright began. Miss Plumley's was a face to figurehead a pirate ship. Her chin – round, forthright, aggressive, determined – alone looked capable of battering through the lower gundeck; while the nose, curved to match the aforementioned top and bottom, had been won in hand-to-hand combat with a Pathan warrior.

But it was the gaze that sent you reeling back in alarm. She had the kind of eyes you see in some fighter pilots: steady, penetrating, and, in the case of her brownish eyes, unutterably fierce.

She had reached her mid-thirties without marrying. No bloody wonder. She reminded me of the nesting eagle that will ruthlessly feed the weakest chick to the strongest member of the brood.

She turned those alarming eyes on me now as she completed her ablutions. "What did you say?" she demanded ferociously.

"I said I'm hiding from Drummond as well."

"Why, what have you done wrong?" she asked, thinking of

drying her hands on the towel, then shuddering and rubbing them instead on her haunches.

"Just trying to get on ops. Sir Drummond and others think I'm too old."

"You do look a bit shagged-out," she said. "How old are you?"

"Nearly forty-six."

"I'm over twenty. Actually I'm over thirty, too. He won't help you, eh? With me he's too helpful. Says he loves me. When I hint that he's got a wife he says she doesn't mind him having affairs, she has her fan club to keep her busy."

"His wife runs a fan club?"

"The General Franco Fan Club. She's a great admirer of General Franco," Miss Plumley said, as she flung her arms around to get the circulation going. "She married beneath her, you know."

"With Drummond I would have thought that was inevitable."

Miss Plumley felt that it was disloyal to her employer to laugh at this, but did so all the same, and appreciatively pawed the dirt floor with her army shoes.

Removing her ATS cap she fluffed her hair. "How do I look?" she asked. There was not a trace of coquetry in the question or in her manner; but equally there was none of irony either, as if she genuinely and naïvely believed that anything short of a head transplant would improve her appearance.

"It's . . . fine, Miss Plumley."

"My name's Guinevere. Anything but Miss Plumley. I hate that name. That's the only reason I'm thinking of marrying Drummond – get rid of that name."

"Good Lord," I said, not knowing whether to be more astonished at her being willing to marry Drummond or at Drummond for having the nerve to ask her, assuming he had.

The canvas entrance to the toilet twitched. A moment later Walter appeared, already fumbling at his furculum. When he saw a woman in the men's toilet he stopped so abruptly that he nearly ran into himself. With his hand still in place, he backed out in mumbling confusion.

"That was Walter," I said. "He's shy."

Guinevere nodded absentmindedly, studying me. "By the way," she asked, "have we met before? Your face is familiar . . ." She slapped her damp haunches. "Got it! You look just like my favourite hunter."

"Thank you."

"I had it shot last summer."

She continued to regard me thoughtfully with her blazing, flint-edged eyes. "So you want to go on ops, eh?" she asked abruptly. "Would you like me to vamp the Drummer – Sir Amyas, that is? He's dippy about me, you know. Do anything for me."

"I'd prefer you not to draw his attention to me, Miss – Guinevere," I said, and explained as briefly as I could.

"That's too bad," she said. "He's pretty influential, you know." She started for the exit. I followed. "He handles a lot of the RAF stuff for the Secretary of State when he's not troubleshooting for his beloved Winnie. Churchill, I mean."

The timing of our egress from the latrine could not possibly have been worse. Drummond was just outside, pacing over the baked grassland with a sapper captain. Together they were consulting the timetable for the aerial demonstration, which was due to start at 1500 hours. Sir Amyas glanced up just as Guinevere and I were emerging from the bog – not exactly arm in arm, but looking fairly companionable.

Not properly appreciating the situation, the sapper captain thought it was his duty to introduce us. "Oh, this is Flight Lieutenant Bandy, sir. He's the man who'll be communicating with the pilot when . . ."

The captain faltered as he became aware that Sir Amyas's complexion had changed from pudge to whitewash, and that his eyes were bulging like a chef's belly.

After a while Amyas found his voice, which had fallen onto the scorched grass. "What's the meaning of this?" he enquired.

Not yet aware of the meaning of this, he sounded almost polite as he looked from me to Miss Plumley, and then to the sordid latrine. So far his voice was restrained. Nevertheless, heads swivelled toward us from all directions, and the sapper captain, a man used to clearing anti-personnel mines, bent his khaki lapel upward and nervously started to suck it.

The minister turned back to Guinevere. But now his fat black eyebrows were starting to writhe like salted slugs. "What the hell d'you think you're playing at, Guinevere?" he asked, though still with that restrained manner. "What were you doing in that lavatory? What were you doing in it with *him*? I'm asking for an explanation. An explanation, Guinevere."

Given Miss Plumley's behaviour in the bog, I expected her to provide a sassy response. Her large uncompromising face was roseate. I assumed it was red with annoyance over being quizzed in so public a fashion, and I fully expected her to start tearing enough strips off him to supply a ticker-tape parade.

To my surprise she remained speechless, not with anger but guilt and embarrassment. The cap she was carrying in her hand was revolving agitatedly. She looked guilty as sin, as if something really had been going on in the latrine.

"It's all right, Amyas," she said almost timidly. "It's just that there wasn't – "

His voice was rising, now. "I'm asking for an explanation," he was saying. "Do you hear? I want to know what were you doing in there, I want to know, I want to know!"

Suddenly he was in such a passion that everybody in the camp, squaddies, cooks, sappers, and the solitary civilian who looked like a spy, were gazing at him in astonishment. If Private Plumley had been his wife and he had caught her snogging with the nearest sergeant-major he could hardly have been more enraged. His hard, lumpy face was glazed with fury. Now he was actually advancing on Plumley, almost as if prepared to biff her on the boko.

Extraordinary. I mean, how could he feel so passionately about her? What on earth did he see in her?

It suddenly occurred to me. Of course! He was an uglyist!

It seemed to be my fate to get in the way. Though this time I had more sense than to say anything. I merely interposed myself and gazed at him in a neutral fashion, to encourage him to pull himself together. And encouragement was needed. His eyes were quite wild. He looked like something with claws that had been distracted from a juicy carcass.

When he found himself glaring straight up my nostrils, it was not a view that entranced him. As his razorlike eyes reached civilization again, he focussed on me properly, and proceeded to slit my throat from ear to ear.

"You again," he panted.

"Yes, sir," I said. "How d'you do, Sir Amyas."

He moved back a pace or two with a trembling hand at his brow, beginning to realize that he had made a spectacle of himself.

His next words were almost faltering. "I still haven't had an explanation what you were doing in there," he said.

"There was no other facility for a lady, sir," I said, more placatingly than ever.

It didn't seem to help much. He made an effort to compose himself, but his expression remained dissonant. "Just what is your relationship with my – my driver?" he asked shakily.

"Oh, we're just good friends," I smirked, turning to Guinevere. And then unable to stop myself from succumbing to mischief once again, I added, "Isn't that right, baby?"

Oh, boy. Another enemy created out of the flimsiest of materials.

Drummond confirmed it. His face rigid, he started to march off; but after only a few paces he turned and said quietly, "Challenging me is going to be the worst mistake you've ever made, Bandy, in a career notable for mistakes, from what I've heard."

It appeared that he, too, had been doing some research.

He treated me to one final laceration from his unblinking blue eyes before turning his back and marching over to the camp commandant, who, for the rest of the afternoon, kept staring at me as if for a last look before they folded the shroud about me.

"I've heard about him," Walter said later. And, with cheerful schadenfreude added, "He'll get you sooner or later."

And Guinevere, now furious at herself for letting everybody see that she was afraid of Drummond, said, "At least he made a giddy goat of himself as well. *Bastard.*"

The Former Naval Person was only twenty minutes late that afternoon. This was pretty good considering that he must have been frightfully busy, ordering the evacuation of Norway, and adjusting to one crisis after another: the German Blitzkrieg on Paris, the Italian declaration of war on Britain, and the sinking of the ship that had been bringing his cigars from Cuba.

But was I ever pleased to see him. At last, here was my great opportunity. If anyone could get me into a fighter squadron, it was old Churchill. He would not deny me just because age had designs on my face.

Though I played my part well ("Hello, Baker Able, receiving you strength five"), the demonstration did not go quite as well as anticipated. Watched by the august visitor and a small group of Red Tabs, the new weapon failed to snip a single wire.

I believe that in a subsequent attempt the weapon did manage to engage the target. Unfortunately, though the wire parted quite neatly, it proved to be a power line. The pilot was electrocuted.

I managed to intercept the Prime Minister just as he was boarding his open-topped car. The outriders were already revving their motorcycle engines by the time I got within range.

"Sir, sir," I cried, as several military policemen started forward in alarm. "Mr. Churchill. You remember me, sir? Bandy?"

He promptly disappeared behind his cigar.

"I'm sure you do, sir," I said. "It was only a decade or two ago. First time we met you were asking me about the situation in France, which was just as bad then as it is now."

"Ah," said Mr. Churchill, his fleshy face a nice pink colour in the sunshine. He nodded and gave me a friendly V for Victory sign which stopped the redcaps in their tracks. But then he gestured to the chauffeur, who immediately started stripping his gears.

To enable Mr. Churchill to stop for a chat, I stood in front of the car and patted the matte-black radiator. "Surely you couldn't have forgotten, sir," I coaxed. "For one thing, I gave you that phrase about blood, tears, toil, and so on."

He emerged from behind his cigar, glaring. "Nonsense," he growled.

"It's true, sir, that was my line. Don't you remember, it was at your house on Cromwell Road. You asked about the situation in France and I used those very words. But I was very magnanimous. I said you could keep the phrase if you wanted."

"Nonsense," he growled again; but there was enough uncertainty in his well-known face to encourage me to continue.

So I also reminded him that we had met on other occasions, most notably upon my return from India. "You asked to see me, sir," I reminded him, "after reading all about my triumphal return after saving India. You would have read about how the crowds had cheered and waved like mad when my wife and I arrived at Southampton. Why, even some dock workers, perched on various girders, made gestures which I took to be approbatory, sir, and the mayor of Southampton gave a speech as stuffed with plaudits and hosannas as a Christmas cake is with candied peel and threepenny bits."

"Get to the point, man," he rumbled.

"I'm just setting the scene to enable you to remember it," I continued, moving closer to the back seat of the car. "Even my train journey from Southampton to London was an occasion for celebration, with a brass band oompahing like mad on the station concourse, you remember, or you would have remembered had you been there. Why, they had even supplied a red carpet, though owing to an untoward movement of the train, my good wife Sigridur and I found ourselves stepping off the carpet and into the guard's van, which was full of bicycles. The guard explained that these were being transported back to London after an outing by the Catford, Putney, and Herne Hill Bicycle Club."

"Mr. Bandy," the occupant of the back seat interrupted, or tried to.

"But I digress," I continued. "The point is, sir, that I want to get out there and biff a few Nazis, but they say I'm too old to fly with a fighter squadron. Now, you weren't too old to fight alongside the Royal Scots Fusiliers at Plugstreet in 1916, were you? Even though you were pretty old even then. So I thought – "

"Mr. Bandy."

"I thought you of all people would see that it's nonsense to keep someone as valuable as me from the front line – "

"Mr. Bandy," the great man whispered, "it's no good telling me all this. I'm not Mr. Churchill."

"What?"

"I'm not Mr. Churchill."

"What?"

"I am not Winston Churchill."

"What? 'Course you are."

"No. I'm a substitute. I'm an actor. I'm being paid to impersonate him, you see."

"A substitute?"

"In case of an assassination or kidnap attempt, or to fool the enemy about his whereabouts, you see."

"You're not Mr. Churchill?"

"No."

"Are you sure?"

"Yes."

"You look just like him."

"That's the whole point. I'm supposed to look just like him."

"You're taking his place?"

"There's a possibility of German parachute troops, you see."

"You're just acting the part?"

"You've got it. At this precise moment the real Mr. Churchill is at Chequers."

"Surely he should be looking after the nation's affairs in this time of crisis, not playing checkers?"

"Chequers is the Prime Minister's official country residence in Buckinghamshire, Mr. Bandy."

"So you mean . . . you're not the Prime Minister?"

"No. Now can I go home to my missus?"

"Yes, of course," I said, stepping away from the car. But then called out, "I don't suppose you could remind him about me, could you?" But the car was already halfway to the perimeter fence, travelling at a quite remarkable speed considering how uneven and hard-baked Salisbury Plain was in the summer heat.

The German army entered Paris and proceeded to swank the length and breadth of the Champs Elysées. The Luftwaffe continued its policy of strafing the civilian refugees straggling along the escape routes. The French government moved from Tours to Bordeaux where the wine was. And the real Churchill made the most amazing offer to the French: if they were willing, Britain and France would no longer be two nations but a single Franco-British union with common citizenship. For some reason he thought that this breathtaking offer might encourage them to fight on. In fact, it encouraged quite a few Frenchmen, terrified at the prospect of having to eat "rosbif" with mint sauce every day, to surrender at once.

Mr. Churchill made no offer to me, though. In the midst of the crisis, where everyone was needed to man the barricades against the totalitarian hordes, I remained as idle as a flatworm. Now there was no work for me at all. If any experimental weapons were being tested, they were not being tested on Salisbury Plain.

The national emergency deepened. Hitler did a little dance in Compiègne forest as he dictated the peace terms to the French, while I helped to prop up the bar in the army officer's mess on Salisbury Plain. The brown jobs wouldn't even employ me as duty officer; they said I wasn't there, officially. And besides, I wasn't a member.

In August the battle began in earnest. After the German attacks on shipping in the Channel, devastating raids on aerodromes that destroyed many of the country's reserve of fighters, and some Teutonic shoot-ups of various mysterious towers and aerials that had something to do with radiolocation, the Luftwaffe switched to mass raids all over Southern England. And all I could do was listen to the broadcasts and the BBC interviews with victorious fighter pilots, and feel as if acid was stapping me vitals.

However, not all was disaster. At the beginning of July, the Royal Navy destroyed the French fleet along the Algerian coast, which helped to restore British confidence and sense of purpose.

And then, suddenly, mysteriously, success out of nowhere. Through the intercession of some anonymous influence I was sent to an Operational Training Unit at a place called Rednal, somewhere in the Midlands. Soon thereafter, assuming I passed the various tests and the medical, I would be sent to a fighter squadron.

I assumed that somehow my exhaustive lobbying efforts with nearly every important person I'd ever met during the course of my travels and travails had finally paid off.

Not a soul came forward to claim credit for getting me out of the scrapyard and into the scrap. Admittedly I wasn't all that curious, though one possibility was that it was Drummond who had relented and given me permission to fly and fight, in the confident hope that I would soon be snuffed out in battle. Which was not unlikely, judging by the casualties, as the aerial battle intensified. I decided that if my patron, whoever he was, wished to remain anonymous, that was all right with me.

Anyway, at the time I was too excited to investigate further. Which is a pity, for if I had successfully pursued the identity of the person who made it possible for me to revenge myself on the Nazis, it would have made a profound difference to my life.

TRYING TO LOOK
INCONSPICUOUS

THE JOURNEY FROM THE Operational Training Unit in Shropshire to the reserve airfield in Norfolk took all day. I was forced to travel in a train hauled by a steam engine that was burning old dog blankets, judging by the odour of the smoke that seeped into the compartment. Plato seemed to like the smell, though.

The final part of the journey from the station to the aerodrome was in the back of a one-and-a-half-tonner that had no springs. The truck was otherwise occupied by so many beery aircraftsmen that there was hardly room for my single valise.

The lads divided their time between patting Plato and staring at my left tit. Below the wings were four and a half rows of gongs. The confirmation had finally come through from Ottawa that I was entitled to wear a score or so of medals and orders. The boys thought I must be an old ENSA entertainer who was travelling in his amusingly exaggerated stage uniform, until I explained that I was a replacement pilot. Whereupon they laughed expectantly, as if waiting for the punch line of a really good joke.

The dominant member of the group was a large, rough-looking LAC who said his name was Tommy Atkins.

"No, no, you've got that wrong," I said. "That was a soldier in the First World War."

"No, it really is, sir. That's my name."

"I'll take your word for it. My name's Bandy."

They laughed dutifully. "It is," I said. "That's my name."

We chatted as best we could in the noisy, jarring one-and-a-half tonner. To a chorus of jeers, Atkins, who had a face like a boxing glove, said that he had joined the RAF to be an SP, but they had made him a rigger instead of a copper. He was currently working on Spitfire airframes. He said that he had nearly been killed in an air raid the previous week.

"That would have been a case of rigger mortis, eh?" I said.

"Oh, very funny," Atkins said; but laughed all the same.

It was still fairly light at 2300 hours when Plato and I showed our orders and warrants at the guardhouse and were given a lift to the mess. And found the bar closed and the mess deserted.

They had closed the bar? At eleven p.m? At a fighter station? Surely I must have strayed into the Pay Corps? And the lounge was similarly forsaken. Not a pilot in sight, drunk or sober. Just a mess steward in a grubby white jacket.

The steward was Rich by name and rich in gravy stains; he also stared as if mesmerized, at my braggart gongs. They did not inspire him to open the bar, though he could see that I was as needful of a drink as an imposter at a temperance meeting. The best he could do was to refer me to the duty officer.

The duty officer duly appeared and was just as ornery. The bar could not be reopened without the CO's say-so.

"So go and get his say-so."

"He's too drunk to open the bar. Nobody uses it anyway. They go down to the pub."

"And I suppose the pub is closed by now."

"'Course it is, it's after eleven," Bernard Greaves said, not exactly in welcoming tones. "So you managed to reach a squadron after all," he went on, staring at my ribbons. "How on earth did you manage it?"

"It appears I have a mysteriously influential friend, Bernard. How's your father these days?"

"I believe he's being seconded to the Ministry of Aircraft Pro-duction," Bernard said offhandedly. Then, unable to contain himself any longer: "I say," he said, squinting against the colourful display, "what on earth are you doing with all those gongs and things? You didn't have those at Camp Borden."

"It's my hobby, Bernard. I collect old medals."

"Oh, I see. Anyway, I suppose I should organize quarters for you. There's a room available in the officers' block across the way there. I'd pick the end room on the left if I were you, as far as possible from the pilots. They can be quite noisy sometimes."

"But I don't want to be as far as possible from the – "

"Pick the room next door to the dentist, old man – he's quiet."

There were, in fact, two bunks available in the room at the end of the lino'd corridor of the officers' quarters. The personal effects of a former occupant, a pilot who had bought the farm just the previous day, had not yet been collected. They were spread out over the taut blanket of one of the beds. The belongings included a one-eared teddy bear.

There was very little sleep to be had that night. First there was the sound of a distant all-clear. I was awake for ages, trying to work out how I had missed the air raid siren that had surely preceded it. There had been no gunfire. Then I was kept busy listening to the dentist next door. The frequency range of his snoring rivalled that of a drill repeatedly glancing off a ridge of bone.

Finally, just as I was snuggling into the arms of Morpheus at 0500 hours, came the snarling of a pack of Rolls-Royce Merlins, followed by take-off effects about five feet overhead.

Blearily at 0600 I fitted myself into battledress, which sported RCAF wings but thankfully lacked the medal ribbons which were attracting too much attention. Thus ungaudily costumed, I wandered over to the mess for breakfast. The mess was deserted. The pilots were out training even at this ungodly hour.

The squadron had recently been in action, but had been withdrawn to this airfield in Norfolk after losing more than half its strength against the enemy Messerschmitts. The survivors were currently absorbing a good many replacement pilots, one of whom was Bernard Greaves.

At 0755, I proceeded along the narrow tarmac road that wound through the camp. It was already tacky in the early August sun. It was going to be another hot day.

The squadron office was one of the long wooden huts that were scattered around the field as haphazardly as toy blocks, and there I waited for my boss, Squadron Leader Daplin. He was at dispersal, busy debriefing a group of sprog pilots, and half an hour passed before he turned up, accompanied by the wing commander. They were both in blue battledress and flying boots. As they clumped into the hut they barely glanced at me before disappearing into the inner office.

When I was finally shown into the inner sanctum I found them both chortling over my service records.

The buff file had been slit open and the innards spread out over a battered Ministry of Works desk. The augury must have been decidedly amusing, for the two officers were laughing like sooth-sayers over the entrails.

"Ah, the man of influence himself," boomed Wing Commander Broseley. His face was mottled, as if it had been dabbed with slices of wet beetroot. Attached to it was an amazing moustache. It was ginger in colour and about twelve inches wide from tip to straggly tip.

"Come in, come in, my dear fellow," he shouted. "Quick, Nick, help him into a chair. Sit down, sit down, my dear fellow, or perhaps even lie down, and let's look at you. H'm . . ." And in a confidential aside that made the windows rattle: "Good Lord, Nick, I do believe he's even older than Rip Van Wrigley."

"I am not," I said.

"Why, have you met the padre?"

"No."

"So how d'you know you're not older than him?"

"Well, somehow he sounds old. I'm only forty-five."

"Forty-six!"

"Oh, yes," I mumbled. "It was my birthday last month."

"Many happy returns," the wing commander boomed. "Including a happy return to the Air Ministry, old man. We don't want you here. The pilots might catch something off you. Like rheumatism."

"We might make him the padre's assistant, sir," the squadron leader said. A cold, slender man in his mid-twenties, he wore a vicious scar that drew down the corner of one eye. It looked like a recent injury. "Or he could run the housey-housey – bingo, or whatever you call it," he said disdainfully. "The chaplain hates that job."

"I came three thousand miles to fly Spitfires, sir."

"Oh, come now, Randy, be realistic," Broseley said. "I can see you're a man of terrific experience. I'm not sure but that I haven't heard of you, even. Have you ever heard of him, Charlie?"

"I'm not sure but that I haven't either, sir."

"But it's quite out of the question, Randy. I mean, you're such a, shall we say, a mature gentleman I have to restrain myself from addressing you as sir. I mean, how would that look in front of the SWO if I fell to addressing a mere flight lieutenant as sir? It would be the end of the world as we know it, or at least the talk of Cranwell."

His tone grew almost sympathetic. "Look, old chap, I gather you're a warrior of long standing with a quite astonishing variety of aircraft in your log books – though I must say a couple of thou isn't a particularly impressive total of flying hours over such a long period – such a *very* long period," he repeated, closing my file with a slap of his large, nicotine-stained hand. "No, it's no good arguing, Randy – "

"Bandy, sir. My name is Bandy."

"Randy, Bandy, let's not quibble. You simply couldn't stand the pace, old boy, and that's all there is to it. Bloody Air Ministry. They'll be sending us Chelsea pensioners next. But quite apart from your old age, Randy, I don't understand this posting at all."

"I'm a bit confused, too," Daplin put in. "I'd've said we had a case of mistaken identity here if I didn't know that the Air Ministry has trouble even with proper identities. Your name's not Brown, by the way, is it? We had a Brown who was supposed to be here last July. Are you sure you're not Brown?"

"No, he's quite pale, really," said Broseley, and had a thoroughly good laugh with himself. Even the squadron leader had difficulty with the joke. "Anyway, we've already established that he's Randy."

"Bandy," I said.

"Anyway, the wing commander boomed, "we can't risk you flying with us, and that's all there is to it. Now cut along, there's a good chap. I've got work to do. Got to catch up with the latest edition of *Men Only*."

"But sir – "

"We'll talk about what to do with you some other time, Randy," he said, smoothing out his kite moustache. And it certainly needed smoothing. "In the meantime take a look around. Why don't you wander down to the flight line and see what a modern aeroplane looks like, eh?"

I gave him one of my straight, blinkless looks. But the sight of my face merely produced a stifled guffaw, though he did his best to turn it into a cough.

"Very well, sir, I'll do just that," I said.

"That's right, old man, you do that," Broseley said, abruptly dropping the jovial act, and turning away dismissively.

Atkins, the burly LAC I'd met in the tender, was working over an aircraft jig when I strolled into the hangar a few minutes later, idly swinging the regulation parachute from my casual hand.

There was a Mark I Spitfire parked outside. I asked if it was ready for flight testing.

"I think it is, sir, but you could check with the flight sergeant."

I didn't want to bother the flight sergeant, so I got Atkins to collect a small crew to help with the battery, chocks, Sutton harness, and so forth; and I clamped myself into the cockpit before he had time to think about it.

I had done only nineteen hours in the Spitfire at the OTU, so it was still an amusing experience, squeezing into the narrow cockpit and wriggling about until the parachute fitted snugly into the moulded seat. And still a pleasure to be fiddling with the fifty-odd switches, tabs, and levers. I couldn't help contrasting the controls in front of me with the ironmongery in my first fighter, the Camel, which had practically no instruments at all.

As I trimmed for take-off, Atkins was starting to worry.

I forestalled his objections. "I'm just doing a few circuits and bumps, Tommy," I reassured him.

"Are you sure it's all right, sir? I mean, nobody's told us."

"Quite all right. So hop off the wing. And tell them to get their fingers out, and crank up the cart."

He did so, but looked worried as I primed the engine and signalled for power. The engine spluttered and banged into life.

My sharp, peremptory tone over the RT bamboozled flying control into giving me permission for a take-off. With fast-beating heart I adjusted fine pitch and trimmed for take-off; then forward with the throttle and a few pounds of boost.

The slender machine accelerated quickly, and it was a relief to bring up the tail and obtain a decent view ahead. In the hot morning the Spitfire took up much of the grass field before lifting over the straggly hedge at the far end.

We bumped about a bit at first, but soon settled down to the usual smooth and contented vibration. We levelled off at 2,000, and started to circle the field. I had done a little formation flying and some air firing at the OTU and was already fairly familiar with the graceful machine. What nonsense it was to say that a gentleman of mature years could not handle a sophisticated modern fighter. Absolute nonsense. My reflexes were just about as sharp now as they had been when, way back there in '17, I flew the Sopwith Camel on fighting patrols, often three times a day. The Camel was a damn sight more difficult machine to fly than this curved beauty, I can tell you.

Sweeping gracefully round the field at 2,000 feet, I checked the various temperatures, then squinted over the side in the dazzling light to locate the administration buildings; and proceeded to dive on them and make a low-level pass at maximum speed to wake everybody up.

Two or three twists, turns, and low-level barrel rolls later there were quite a few upturned faces at dispersal, at the aircraft parking bays, on the drill square, and outside the hangars.

I continued to throw the machine into every manoeuvre I could think of. Admittedly there were not many of them, as I had never enjoyed stunting – it made me squint. Still, I was desperate to prove myself and it was a pretty impressive display.

A few of the manoeuvres were decidedly reckless for someone with fewer than twenty hours. I blasted across the field upside down for nearly half a minute before rolling upwards. That scared me so much I gave up after beating up the tower, where they were watching through field glasses. Turning onto final I banked on sharp, pointed wingtips as if to turn the machine into a Catherine wheel.

And forgot to lower the undercarriage.

The Spitfire slithered to a stop on its belly, bending the propeller and forcing them to send the sprained engine back to the disgusted fitters, who had only just finished repairing it.

"That settles it," Broseley said. "You're in charge of the bingo games."

SCRAMBLING

BY THE THIRD WEEK in August, the aerial trespass by the Luftwaffe showed no signs of flagging or abating, and if our experience was anything to go by, the battle was being lost. Our new base in Essex was bombed and strafed four times in a week, rendering it useless for crucial hours at a time. And our squadron casualties were approaching 10 per cent per day. In one of the raids, the sergeants' mess received a direct hit and two of our sergeant pilots were injured, and one killed. These losses, together with the delay in receiving replacement pilots, threatened to put the squadron out of business entirely. It was in these circumstances that I was tannoyed to Broseley's office one morning.

His office was usually blue with cigar or cigarette smoke, but today it was nice and airy. I sound found that this was because most of the glass in the window had been blown out. The wall opposite the window was badly damaged by blast.

"There's a Spit being delivered this morning from the factory," he said, looking down at his desk and pushing sheets of paper around it with his large, stained forefinger. His normally booming voice sounded as if it hadn't slept for a week. "I've nobody else to give it to. Do you think you could make it last for a few days without pranging it?"

I didn't understand at first. "You want me to collect it from the factory, sir?"

"No, dammit, I want you to fly it." He looked up sharply.
"Assuming you still want to fight."

"Ah," I said with a long sigh. "You assume correctly," I said.

"Daplin doesn't think it's a good idea," the wing commander
said, sounding thoroughly hostile. "He considers you unreliable."

"He's just jealous, sir. He wants to be considered unreliable
himself," I said, distracting Broseley with chatter in case he was
already regretting the offer, and was about to withdraw it.

Instead, he sat down wearily and reached for the telephone.
"Well, do your best, Randy," he said, and waved for me to get the
hell out.

Which I did, walking on cushions of air.

This was the day that the attacks directly upon the RAF airfields
ended, at least for the time being. Instead, the Luftwaffe turned its
attention to the cities of southern England, particularly London.

The change in strategy might have had something to do with the
RAF raid on Berlin on August 26 – more leaflets, for God's sake, but
a few bombs as well. Maybe Hitler was miffed. He must surely have
been annoyed at his air chief, Hermann Göring, who had promised
faithfully, cross his heart and hope to die, that the RAF would never
touch Berlin. But whatever the reason for the switch of targets it
was a Good Thing for the country. Hard cheese on the civvies, but
lucky for us.

The first time I flew against the enemy was in the Sopwith Camel,
which was made out of dope and piano wire. On that memorable
day in 1917 I was allocated a position at the arse end of a ragged
quintet, and I neither saw nor understood anything that happened during the course of the flight, or, indeed, over the next
dozen flights over enemy territory. The other pilots kept changing direction or diving or split-arsing for no apparent reason.
They told me that the sky had been full of enemy aircraft. I had
seen none of them.

It was like that all over again, when at the end of August I flew
with the Spitfire squadron for the first time. I perceived almost

nothing from the cramped cockpit. I was as useless then as I had
been twenty-three years previously. When we straggled back to
our Essex base singly or at best in pairs, and the overexcited pilots
gathered at the briefing hut and described the various aerial com-
motions we had been through, I could contribute nothing. I had
failed to notice a formation of bombers said to be sixty strong.
Equally shameful and far more dangerous was a failure to see the
enemy fighters lurking overhead. I had not even been aware that
my flight had been shot at by a pair of Bf 109s until they told me.
I had hardly seen a darn thing.

I don't know. I was beginning to wonder if I was quite as eagle-
eyed as I'd thought.

While waiting my turn to report to the intelligence officer, I listened to a couple of RAF pilots, hoping to learn something useful.

"Where'd you hear that?" one of them was saying.

"From S2."

"Duff gen merchants."

"Too true."

"Bad show!"

"Dashed bad show."

"Pure line shoot."

"Quite. Gerald get back?"

"Had it."

"Prang?"

"Flamer."

"Hard cheese. Good bloke."

"Roly too."

"Flak?"

"Clag. Lost."

"What a bind."

"Quite. See Lofty bail out?"

"Dead sticked."

"Wiped the crate."

"Quite."

"Should get a gong."

"Or a rocket."
"Beer?"
"Green Man?"
"You're on."

On my third trip Nicholas Daplin, after surreptitiously kicking
Plato under the pretence of pushing the old mongrel aside, came
over to listen to my report to the intelligence officer. "You're not
doing too well, are you, Bandy?" he observed. He was holding a
tightly balled handkerchief in his hand.

"At least he got back," said an FO named Joffee, a large and
sophisticated bruiser from Toronto who had difficulty squeezing
into the Spitfire cockpit, especially after he'd had half a dozen pints
at the local. He had a hippopotamus chin and his nose was so bent
that he looked as if he were perpetually turing right.

"And even remembered to lower his undercart for the landing,"
Daplin said; and added, "And why didn't you answer when I called
you on the RT to move in closer?"

"I was preoccupied."

"You were preoccupied, *sir*. Preoccupied with Waafs in blue
knickers, were you?" said Daplin, who seemed obsessed with
servicewomen's underwear. He was always talking about knickers
or panties or, as he sometimes called them, trolleys, presumably
because they went up and down.

"You'll have to do better than that, Bandy," Daplin said, drawing the balled-up hanky out of his fist with his teeth. Joffee looked
at him.

I explained with as much dignity as I could borrow from the
mess funds that I had been sticking to young Greaves's tail, acting
as a whisk to keep the Hun flies off him until he had gained some
useful experience. Cyril Greaves had asked me to look after his son,
and had been touchingly grateful when I promised to do so.

Daplin knew that I was on friendly terms with an air vice-
marshal. It seemed to be another sore point with him. "Oh, yes, we
all know you suck up to the brass," he said. "Well, I hope you don't
think it'll get you any preferential treatment here. And another

thing: there is to be no wandering off independently. This squadron is noted for its discipline, on the ground and in the air, and I'm not putting up with adventurers who think that just because they once held high rank they can do what they want. I shall be watching you, Bandy.

"And keep your wits about you, next time you fly. I expect today you were daydreaming about that new nurse at sick quarters I saw you out with," Daplin said.

He had seen me dining out with the nurse in question, if you could describe a trip to a glum café for pilchards and wet potatoes as dining out. "Daydreaming about gently smoothing her thigh," Daplin said, dabbing at the dollops of sweat under his eyes, "until they open up and she unbuttons her tunic to give her bosom room to heave, and . . . I expect that's why you were preoccupied, and failed to notice the enemy."

Odd chap, Daplin. He seemed to believe one was thinking about sex all the time, instead of just in one's waking hours.

"I can't quite put my finger on it," I said to Joffee after Daplin crashed out of the door. "But I'm beginning to suspect that Daplin doesn't entirely approve of me."

"I can put my finger on it," he replied. "And it's all very understandable," he said in his reasonable tones. "He hates you. He hates your face. He hates your voice. He hates your character, your personality, your connections, your life, your flying, and your dog."

"I can't think why. Plato is a very inoffensive old thing."

"Personally I think Daplin's trouble is that he was shot down twice in France. It is my informed medical opinion," Joffee continued, "as a biologist of note — I once cut up a dead vole and made several scientific observations before I was sick — that Daplin's experience on Fairey Battles jarred his sex hormones loose."

Bernard Greaves was no happier with me than Daplin was. "Dammit, Bandy, you keep giving me heart failure," he complained over the mess coffee after a morning of three separate, frantic scrambles. "Every time I twist round to make sure there's no Hun on my tail, there you are. I mean, dash it all, you don't have to be that close, do you? I don't need nursemaiding, you know."

"The Jerries use wingmen, Bernard. And with all their experience, they should know."

"He's talking rubbish," Daplin said loudly from another part of
the lounge. "I knew it – he's just a windbag." He smirked across at
me. "You haven't been here long enough to notice anything like
that, Bandy."

"That's true."

"There you are, then."

"I saw it in Spain, Squadron Leader."

While Daplin was busy flushing, several pilots huddled closer.
"You were in the Spanish Civil War?"

I admitted I was.

"Which side were you flying for?"

"Government. Though they made it kind of difficult for us volunteers to help them," I said, unhappily remembering.

The pilots encouraged me to yarn about my experiences in the
Iberian peninsula. One of the things I mentioned was that by the
end of the war, the Germans, who were fighting on Franco's side,
seemed to be adopting a much looser flying formation than had
hitherto been the norm.

"Is that right?" Joffee said thoughtfully.

"That's bloody rubbish," Daplin said, so furiously that everybody
looked at him in surprise. His face was white and pinched, and
he seemed to be quivering with anger. "Don't listen to him," he
shouted. "We've nothing to learn from the Hun, nothing."

He looked sick and hunted, as if it had occurred to him that if
we had nothing to learn from the Germans, how come they had
managed to shoot him down twice?

As soon as he quit the lounge, a few of the pilots continued to
ask questions about what else I'd seen in Spain. One of them, Tom
Dirkin, confided in an undertone that, "Maybe they're right, maybe
we shouldn't bunch up so tight. As things are, we don't seem to be
doing too well with our tactics."

He was an angry man. His family lived in London and had been
bombed out. He glanced around cautiously, and muttered, "We

seem to be more interested in correct RT procedure and keeping nicely spaced than going after those bastards."

By September we were being scrambled as many as five times a day, and vectored toward great packs of bombers. And I was still of very little use, failing to observe everything that was going on around me. Even in chaotic Spain I'd done better than this. And I couldn't use the excuse that I was concerned with protecting Bernard. Invariably I was losing sight of him the moment we started split-arsing.

I even wondered for a mo if I was being too cautious. I was certainly doing my best to avoid being snuck up on. I knew how easily a fighter pilot could be done in by the one he never saw. My excuse for concentrating on preserving my own hide was that I couldn't be of much use to anyone if I was dead.

My other excuse was that Squadron Leader Daplin confused me. Half the time he seemed to be stooging around from Essex to the Kent coast to no real purpose. Yet he was following his instructions from the Sector E controllers to the letter. In spite of which we never seemed to get much closer to the bombers. And we didn't seem to be trying hard enough to claw for height in order to reach the Messerschmitts glinting overhead in the sun.

After a dozen or more sorties the nearest I came to actually fighting was when Flight Lieutenant Joffee, or Toffee Apples as the others called him, was leading the squadron. He dived onto what seemed to me to be nothing more dangerous than a cloud. But when we fell out of it, there proved to be a trio of Heinkels underneath, heading for home.

After a long burst, Joffee sent one of them down in flames. Sergeant Toye accounted for another. Bernard tried to get at the third, but either his shooting was amiss, or the Heinkel pilot was too evasive, and the twin-engined bomber got away.

So once again I achieved nothing. Worse, when I landed back at the field I pulled a trapezius muscle whilst clambering out of the cockpit. I had to be helped to the ground by one of the erks.

"Poor old soul," I heard someone say.

Then I got told off by Bernard, who said that before he engaged the Heinkel he had very nearly been shot down by a 109. "You were supposed to be watching my tail," he complained.

"It's impossible to stick with you all the time, Bernard," I said drably, but, in between my eeks and ouches, I felt appalled – for I hadn't noticed the 109.

Daplin joined in. "Our influential friend was probably too busy thinking about Waafs' knickers," he said. "Well, all I can say, Bandy, is if Pilot Officer Greaves goes for a Burton, we'll know who to blame, won't we?"

Every day, as the fighting over Kent and the Channel grew more and more desperate, I seemed to be an increasing liability rather than an asset. Because of the wrenched muscle, I couldn't even run to the aircraft with the others. Now, on top of my aerial incompetence, it looked as if I were going slow, showing no enthusiasm for the fight.

"Get a move on, Bandy," Daplin shouted as he hastened past on the way out to his own Spit. And, on our return: "Too shagged out to run, are you?" he asked. "At it again with that nurse, I suppose – exploring the fault line inside her knickers, were you?"

"She's giving me physiotherapy, sir, for my back."

"That's what they're calling it now, is it? I say, Daphne, let's have your pants off for a spot of physiotherapy, what?" Daplin said, looking around to see if anyone else considered this amusing.

Toffee Apples, at least, was unamused. "That man is seriously disturbed," he said. "And he seems obsessed with you. I'd complain to the station commander, if I were you."

He was referring to Group Captain Mince. But I was inclined to keep clear of him. He was already suspicious of me. He had intercepted me one day to ask if I was sure I wanted to continue on operations. "You're a bit long in the tooth for this sort of lark, aren't you, Bandy? Of course, I too would dearly love to be out there fighting the enemy," he said, "but I recognize my limitations."

"You do?" I said in surprise. I didn't think Mince had any. He looked after himself so well.

Group Captain Mince was tall and handsome, with a manly, square-jawed face and a dignified demeanour. Even his hair was dignified. It was also so plentiful that I felt stabs of pure jealousy whenever he removed his gold-braided cap. I seriously considered spreading a rumour that the distinguished touch of silver at his temples was counterfeit: that Mince was highlighting it with silver polish.

Worse, though years older than me, he looked in much better shape. I looked ready for the glue pot. He looked like an ad for Patem Peperium, the Gentleman's Relish. Group Captain Mince was an extremely fit man. He maintained the fitness through an energetic regime of compulsory outdoor PT classes and physical jerks in the gym. He also ran the cross-country exercise every Sunday, the Squadron Treasure Hunt (the treasure being a recording of Schönberg's music), and insisted on at least two soccer games being played per week, regardless of the weather.

Of course, he didn't actually take part in any of these activities himself. The exertion was for everybody else. He believed that the nervous energy he expended in organizing the events was sufficient exercise for him.

The annoying thing was that he was right. Making everybody else sweat kept him in excellent condition.

"I saw you hobbling out to your plane this morning," Mince said in his clean, hygienic, and well-tailored voice. "You're obviously in no shape for this sort of game, Flight Lieutenant."

"It's my back, sir."

"I know it's your back. I'm not denying it's your back. What I'm saying is that your back's turning into a humped bridge."

"I sprained a muscle, sir, getting out of the plane."

"I see. So not only do you have difficulty reaching your plane, but when you do, you have trouble getting out of it again. Really, Bandy, even for a man of your age – I don't suppose you speak Serbo-Croatian, do you?"

"Huh?"

"Serbo-Croatian? Do you speak it?"

"Not really."

"Pity. You could have applied for the job."

"What job?"

"What job, *sir*, if you please. They've been calling for volunteers who have a knowledge of Serbo-Croatian. It might have been just perfect for you, if you'd been able to speak Serbo-Croatian," Mince said. And setting me a good example by straightening his own back, he marched off for his afternoon siesta.

On the following day, Daplin accidentally led us right under a pack of 109s.

Just as our air controller, code-named Midway, was using their clever "radar" machinery to inform us that there were bandits in the vicinity, we were bounced right merrily.

Suddenly it was every man for himself. But this was something I knew about. With the Spitfire's turning ability and my dedication to the preservation of my hide, I managed to keep out of danger for the all-important first few seconds of milling confusion.

The sky was full of twisting, turning machines. A solitary Spitfire appeared on the left, wobbling close. The canopy was open. Was he crazy, flying straight and level like that in the middle of a dogfight?

Then I realized that the pilot was bailing out. White smoke streaming from his engine. Glycol coolant.

As the plane started to go down, and the pilot jumped I saw the letters on the fuselage. It was Bernard's plane. I hadn't even managed to protect Cyril's beloved son.

At least he was out of the plane. But this was no time to admire his swinging descent. I got mixed up with a 109, but managed, by using both hands on the doughnut-shaped grip of the control column, to get roughly behind him.

Unless the reader has missed the sublime opportunity to read the previous volumes of *The Bandy Papers*, he or she will know that I have been a first-class shot ever since shooting the Professor of Surgery in the back during officer training manoeuvres in Toronto's Don Valley. Yet I had not done at all well during firing practice recently at OTU. Unless I was squarely behind the target – and that hardly ever happens in high-speed combat – I seemed unable to work it out properly in the Spitfire's glowing reflector gunsight. Nor did I get it right now. You'd think one could hardly miss with the Messerschmitt only seventy-five yards ahead. Giving it twenty-five degrees of deflection I pressed the tit for three long bursts from the eight machine guns, which chattered and sent smoke streaming back over the wings, causing the cockpit to fill with cordite fumes, which I could somehow smell even through the oxygen mask. I gave him ten whole seconds of explosive bullet, and only just managed to register a few red sparks along his starboard wing before he did one of those fast dives out of range that 109s were so good at.

Luckily I had an excuse ready: a very inelastic shoulder muscle. And in combat, every muscle counts — especially the sphincter muscle. All the same I felt very discontented, and searching around for an excuse I blamed the tools. Machine guns simply couldn't do enough damage to a metal kite. What we needed were cannon. Some upcoming marks of Spitfire had cannon, why couldn't we have cannon, I could have blown that wing to buggery if I'd had cannon.

And the Jerries had cannon. I knew this because while I was blaming the Air Ministry for not having cannon, cannon tracer started to rule untidy lines just above the canopy. Feeling as if I'd swallowed an alarm bell and it had stuck in my gullet, I rolled the kite before I had a chance to panic and hauled the stick into my guts; stabbed the rudder into a turn; and darted off sideways and downwards toward the clouds in so fast and cowardly a fashion that the altimeter could hardly keep up. Strangely, though, when I looked at the airspeed indicator I only seemed to be doing 20 mph. That didn't seem right, somehow. Then I realized that the needle must have gone right round the dial and started up the scale again. Pulling back the stick took quite an effort. The aircraft was shuddering as if it, too, was in a funk. I must have been going down at nearly 500 mph. As often happened, my mind, in its fear and agitation, was chattering like a ninth machine gun. The words on that railway poster kept haring through my head: *Is Your Journey Really Necessary? Is Your Journey Really Necessary? Is Your Journey* – Pretty stupid, that. After all, you were already at the railway station, ready to go, what did they expect, did they expect you to read the poster, then turn and go home? Practically everybody travelling nowadays was on some sort of war service. Imagine some erk deciding not to report at the guardhouse at 2359. "Well, you see, Sergeant, I saw this poster, and it got me thinking . . ."

Emerging finally from the clouds I found I was only 2,000 feet up – and still diving, even though gradually pulling out of it. And heading straight into the barrage balloons from which London was suspended.

Barrage balloons could cause considerable unease in the manliest of fighter bosoms, and mine was no exception. I'd heard tales of pilots blundering in fog or rain into their forests of steel cables. From the ground they looked like white, sluglike vestigial organs hacked from giant corpses: ridiculous. They were not ridiculous as far as the stressed metal wings of small fighter aircraft were concerned. At the craven speed I was going I was in the midst of them before I had a chance to turn. One of them was directly ahead. I turned the Spit onto its beam ends. Crawling skin informed me that the cable had sliced past, though I didn't see it. Then I was climbing again and wishing the supercharger blasted in at angels 2 instead of 18 or 19.

Not content with almost cutting me into bacon slices, a Bofors gun took potshots at me from the eastend docks as I hurtled past and upwards. Straight toward a Junkers dive bomber that had just shat onto those same docks.

As usual, Squadron Leader Daplin came over to listen to my report to the IO. "And did you get the dive bomber?" asked the IO.

"No, 'fraid not," I said. "I think I got it in the sights okay, but when I fired all I got was a hissing. I'd used up all the ammo."

"Well, at least the hissing was appropriate," said Daplin.

WALSINGHAM MANOR

IN AUGUST I RECEIVED an invitation to spend the weekend at a place called Walsingham Manor, which was somewhere in Buckinghamshire. The invitation was from a Lord Houghton.

Who was that? Could it be that my secret benefactor was about to expose himself? Apparently not. An explanation came during a telephone call from Air Vice-Marshal Greaves. Houghton's daughter was none other than Guinevere Plumley. The invitation was really from her.

I was tempted to enquire why Lord Houghton wasn't called Plumley, or Guinevere wasn't called Houghton; but I couldn't be bothered trying to understand the subtleties of English lineage. What I was curious about was why Miss Plumley wanted me, as I'd only met her once in a lavatory.

Still, I was happy to accept. It would be my first social outing since arriving in England. Besides, Greaves seemed particularly keen on my going. Gosh, that man really loved me. He even provided transport. A friend of his had an Armstrong-Siddeley that had belonged to his RAF son who had been killed in an accident in 1938. He was willing to sell the motor car to a serving pilot at a good price. "I'll tell him you're a worthy recipient," Greaves said in the subservient tones he fell into whenever he was conversing with me.

"Thanks very much, Cyril. How's Bernard, by the way?" I asked. Plopping onto the earth in his parachute, Bernard had braced himself too hard against the impact, and had suffered a compound fracture of the leg. He was now out of hospital and recuperating at home.

"On the mend, his mother says," Greaves said briskly, and went on to remind me once again of the date for the house party. To which I assumed that he, too, had been invited.

In due course I was interviewed in London by Greaves's friend and found to be worthy of the Armstrong-Siddeley. I paid him a ridiculously low sum for a splendid, two-door beauty in dark green. It had not been driven for two years but the owner claimed that all that was needed to make it fit for the road was for the chrome and stainless steel to be painted over, and for matte black hoods to be fitted over the giant headlights to make their illumination less visible from the air, as demanded by the emergency regulations.

In this splendid vehicle, and on the appropriate Saturday, I set out, armed with a sheaf of petrol coupons and a thirty-six-hour pass, for deepest Buckinghamshire. I located the property with the usual difficulty. It was late afternoon before Walsingham Manor tottered into view.

It proved to be a huge wooden barn of a place, all black timbers against crumbling white plaster, on so large a scale that the chimneys looked like extra houses that had been plopped onto the roof. I didn't think much of the joint. It had been interfered with over the centuries, but as usually happened when subsequent owners tinkered with the original design, not very harmoniously. The long façade, for instance, was positively cluttered with bay windows.

The driveway, however, was excellent. The lawn-bordered stretch that served the front entrance to the house was freshly coated with white gravel. It was the purest gravel I'd ever crunched over, sparkling in the slanting sun as if it had been sown with silver nuggets.

The butler, in a striped waistcoat, had a purple face and a thatch of white hair that made him look like the top prize at a coconut shy. Already at the front door as I drove up, he was busily cleaning the bootscraper outside the oak and iron front door. The bootscraper, which was in the shape of a cringing serf, was so caked with dirt that anyone unwise enough to use it would have transferred prodigious amounts of muck and slubber to his footgear.

As I parked opposite the entrance, the butler, hunched over the bootscraper, gazed unhappily at the green car. Still bent over at a bugger's angle, he continued to cast sidelong frowns at the car as I climbed out of it and stood there, stretching and rubbing my back. He failed to speak until I had bid him good evening and had given him my name. Whereupon he announced that his was Davis and would I mind parking my motor car beside the others; and he pointed to where a few cars were parked on a weedy part of the driveway to which the pristine gravel did not extend.

I felt a bit huffy at this. After all, I had only parked outside the front entrance so he wouldn't have so far to carry my heavy valise.

"It's the gravel, sir," he explained, applying a coat of blacking to the cleaned-up serf. "It has only just been laid, at considerable expense."

"You'd prefer that the guests not drive their cars onto the driveway, would you?" I asked, as I reached into the "boot" of the car for my valise.

Immediately I regretted the snotty rejoinder. I should have remembered that an antagonistic servant could make all the difference between a comfortable stay and one riddled with pother. And Davis was certainly looking displeased, as he straightened up from his labours.

Or rather, as he attempted to bend himself straight. But he seemed to be having difficulty with his back. To restore himself roughly to the vertical he was forced to place his knuckles against his lumbar vertebrae and push inward. Even then, a series of eeks and ouches proved to be an essential part of the process.

Unfortunately, though the charming physiotherapy I was receiving had ameliorated my muscular difficulty, I was still somewhat unpliant. As I heaved the valise out of the boot it snatched at my sprained muscle. The result was that I, too, emitted an almost identical series of suppressed yelps.

When I next glanced at Davis's purple phiz, I could see that I had further offended him. He was convinced that I was making fun of him.

I hastened to explain. "Pulled a muscle. Few days ago," I squeezed, trying to undo the damage; but it was too late. I was already down in the guest book as a difficult customer; probably the sort of person who would tip him no more than a half crown for the entire weekend, assuming I didn't sneak out without giving him anything at all.

The start to the weekend was even less auspicious than that. Davis was now gazing at my beautiful green car, but wearing an expression that was far from admiring.

"What?" I asked.

He continued to stare at the car. It was only then I noticed that it was leaking. Oil was trickling out from under the engine and onto the gravel. Already a great black patch was spreading over the glittering, virginal surface.

"Oh, dear," I said.

"Indeed, sir," he said; and turned his back on me, and walked back into the house. Without even offering to carry my valise, either. In fact, he would have closed the front door in my face had not Guinevere Plumley emerged at that moment. Whereupon I proceeded to stare as if I'd never seen her before.

The thing was, I had retained only a partial memory of Miss Plumley's appearance, mainly the parts south of the collarbone. Those, especially the southern hemispheres, were inclined to stir up a positive cauldron of assorted hormones. Even now, in her riding breeks and an old green pullover, her riproaring figure tended to liquify my old knees. The wool of the pullover was fine enough to allow her bust to boast of its proportions to a braggardly extent, while the britches helped to balance the books, wrapped as they were round a bottom as perfect as that – or those – on your typical Grecian statue.

Unfortunately one could not avoid looking at her face sooner or later, and, Good Lord, was she ugly! No, that was unfair, it was far too dramatic and characterful a phiz to warrant such a word.

With her fierce gaze, her mighty chin, and hooked nose, she looked like an admiral in drag. You half expected her to start bawling things like, "Splice the halliards, Mr. Chrétien! Avast the starboard tackles and break out the rollocks!" She would certainly have had the voice for it, one capable, as someone once said of mine before I became utterly civilized, of being heard the length and breadth of a battleship.

She demonstrated it the moment she emerged from that vast Elizabethan pile. "I say," she boomed, "what a gorgeous car."

"I'm afraid it has misbehaved on your driveway," I said, feeling wan while I recovered from her appearance.

"Oh, my word," she exclaimed. "We'd better get that seen to right away."

"Yes, I certainly can't drive away without oil."

"I meant get the gravel cleaned. Davis was very proud of his new driveway. It's his. My God, what a mess."

"What d'you mean, it's his?"

"He was so ashamed of the state of our driveway that he paid for the lorryload of gravel."

"But your father will reimburse him, won't he?"

"No. He told Davis he couldn't afford it. And it's true. It's Davis who has all the money. Daddy doesn't have any at all."

"Oh," I said, finding it no more peculiar than most things that happened in the English countryside.

She was staring at me with a frank interest that had me checking a certain vertical row of buttons. "My goodness," she said in a voice calculated to warn ships away from the rocks, "you do have a lot of medals. What a delicious assortment of fruit salad. That will impress Mummy – she's all for ostentatious display."

She took my arm, almost lifting me off my feet in the process. "Look," she said, lowering her voice a few hundred decibels, "I wanted to catch you before you met anyone, so you'd know what was going on."

"Why, what is going on?" I asked; but before she could answer, a woman appeared in the doorway and called out, "Come along,

you two, stop conspiring out there. I presume you're Mr. Bandy.
You're very nearly late for afternoon tea, Mr. Bandy. Come along,
Guinevere, that's quite enough of that."

Quite enough of what? I wondered. Meanwhile my heart had
gone down for the third time at the sight of Guinevere's mother.
Tall and grey, and with bones sharp enough to carve a turkey, she
wore the expression common to quite a few women of her class. It
was the affronted look, the kind suggesting that you had just
requested her to clean out your chamberpot.

The voice, too, was intimidating: weary, drawling, teetering on
the verge of edginess. She used it to good effect as we entered the
house and started across the dark wooden hall. "You're too late for
a wash and brush up, Mr. Bandy," she said.

I thought for a moment she was telling me that I was irre-
deemably grubby, until she added, "You'd better have your tea
before you go upstairs, or everyone will have scattered by the time
you get down again." And hauling both Guinevere and me along
by the hawser of her bossiness, she led the way into the lounge
where the rest of the company was gathered.

This was a long, narrow space; so long, in fact, that an old grand
piano had been placed at the far end to elucidate the perspective.
There were several windows down the lefthand side of the room,
all of them slightly drunken. As for the wood plank floor, it was so
far from being horizontal that any dropped object capable of
motion was likely to roll, not merely to one side, but out of the
room entirely. I felt quite disoriented, until I learned to stand tilted
over at angle, and also slightly backwards, i.e., roughly parallel to the
other guests.

The company consisted of a young girl in a party dress, a country
gentleman or two, and no fewer than four overdressed ladies with
teacups and Eccles cakes. I took to them right away when one
of them said, "You look very young to have so many decorations,
Mr. Bandy."

I'd received so many rude remarks lately about my raddled
mug that my response was cautious. "You don't think I look old?"
I asked.

"Oh, no," another of the nice ladies said. And a third, who was not quite as nice as the others, said, "Why, how old are you?"

"Forty-six – but only just."

"H'm," she said. While the really nice lady said, "You look much younger than that."

For the rest of the evening, whenever they were within range I would say, "So you really think I look young for my age?" and three-quarters of the ladies would dutifully reply, "Oh, yes, definitely." Though after a while they started to look preoccupied whenever I was in the vicinity. They would talk about St. John's wort, stone parsley, and bladder campion and things like that, instead of taking an interest in my youthful looks.

Also among the company was a pink young man in army uniform who was standing on one leg. I assumed that they had been playing charades and he was illustrating the pink flamingo; but nobody seemed to be paying any attention to him except the four-teen-year-old girl in the party dress, and even she looked more interested in a plate of cucumber sandwiches that she was steadily despatching.

Lord Houghton was also in evidence, though only just. He was standing by the empty fireplace – empty except for an iron grate the size of a megalosaurus skeleton. He had watery blue eyes, a bald napper, and was attired in a blue-green Harris tweed suit that could not have been lumpier had it contained a hundredweight of coal.

"How do you dare?" he demanded.

Oh, God, he hadn't wanted me here. He'd been against inviting me. Guinevere had invited me on her own, without asking him.

But then I realized that he was merely employing the conventional greeting.

The moment I responded, he looked as tired as anything, and leaned harder than ever on the marble mantelpiece; or rather, on the marble caryatid sort of thing that acted as one of its supports, for the mantel itself was much too high for him. He was hardly more than five feet tall. His daughter was nearly a foot taller.

Meanwhile I kept looking around for AVM Greaves, but there was no sign of him. I wanted to ask Guinevere where he was. I was also anxious to learn from her what was "going on." But she was talking to the pink lieutenant, who was obviously terrified of her, judging by the way he had backed against the panelling with his arms spread along the woodwork, and the way he was listening to her as if any incorrect responses on his part would merit a thorough thrashing.

I started in that direction, but Arthura, Guinevere's sister, intercepted me. She had her sister's jutting chin but was otherwise quite symmetrical. "Have a cucumber sandwich," she said, offering me an empty plate.

She then started theatrically, as if she had only just noticed that the plate was unpopulated. "Oh, dear," she said, "I suppose Lane was unable to get cucumbers at the market."

"What, not even for ready money?" cried Guinevere; and the two girls chortled confidentially, and giggled even more at the sight of my blank expression which hadn't caught the allusion to the opening scene of *The Importance of Being Earnest*.

The girls seemed very fond of each other, considering they were sisters. Perhaps the non-competitive age gap between them had something to do with it. Arthura was a good twenty years younger than Guinevere.

She was also rather more graceful in her movements. She floated. Guinevere tended to knock into things.

Now they were holding an even less comprehensible conversation. "Mumchuck's not very pleased with you," Arthura was saying to Guinevere.

"She's notchuck?"

"No. She was saying nice things about you. That's always a bad sign."

"I suppose it's because I invited whatsachuck for the weekchuck without consulchuck."

"That would certainly do it. Look out, there's Nanny."

I looked around but failed to identify the girls' nanny. When I turned back, Guinevere was talking to Davis. She was trying to console him over the fouling of his driveway. "I'm sure Mr. Bandy will offer you something to cover the cost of cleaning it up," she was saying.

He didn't look the least reassured, and in fact treated me to a most unfriendly look. Arthura was also looking at me as if memorizing me for a police artist.

"What's this chuck business?" I asked her. "Consultchuck, and all that?"

Instead of answering she had a question of her own. "You're crazy about Gwinny, aren't you?" she said.

"Good Lord, no."

"You're too late. The Drummer wants her."

"What band is he in?"

"I refer," she said loftily, "to Sir Amyas Drummond, CBE, MP. He's madly in love with Gwinny. He's been trying to entice her into bed for months, you know."

"Really?"

"He's offered to set her up in a *pomme de terre*."

"In a what?"

"You know – in a little flat. Like they do in Paris."

"Ah, got you. A *pièd-à-terre*."

"What are you talking about?" Guinevere said to her sister. "What are you telling him?" She looked at me. "You have to watch her, or she'll slander you the moment you look at her."

"All I said was, the Drummer is madly in love with you," Arthura said.

"I don't want to talk about it," Guinevere said, and proceeded to do so.

It seemed that she was still annoyed at herself over the Salisbury Plain incident. "I just hate it, showing I was afraid of him," she said. "Showing my weakness."

"Why, what happened?" asked Arthura.

Ignoring her, Guinevere said to me, "All the same . . . I know you think he's ghastly, but he's a lot more attractive to women than you'd think."

"Ugh," said Arthura, and pretended to be sick into somebody's hat.

"It's not easy to resist a man who goes after you so determinedly," Guinevere said, "even when you don't like him."

"Never mind him," I said. "Are you going to tell me now about what's going on?"

But there was a fresh distraction: a nice old body had approached. She had warmly welcoming brown eyes, and a bosom suitable for small children to shelter under. This was obviously the girls' dear old nanny.

She gazed up at me with a sweet smile. "How d'you do?" she asked, looking as if she would like to give me an infusion of comfort, too. "You must be Gwinny's friend, Bartholomew?"

"Yeth," I said, pressing her old hand, and feeling I ought to iron it flat and place it between the leaves of *The Romance of Proctology*.

"I've heard all about you from dear Gwinny. She says you are the most fascinating man since Ellsworth Prouty Conkle."

Before I could ask who the hell that was: "Have you met every-one yet?" she added, looking around vaguely. "I'm afraid you're going to miss Lord Houghton. It doesn't look as if he'll find his way home in time."

"I've already met him. He's over there."

"So he is. I didn't see him come in. Tell me, what do you think of him?"

"He's very."

"Yes he is, isn't he? Though he was quite well-known in academic circles – or," she added with a mischievous twinkle, "should I say academic squares? – until he joined the government. His field is medieval politics. So they conscripted him onto various government committees and commissions, as soon as war broke out."

"They felt that medieval politics would help the war effort?"

"Yes. Until they discovered that scholarship had addled his brains."

I reared back a bit at this rather unnannylike remark about her employer.

"Mind you," she added, "some would say that being addled was a further qualification for government service. But that would be a terribly cynical attitude to take, don't you think?"

"Indubitably."

"But tell me, dear, what do you think of our Gwinny? Isn't it just amazing how well she's got on?"

"It certainly is, ma'am."

"She has only just joined the army, and already she's a private."

"Gosh."

"And chauffeur to a government minister, too. I don't know how she gets these jobs. Do you?"

"No, I don't."

For the first time her sweet smile faded, and she moved as close as her motherly bosom would respectably allow. "Are you acquainted with Sir Amyas Drummond, Bartholomew?"

"I've met him a couple of times, ma'am."

"He says he loves her. He's certainly been pursuing her most devotedly. But does she love him? I don't understand Gwinny at all, she's very mysterious. This invitation of hers, for instance. I mean, how could she, knowing how I feel?"

I certainly knew how I felt: disoriented. There seemed to be all sorts of undercurrents flowing around.

"I don't suppose you know why she invited him?" Nanny enquired.

"I'm sorry, I'm not with you. Who invited who?"

"Gwinny. Sir Amyas."

It was getting steadily worse. "Gwinny," I stated.

"Yes."

"Is going to invite Drummond?"

"She already has. He's been here since Friday evening."

"Sir Amyas? He's here?" I asked, looking around in alarm.

"Not at the moment, of course. He had to dash back to London on some errand or other. I'm sure he thinks the country can't carry on without him. But he'll be back in time for dinner."

"Excuse me, Vera," I said – Guinevere had mentioned that Nanny's name was Vera – "but is this some of Cyril Greaves's doing?"

"Air Vice-Marshal Greaves, you mean?"

"I'd like a word with him, Vera, if you'll just tell me where I can find him."

"With the Ministry of Aircraft Production, isn't he? You might find him there."

"No, I mean here in this house."

"He's here? Don't tell me Gwinny's invited him as well?"

"He's not here?"

"What do you mean, he's not here?" she demanded. "You just said he was."

"Was what?"

"Was here."

"Oh, I see, Vera," I exclaimed, enlightened. "He was here, but now he's not?"

"Not what? And where does Vera come into this?"

I took a deep breath. "Let's start again, shall we?" I said authoritatively. "I gather that Cyril Greaves is not here at the moment."

"Not as far as I know. Why, were you expecting him to be?"

"So Greaves isn't here, but Drummond is, is that right, Vera?"

"I've just told you," she said impatiently. "Sir Amyas Drummond is here, but he's not here at the moment. And why do you keep calling me Vera?"

"Well, Gwinny said her nanny's name was Vera."

"Yes?"

"So?" I said in a QED sort of voice; just as Guinevere came up and said, "Cook wants a word with you, Mother."

"Oh. All right, dear. I've been having such a nice conversation with Mr. Bandy here." And with an edge to her voice she added, "He doesn't understand it either – why you would invite Sir Amyas Drummond for the weekend when you say you hate him."

"It's politics, Mother," Guinevere said curtly. "Nothing to do with you."

"It has a great deal to do with me, dear," Lady Houghton said, "when you invite someone I detest to my own home."

"I told you, it's politics, Mother. I can't say any more than that. Excuse me, I'm just going to have Mr. Bandy shown up."

"Shown up?" I whined. "But I haven't done anything."

"To your room."

"Oh – to my room."

"Davis," Guinevere called out. "Show Mr. Bandy up to his room, will you?"

Davis nodded and gave me a particularly nasty look. Any more of that, I thought to myself, and his damn gravel could stay black with oil.

On second thoughts, though, I decided to butter him up like a crumpet. "Excuse me, Mr. Davis," I said in a toadying voice, "but who was that lady who greeted me at the front door, who escorted us into the lounge? The one over there, making Arthura cry?"

"That's Vera, the children's nanny," he said curtly.

"That's what I thought," I said.

Ever since my first traumatic experience with the ablutionary facilities of the ancient Britons I had treated their plumbing with considerable caution. The bathroom in this tottering house, along the corridor from my bedroom, was certainly one to be wary of. To begin with, it was apparently without electric light. The only illumination was provided by the shivering flame of a kerosene lamp, which added its own insalubrious smell to the built-in odours of mildew and other sorts of dampness. Even the ceramic tiles looked mouldy.

I had thought of relaxing in a nice hot tub before joining the others for dinner; but upon inspecting the tub in the light of the oil lamp I caught sight of a gigantic, deformed spider. I think it had seven extra legs; it looked like a rugby scrum in insect form. As it scuttled for cover into some toxic fissure I decided that I didn't really need a bath after all, as I'd had one in 1939. I would have a stand-up wash instead, at the basin, which, though equally stained, was at least free of arachnids with genetic problems.

First, though, I tested the faucets, and was easily able to tell which was the hot tap and which the cold. The hot tap was the one issuing gasps of superheated steam calculated to blister an armadillo. However, the steam condensed fast enough in the basin, and the cold water flowed efficiently.

Satisfied that all was miraculously in order, I stripped to the buff, and was busily soaping me vitals – when I felt something grope me in the dark. Something moist and slimy was creeping slowly over my dorsal surface.

I was already primed for something unusual to happen. Though it was a warm summer evening outside, the air in the house was murky, and the atmosphere unwelcoming. It seemed to me that the passages were full of evil shadows. Guinevere had mentioned that there were secret passages everywhere. In addition, Arthura had informed me with suppressed relish that there were rats in the attic, white slugs in the cellar, and ghosts of people who had come to violent ends everywhere. So when the thing so obscenely flopped against the already crawling skin of my bare back, I emitted a cry of surprise, and turned to see what it was.

Actually, a little more than surprise was involved, and I did not so much turn as whirl like a ceiling fan, in the process knocking the oil lamp to the floor and plunging myself into even more frightening gloom.

At which point Guinevere rapped at the door, and asked if she could enter, a permission which was readily granted despite my state of stitchlessness, not to mention foaminess, which made me look like a sex maniac with hydrophobia. She appeared, bearing a small light bulb. "I thought I heard you scream," she said, shouldering me aside in the gloom.

Climbing onto the wooden side of the bath, she drove the light bulb into the socket dangling high overhead. "Finally got the fuse mended," she said.

"Thanks very much," I said. The twenty-five-watt glow made the bathroom look worse than ever.

But at least it enabled me to ascertain that the thing that had slimed me was merely a length of dank wallpaper that had drooped down from the wall above the bathroom's cracked tiles.

"Don't tell me," I said shakily. "You've come to say that this is the old bathroom and you don't use it any more. You have a nice new bathroom further along the passage."

"Well," she said, picking up the oil lamp and replacing it on a semicircular table with a marble top, then pushing a dead mouse out of sight under it with the point of her silver slipper, "there is another bathroom on the far side of the house, but it's no better than this one."

She was already dressed for dinner, wearing a silvery frock that was clinging for dear life to the mammary slopes. Down in the forest, something stirred; but only for a moment. I could hardly avoid braving her rampaging features. When I finally did so, I couldn't help starting back slightly, the way an old friend from my film days, W. C. Fields, could start so defensively.

The odd thing about Guinevere was that she seemed quite unaware of just how aesthetically schizophrenic she looked. Like the way she was now modelling her dress with a revolution of swirling skirt. "Well, what d'you think?" she asked almost coyly.

"It's a lovely dress, Guinevere," I said as my eyes fell, panting with relief, to those sublime breasts of hers which seemed to be unfettered, owing nothing to either artifice or engineering.

"You may call me Gwinny," boomed she. "And I can see you appreciate my Turks."

"Turks?"

"I call them my Turks," she said. "It's something called rhyming slang, you see. Breasts – breastworks – Turks. Get it?"

"With difficulty."

"I just made it up," she said, her voice fading as she looked into my eyes. Which were forced to look back into her ferocious equivalents.

Her burning brownish eyes, which could penetrate like a thermal lance, had suddenly gone all misty for some reason. That phrase about eyes being the windows to the soul suddenly made a bit of sense. It was like looking through the grill of an iron cell into a pastoral romance by Fragonard. And her voice, too, had gone all soft as she said, "You'd better hurry. Dinner and all that."

But then the moment was shattered by a guffaw as she looked down and said, "Though I can see you're already in a hurry."

It was only then I remembered that I was attired in my birthday suit. I turned away to hide behind a face cloth. I must have been looking down her dress too long.

"Wait," I croaked. "Haven't we something to talk about? I'd like to know – why is Drummond here?"

"It's all part of Cyril's plot. But don't worry, darling, it's nothing to do with you. Or only partly. It's just that – "

She stopped as the doorknob rattled and the young lieutenant, whose name was Ronald Bilton-Sande, entered. "Oh, sorry," he said, backing away in fright at the sight of Gwinny.

Then he noticed me – nearly all of me. Only my privates were not on parade.

"Oh, hellair," he said. And his pink face with its blond moustache and small chin went pinker still. "Carry on, Sergeant," he said, loud with sweating embarrassment as he contracted into the corridor.

"We're not carrying on. What the devil do you mean, carry on?" Guinevere said, advancing on him in her habitually menacing fashion.

Mong joo, no wonder she had reached the age of thirty-five without marrying. Judging by a certain awkwardness in her movements, or at least a lack of physical assurance, maybe she'd never even broken her duck, sexwise.

Broken her duck, that was a cricketing term I'd recently picked up and was now using rather indiscriminately.

Drummond returned to Walsingham Manor at around eight o'clock that evening. He had barely time to change before dinner was gonged.

It was in the dining room that I was formally introduced to him just before we took our places. And, praise be, he failed to recognize me.

Perhaps it was because he did not expect to encounter me in civilized surroundings. Now, if it had been a jail cell or the dining room of a sewage farm . . . But more likely it was because he was still decelerating from a hectic day, while I was camouflaged among several other guests who meant nothing to him.

I must admit he looked damned impressive, despite his rushed air. In contrast to Lord Houghton, who resembled a waiter in a Charlie Chaplin film, Drummond's evening dress was perfect, and his carriage dignified and authoritative. Moreover, his manner was entirely charming. I could hardly believe it was the same person who had so brutally and contemptuously humiliated Air Vice-Marshal Greaves in public. He seemed a different man entirely.

Because he'd been unable to join us for drinks before dinner, he carried his tumbler to the dining table, and proceeded to amputate three fingers of Scotch in three minutes flat, before turning to the various wines on offer. As wartime cellars emptied, wines were becoming something of a treat.

I myself was being particularly abstemious that evening. I wanted to keep a clear head for the dangers that lay ahead, as soon as Gwinny told me what the dangers were.

I had another reason for making do with just two or three double whiskies and a few sips of the wine. The dining-room floor was so tilted that I feared I might develop *mal de mer*. The incline was so marked, in fact, that it took something of an effort to climb the slope to the dining table. One thin, frail lady had to hold onto the table to avoid sliding backward into the panelling.

Davis The Butler, however, was fortunate in having the use of a velvet rope along the wall, the equivalent, I thought, of the storm lashings of an Atlantic liner. Even so, he had trouble sometimes in reaching the table, especially when he had awkward dishes of food to carry, some of it quite warm. "Davis The Butler," incidentally, was how Arthura addressed him. "Would you bring me the latest edition of *Tit Bits*, Davis The Butler?" That sort of thing.

Arthura was seated opposite me at Lady Houghton's end of the table. I was thankful to have been placed as far from Drummond as possible. Even so, I made an effort to be especially circumspect, not wishing to draw the slightest attention to myself.

I hadn't reckoned on Arthura. I rather liked Arthura – until it came time for my amusing contribution to the general conversation.

It came while Lady Houghton was busily apologizing for the dearth of decent help. "Davis is our only remaining servant," she was explaining sorrowfully. "Apart from the maids, of course. Let me see, what are their names? I know one is called, May, and another is Joan, and the third is – "

"July?" I suggested.

Arthura sat up straight and looked at me, as Lady Houghton said, "No, it's not that. It's the one who acts as cook. What's her name again?"

"Cook?" suggested Arthura, glancing at me.

"Yes, dear. I'm trying to remember her name."

"Whose name?"

"Cook's name, dear."

"It's Cook," Arthura said; but inevitably she went too far with the Abbott and Costello routine, and got told off by Vera The Nanny.

I had hoped to be within groping distance of Guinevere; but Gwinny had been placed beside the guest of honour. She seemed to be making the most of it: verbally fawning on Drummond to a sick-making extent, as we used to say in the Twenties. I wasn't paying any attention to them, of course. It was a matter of complete indifference to me how disgracefully she behaved, or who she blarneyed, softsoaped, or sucked up to. I was totally indifferent to the way she kept touching him; resting her hand every two- and three-quarter minutes on his forearm, tapping his wrist with a coy forefinger, laying the balance of her digits on the back of his warty hand. Peering up his filthy nostrils at the hairs and the gockies. Gazing at him with unalloyed admiration, laughing indelicately at his fribbling trifles or listening gravely to his political piffle, and no doubt occasionally allowing her obeisant patella to contact two or three of his lower limbs under the dining table, or even allowing him to knead her shameless thighs. But as I say, I wasn't looking, it was nothing to do with me.

I could hardly be unaware, though, that the politician was lapping up the homage like a spitty toad, his face glistening red with the pleasures of flattery, a face that was starting to match the colour of the claret with which he was so unrestrainedly strumming his uvula.

In between his benign-uncle responses to Gwinny's adoration he was expounding on the subject of democracy. It seemed that he did not much believe in democracy. It was an itinerary for ultimate decadence, moral and physical, which would end in the collapse of the social attitudes that guided human behaviour. He cited the Turks (which gave me a jolt) as being properly disciplined, and even introduced a little personal material into his eloquent arguments. "I am not exactly biased in their favour in speaking of Turkish accomplishments," he said, looking around with a carefully crafted smile. "I was captured by them at the Dardanelles, and I can assure you I was not treated indulgently. I will mention only one ordeal. When I complained about the theft of Red Cross parcels, I was hung upside down and beaten on the soles of the feet – "

There was a gasp from the company. "Oh, I say, sir," said Second Lieutenant Bilton-Sande. And Guinevere put her hand over Drummond's great fist and squeezed it comfortingly.

I felt a lot better though when, at that precise moment, Lord Houghton, asleep at the head of the table, emitted a snore like an iceberg grinding along the Titanic.

I fell instantly in love with Lord Houghton.

As I say, it was Arthura who got me into trouble. It occurred during the pudding stage of the meal – Spotted Dick with alcoholic sauce. To help the girl recover her composure after being told off for doing an Abbott and Costello, I began to relate the latest gossip about our SWO.

"What's SWO?" Arthura asked, too loudly. I had been trying to keep the chat low and confidential.

"Stands for Station Warrant Officer," I said.

"I can't hear you, Bartholomew," said the little madam. "Speak up."

She had achieved her goal. We had everyone's attention by now.

"The Station Warrant Officer," I explained, speaking only a little louder, "is quite a big cheese, administratively speaking, on an RAF aerodrome."

"Aerodrome, Bartholomew? What's that?"

"You know, where our planes are based. Anyway, about the SWO
– he was a big burly chap, absolutely terrific at drill. He was – "

"Drill? What's that, Bartholomew?"

"Leave Mr. Bandy alone and let him get on with the meal," her
mother interjected.

But she persisted, and I was forced to explain that drilling was
"when they march the men up and down."

"Up and down what, Bartholomew? A staircase, a plank, what?"

"Up and down the parade ground, Arthura. Anyway, a short
time ago, the SWO got married, you see. And, after, on his wedding
night – "

Further along the table Vera The Nanny stiffened, and glared.
Davis The Butler was glaring at me as well. And other guests were
craning over for a better view of me.

By then I had lost all confidence in the story. "Oh, it's nothing
really," I said. "Not worth telling."

"No, go on, Bartholomew," said Lady Houghton.

"Please, Bartholomew," Arthura said, winsome as Shirley Temple.

"Well, it's . . . Well, on his wedding night," I faltered, "the SWO
– no, really, it's not all that good a story, Arthura."

"No, go on, go on!"

"Well, while his bride was summoning up the courage to undress
in the next room, the SWO suddenly bellowed in his best parade
ground voice, 'All right, all right, let's be 'aving you!' Whereupon
his missus fell down and had a fit."

The silence was deader than ever. "Well, I told you it wasn't," I
mumbled.

"What did he mean, 'Let's be having you?'" Arthura asked.

"Well, I . . . it's the sort of thing he would, you know, call out
to the recruits, as he, you know, had them walk up and down the
parade ground."

"But his bride wasn't a recruit, surely?"

"Uh, no."

"So why would he say that to her?"

"Well . . ."

"Also," Arthura said in her primrose voice, "why would he even say it to the recruits, when all he was supposed to do was teach them to walk up and down, and – ”

"Shut up, Arthura, and eat your Spotted Dick," said Guinevere. But that didn't help much, either. Scarlet-faced with suppressed giggles, Arthura had to flee from the room.

At which point Drummond, looking exceedingly peeved at having the conversational initiative wrested from him just as he was reaching the climax of his interesting analysis on the need for greater discipline in society, suddenly recognized me. With a look imported directly from Hades, he opened his mouth to speak. But a useful diversion occurred just then. Lord Houghton fell off his chair.

When Guinevere finally let me in on the plot and described the scheme that she and Cyril Greaves had cooked up between them I was rendered quite speechless at its juvenility.

I was not told about it until half an hour before the plot was to be hatched at midnight. I was proceeding in a northwesterly direction along the corridor leading to my room, comfortably warm after reducing Houghton's cellar by a bucket or two of brandy, when I was intercepted by Guinevere. She was in the act of rushing headlong into a filmy nightgown, flinging her arms around her head as if semaphoring from a corvette. "Come to my bedroom right away," she hissed.

"Eh?"

"It's on the far side of the house – down this way, turn right, then first turn on the right, and it's the second door on the left."

"What makes you think I'm interested in going to your bedroom after your behaviour tonight?" I asked. "Was that the second turn on the right, and first door on the left?"

"Why are you being so snotty all of a sudden?"

"Letting his hand stray down your back, for one thing."

"What? For heaven's sake, Bart, you don't think I was seriously making up to the Drummer, do you? Look, come to my room and I'll tell you all about it. Come on, hurry, there isn't much time left!"

She dashed off, still talking, apparently under the impression that I was following. But the sight of Lieutenant Bilton-Sande had stopped me dead. He had emerged from the bathroom. His towel was draped over his khaki shirt, the sleeves were rolled up, and he looked as if he were just back from several sabre fights in Heidelberg. There were cuts all over his face.

"Thought I'd better practise shaving for tomorrow," he said, dabbing at his chin. "Servant usually does it in the morning – Private Tannin. Should have brought him along, I suppose."

"I'd get that ear stitched if I were you, Ronald."

"Yes, I suppose. I suppose you're right. I say, old chap, did you see the way that Ministry fellow was touching up Gwinny?"

"Yes, I did."

Ronald was blushing all over his face – the parts of it that weren't already stained with blood. "I mean – bit much, don't you think?" he said. "Feeling her up with her father only a couple of feet away. Mind you," he added despondently, "she didn't seem to mind all that much."

"No."

"Well, goodnight old chap," Ronald said. "By the way, don't turn on the hot tap in there. Blew my shaving mug to bits. Goodnight again."

I was still standing there when Guinevere reappeared. "Well, aren't you coming?" she whispered angrily. Then: "Oh, for God's sake. Look, let's talk in your room," she snapped, and slippered down the corridor to my door. "Well, come on!"

Because the frame was askew, the door was difficult to open. She shoved angrily at it and almost fell into the room.

And that was where she described the scheme that she and Cyril Greaves had cooked up between them.

"You're mad."

It was simple to the point of idiocy. Her contribution was to lure Sir Amyas into her bedroom on the far side of the house. The moment he climbed into her bed she was to emit several screams. That, she said, was where I came in. At that point in the proceedings I was to burst in and accuse the minister of gross misconduct.

She had already hinted to the victim that midnight might be a suitable time to come visiting.

I looked, feeble with astonishment, at my watch. It was 2340 hours already.

"Naturally," she said, "my hints were just ambiguous enough to allow me to claim that he had got it all wrong – that the most appalling misunderstanding had taken place. You know, so he wouldn't be able to claim that I'd entrapped him."

"You're crazy."

"Don't blame me. It's Cyril's idea."

"Greaves? What's in it for him?"

"Naturally he would have preferred to burst into my bedroom himself."

"He would?"

"And catch Drummond red-handed, so to speak. He didn't want to involve you. But Drummond would have been too much on his guard if Cyril had been anywhere near here this weekend. He knows how much Cyril hates him. Cyril has made some very unwise threats and Drummond has heard about it."

Wearing a mulish expression, I started kicking my valise. Which, incidentally, had not been unpacked. It was still where Davis The Butler had left it, cowering by the four-poster.

"So I'm elected to catch the scoundrel in your bed, is that it? With you screaming your head off."

"Actually I'll be screaming quite softly – I don't want to make too much of a scene."

"Very delicate of you. So I act the part of a scandalized guest, attracted from the far side of the house by your faint screams."

"I was thinking of you more in the part of a jealous lover, Bartholomew," she said softly, moving her nightgown much closer. "I know you're already jealous. Perhaps soon you can prove the lover part."

"Never mind that. Perhaps you'd be good enough to tell me what happens after I burst in."

"Well, it's obvious, darling. You squeal on him. You write to

Cyril, describing the infamous scene, and Cyril feels he must show the letter to his boss, Lord Beaverbrook. And the Beaver, who is a close friend of Churchill's, shows it to the PM. And, bingo, Drummond is out on his fat sit-upon, utterly disgraced. It's quite simple, really."

"And what's in it for you?"

She put her arms around me, mainly, I think, so as to discourage her face from giving away its secrets. "I have good reasons, Bart, but I can't tell you what they are," she said, her voice muffled against my chest.

Despite my feelings about Drummond, and despite the blackmailing embrace, the dizzying perfume from her ethereal folds, the delectable pressure of her breasts, I had no intention of falling in with the ridiculous plot. It was the sort of scheme that, however simple it might sound, always went wrong. I knew. I'd been involved in quite a few simple schemes in my time.

"It's the most ridiculous – " I began, just as there came a rapid tattoo on the door, and the voice of Guinevere's nanny. "Guinevere," it was saying, "is that you? Are you in there? I know you are, I heard you next door. That's not your room. You come out of there this minute!"

The doorknob rattled. "Oh, Christ," Guinevere said. "And the bloody door's not locked."

Whereupon, grabbing my arm, she rushed me headlong toward shelves filled with bound volumes of Law Society Reports, 1823 to 1909. She didn't seem to realize that I was in no mood to read even fairly recent law society reports, and continued to rush me toward them. Meanwhile, the doorknob continued to rattle, and in fact the entire door was vibrating, as Vera The Nanny attempted to overcome the expansion or possibly contraction of the surrounding woodwork.

"You open the door this instant, do you hear?" she was calling out in a voice like a *Flammenwerfer*. "You're with that air force man, aren't you? I'll tell your mother on you, so I will. You let me in this minute, do you hear?"

"Yes, yes, Nanny," Guinevere called out. But instead of doing so she clutched at some fancy scrollwork to the right of the bookcase. "Nanny, wait a minute, the door's stuck, I'll just get it open," she called out over her shoulder. "I'll be with you in a minute."

At which point the bookcase opened wide, and Guinevere was whispering, "Just wait in here until I get rid of her!" Simultaneously she placed her all-too-competent hand in the middle of my back and propelled me, with a force that could have overcome the inertia of a Sherman tank, into the pitch black space beyond.

ANOTHER VIEW OF SAME

WALSINGHAM MANOR, I GUESS, had been built in the days when people might need a secret passage as an emergency escape route from their debtors, bishops, tenants, or wives. Or perhaps it was to enable the master of the house to spy on his guests, and watch them undressing. Whatever the reason for Swiss-cheesing the joint, as I stood there in the darkness I thought bitterly that they might at least have put in a bit of lighting. It was stovepipe-black in there. Even though I was only a foot away from my bedroom not a chink of light showed through.

After being thrust so rudely into the woodwork, I had remained perfectly still for minutes on end, in case the slightest sound, particularly the slightest sneeze – it was damn dusty in there – alerted the dreaded Vera to the presence of this particular rat in the wainscotting. Though the passage seemed pretty soundproof as well as light-tight. I could hear nothing of what was being said out there. All that seeped through the wall was a muffled woofling. The woofling sound went on for so long that I got tired of waiting for Gwinny and Nanny to return to their own rooms. I went exploring; not very far, of course, in case I got lost.

This was a progress accomplished entirely by touch. Dusty Tudor laths, gritty Elizabethan plasterwork, frangible Jacobean lattice, crumbling Cromwellian brickwork, and an amazing tactile diversity of building materials, studs, and supports, formed themselves under my wavering hands, or buckled my ankles underfoot. Every now and then I was treated to a brisk shower of dust, which, for some reason, smelled of smoke.

I was careful to make mental notes of the directions I was taking through the secret passages. For instance, after I had faltered only a few yards I espied a chink of light on my left, escaping through some wattlelike material. I widened the hole enough to obtain a view, not of a bedroom, but of a moonlit garden. Vegetables, I think. A high-angle view, of course, as I was on the second floor.

I made a careful note. A few yards from my bedroom – moonlit garden on left. So, coming back, the chink of light would be on the right.

Mind you, it was not easy keeping track. The passage changed direction several times. It also sloped up and down. Every now and then it might rise one or two feet by means of crude steps or heaps of debris. Presumably this was to accommodate the changes in the levels of the sloping floors.

I wished now I hadn't given up my pipe. Then I would have had a box of matches. With a box of matches I could have seen where I was going. Still, I wasn't doing too badly. If I failed to find any other exit from the warren I could always return to my own room. In fact, just to make sure that I knew where it was, I retraced my steps, keeping an eye open for the chink, and feeling about on my left for the distinctive stretch of brickwork outside my room. I had made a particular note of that before setting off, the distinctive stretch of brickwork. Beyond it was the bookcase in my bedroom.

On the way back, though, the passage suddenly came to an end. I ran into a brick wall that hadn't been there before.

There was only a momentary panic. Wide-eyed with placidity, a set of grimy knuckles jammed in my mouth to stifle an apathetic yawn, I composed myself in a manly way. If the worst came to the worst I could always break through a wall into somebody else's bedroom.

Naturally I would be careful not to break through the wall over-looking the vegetable garden, which would mean a drop of about thirty feet, as the garden was a good thirty feet down. I would be careful not to do that.

Really, claustrophobia was quite irrational. There was nothing to worry about, really there wasn't. No reason to fear that I might be trapped in the walls forever, like Montresor's Po. I mean, Poe's Montresor. Or, no, it wasn't Montresor who was walled up, was it? It was Montresor who had walled someone else up, wasn't it? Chap called Bandy, was it?

Anyway, it was best not to think about that, at a time like this, or, indeed, at any other time. And it was important to conquer the impulse to panic. After all, the secret passage network couldn't be all that extensive in a huge house like this with its endless . . .

Oh, all right, go ahead and panic.

No, but, you know. By now it must have been at least an hour since Guinevere had embedded me in the wall. And I'd been feeling my way forward, onward, ever since! Oh, God. Steady the Buffs.

Unfortunately by now I hadn't the faintest idea where I was. While my exploring hands were encountering all sorts of building material, some of it crumbly, some of it smooth, some of it splintery, some of it sharpish, none of it provided me with a navigational fix. At one point I thought I'd found a way back to civilization when my hands scraped along a stretch of extruded mortar. It felt as if it were attached to a real wall. And if it was a real wall it must have a doorway or other opening in it somewhere.

No, it didn't.

Come, think. Where might you have gone wrong in retracing your steps, lad? What about the chink that had provided the view of the garden – vegetables, I think. If I could find that I would be only a few yards from my room. Good. Now we were getting somewhere.

I found it! Oh, God, here it was, my chink of light! Yes, there was the garden, far below, smothered in blessed moonlight.

The only thing was, it was in the wrong wall. As I was returning, it should have been on the right. Instead it was on the left. Plainly, the moon had made a mistake, somewhere.

Ah, but wait! If the chink was on the left, it meant that I had already passed the distinctive brickwork that marked the location of my bedroom. So if I walked backward, I would be home in no time at all.

And, by George, I found it. Admittedly there was no distinctive brickwork, just some sort of panelling. But I was not concerned with minor details at this point. It was my room all right, poorly lit but plainly visible through a crack in the panelling, complete with its dark wallpaper and huge, faded carpet.

I was so relieved to have found my way back that it quite overwhelmed a vague puzzlement as to how I'd managed it. I was too weary to work it out. All I cared about was finding a way into the room without smashing through the panelling and creating a dirty great hole in the wall which might be difficult to explain to my hosts.

And here it was. My hand encountered a simple wooden lever arrangement. When pulled down it swung open a section of the panelling. Reeking with relief, I stepped into an empty alcove. I was home.

And so fatigued by then that I was tempted to snuggle straight into the four-poster. Fortunately I caught sight of myself in a mirror. I looked like something risen from the grave, staring-eyed, covered in dust, decorated with whitish cobwebs.

I wasted no time in tiptoeing into the corridor on my way to the bathroom, not wishing to disturb anyone at three or four in the morning. Except it wasn't. When I checked my watch I found that it was only five to twelve.

Five to twelve? You mean to tell me I'd been in the walls for only twenty minutes?

I was in no shape to argue with my watch. Entering the corridor, I turned right for the bathroom. But somebody had shortened the corridor by twenty feet. It used to be thirty feet long. Now only a few feet of blackened flooring and threadbare carpet met my heavy-lidded gaze.

So I turned left, though I could have sworn that it was a right turn out of my room toward the bathroom.

Well, at least the bathroom was still there . . . on the wrong side
of the corridor . . .

Shaking my head to disperse the fog inside, I entered the bathroom, and once again performed my ablutions stripped to the buff;
and then lurched back into the corridor and turned right – no, left
– and into my room on the left – right.

But where was my valise? Davis The Butler had dumped it
unceremoniously by the bed. I guessed he must have decided to
unpack it after all.

But if he had unpacked it, where had he put the stuff, particularly my pyjamas? There were two chests of drawers in the room,
but no sign of my clothes.

Well, just for that, I wouldn't wash his gravel for him.

Though tottering with fatigue by now, there was still room for
a lot of annoyance. That bastard, Davis. Every time we had encountered each other this evening, he had glared at me. Now, out of pure
spite, he had hidden my personal effects.

I would have to go to bed pyjamaless; and as this was England,
the bed was bound to be damp. Boy! He sure as hell wasn't getting
a tip on Sunday night!

Actually, the bed was quite comfortable, scented and quite warm.
But I had been in it for only two minutes and was just starting to
relax and grow drowsy, when – alcove?

A panelled alcove? There hadn't been a panelled alcove over
there. There had been a bookcase, stuffed with red volumes.

I lay there in the darkness, thinking about it. And about the corridor outside. I was certain that earlier in the evening when I left
the bathroom I had turned right, walked along a passage, and into
my room, which had definitely been on the left. Instead, these
directions had been reversed. What did that mean?

After all the sherry, whisky, hock, claret, port, and brandy, before,
during, and after dinner, and all that healthy exercise in the secret
passages, I was exceedingly reluctant to get up again and investigate.
All the same, it was peculiar . . .

Blessed drowsiness. But Morpheus was not to be embraced just yet. As my eyelids clanged shut there was a clicking sound on the far side of the room. And then a creaking noise as the door was opened. Then it was being closed just as surreptitiously.

I forgot all about breathing. Despite the special adhesive, my hairpiece detached itself from my scalp and flew twice round the room. Sweat beaded my brow, to form a diamond necklace.

There was a distinct rustle of movement. Somebody was feeling their way across the room. I could sense rather than see her. The sense turned a good deal more concrete when the earth moved for me. Or rather the mattress. It sank several inches as the visitor sat on the edge of the bed.

Now she was swishing back the covers and climbing so dexterously into bed despite the pitch darkness that one could not avoid the suspicion that these motions were born of long practice. But then the faint odour of tobacco came drifting across the pillows, and I knew who it was, but not yet how it had happened.

He murmured some muffled endearment, but I was in no mood to respond, especially after I felt something gristly press against my thigh. Whereupon I decided to respond after all. I screamed.

There was a muffled oath from my bed partner; and as I leaped out of bed on one side, he rolled out of the other, swearing dreadfully.

Simultaneously the bedroom door was flung open, a practised hand felt for and switched on the light – and there stood Guinevere in the nightdress that swelled so fetchingly in the thorax region. And there also stood Sir Amyas, also in a nightgown, which also swelled, though not so fetchingly, in the pelvic region. Standing by the bed in more ways than one, his meaty face wore a look of utter bewilderment and only dawning consternation.

"So, Sir Amyas, this is where your inclinations really lie, do they?" cried Guinevere in a passion, while carefully closing the door behind her so as not to disturb the neighbours. "A pervert! I would never have believed it if I hadn't seen it with my own eyes!"

"What d'you mean?" Drummond said hoarsely, trying to conceal his excitement – though shock was ensuring that there was now little to show in the way of evidence.

"A pervert of the worst kind," she cried, as if there were degrees of degeneracy, and Drummond was at the top of the list. "A bugger!"

"I beg your pardon?" he shouted back indignantly.

"And so you should! I wonder what other perverted debauchery you were about to indulge in, when I heard one of you cry out in what must have been ecstasy, and I rushed in here to see if I could help, only to find you and that man there." She pointed in my direction. So did her writhing eyebrows. "Oh, oh," she bellowed, *sotto voce*, "I just can't bear to think about it."

I looked behind me in a bewilderment almost as great at Drummond's, thinking someone else must have emerged from a secret passage, but her finger was still pointed straight at me.

"The pair of you are nothing but foul perverts!" she informed us. "Oh, I am sickened to the very soul. I could believe it of him, I suppose, but you of all people, Amyas, a man I had come to love and respect. How could you do this to me?"

"I don't understand," Drummond stammered. "This is your room, isn't it? You said – " He stared at me. "What's he doing here?"

"I don't wish to know what he's doing here, except he has no right to be here, and I'll take that up with him later. But isn't it more to the point what you've been doing here?"

"But you asked me. I mean – you said – you seemed – "

"Are you daring to suggest that I invited you to my bedroom?"

"Well, I – I thought – it seemed to me – "

"Oh, this is insupportable," she cried, near to swooning with shame. "You have the nerve to pretend that I actually invited you to sully my boudoir with the nearest junior officer?"

"I got the distinct impression – "

"If I seemed to be proffering such an invitation during the course of the evening, then you have very much misunderstood, Sir Amyas. How thankful I am now that I was not ultimately tempted to give way to your surreptitious caresses and other insinuating ways, now that I have plumbed the depths – fortunately with my eyes only – the coarse depths of your perverted nature," cried Guinevere, who was surely taking a course in Victorian literature.

Only now did Drummond begin to feel the point of her accusations. He turned and stared at me, then back at Guinevere, and said hoarsely, "My God, woman, you don't think – you're not suggesting that he and I – that that dreadful man and – in this bed – we –?"

"Don't come the innocent with me, Sir Amyas," she cried, before realizing she was raising her voice and in danger of attracting outside parties. She turned down the volume to an atmospheric crackle. "I saw you together! And look at him!" she said, pointing again at me. "What else am I to believe?"

For the second time that evening I realized I was standing obliviously naked before her.

"Look here," I croaked.

"I've already looked there!" she answered, "and it's frightful!"

"You say this is your room?" I asked feebly, picking up a pillow and holding it before me.

"And don't you try to get out of it, either," she cried. "You're just as foul as him, you, you sodomite, or catamite, or vegemite! And now both of you – get out of my room! Not that I'll be able to sleep in that bed, now that you have despoiled it with your unspeakable practices. Oh, God, the very thought of what you were doing sickens me," she said, issuing a shrewd sob.

"Guinevere," Drummond cried.

She risked raising her voice to a hysterical strangle. "Get out," she screamed. "Get out of my room before I call my nanny!"

Sir Amyas and I shuddered, and while still protesting our innocence, made preparations for a hasty departure. Or rather, Drummond continued to protest his innocence, while I tried to work out how I had managed to cross through the secret passages to the far side of the house and emerge into Guinevere's bedroom rather than my own.

I don't suppose Drummond slept much that night, through wondering just what his beloved Guinevere intended.

He found out the next morning. She informed him that it was her duty to expose him for the good of the country. The authorities would receive a full report on the incident involving a minister of the Crown and a junior officer.

He was distraught, and protested his innocence in the most desperate terms. She refused to listen to him. I was aware of this because I overheard them in the tool shed beyond the vegetable garden. I had been directed there by one of Lord Houghton's surviving maids, the rest having become land girls, shell-fillers, or canteen workers selling Woolton Pies, the new austerity dishes invented by Lord Woolton, Minister of Food.

When Sir Amyas emerged from the tool shed, a large chalk and flint structure, he looked so sick that I actually felt a tweak of compassion; or at least I felt it until he directed a look of hatred full upon me. "You did this," he said unsteadily. "You're behind this." And though I squeaked that it wasn't me, sir, he added in a low, juddering, but distinctly malevolent voice, "I'll make you suffer, you jumped-up colonial fraud, if it takes me the rest of my life. I'll make you pay."

As I watched him stump away toward his waiting car, straight across the emergency regulations garden with its regimented rows of cabbages, onions, leeks, and the austerity carrots, which were not allowed to grow longer than six inches, I must confess I experienced a wee kinky of apprehension. As if there weren't enough dangers in my life as it was.

I didn't realize that I was in almost as much trouble as Drummond until I marched into the tool shed to remonstrate with Guinevere. I said that surely even Drummond didn't deserve such treatment.

Dressed in brown corduroys and the same green pullover that she had worn the previous day, she was standing at a long work bench sharpening a sickle. The entire length of the bench was cluttered with household and garden tools, vices, plant pots, seed packets, disassembled machinery, and sundry lengths of metal gritty with rust.

"You don't understand the situation," she said defensively. "I'm not doing this for fun, you know."

"What d'you mean?"

"I can't tell you what I mean," she snapped. Then her voice and manner softened, and she said she was sorry to have placed me on stage, as it were, rather than in the grand circle. It was just that she had been forced to improvise when I had wandered through the secret passages and emerged into the wrong room, a puzzling development but one which she had proceeded to exploit for all it was worth.

"Or perhaps it wasn't a mistake – you were waiting for me to hop into bed with you?" she asked, sounding – Good Lord – almost hopeful.

"I thought it was my room," I muttered. "It seemed the same, except for the books."

"And the pictures. And the shape of the room. And the colour of the wallpaper. And the – "

"I was never in my room long enough to see what it contained."

"Anyway, it's all worked out quite well. Now we have Drummond where we want him."

"What d'you mean, we?"

"Now he'll have to resign," she said with satisfaction, running a stone vigorously along the gleaming blade of the sickle.

"That's all very well," I protested, "but what about me? If it gets out why he's resigned – and it will, there'll be too many questions asked – my reputation will be ruined as well."

"Oh, nonsense, sweetie. You're not important enough."

"Nevertheless it will put a stain on my character."

"You have so many already, nobody will notice."

"A stain," I persisted, "that will follow me for the rest of my life."

"That's silly, how can a stain follow you? Unless it's on wheels."

"I just don't wish to be known as a pervert, Guinevere."

"Call me Gwinny."

"You can't do this. If you ruin him you'll ruin me as well."

"We must all make sacrifices for the war effort, Bartholemew."

"What?"

"Darling, nobody will care that you're a rampant homosexual,"
she said reassuringly. I winced. She didn't even notice. "People will
soon forget about you. The main thing is, we'll have put the
Drummer out of action."

"I just don't understand why you're doing this."

"Just take it that I'm helping Cyril to get his revenge, that's all."

"Cyril?"

"He was thrilled at the opportunity to get the Drummer."

I stared at her, feeling chilly, though it was already a hot August
morning. The chalk and flint building was almost stifling, and
humming and moaning with bluebottles and wasps.

"But you say that's not the real reason?" I said at last.

She laid aside the sickle, and picked up an even more dangerous
implement, a scythe, and began to sharpen it with hard, rasping
strokes.

At least she had the decency to avert her face. A face that I had
begun to get used to, and even to admire for its power.

"And who else are you doing it for, Gwinny?" I asked.

"I'm doing the country a service, Bartholomew. That's all I can
tell you."

I was quiet for a moment; then: "And you're ready to see me go
down with him, are you?"

"Only a little way down, Bartholomew," she wheedled. She
smiled, though even she could not help the flush on her rippling
cheeks. "Don't worry about it, darling," she said. "Anyway, it may
never get out about your being degenerate."

"About me being . . . ? Good grief, Gwin . . . !"

"Well, after all, I did find you in bed with him, didn't I?" she said.

"But Christ, Guinevere – !"

"I mean, there's no getting away from it, is there?" she said accusingly. "You were there, stark naked. Really, I'd never have thought it of you, Bartholomew. Never."

I started toward her; but then decided not to kill her after all, at least not while she was so well-armed. She had a very long, freshly sharpened scythe in her hand. But of course it meant that I was doomed to be labelled a pervert forever.

Toffee Apples and Me

EVERY DAY NOW, THIS feverish September, we awoke with the feeling that the Battle of Britain, as they were calling it, was reaching a climax, and that the conclusion was near. The trouble was, we also felt that the conclusion might not be favourable to our side, if our experience was anything to go by. My squadron, at least, was on the debit side, losing more machines than the enemy, with the pilots growing dangerously fatigued by up to five sorties a day, yet without the energizing of success as compensation for the nervous strain and the almost daily loss of friends and companions.

As the squadrons and the Staffels clashed, a cat's cradle of contrails laced the cloudless skies above the hops and the poppies and the scorching downs of Kent. They were even advertising the show over the air: eye-witness descriptions of the mass battles overhead, and commentaries on individual scraps between the home side and the visitors. The BBC listeners could hear the snarl of Merlins or the rising whine from mortally wounded aircraft, and even the sky-high sputter of machine-gun and cannon fire.

On the Tuesday after my thirty-six-hour pass spent at Walsingham Manor, the sector controller sent us out three times. The third sortie came quite late in the evening, a single squadron show led by Daplin. We were vectored onto a truly enormous formation of enemy bombers, and we all had the feeling that this was it: the battle was to be won or lost over the next few days. If we lost, the invasion would come before the army could make up the loss of their equipment in France, and tyranny would rule for a hundred years.

We had been stooging up and down in tight formation, shadowing the hordes of German bombers for nearly half an hour, when I decided I'd had quite enough of this. Without further thought I put the wing over and dived toward the thickest part of the bomber formation. After a moment, Joffee followed, and then Sergeant Toye and one or two others. Daplin's voice, rasping angrily over the RT, soon faded.

I was going so fast the aircraft shuddered violently. I pulled up, practically draining all the blood into my sweaty socks, and the sky darkened for a moment before turning brighter than ever. Hauling back the stick with both hands I used the speed to climb toward the Heinkel bombers. A vulnerable belly steadied itself in the red sight.

I was aware that some 109s had come tumbling down after us, but I was just too browned off to care. I ignored my favourite rule, which was never to get into firing position without checking to ensure that there was no one behind me with a negative attitude. I didn't care whether there was anyone behind or not. It just seemed more important to do something about this new armada.

The plane shuddered again, this time from the vibration of the guns. The bomber in my sights blew up almost instantly, hurling its tail to one side. The tail went into a little spin of its own.

Within half a minute the skies had miraculous cleared of all the hundreds of friendly and enemy machines, except for just two other aircraft, a Messerschmitt on the tail of one of ours. I shouted a warning over the RT, but the Spitfire went down anyway, smoking and spinning, and disappeared below the clouds.

By the time I had thumped back onto the grass again I was very close to acknowledging that I was getting too old for this sort of thing. I was plum-tuckered and shagged-out after a mere two weeks of hard work in the blue skies, a fatigue that the weekend in Buckinghamshire had done nothing to ameliorate (ameliorate was my latest favourite word; I was now using it on every conceivable occasion and on some that weren't conceivable).

My morale was not exactly enhanced (another favourite word) by Squadron Leader Daplin's castigation (another) to the effect that I had broken formation and put the whole squadron in danger. He made sure that the dressing-down was in public. "You thought you would go for some derring-do, did you? The great once-upon-a-time ace, going to show us how it should be done. So you got one bomber, but what did it cost? Three of our pilots, your friend Dirkin among them! You happy now, Bandy, now you've shown what a fine aggressive flyer you are? And you see where's it's led – the loss of three of the best pilots in the squadron. Through your selfish, egotistical lack of self-control and discipline and consideration for others."

There was more of the same, most of it unanswerable, though as it happened one of the three pilots he was referring to was returned to us by the rescue services unharmed, though somewhat the worse for wear, alcoholwise.

All in all, 1940 did not seem to be a vintage year for your hero, on the political as well as the military front. Every day I expected to read in the papers about the resignation of the Parliamentary Under-Secretary of State for Air. Following which would come the nasty rumours as to why he had resigned, and speculation as to who else was involved. Ah, well, it would make a change from "a guardsman in St. James's Park."

It wouldn't be long before they connected me with Sir Amyas Drummond. I would enter the mess one day, and there would be a sudden silence, and a shiftiness. There would be lots of space around me at the polished mahogany mess table. Then when I was walking around the base one day there would be a kissing sound from a group of erks. Next time I went into a shop to buy a newspaper they would offer me a copy of the *Pansies Gazette*. After that there would be an anonymous letter from Canada, requesting me to stay away if I knew what was good for me. They didn't want my sort in the country to sully the snowbound wastes, or give lumberjacks who were okay other ideas.

On the morning after Daplin had given me such a bollocking, the whole squadron was called to the briefing room. We waited for quite a long time for the wing commander to arrive. As we lolled about in our blue uniforms with white polo-neck sweaters, I pretended to be interested in the maps that papered the walls, and the propaganda posters warning us to be careful what we said to the German spies in the bus queues, but I was as uneasy as everybody else. I felt certain that they had found me out and I was for the chop.

"Something's up."

"Seems so. Even the squadron cat seems jumpy this morning."

"You'd be jumpy, too, if you had fleas."

"I hear it caught them off Group Captain Mince," said Sergeant Toye.

Normally, this remark would have brought quite a reaction, considering how fastidious Mince was. But everyone was too tense to laugh.

"He was up with us yesterday evening," a pilot said. "The wingco, I mean."

"Broseley was flying? I didn't see him."

"He was there, all right."

"Cripes, things must be worse than we thought."

"Look out!"

Broseley had finally arrived, accompanied by the intelligence officer.

We stood to attention, and a dead silence fell. The only sound came from Broseley's boots as he strode heavily to the front of the room. On the platform he turned to face the assembled pilots, to announce that Joffee was taking over the squadron.

Daplin had been sent off on leave, and had already departed. Along with him had gone two pilots whose performance had been less than promising. They had not shown the requisite moral fibre.

"Enough said," said Broseley; who, naturally, had a good deal more to say, about how a new drive and enthusiasm were needed in the outfit. "I've been watching you people. Your aerial discipline has been just wonderful. It would bring joy to the hearts of the advanced training wallahs. Really wonderful. Watching you yesterday, I felt quite choked up."

Without warning he slammed the table with his great fist. The company started as one man. "I'll have no more of it!" he said. "What we want now is some very untidy work from all of you. What I want are people who will really go after those bastards who are using our sky as if it belonged to them."

He slammed the table again, and everyone trembled. "What I want," he said in a voice so powerful it vibrated his monstrous moustache, "are people who care enough about the folk in the East End of London who are getting pulverized in their houses, or hurt, or killed, day after day, morning, afternoon, evening, and night. What I want are pilots who care enough about those people to make sure those bastards behind their crooked crosses don't get back to knackwurstland to boast about it. Right, Joffee?"

"Right, sir! Damn right, sir!"

"And you, Bandy!" he bawled. "You're taking over B Flight from Joffee. And like the commanders of A and C Flights, if you're not followed by pilots who are prepared to go right into the middle of those bombers' formations, then I expect you to report them to me, so I can get rid of them pronto.

"All right," he said, in somewhat more moderate tones. "Come up here, will you, Apples. And you too, Bandy. In fact, I'd like to hear what you, Bandy, have to say to your pilots."

"Me?"

"I'm interested in hearing right now what you would want to say to them."

"You want me to give a speech, sir?"

"No, I don't want you to give a bloody speech. I want you to say something useful before we get back to business."

"All right," I said. I didn't know why he wanted me to address the multitude. However, having been a politician at one time, I was always willing to bluster and hector. So: "All right, folks," quoth I from the platform. "First of all, I know you think I'm the ancient mariner. Well, until now, I've certainly been inclined to follow the ancient rules about air fighting." God, that wasn't too impressive a sequitur. "Now, tacticswise, I haven't seen anything so far that's much different from the First World War." Someone groaned faintly. "Except that now one has even less time to think."

This was awful. I was facing a sea, or at least a pond, of blank faces. I hurried on, sweating. "Anyway, all I have to say is that, after this battle is over, I shall be returning to all the old rules that have kept me alive for so long. Things like using the sun as cover, and constantly checking behind you, and on ops never flying straight and level for more than a few seconds, and all the other useful tactics that make the difference between the pilot who goes for a Burton, and the one who makes it into his dotage at the age of forty-six, or even older."

I took a deep breath, and continued in as sincere a fashion as my whining drawl would allow. "But right now I'm saying the hell with all the rules and tactics. We'll come back to them when we can afford to. But right now we can't afford to. We have the biggest emergency since the year sixteen . . . whenever the Spanish Armada was. If we don't win this one, we lose everything. So until the crisis is over, we're going to forget all the rules – and go out, and at any cost, *get those bombers.*

"We simply must win this one, fellows, and that's all there is to it," I finished in a decidedly lame diminuendo.

The operations centre in Ongar had been asked not to send us once more unto the breach, dear friends, until Broseley had finished sorting out the squadron. Three o'clock in the afternoon found us still hanging around the flight hut at the edge of the aerodrome, expecting to be hurled aloft at any moment. They were saying that huge air battles were taking place over Kent and even over London, and we were expecting the order to scramble at any moment. In the meantime we larked about nervously. I got a fastball game going between members of my flight until I nearly broke a leg falling over Plato, who had volunteered to join the team as well and kept getting in the way. Grey-whiskered Plato, an adorable old dog, had now become the squadron mascot rather than my personal pet.

After that near mishap, we lolled about in our deck chairs stolen from Southend-on-Sea Corporation, gossiping and conjecturing.

Still there was no word from Midway, the code name of our controller. Tense as animal traps, we feigned nonchalance under the
burning sun.

The phone rang. I started so violently that for a moment I
thought I had undone my trapezius muscle. "Scramble!" Then the
dash to the aircraft, parachute butting my behind, ground crew
darting out from the shade of the wings.

Two minutes later I was busily pumping up the undercart – no
hydraulic gears in this early model – and climbing on full throttle.
All three of the squadrons that shared our field were aloft. Every
day our fighter formations were growing larger in an attempt to deal
with the Luftwaffe's mass tactics.

Just as the supercharger punched in at 19,000 feet, Midway came
on the line, calling Bob Broseley. "Hello, blue leader. I can offer
sixty-plus bandits in your area, can you deal, over?"

Broseley's voice sounded calmly over the RT. "Blue leader to
Midway, give course and direction if you please."

Learning that the enemy formation was slightly above us but
travelling in the opposite direction toward central London, we
turned, still climbing; and five minutes later, right over the winding
Thames, we caught up with a great cloud of Junkers and Heinkel
bombers. They were in a jiggling square formation a mile wide,
with packs of ravening Messerschmitts another few thousand feet
overhead.

Not every sighting of enemy aircraft led to a fight. Many a time
the Hurricanes and Spitfires returned to base with the patches over
the gun ports intact. Not this time – the familiar shivery excitement
told me so; the dry mouth, the fluttering heart, quickening breath
thunderous in the oxygen mask. At the same time I felt more
confident than at any time since arriving at 6 OTU so many eons or
weeks ago. As our squadron manoeuvred into position, trying to get
up-sun, I glanced over my shoulder to make sure my wingman was
in place – Pete Siomontschuk from Edmonton – he was down as
Petechuck because nobody could pronounce his name – even he
had trouble with it after a few Johnny Walkers. I waved to him, then

with the same shaky glove I flicked the gun button to ON, and sank the seat to its lowest position.

Two minutes later, keeping one eye on the Messerschmitts, one eye on the bomber formation, and one eye on Lady Luck, we put the wings over and attacked — against the sun, but there was no time for aerial niceties. I think everybody was in a hurry to get at the Nazis before they released their bombs over the centre of the city. They had already beaten up the East End. Great fires were burning down there, smoke billowing from the poor workers' houses around the docks.

Broseley did his best to plunge us through the centre of the enemy formation, to break it up. Rather too closely followed by Petechuck — he was taking his duties as guardian very seriously — I picked out a round-nosed Heinkel, held fire until I was only a couple of hundred feet away. My old shooting skill was back, at last. With twelve degrees' deflection I was hitting him squarely near the wing root. I suppose his gunners were shooting back, but I didn't notice.

The Heinkel caught fire, and twisted out of my line of sight. Pete later confirmed that it had gone down.

I was about to use up the remaining ammo on another Heinkel but had to bank away when some purposeful Messerschmitts came down from their eyries.

Amazingly, Petechuck, instead of freelancing on his own as he was expected to do, was still with me as I engaged a second Heinkel, this time from head on. Eight lines of machine-gun bullets shattered his Plexiglas nose, and must have eaten down the length of the fuselage. The twin-engined bomber blew up just as I was diving under it. It had obviously not released its bomb load. But what was good for the workers was not too good for me, for in disintegrating, the bomber must have taken away most of my tail. The Spitfire went into a whirling spin.

There was no response from rudder or elevator and for a while I knew what it must be like to be a sample in a centrifuge. After a while the ailerons helped me to get out of the spin, but it wasn't much of an improvement. Now I was in an uncontrollable dive. So I closed up shop, hauled back the canopy, and got out as fast as I could.

Without much leeway, vertical division. When the chute stopped swinging and I looked past my flying boots, I was surprised to discover that I was only about fifteen hundred feet above the sunlit smoke that was drifting over central London.

But, oh, joy. I had survived. By gad, I felt good, if still somewhat weak with fright. This was only the second time I'd had to bail out. I let out a yell and waved my arms, and began to sing that ridiculous song about hanging out the washing on the Siegfried Line; and I even recited a bit of poetry, lines by the Canadian pilot John Magee that were to become the most widely quoted of all aerial verse: "Oh! I have slipped the surly bonds of earth/And danced the skies on laughter-silvered wings." Mind you, at moments like this, I didn't find the earth all that surly, in fact I was looking forward to making its acquaintance again, any moment now. Also, I wasn't too keen on flying a plane with laughable wings. Still, it was a good poem, I guess – stirred up a bit of sentiment in even the toughest flying breast.

That other parachuting occasion was as far back as 1918 when my brigade commander, Arthur Soames, or Arser, as his sexy French wife, Marguerite, called him, had manoeuvred me into volunteering to test Britain's first operational parachute. It was Cyril Greaves who had been piloting the plane I had jumped out of. Now *that* was a frightening experience I can tell you, especially after I had plopped down into the park where Brigadier Soames had his HQ. I landed right on top of his prize peacock, killing it dead. "He's gone and jumped on my cock," I remember him screaming at his staff.

It suddenly occurred to me with a stab of alarm that if luck plotted its usual course, something equally upsetting would happen within the next few seconds. It would be just my luck if I landed on the Canadian High Commissioner. Or – oh, God, no – on Amyas Drummond. Please, no – not Sir Drummond. I looked down anxiously to see where I was – Drummond was bound to have a flat hereabouts in central London. And, oh, Lord, once again I was falling into a park.

Because of a scarcity of seconds and an excess of smoke I was lashing into the treetops before I could work out which park it was. The leafy branches thrashed wildly around me as braking gravity hacked me through the gritty branches and the foliage. Then I was being brought to an abrupt halt about ten feet short of the ground with a jarring suddenness as the canopy tangled.

I took stock, hanging there for a moment like a glassy-eyed rabbit outside your typical English butcher shop. The first impression was one of sound: fire engines and the steady wail of the all-clear siren. The second was of taste and smell. I smacked my lips, tasting the air like a wine-taster, sampling the odour and flavour of the smoke that drifted thinly across the park. Good colour. In the filtered sun it was quite an attractive bluish grey. But the bouquet left something to be desired, being of burning laths and horsehair lagging. Victorian, I should say, with just a touch of Gothic Revival. Belgravia 1940?

However, this was not getting me onto terra firma. I looked around and almost immediately noticed a denuded branch two feet away. I had just finished perching on it and shrugging out of the parachute harness when I became aware that two neatly dressed upper-class girls of about ten and fourteen respectively had come running up; or rather the younger one had come running, while the elder had walked up with a restraint unusual in one so young. I knew she was upper class because it was obviously an upper-class garden I'd fallen into. It was so large I couldn't even make out the perimeter, though admittedly the boundary could not have been far, for the ringing and clanging of the fire engines was quite close.

Now the kids were standing under the tree, staring up at me. "You're not a German, are you?" asked the elder rather censoriously. Both girls were dressed in simple blue frocks that made them look even younger than their height and development suggested.

"Canadian," I said, brushing myself down as I sat perched on the branch like Robin Redbreast. I was wearing a new battledress and an expensive white polo-neck sweater and was concerned to keep them clean and tidy.

"Oh, dear," she said. "I have heard that Canadians are very rough and unruly."

"That's the army," I said. "We aviators are faultlessly circumspect. By the way, you don't have a ladder, do you?"

"Of course we don't have a ladder," she replied haughtily. "What a silly question. As if we were in the habit of carrying a ladder around with us."

"For one thing," said the smaller girl primly, "we're not allowed to carry ladders, are we, Lilibet? We have people to do that for us, you know."

The younger one was the prettier of the two and had an attractive smile, though it was perhaps a shade deliberate. I thought I preferred the older girl, even if she was rather toffee-nosed.

Both of them had the most exquisitely clear white complexions which had obviously been well-protected from the vulgar gaze of the sun.

"Well, are you going to stay up there all day?" the older one demanded.

"I'm thinking about it, Miss."

"Well, don't think about it too long, or Papa might mistake you for a grouse and shoot you."

"That's right," said the little girl. "He's very fond of shooting grousers."

"Grouse," the one called Lilibet corrected her. "The word is grouse."

"Shouldn't that be grice?" I suggested from up the tree. "Like the plural of louse is lice?"

"You are really very silly indeed," Lilibet responded, though a little hesitantly as if she were not quite sure about it.

The little girl hopped about on one foot for a moment, then said, "Aren't you ever going to come down?"

"Well, if you girls don't have a ladder on you, I guess I'll have to climb down," I said, just as the branch snapped. There was a loud crack and I took the most direct route to the ground, and – fulfilling the fear expressed earlier – almost fell on top of the younger girl, close enough to send her, too, sprawling.

Fortunately, after her first alarm, she found it funny, and giggled as we picked ourselves up and plucked leaves and twigs off ourselves. Her sister, though, was not amused. After making sure that her sister was unhurt, she turned and told me that I should have been more careful.

"It was the tree's fault," I whined. "It snapped."

"Our trees are not in the habit of snapping," she snapped. "We have a gardener to make sure that our trees are always in good working order."

"Well, this one wasn't," I sulked. I'd hurt my elbow in the fall. "It must have been a dead branch."

Just then a neat, worn-looking man in slacks and a fawn sweater appeared through the trees.

I started to feel uneasy. He looked awfully familiar.

"Hello," he said hesitantly, glancing up at the spread of parachute silk above us.

"Hi. My name's Bandy, sir. Bartholomew Bandy. Had to bail out. This your garden, sir?"

"Y . . . yes."

"Papa," said the younger girl, "he's broken our tree. Look at that," she cried, pointing to the branch I'd been sitting on, but which was now lying on the ground, dead.

"Snitch," I said; and was just about to stick my tongue out at her when it hit me who the man was. Which also told me where I was: the bloody back garden of Buckingham Palace.

The King was regarding me with a frown. "Bandy," he said. "My father used to talk about a man c . . . called Bandy. A . . ." He waited for a moment to allow the syllables to catch up. "I remember him saying that this fellow Bandy kept turning up at the palace demanding more medals. My father said he got quite tired of ind . . . ind . . . indulging Bandy's insatiable appetite for orders, crosses, and sashes."

It was too late now to start curtseying or whatever one was supposed to do in such circumstances. So in keeping with the informal occasion I stayed casual. "Actually I got on quite well with your dad, sir, even if he was a gruff old chap. But then of course he was Royal Navy. They're all gruff."

"Well, really!" said Princess Elizabeth. But King George the Sixth's prematurely worn features relaxed into a delighted smile, and he promptly invited me into the palace for a nice cup of tea. And it was a nice cup of tea, too, even if they had run out of sugar.

THERE'S ME IN THE BLACKOUT

HERE IT WAS NEARLY 1941, and still the Parliamentary Under-Secretary had not resigned. In fact, with his gift for self-promotion, Sir Amyas seemed more prominent than ever. You could hardly line a birdcage with newsprint without reading about some eloquent speech of his. Which was all the more remarkable considering that newspaper space was so precious. The papers had now been reduced to four pages, with just the occasional extra sheet for the posh dailies.

I tried to get in touch with Greaves to find out what was happening, but he seemed to be in a snit and wouldn't answer my calls. Finally, I awarded myself a forty-eight-hour pass, and drove up to town in a thoroughgoing fog. Trying to locate Cyril's flat in a pea-souper did not exactly soothe my mood. Long separated from his wife, Greaves was living alone in a flat close to the Royal Albert Hall. It belonged to one of his many aunts who had retreated to her country cottage to escape the bombing.

When I finally found the damn place in the fog, it was like entering a rain forest. The vast flat was so filled with vegetation that a machete would have come in handy to get to the drinks trolley. Though I knew something about flora – I could recognize a rose or a tulip within seconds if they were nicely wrapped in cellophane – most of the items were unfamiliar. Cyril claimed that many of them were rubber plants, but that was patently absurd. Anyone could see that they were real. I did, however, recognize several similar items that were spraying armfuls of pink petals out of a row of brass planters. "Ah, yes, Christmas cacti," I informed Air Vice-Marshal Greaves, who looked surlily impressed until he noticed the name on the stick in one of the brass buckets.

The similarity to a rain forest was emphasized by the wet mist – much of the London fog had seeped inside – and by the heat. Cyril's aunt had installed that great rarity in Britain, central heating. It was turned up so high that the parquetry under some of the radiators was smouldering. What with the calories and all the oxygen that was being produced by the foliage I knew it would be quite a relief afterwards to get back into the fog.

I'd had the impression for some time that Cyril was not pleased with me. This visit confirmed it. "We could have destroyed Drummond if it hadn't been for you," he said.

"How? I thought Guinevere was all set to scupper us both, him and me."

"Well, she didn't," he said sulkily. "She betrayed me instead."

"I've been trying for weeks to get in touch with her, but even her mother doesn't know where she hangs out. And the Army doesn't know either."

"How would they know anyway?"

"Well, she's in the army, isn't she? She wore an ATS uniform."

"For God's sake, Bandy," Greaves said pityingly, "you'll be trusting a company next because it's called a Trust Company. You know what she is."

"How d'you mean?"

"If you don't know by now you must have the brain as well as the appearance of a horse."

Dear oh dear. Where were the days of yore when he regarded me with a reverence bordering on idolatry? Today he was positively hostile.

"And another thing," he said sharply. "Just what are you up to? Are you a Red, or something?"

"A Red?"

"They've been asking questions about you, Bandy – or should I say Comrade Bandy?"

"Who's been asking questions?"

"Who do you think would ask questions about spies and subversives?"

"What on earth are you gibbering about?"

"You mustn't talk to me like that, Bandy. I'll have you remember I'm very much your superior officer."

"Sorry. So what the hell are you gibbering about, sir?"

"They have proof of your communist affiliations."

"My communist . . . !" I went for a brief walk through the tarantulas and Miocene flora. "Good God, Cyril, you've known me for twenty years. Have I ever shown the slightest leaning in that direction?"

"Not leaning could be your cover. Did you ever attend Cambridge University?"

Ignoring the irrelevant question I shouted, "This is the goddamn limit. You know damn well how I feel about the Reds."

Remembering the dreadful way I had been treated by the Bolsheviks – imprisoned, starved, beaten, given the freedom of Moscow – Greaves subsided a little, and even had the grace to look ashamed. "I suppose there must be a mistake," he muttered.

"You suppose so?!"

"All right, I know so! But they seem convinced you're a subversive. They say that if they weren't so preoccupied with the Germans they'd have probably hanged you by now. It's only because they're still hoping to get the Russians on our side that they haven't done anything about you."

"Where did they get this idea from?"

"I don't know," he replied irritably. "Anyway, that's their problem."

"It's very much mine, too," I said heatedly. "And where does Guinevere come into all this?"

"She betrayed me, that's what she did."

"How?"

"She refused to testify about you and Drummond being caught in bed together."

I took a deep breath. With all the oxygen in the room it made me dizzy.

As Greaves had still not invited me to make myself at home, or even to offer me a drink, I sat down, firmly, on his air force cap.

"Let's start again, shall we?" I said. "You – "

"Hey – mind my cap!" he cried, rescuing it from under my bum.

"Cyril, you know the circumstances that led up to that bedroom scene?"

"Look at that! Look what you've done to my cap!"

"Never mind your blasted cap! You're saying Guinevere didn't go through with the accusation against Drummond after all?"

Greaves continued to caress his precious cap as if it were a prize Pomeranian, but otherwise remained angrily silent.

"But why didn't she follow through, Cyril?"

He muttered reluctantly, "She said she just couldn't do it to you, that's all."

"Oh?"

"At least," he conceded, placing the cap safely on a sideboard, "she had the decency to feel ashamed of her conduct."

"For being prepared to disgrace me?"

"No! For *not* being prepared to disgrace you," he said, reaching out and plucking a rare orchid from its stem. "Though as I say, she had the grace to apologize for not going through with it and ruining you." He detached a glowing orange-and-white petal, and started nibbling obsessively at its meaty texture. "And the result was that swine Drummond is still in power."

I said wonderingly, "She let Drummond off the hook to . . . save me . . . ?"

"And now she hates you. Justifiably, in my opinion."

"Hates me? Why?"

"For stopping her from doing her duty."

I sat there, trying to figure it out. Guinevere felt that I had betrayed her by forcing her to let the side down, was that it? But what side was it that had been let down? Or to put it another way, as the Bishop said to the actress, she now hated me because it was for my sake that she had decided not to ruin Drummond, was that it? It was all too much for my horse brain. So I merely looked around for something else of Cyril's to sit on.

After a while his bad temper subsided and he offered me a drink. He then went on to consider other means by which he might dish the Parliamentary Under-Secretary.

"I've been thinking," he said. "I've found out that Drummond often goes shooting up in Scotland on the Earl of Troon's property."

"What about it?"

"What I was thinking of," he said, "was that you could join in and accidentally, as it were, shoot him."

"Shoot him."

"Yes."

"Shoot Drummond. With a gun."

"Of course with a gun! Don't be so ridiculous."

"I see. I get an invitation somehow from the Earl of Troon, and promptly blast one of his guests with a shotgun, is that it?"

"No," he said thoughtfully. "What I had in mind was, you could do it from your Spitfire."

"From my Spitfire."

"I hear you haven't lost that deadly aim of yours," he said with an encouraging smile that came nowhere near his eyes. He continued to gaze at me with a look of such respectful supplication, however, that it quite took me back to the good old days when he practically grovelled at my feet in adulation.

"So," I said, "the idea is for me to join in the shoot with my eight-gun Spitfire?"

"I don't see there'd be any risk," he wheedled. "You could come in low, and be out of the area before they had a chance to identify your aircraft. Wait, where are you going?"

"Oh, just along to the nearest loony bin, to see if they have a vacancy. Whether it's for me or you I'm not quite sure," I said, and departed soon after, trying to slam the door; but it had a pneumatic fixture that prevented it from doing anything except to emit a hopeless sigh.

1941 was the year I was able to relax my annual resolution to cut down on the booze. It was obvious that my face had sufficiently benefitted from the alcoholic restraint. In the mirror it looked back

at me with only a few hints here and there of its former dissipa-
tion. "You're looking years younger," said someone who wanted to
borrow a fiver for a trip to the West End. "Hours, anyway," said
Sergeant Toye.

Now that the immediate danger was over – aerial photographs
showed that the invasion barges in the French and Belgian ports had
finally been dispersed – the pilots of our squadron had established
Friday evening as Binge Night. Mind you, every night was that sort
of night down at the Pig and Trough, but Friday was especially
bingeful. It was sometimes so riotous that word had spread, and
pilots from other squadrons were starting to show up.

At first I had lamented that squadron booze-ups weren't what
they used to be. As I kept telling the fellows, it was much better
when we held them on the aerodrome, right there in the mess,
where there were riotous ceremonial speeches, celebrations to
honour pilots whose gongs had just come through, and rousing,
emotional toasts to the KingGodBlessHim.

"At least the pub gets you off the station for a couple of hours,"
said Hector McCurdle.

"So pubs aren't good enough for old Bandylegs," said Broseley
on this particular evening. "You prefer the Café Royal, I suppose."

"You're drunk, Boozeley."

"That's Broseley, you pie-eyed piebald."

I froze and half raised my hand, thinking that he was slyly referring to a certain person's hairpiece; but the wig was as firmly in
place as ever. Nobody had the faintest idea that half my head had
gone.

Did I say half my head? Half my hair, I meant. All the same, my
head did feel a little like that tonight. A particularly boisterous
party had developed, to celebrate our latest success. We had shot.
down five e.a. without loss.

I was also revising my New Year's Resolution because Mr.
Meakin, proprietor of the Pig and Trough, had received a case of
Johnnie Walker from a patriotic friend in Kilmarnock, and was
keeping it specially for "My Boys," as he called us.

Tonight I had certainly had my share. And Finnegan's share . . . and Brooke-Gaitor's share, and Thompson's, and Scotty's, and . . .

"Incidentally," Broseley said, "incidentally . . ."

"Incidentally what?" asked Squadron Leader Joffee.

"What d'you mean, incidentally what?" Broseley demanded. I think he was frowning under his moustache.

"You said incidentally."

"You said it too, Apples, I stinktly heard you."

"No, you — oh, forget it."

"I can't forget it," Broseley said tragically. "It will stay with me for the rest of my life."

"What will?"

"I don't know. I've forgotten. Oh, yes — " He turned roughly in my direction. "What I was going to say was that a profound mystery surrounds you, Bartholomew Bandy," he began. But then looked offended. "But I'm not going to say it now, because Apples is being so rude."

"A mystery?" I asked with an incredulous laugh. Then, soberly: "Yes, I know what you mean. There's something odd going on in my life, and I don't know what it is."

"Zactly. Like for instance I expected somebody entirely different from you when you first arrived in your wheelchair. I expected a much younger person would replace as a turn-up pilot."

"Thank God he didn't," said Sergeant Toye, "or we would never have had the privilege of hearing Mr. Bandy render 'When There Isn't a Girl About' on the pianoforte."

There was an uproar of laughter at this. I gave Toye a look. "Who let Toye into this select gathering?" I demanded. "Who let in this common sergeant?

"No, but you're right, Boozeley," I said, taking another swig. "I feel as if I'm being manipulated by fate."

"I know him quite well," Broseley said. "Air Marshal Fate. Gloomy chap." And he sniggered to himself.

"People keep getting the wrong idea about me. I keep getting calls from Records, and they sound as puzzled as me."

"Puzzled about what?"

"That's it. I don't know. It's so . . ."

"Puzzling?"

"Zactly. Listen, everybody," I called out. "Shall we have a singsong round the piano?"

"No!!"

"I used to play in a mess . . . in our old mess. This was after I acquired a piano – "

"Oh, God," said Brooke-Gaitor, "it's not the story of how you stole the brigadier's piano again, is it?"

"Why, have I told it before?" I said, as somebody said into my port earhole, "Bart – somebody wants to see you."

"What? Who?"

"The civvie over there."

As soon as I managed to focus on him, the civilian turned and walked though into the next room – the lounge, public bar, saloon, snug, private bar – whatever it was.

I proceeded with all due care and attention in a roughly souse-westerly direction toward the same lounge (public bar, saloon, etc.), which had comfortable sofas, and tables that were almost undamaged.

There was only one other person in the place. This must therefore be the civvy who had just walked in there and who wished for an audience. I walked over to him in a faultlessly crooked line. It would have been a mistake to walk over in a straight line as there were numerous sofas and tables between me and the person in the shadows and the dark suit.

Arriving dead on time, I peered at him closely, and failed to recognize a single feature, or even a double feature. It occurred to me that this was because I had not previously encountered him.

"You are Mr. Bartholomew Bandy," the man said, "I take it?"

"You take what?" quoth I challengingly. "What have you taken?"

"I was confirming that you are indeed Bartholomew W. Bandy, sir."

"There was no need to confirm it. I definitely am him, or he."

"You are not quite what I expected, Mr. Bandy," the visitor said, handing me his card. It was a very nice, expensive card. I peered appreciatively at the embossed lettering, running my fingers over the lettering as if it were braille and I were fairly blind.

I almost felt like running my digits appreciatively over the visitor as well, as, like me, he was so beautifully cut. His suit was superbly fashioned. It could not have come from anywhere but Saville Row, or possibly Burton's, The Fifty Shilling Tailors, or a particularly fine market stall. The material was darkest grey, with just a hint of a stripe – actually several dozen stripes – unless of course it was a single but continuous stripe that wound backwards and forwards in more or less parallel lines, except where the stripe reversed direction, in which case there would be several loops.

Inside said suit was a figure neat and compact. Quite a good-looking chap he was, with presence and personality, and so open and frank a face that I immediately put him down as a spy, possibly a member of MI5, MI6, MI9, MI13, MICe, or SMIT(n).

The dark gentleman seemed in no hurry to state his business. Recovering from his surprise, he invited us both to sit on one of the sofas, and proceeded to chat inconsequentially about this and that for a minute or two while he occupied himself with summing me up, and arriving at a handsome figure.

I grew warier still when he confessed to being employed by the Foreign Office, which, as everybody knew, was filled with pansies and Arabists. For an uneasy moment I thought he might be a pansy himself. He had moved very close to me by now, ostensibly to keep the talk confidential. Maybe he thought I was one of them, having heard about what had happened in the bedroom in Walsingham Manor. Except, of course, that nothing had happened.

After a while, upon listening carefully to our conversation, I discovered that we were having a nice chat about Russia. He seemed genuinely interested in my opinions. Which was strange, as I was doing little more than agreeing with his opinions, including the one to the effect that Russia must have been an interesting place to visit before the Revolution.

I continued to play along in order to find out what he wanted. He had certainly not come up from London just for a nice chat.

Trouble was, I was finding it difficult to concentrate. My eyes kept rolling in opposite directions, like a stripper's tassels.

I waited patiently for my eyes to subside and for him to speak his mind. But he kept on and on about Eastern Europe and its problems and prospects. "You're really pro-Soviet yourself, aren't you, Mr. Bandy?" he asked suddenly, all the rust abruptly disappearing from his steely eyes.

"I yam not. I've been a distink enema of them for going on twenty-two years, give or take a Bolshevik."

"I understand," he murmured, smiling, "that's your cover, isn't it?"

"I know what you're trying to do," I said loudly.

"Shhh," he replied, somewhat absurdly, considering the racket from the chaps next door.

"You're from MI pick-a-number, any number, aren't you?" I cried. "Trying to entrap me, that's what you're trying to do." And I rose steadily to my feet, though it took a while.

"This is entirely unofficial," he said. "You don't have to worry that I'll expose you as a supporter of Soviet democracy and the cause of world peace. You'll see – nothing will come of this meeting unless you want it to. I don't expect you to admit straight out that you're doing a triple."

"A triple?"

"Maintaining that you're a communist – "

"But dammit, I don't maintain it," I protested in a firm mumble, still trying to halt my eyeballs.

"Pretending to be one," he continued, "so that people will think it's a cover and you're really hostile, when all the time you really are a communist and pro-Soviet. I know you can't admit straight out that your loyalties are to the cause, without bourgeois pretensions to outmoded nationalism, but – " and at this point he rose and touched my elbow in a friendly fashion – "when you see that nothing will come of my personal knowledge that you are on the right side, perhaps you might care to get in touch with the person named on the other side of my card?"

By then I was spluttering with indignation. I started to protest heatedly at the accusation that I had sympathy for international socialism, or any other ism, for that matter. But, "That's good," he whispered giving my elbows another little squeeze. "Confuse them by maintaining your allegiance to communism while at the same time indicating the opposite to the opposite." And with a conspiratorial wink he departed, leaving me thoroughly annoyed and confused as to what I was being thoroughly annoyed and confused about.

I nearly called him back to deny everything he'd said in the hope that the denial might apply to the parts of what he had said that ought to have been denied. In preparation for which I focussed blearily on his card so that I could dress him down by name.

Boris, it said on the card. No address. Just that and a telephone number.

Well, Boris, you agent provocateur, if you thought you could get me to admit to being a Red (or was it to admit to *not* being a Red to establish that I really was one?) so you and your security men could go on persecuting me with a clear conscience, then you've another think coming.

It was obvious what they were after. Having failed to obtain proof that I was a communist, they were hoping to get me to admit it – or deny it – or confirm that I was a Red by admitting that I was. Or wasn't.

I was about to tear up the card in fuzzy annoyance when I realized that Boris wasn't the man's name at all. That was the name scrawled on the back of the card. The proper name was on the other side in the embossed type: H. A. R. (Kim) Philby.

Strangely enough, a few days later when I looked for Boris's number on the back of his card, it was no longer there. Must have been written in invisible ink, or something. Very strange.

Amazing that in a city of eight million or so, I should bump accidentally into Guinevere. Though I guess the odds weren't quite as amazing as that, as most service people congregated in a comparatively limited area of the city, usually the West End. In my case it was Westminster.

It was a freezing night, and the air raid alarm was howling as I emerged from the St. James's Park underground station. The anti-aircraft guns in Hyde Park were already banging away.

I darted back into the tube. And there she was, jammed among others who had taken shelter. She was against the far wall, her back against a poster reading CARELESS TALK COSTS LIVES. (Under this somebody had written *Careless Lives Cost Talk*.)

She was wearing a long black woollen coat and a close-fitting red hat with a drooping black feather. Though her eyes were as pugnacious as ever, and her eyebrows bristling like warthogs, her face was paler than usual, making the vermilion lipstick almost fluorescent even in the dank gloom of the Tube.

"Hello, Bartholomew," she said, as calmly as if we had arranged to meet on the station concourse. "I've been hearing all about you."

"Once and for all," I burst out, "I am not a communist!"

Several people turned and looked at me. One of them scowled – probably a Party member thinking I was denying them thrice.

"I was referring to your flying exploits."

"Oh."

"How many is it now?"

"I don't know – six or seven." I took a deep breath to help me recover my aplomb. "You're a civilian again, I see."

"Yes," she said, scowling as a seven-foot all-in wrestler wearing an LDV armband accidentally bumped against her. For a moment I feared she was about to beat him to a pulp.

"Why don't you come clean, Guinevere, and admit you're in Intelligence."

"Please don't be short with me, Bart. I'm cold and hungry, and miserable."

To my astonishment this brute of a woman with her glorious figure and her hook-nosed, bulldozer-chinned assault of a face sounded quite forlorn. And for the first time I found myself looking at her as a woman rather than as a walking ad for plastic surgery. The fierce bright eyes had dimmed to a ten-watt vulnerability.

I felt a strange sensation, as if I were turning into a serving of mushy peas. For a ghastly moment I even felt like giving her a hug to help warm her up. Which, apart from anything else, would have been dang silly as I was probably colder than she was. I'd miscalculated the weather again and come out in my blue raincoat rather than the hideous service greatcoat.

As if it, too, was chilly, the ground shuddered. Then came the dull thump of explosions. A stick of bombs falling, not far off. One. Two. Three.

I breathed easier. They were receding.

My alarm wasn't receding, though. For a dreadful moment I had come close to finding this normally ferocious beldame almost appealing. For God's sake! What was happening to me? Tonight she was even being considerate. When I glanced at my watch she said with an obvious effort at insouciance, "Don't bother about me if you have an appointment."

"I was thinking about my hotel. If I don't get there soon dinner will be off."

She looked away. Her eyebrows sank dejectedly onto her eagle beezer. To my fury I heard myself saying, "Would you care to join me?"

"Are you sure you want me?"

"It's not far – Buckingham Palace Road."

"Well, if you're sure, Bartholomew . . . ?"

Dodging an officious ARP warden ("'ere, where d'you fink you're going?"), we sneaked out of the subway. It felt colder than ever, and I found myself huddling against her, to take advantage of her overcoat and her superstructure.

Searchlights were fingering the sky. In the direction of the river a huge fire was raging. The sky was bright orange. A few hundred yards away another fire was building up, somewhere near the Ritz. Fire engines were clanging. Someone blew a halfhearted whistle that sounded like a lonely bird. We walked quickly, Guinevere seemingly indifferent to the tinkle of the ack-ack shrapnel that was raining down. I myself was twitching like a rabbit. Like the old grey mare my nerves weren't what they used to be.

We had quite a decent dinner at the hotel. "My son's in the Air

Force," the waiter said. "A wireless operator. He can do twenty-five words a minute. That's supposed to be very good."

"Absolutely. I could only manage about four words a minute."

"And you with all those medals."

"Yes. I'm afraid none of them is for wireless operating."

At the next table somebody was saying, "There's a big fire on Page Street."

"Page Street?" said the man. "My God, I hope it's the Westminster Hospital and not my club."

Guinevere was listening to an orchestra of retired cat lovers at the far end of the restaurant. Judging by her expression she considered that the musicians ought to be drowned. But when she turned to me she looked as if she was coming to a decision that would take a great deal of courage. But for the moment all she said was, "You're very good with unpretentious people, aren't you."

Her spirits seemed to have revived. She looked as happy as her face would permit. "It's lovely and warm in here," she said. "I wonder how they get the fuel."

She grew so relaxed over the chocolate pudding (made from cocoa and asbestos) that she even talked about herself. In so doing she let slip enough detail for me to guess how she might have gotten involved with Intelligence. (Unless, of course, she was engaged on some operation that required her to be indiscreet – you could never tell, with mince pies.)

Anyway, she revealed that, upon leaving the Cheltenham Ladies College, she had gone up to Oxford, and had done well there; so well that they had kept her on in the modern history department (much to her father's disgust. A medievalist, he didn't think anything worthwhile had happened in history after Snorri Sturluson had written *Heimskringla*).

In the mid-Thirties, Guinevere was approached by her favourite teacher at the Cheltenham college, a Miss Cumbersome. Miss Cumbersome had done work for the security services in the First World War, and had continued to work for them after the war as a hunter-gatherer. She had recruited Guinevere at Oxford.

Apparently, Oxford and Cambridge were good places to meet people who had a sufficiently high turpitude quotient gained over years of academic infighting and intrigue. Another reason why Miss Cumbersome had kept Guinevere in mind for so many years was that Gwinny had been good at inventing complicated indoor and outdoor games, where only she was certain of the rules.

"Good training for MI5, eh?" I said.

She frowned, and said, "I'm talking too much. And you seem to know too much about the business."

I didn't mention that I had done a little work for British Intelligence between the wars. Later I realized that I should have spoken up. It might have made things a lot easier for me, in Quebec.

So far the dinner had been a success. I was even starting to get accustomed to her face. Even the coffee was good that evening. Strangely enough, coffee was unrationed and freely available in the shops, while the tea ration was down to two ounces per person per week. Yet still these peculiar islanders refused to switch to such plentiful supplies.

"I met Cyril the other day," I said.

"Yes, I know."

"He wants to kill Drummond. Do you think there's something wrong with him?"

"With Cyril? No, why should there be?"

"I just told you. He seems bent on killing the Minister. Except he wanted me to do it."

"Did you accept?"

"'Course I didn't. Whaja take me for? I'm a decent, sensible, tolerant, live-and-let-live person."

"You've reformed, eh?"

We smirked at each other. Her smile faded. "You have a room here?" she asked.

"Yes."

She took a deep breath, which, with her chest, was always a fine spectacle. "Could you put me up for the night?" she asked in a voice that was meant to be discreet but which in fact swivelled heads from as far away as the string orchestra. Now she was blushing like the proverbial bride, looking down at her hands which were all-in wrestling. "I don't feel like going home."

She must have noticed the fear rising and the blood draining from my face. "I'm sorry," she said quickly. "Forget what I said."

I started to gibber. "No, no, forget it," she snapped. "I know perfectly well I'm as frightful as the Gorgon's mother-in-law."

"Not at all – "

"It's just that not once, not once has a man ever – " she began; she stopped, and started again, but looked down at her hands, her face a mottled red. "You feel desperate, sometimes, if only for, for a pair of arms around you. Hell, I'd settle for one arm and half a compliment."

"A man has never?" I whispered, encouraging her to lower her booming voice. Even the orchestra had stopped playing and were aiming their ear trumpets at us.

"Thirty-six years old," she said, and laughed into her lap.

There was a longish silence between us. The entire dining room looked thoughtful. It was now my turn to take a deep breath.

At ten pip emma she collapsed back on the pillows, damp and panting, her hazel eyes like misted-up mirrors. And after a while she said, "Oh, Bartholomew . . . !"

"Wot?"

"It left nothing to be desired."

"M'kew."

I looked down at her rather more healthily flushed face on the pillow. And, *Oh, my god – she was beginning to look good.*

At 2300 hours, after further tuition, I said drowsily, "Cyril said you hated me."

"Not really," she said, snuggling against my shoulder, "even though you did force me to appeal to my better nature."

"I'm glad you won the appeal. I didn't fancy being exposed as a pansy. Not least because Group Captain Mince might have lectured me on the advantages of heterosexual relationships, citing him and his wife as good examples."

The bed shook; but it was only her, laughing. "Mind you, there's a lot of queer things about you," she said, tickling my earhole with her breath.

I leaned up on one elbow, and reached over to pull down the bedclothes for another helping of nakedness. "Gwinny," I said, "I was your first lover? But what about Drummond? Didn't he . . . ?"

"No. I was too frightened."

"But he really loved you?"

"In spite of this frightful phiz, you mean? Yes, incredibly enough, it seems so," she said, embarrassedly covering herself, but making up for it by reaching down and enclosing my temporarily indifferent member in her cool hand. "Changing the subject if I may − I suppose Cyril's plot to compromise Drummond wasn't entirely a washout. Amyas is now very grateful to me for not squealing on him. Which might come in useful."

"How can he be grateful, after you threatened to expose him?"

"Lie down, will you, you're letting all the warm air out. Well, look at it from his point of view. I was just the wronged woman, that's all he knew. So why wouldn't he be grateful when I said I believed him, and wouldn't snitch on him?"

"M'm."

"I did it for your sake, Bartholomew. So you owe me a lot."

"Maybe it was the other way round," I said. "Maybe you let him off the hook for your own professional reasons? And I was just a bonus?"

"You mistrustful beast," she exclaimed, still holding on. "How can you be so cynical?"

I placed my head back on the pillow − carefully, in case the hairpiece had become dislodged by the evening's gymnastics. "I know," I said. "I often have unworthy thoughts."

She gave it a tug, as if summoning Davis The Butler. "I really did do it for you, Bart, against my better judgement. I'm growing very fond of you, even though you're totally unsuitable. You wouldn't fit into my crowd at all.

"But at least," she added sleepily, "I've eliminated the suspicion about your sexual orientation," she said. "You certainly don't need any advice from Group Captain Mince."

"You've eliminated the suspicion?" I snorted. "Dammit, woman, you're the one who created the suspicion in the first place, out of nothing."

"I suppose so. One tends to forget unimportant details," she said, as I drew her closer in order to tickle the base of her spine. And then to haul her leg over my hip.

"Another thing I'd like to know," I said, "is where are all the other suspicions about me coming from? About me being a Red. Is it some game you people are playing?"

"Don't start that again, Bartholomew," she said.

"You mean this?"

"No, no, you can start that any time. I meant . . . don't start on politics."

"Or is Drummond behind it?"

"Not so far as I know, though you're certainly on his mind. Now he not only detests you, he's afraid of you, as well. That you'll spread rumours about him that could get him sacked."

"I wouldn't, because it would get me in trouble too."

"He can't be sure of that. I expect," she said, pausing for a few groans and whimpers, "that he'll get you, one of these days."

Shortly before Hitler attacked the Soviet Union, instantly transforming that ghastly man, Stalin, into Uncle Joe, our heroic and lovable ally, I was sent to take charge of a newly formed Spitfire squadron in Kent. I had hardly taken up my new duties that summer when I received a telephone call from the Air Ministry to the effect that the police in a place called St. Mary's were holding a man who claimed to be a senior RAF officer. He had been arrested under suspicious circumstances the previous evening.

The prisoner had refused to explain himself, though he had spoken my name. So would I proceed to the police station to verify that the suspect was utterly loopy, and would I call them back as soon as I had established that the prisoner had no connection with the RAF.

"Where is this town, St. Mary's?"

"It's a village. Somewhere in Kent."

"Thanks a bunch. But look here, I'm supposed to be flying in half an hour. It'll probably take me hours to get there. And I can never find my way anywhere, with all the signposts taken down."

"Look on it as a nice little break from the tedious routine of shooting down enemy aircraft, Squadron Leader."

"Bah."

I would have protested further at being sent on an errand that could surely have been handled by somebody a little less busy than I was, except that I don't think the caller from Ad Astra house was entirely confident that the prisoner was doolally. And I admit that I felt a little uneasy, too. Just as I had feared, even in the fast Armstrong-Siddeley, it took hours to locate St. Mary's. It was a tiny village with a little rustic police station. There were roses round the door, and a garden, tended by a constable, dotted with busy lizzies.

I was welcomed by a portly sergeant with a steaming mug. "Good morning, sir," he said cheerfully. "Thought you might like something strong, like a mug of cocoa. Just powdered milk, but it's real sugar. We get an allowance from the Chief Constable's Air Raid and Suspicious Persons Budget.

"The accused," he continued, "was picked up loitering near the gates of Tenterden Lodge at nine o'clock last night. That's about five, no, four and a half miles from here on the A41. He was attired in a suspicious manner, and upon being formally arrested and searched this weapon was found on him," the sergeant said, producing a gigantic revolver.

"Good Lord."

"Be careful! It's fully loaded."

"I'm surprised it's not on a gun carriage."

"Yes, sir. After being questioned at some length, the accused claimed to be – " the sergeant referred to his charge sheet – "an air vice-marshal with a CBE, DSO and one bar, and DFC and one bar. That was all we could get out of him. Or at least all that was coherent. But subsequently my constable overheard him muttering

somewhat disrespectfully about a Squadron Leader Bandy. Whereupon we made application to the Air Ministry – in London," the
sergeant added, as if there might be air ministries all over the
country, "and they very efficiently narrowed it down to you, sir.
Now would you care to inspect the prisoner, sir, to ascertain – "

"The place he was found near – Tenterden Lodge. Who lives
there?"

"The gentleman was not in residence at the time, and we have
seen no reason so far to contact him, whether for identification pur-
poses or – "

"Yes, but who is he?"

The sergeant looked offended at what he plainly regarded as my
peremptory tone. "I was coming to that, sir," he said. "The gentleman in question is well-known in the neighbourhood, and indeed,
holds a high position in the – "

"Sir Amyas Drummond, by any chance?"

The sergeant looked more offended than ever; and I realized that
my eagerness had been a mistake; for the copper now started to look
thoughtful. He observed, half to himself, "Yes, that is correct. A
Minister of the Crown. Perhaps I had better inform my immediate superior about this."

Which I didn't feel was at all a good idea. I tried to make light
of it, but the damage was done.

"Would you now care to inspect the prisoner?" the sergeant
asked stiffly.

"Thank you, Sergeant," I said. "By the way, what did you mean
when you described the man as being suspiciously dressed?"

"You will see in a moment, sir."

Which I did. Air Vice-Marshal Greaves was attired in a striped
jersey and dark trousers. He even had a mask, dangling round his
neck from a black cord, though he had not actually been wearing
it when apprehended, nor had he been carrying a sack with the
letters SWAG on it.

"At first my constable thought it was some college jape," the
sergeant said, "dressing up like that. You know what the toffs are like,
knocking off policemen's helmets and so forth. But the prisoner

appeared to be sincere about his apparel. Though you will observe that the stripes go the wrong way."

"The wrong way?"

"The apparel of your typical stereotype of the masked burglar," he said, "shows the stripes of the jersey as being horizontal. But as you see, the stripes of the accused are vertical."

"Yes, that's a mistake. Vertical stripes make you look slimmer," I said.

The sergeant was now regarding me almost as suspiciously as the prisoner. "Yes, well . . . if you will be so good as to either confirm or deny that you are acquainted with this man?"

I looked at him placatingly. "First, may I have a few moments alone with him, Sergeant?"

When we had the cell to ourselves, I said, "Well, Cyril, here's another fine mess you've gotten into."

He looked away, his hands aimlessly fiddling.

"Were you intending to shoot Drummond yourself?"

"Someone had to."

"What are we doing to do about it?"

"Do about what?"

"This. You being arrested. How are we going to keep this out of the news?"

"That's your affair. I shall be quite happy to waylay him some other time. Do you think they'll give me my gun back?"

I paced up and down the cell, which quite took me back to the good old days in the Soviet Union, thinking that I would have to handle the situation very sensitively.

"Cyril," I said, "how do you feel about lunatic asylums?"

"What?"

"You know that's where you belong, don't you?"

"Do I? Did I escape, or something? Is that why they've locked me up?"

I stood still for a moment. Then: "Something like that," I said. And, after another pause: "Cyril? Would you like me to take you home?"

"To the asylum, you mean? Why, do you belong there, too?"

"No, I meant get you out of here. We'll see a doctor."

"Bernard is dead, you know."

"What?"

"He was killed the other day."

"Oh." I sat abruptly on his bunk. "Oh, Cyril."

"Shot down, did I mention that?" He looked at me blankly. "We didn't get on all that well, but . . . I was away from home so much, you see. That's how my marriage pranged . . . but he was all . . . he was all."

I put an arm around his shoulders. After a moment he leaned against me.

Trudging Along

ANOTHER NEW YEAR COMING up. Three weeks to go.

As the Spitfire turned downwind, silver tracks crept up the Perspex. Rain again. After being kind during much of 1940, 1941's weather had reverted to its old British ways. It had been raining on and off all week now. Curtailing operations. Thank God.

In spite of the enforced rest, I was shagged-out. They were not entirely wrong about middle-aged gents being unsuitable for combat. I was tiring much more easily. And being tired, now that we were flying sorties over France, was a visa to oblivion, or at best, a reservation in a stalag luft.

Even the new mark of Spitfire I was flying, with the more powerful engine and the four cannon, brought no thrill, as the song had it. Not that I was turning fatalistic, the way some pilots did, behaving as if death might be a nice change. I hadn't come this far, through several wars, several marriages, and several hundred crises to give up just yet. Ah well, back to the station for a quiet evening.

Crosswind, and a quick look around to make sure there were no hit-and-run bandits in the circuit, before lowering the gear. But there were two Spitfires ahead of me. I kept an eye on them until their tail wheels were safely down. I could read the letters on their fuselages, and realized I hardly knew either of them. I had brought four pilots from the old squadron when I moved here: Hector McCurdle, Sergeant Toye (now a Flying Officer), Bill Coombs, Tam Maiden. Only Toye was still with us.

Among others whom I had come to know reasonably well, Group Captain Mince was still Group Captain Mince at the old station, Bob Broseley was in command of the Henley Wing, and Brooke-Gaitor had been shot down and taken prisoner.

In the great air battles of 1940 and 1941 I'd abandoned caution and persuaded the others to fly recklessly. But increasingly now I believed in the German rather than the British tactics. In WWI, the Jerries had rarely come barging over our lines, looking for trouble. They let us come to them and take the risks. So we had created our own disadvantage. And that aggression, which had been unnecessary, had gone on for years, with lousy results as measured against the cost. I feared that we were making the same mistake all over again.

Today's operation was not a bad example. We had shot up a railway siding that might – or might not – have been transporting Wehrmacht equipment. Two of my pilots had gone in, in exchange for German losses that could probably be made up in a few minutes in a German factory.

I was making representations about it to the brass. I wasn't demanding that we stop being nasty to the Germans. All I was saying was, consider the exchange rate between the actions and the costs. As poor old Greaves had said –

"Red leader, look out!"

Jesus! Only just in time, I pulled up and over a perimeter hut, and slammed on power, hauling up the gear by sheer reflex.

As I was now too high on final, it meant I would have to face the shame of going round again.

Heart thudding, sweat spreading under the eyes, I cursed myself; tore strips off myself. Good God, man! Good God. How could you have been so dozy?

As I flew round again, I wondered what excuse I could make to explain such an unforgivable lapse in concentration. Could I pretend that I had been revenging myself on the radar operators or something, giving them a fright in retaliation for . . . ? No, I couldn't do that. I would just have to sweat it out. If anyone made a remark I would treat them to a look of pity, as if it were perfectly obvious why I had very nearly crashed into the radar hut.

As I taxied past the main building I saw a small group of officers huddled in the main entrance. They were watching my particular aircraft. Oh, Lord, had they seen the balls-up? I sweated cobs all over again, and cursed when I saw that one of the officers was Bob Broseley.

Perhaps they hadn't seen anything? After all, it was pretty misty with rain. Anyway, what the hell were they doing here, hanging around doorways instead of getting on with their work? Were they waiting for me? Was it a delegation bearing bad news?

I wondered if I could avoid them. Maybe sneak out the back way, grab the car, and take off for the nearest pub. Which reminded me. I was drinking too much. Again. Booze might increase the jollity of squadron get-togethers, but it sure didn't increase your chances of surviving the next rhubarb.

Why the hell had I tried so hard to get into the fight? Though I knew the answer to that. It was what they had done to Sigga.

As I stepped down onto the port wing root, Tommy Atkins, who had also come with us from the old squadron, came lurching up. "Two of the kites look badly shot up," he said.

"And two down. Mr. Yates, and Mr. . . . " But I couldn't remember the other pilot's name, and so felt even worse.

"That's not too good is it, sir? Out of twelve."

"No, it's not, Tommy."

"But you don't have nothing to worry about. You do a terrific job, keeping everybody going, sir."

I managed a smile, and straggled away from the plane with my parachute and my half-eaten bar of chocolate. I had been taking choccy bars on ops ever since 1917. Here I was, still doing it, a quarter century on. Nothing else to show for my entire life, no wife or home or even country, nothing to show for it but a bar of chocolate. Eh, shaddup, you self-pitying veal cutlet.

The party huddled in the entrance of the main building was almost certainly waiting for me. I trudged toward them through the thin, soaking rain, removing my helmet as I did so – very carefully, as the last time I whipped off the helmet, the hairpiece, soaked with sweat, came off as well. This tragedy was very nearly witnessed by two WAAF dental technicians.

Yes, it was Bob Broseley in the entrance. "What are you doing here?" I enquired.

His reply was low-key and mysterious. "I wanted to be here when you met," he said. And: "It explains quite a bit about what's been happening."

I looked at him, then at the other two officers. One was a tall young fellow, hardly more than a boy, with an interesting though far from handsome face. The other was Guinevere Plumley – dressed up as a WREN officer.

"Well, well, what are you doing here?"

"Never mind me," she said. "What about him?" And she gestured at the young pilot officer.

He looked familiar, but I couldn't think of his name. Not that that was surprising any more, when I couldn't even remember the name of the pilot who, half an hour ago, had gone spinning into the drink off Dunkirk.

"Bartholomew Bandy," said Bob Broseley gleefully, "meet Bartholomew Bandy."

I stared at him as if he'd gone off his trolley; then back at the serious young man with the pilot officer's thin stripe and the RAF wings – and the Canada flash on his shoulder.

Except – should it have been a U.S.A. flash? Me in 1922, 1923 . . . flying the U.S. Mail . . . teaching Cissie Chaffington to fly . . . stunting the Vimy (how reckless I was then) . . . acting in the filums . . . building the Gander monoplane . . . Cissie Chaffington . . .

"Oh, my God, it's not . . . You're not Cissie's son?"

"Bartholomew Wendell Bandy," the boy said, speaking in a whining drawl that made me start.

"That must've been why there was a certain amount of confusion," Guinevere said, plainly thrilled at my appalled expression. "With the Air Ministry having two Bartholomew W. Bandys on its books."

"Father!" cried Bartholomew W. Bandy.

A PAIR OF LOOK-ALIKES

TO SHOW THAT THE sudden appearance of a son might have been anticipated by the alert reader, I need only make reference to a previous volume of my memoirs, *This One's on Me*, in which I observed that the prospect of Bandy progeny genuinely frightened some people. I knew this because they had told me so. *The thought of another Bandy loose in the world is just too ghastly to contemplate, they had said. Actually I had a child, but it had been taken over by the mother's billionaire parents.*

That's what I wrote on page 355.

I had always wanted a child. I'd been on the lookout for one ever since my first wedding night. Preferably not a girl, in case she inherited my thoroughbred looks, which would have given her a hard time in school: the kids would have made whinnying noises at her. I wanted a son who could take care of himself with his fists, knuckledusters, tear gas, and so forth. That was one reason I was eager to marry Cissie Chaffington when I learned that she was pregnant.

Unfortunately her parents interposed themselves between me and the wedding cake. They detested me. In fact, every one of Cissie's forty-seven relatives detested me, except for Aunt Ruth, who was prejudiced. The paternal hostility stemmed originally from an unfortunate incident in Ottawa when Mr. Chaffington came to visit, and I took him a gift which turned out to be a bomb. As I recall it was from some anarchist friends of his. From then on his attitude was decidedly unfriendly, a hostility that tended to be inflamed rather than soothed by the balm of time as fresh areas of conflict opened up between us. And Cyrus Q. Chaffington was not a forgiving man.

The Chaffingtons took over the child as soon as it was born, re-established a lifelong hold over Cissie, and swept mother and son off to California. It may be hard to believe that they could manage such an injustice when their opponent was none other than Bartholomew Wolfe Bandy, warrior and crusader against nastiness, or that the Hero of Jhamjhar would put up with such arrogance and spite. In fact, the Chaffs could manage it quite easily, because I had returned from captivity in Russia with hardly a bean; and without money you are helpless against the rich. And the Chaffingtons were as immensely rich as they were immensely influential. Squadrons of lawyers and state governors formated on their sway and power. For instance, in 1921, one word from Chaffington was enough to get me fired from the U.S. Mail Service, and another word put me in the humiliating position of being threatened with deportation from the United States.

So they took over the child, and their only daughter, Cissie, a kind, gentle beanpole of a girl who had just enough strength to oppose their efforts to have the boy's name changed by deed poll so as to expunge even my moniker from their genealogical tables. Otherwise her resistance collapsed entirely, as did, later, her health.

When I was finally able to accumulate some coin of the realm, mainly by smuggling liquor into the U.S. by air – an ironic, pleasing but definitely unwise activity, as Chaffington was a supporter of Prohibition – I attempted to fight the legalized kidnapping in the U.S. courts. My claim was easily thrown out – the U.S. Attorney-General was a crony of Mr. Chaffington's.

After the failure of two appeals I was forced to give up, not least because I myself was in danger of being thrown out of my own country as well, owing to a misunderstanding involving the then Prime Minister of Canada, Mr. Mackenzie King – who, for God's sake, was *still* Prime Minister, all these bloody years later, if you can credit it.

I managed to accumulate a fair packet of dibs by the time I had bombasted back from India in the late Twenties. In fact, I was wealthy for a while, richer than a plum pudding. But Cissie was dead by then, and the American courts were darned if they were going to hand over an American child to a furriner, especially a British Imperialist Aggressor, as the Chaffington press characterized me. After that I gave up – without ever having seen the boy.

Obviously the boy knew nothing of my side to this sordid story. Chaffington had seen to that. So it was hardly surprising that young Bart was behaving now as if I had deliberately neglected him all these years. When we went to my quarters to talk in private, he did very little responding, and his attitude was decidedly un- friendly. At first I hardly noticed, I was so excited at meeting my son for the first time. It was only when we repaired to the Pig and Trough that it occurred to me that I was doing most of the talking and that his few answers were cold and sullen. His hostility toward me had, if anything, increased since he first clapped eyes on me six hours previously.

Taking him down to the pub didn't help much. He was a tee- totaller like his grandfather, and wouldn't even touch ginger beer because of its name. The landlord, Mr. Meakin, had great difficulty in finding an alternative soft drink among his stock.

"Do we have to sit in this crummy joint?" said young Bart in his American tones, which were so loud that even I winced a bit. He had the projection of a Victorian actor-manager in full flight in the role of *The Drunkard's Son*.

"Doesn't it thrill you," I replied gently, "to be sitting in a hostelry that was in business when Geoff Chaucer was Justice of the Peace?"

"Geoff who?" he asked, looking dumb – deliberately. He knew who Chaucer was, all right. He'd had the best tutors money could buy. But this was just another example of his determination to upset me one way or another, in the hope that I would confirm his profound belief that I had turned my back on him the moment he was born.

"It's so smoky in here," he said, waving and coughing. He didn't smoke either.

"There's a Lyon's Corner House just down the street," I said, "if you prefer."

He shrugged indifferently. "I guess if you guys are used to holing up in this place," he muttered.

Now he was looking suspiciously at my glass. "You drinking whisky?"

"Yes, while they still have any. They're down to *Tam O'Shanter's Mare's Tail* by now."

"It rots your brain. Every single drink destroys one more brain cell. Three drinks, *poof*, three more brain cells gone."

"Who told you this?"

"Grandfather. It's true. Ten drinks, ten cells. Before you know where you are, *bang*, a whole segment of your brain gone."

Jesus Christ. I was back in Beamington, Ontario, at the age of twenty-three, being told the same thing by the local doctor.

"Bart," I began.

"That's Bartholomew, if you got to. Though really as my superior officer you should be calling me Bandy."

"I'm also your father."

"That remains to be seen."

I had already attempted to describe the measures I had taken to restore him to my care. He was too set against me to listen.

"All I know is, Mom was real unhappy about you."

"I wanted her. I wanted to marry her."

"So what stopped you?"

"Your grandfather."

"Sure."

"You must know how powerful he was."

"He was always real good to me. At least – " He stopped.

I waited, but he had clammed up. "Don't tell me," I ventured, "that you found out what he was like?"

"He was good to me," the lad said defiantly. "He was great. That's all there is to it. I'll never say a bad word about him. I won't give you the satisfaction."

I went over to the bar. Mr. Meakin beamed and suggested I must be overjoyed to be reunited with my son.

"It's all over the town, Mr. Bandy. Everybody's talking about it. You must be so proud."

"Sure am," I said, downing the Scotch (a double) in one gulp. "Make it another, Mr. Meakin," I murmured, casting a guilty glance over my shoulder and hoping that the loss of another two brain cells wouldn't show by the time I got back.

"He's a fine-looking lad," Mr. Meakin said doubtfully. "Tall. Everybody's so pleased for you, Mr. Bandy."

Back at the scarred bench in the corner, Bart was looking at a picture of his mother in his wallet. "Could I see?" I asked, holding out my hand.

He handed over the wallet as reluctantly as if I were a footpad. "Yes, that's Mother," he said. "I'm surprised you even recognize her."

"I've tried to explain, son."

"Look, I don't want to be called 'son,' if that's okay with you."

I was about to hand back the wallet when I saw the card struck in one of the pockets.

"Communist Party? You're a member of the CP?"

"I am."

"Christ, no."

"I don't approve of blasphemy."

"But a Party member? How could you?"

"Listen – sir. How could I not? After the gutless way the capitalists behaved toward Hitler and that gang before the war."

"I know. But – "

"And the conditions of the steel workers in Pennsylvania. And . . ." And he listed other assorted social, political, and economic injustices.

"I've been a member since I was sixteen," he said defiantly.

"Who got you into it?"

"I didn't get it from anybody. It was after I read John Strachey's *The Theory and Practice of Socialism and Capitalism*. And a lot of other great works. They all agreed that capitalism was doomed and there was only one way forward, and that was through socialism to communism.

"Communism," he explained, "is of course the ultimate state of socialism, at present just an ideal. But there's no doubt the Soviet Union is on the right track. They're getting there."

"My son the communist."

"Yeah, I heard how you sneer at anything that might improve the lot of mankind. And how fanatical you are about the U.S.S.R."

"With good cause."

"So they took you prisoner for a few months. So? I mean, what right had you to be there in the first place? You were intervening in their civil war, right? And, anyway, they let you go in the end, right? They gave you the freedom of Moscow."

"Who told you all this?"

"Mother. She really loved you," he said, looking at me with something so close to hatred that it quite stapped me vitals.

"Anyway, I'm not going to argue about it," he said. "Whatever you think, the Soviet Union is the only hope for the world. They're the upholders of peace and all standards of decency and fair play in the world."

"And how do you feel about the pact they made with Hitler that started the war?"

"That's a distortion formulated by the capitalist hyenas of Wall Street. That was an example of Soviet realism, the only course open to them at the time. Now, of course, they are single-handedly defeating the fascists in their Great Patriotic War. Upton Sinclair says that — "

"Anyway, we shouldn't be talking politics in our first real get-together, son."

"What else is there for us to talk about? And quit calling me 'son,' will you? You got no right. After eighteen years not caring one goldarn about Mother. Or even me."

"If I can't call you son, what am I to call you?"

"You may call me Comrade, if you wish," he said, with just the faintest hint of mischief in his otherwise long, blank, haughty face.

"Maybe," I suggested, "I could address you by your service number. What's your last three?"

"772."

"So maybe I'll call you 772 Bandy," I suggested, with a winning smile.

It lost. I'd have done better to have tilted onto a starboard buttock and farted.

Moreover, the attempt at intimacy was worse than a wet kiss. His face turned cold as mutton. "Call me whatever you like," he muttered, unbuttoning the top pocket of his smart blue uniform and then buttoning it again. "What do I care? You mean nothing to me."

Though I didn't know it, I was to have little time this year to get acquainted with 772 Bandy. The little opportunity I had was unsatisfactory. Though he had gone to some trouble to find me the moment he arrived in England, it was mainly so that he could release some of the pressure of his feelings. He was bitter as cyanide at being abandoned, as he saw it, by a father he might otherwise have admired for his flying skill. My father, the ace fighter pilot. And now that we had met he had a chance to tell me that I was a deuce.

His hostility was such that he would seize any opportunity to deny me the slightest satisfaction in our relationship. For instance, I was more than a little curious to find out how Chaffington felt about his grandson being a card-carrying member of the Party. Chaffington must have had a frothing fit when he heard about it. But seeing how greedy I was for a description of Chaffington's discomfiture, the boy, with every appearance of vindictive satisfaction, immediately closed up shop. Nor would he give the slightest clue as to Chaffington's reaction when he learned that a member of his family had joined the RCAF and gone off to fight for the hated British Empire.

Incidentally, Chaffington had been in the news quite recently, once again dismaying the British government. Three or four days ago, he had made a speech in Washington confidently asserting that the United States would not join the war under any circumstances, and his newspapers would continue to oppose the aid that President Roosevelt was giving to the United Kingdom.

He had delivered the speech on December 2, 1941.

It was only a few days later that the appalling news came in: They were going to post me back to Canada. Worse, I heard the news from my pilot officer son, and the more dismayed I looked, the happier he became.

This was during a trip we had taken into the Kent countryside. I wanted him to see one of the great castles of England, which was still being occupied by a family that had owned it for six hundred years, give or take a bailiff or two. He perceived only the capitalist privilege. "They'll be swept away," he said, "when power is restored to the people."

It was only then that I properly appreciated how absurd the Air Ministry had been in getting their B. W. Bandys mixed up, to the extent that they could actually believe that I was a Red under the bed.

As we strolled around the castle in a fourteen-carat gold sunlight, I told him a little about that snafu, and asked if he had ever been mistaken for me. His only response was to shudder ostentatiously at the thought. I made several further attempts at cosy conversation. Still he would not open up.

Finally I said gently, "772 Bandy, if you find me so distasteful, why are you spending all your leave with me?"

He went off like a Very light. "Jeez, I'm sorry – I won't bother you any more." And he turned to rush off.

I only just managed to hold him back. "Bart, I like having you here," I cried. He was hauling away from me so persistently that my heels were scoring through the gravel. "It's just great, honest. I just wonder what's in it for you, when you never seem to be enjoying yourself."

My unhappy eighteen-year-old son was finally braked to a halt. He stood there, looking down at the disarranged gravel, shoulders hunched as if I had threated to knout him.

I tried to put an arm round his shoulders. "Cut it out," he shouted, and for a moment looked as if he were about to hit me.

So I thought I'd better talk about the weather. I pointed out that not only was it not raining for once, but there was even a little sun.

"Quit calling me 'son,'" he said out of sheer force of habit. Then, looking sheepish: "Oh, you mean . . ."

"Look, do I have to go on calling you 772 Bandy?"

"I don't see that it matters, Father. We won't be seeing each other much longer."

"We won't? Why not?"

"Well, I'm staying over here, you're going home."

"I'm going back to Canada?"

"So they say. First I'll be going to an OTU, then I guess to a squadron. Unless, of course, the fascist authorities decide to persecute for my socialist faith, and deny me – "

"Never mind about you – what's this about me going home?"

"This girl I met at the Air Ministry, she said they were posting you back to Canada. On orders from some big-noise politician, or somebody."

It was my turn to stare down at the gravel. "Drummond," I said.

"Yeah, that was the name. You know him?".

Drummond, having failed to polish me off in the air, had now decided to ship me out of the country in the hope that I would be torpedoed. And right now, given what was going on in our convoys across the Atlantic, his odds looked quite promising.

I stared at 772 Bandy, wondering how many more shocks were in store for me.

As it turned out, there was only one more: the news that Air Vice-Marshal Greaves had been declared fit for duty.

The suggestion that he was suffering from a nervous breakdown, they said, was nonsense. He had passed the medical with flying colours. As for the business of the striped shirt and the revolver, that had been a misunderstanding. Air Vice-Marshal Greaves was as normal as anybody in the Air Force. He was filled with aggressive spirit and was thus upholding the finest traditions of the Service.

In fact, they had put his name forward as the new Chief of Bomber Command; though in the end the job had gone to somebody else, a chap named Harris, who had even more of the spirit of aggression than Cyril Greaves had.

PART II

ME IN MY PINNY

IT WAS FIFTEEN MONTHS before I saw Bart again. I was back in Canada, just as he'd predicted, and he arrived in a cargo ship that was bringing the latest batch of entrants to the Commonwealth Air Training Plan. I picked him up in Montreal and drove him to Ottawa in my used Plymouth. I had a ground-floor apartment out west on Crawley Avenue.

"This'll be your room," I said. "Bathroom's just outside, the door on the left. Dinner'll be ready soon. I've made it myself."

He sniffed the air. "What are you cooking – tomcat?"

When I first greeted him in Montreal he had so far forgotten himself as to actually smile. For a moment, his face had lit up like the sun coming from behind the cumulus. Luckily he had remembered just in time and had quickly recovered from this physiognomical blunder. Still, the expression had been there for a moment, however soon quelled.

"Not too many good restaurants around here," I said. "Not too many in the whole of Ottawa, actually. But at least you'll be able to get steaks again. And bananas. Gosh, did I ever miss bananas when I was over there, eh?"

He went and stood outside the apartment to enjoy the dry heat of an Ottawa summer. Having grown up in a warm climate he had found the Britannic elements a hell of an ordeal. Here the temperature had not dipped below ninety degrees Fahrenheit for over a week, and had touched a hundred on two occasions. After a particularly hard winter I was enjoying it myself, revelling in the dazzling light, the heat-bleached sky.

"It's good to have you here, 772 Bandy," I said.

"Have you been drinking?" he demanded.

"Just a quick nip or two."

"You must have rushed to the liquor cabinet the moment you got in. Are you an alcoholic yet, Father? Answer yes or no."

It was true that I had wasted no time in going through the rye, och aye – I was so nervous about meeting him again. Me, with hardly a nervous nerve in my system? But yes, I was. I wanted so much to make a friend of him, though I suspected that with the lifelong hostility drilled into him by the Chaffingtons, the moment might never come.

I decided that a subtle change of subject might be in order. "Good flying weather," I said.

"In this heat?"

"No, you're right, B.W., it's not very good flying weather."

When he remained silent, I hurried on. "I go up whenever I can, at Uplands. Though I'm not expected to do more than the minimum to keep up my flying pay."

"Yeah, a guy's got to think about money. Money's the only thing that matters," he said with the lofty contempt of a youth who didn't have any. Then, having made it plain that I had ruined his solitude by joining him outside, he went back into the apartment, feeling his way carefully. My heart bled for him in his blindness.

I had been in the civil service city of Ottawa now for well over a year, and in all that time I had done absolutely nothing. Drummond had gained his revenge, all right. I had received my comeuppance. He had spared me the final curtain call, the last trump, the bitten dust. While the war hung in the balance in Europe and the East he had eased me back into the land of plenty, and provided me with a cushy billet in my own hometown. I had received yet another medal (in the post). I had received a raise. I had been promoted. No wonder I was drinking like a dromedary. They had made me senior RCAF recruiting officer concerned with applicants from the U.S.

Except that there weren't any. The United States had been in the war for about eighteen months, so naturally Americans were joining their own air force, not ours. But did that make any difference to my duties? Not a bit of it.

A dillydally of days, a malingery of months had gone by, and I was still stewing in my office on Wellington Street, doing SFA as far as the war effort was concerned. The days loitered past at a maddening pace. I thought of resigning my commission and going in for something rather more challenging, like running an infants' Bible Class or worming Chihuahuas. All I had to look forward to were my biweekly visits to Laurier Street. I had a young mistress along there, a French-Canadian girl who liked to practise her English and clean out her navel with a toothbrush. Until one day I paid her an unexpected visit and found her canoodling with another chap. Bit humiliating, that was – he was even older than me.

On top of such assorted frustrations, there was the anxiety over my son's safety. For a while he had, in fact, remained relatively safe. I was secretly delighted when I heard that he had not done well at OTU and had been held back from actual operations until they could decide what to do with him. Throughout most of 1942 they had kept him busy driving twin-engined Ansons, transporting flight crews hither and yon – and frightening the shit out of them with his flying, according to one source. People wondered how on earth he had managed to earn his wings in the first place. The fact that he had qualified as a pilot at the age of sixteen in the United States and so had his ticket when he joined up in Canada might have had something to do with it. "But he must have qualified at a damned easygoing flying school," said one instructor.

While appreciating his frustration at being given joe jobs, and while expressing hypocritical sympathy for him in my letters – which he mostly failed to answer – I was delighted that he was being kept out of the slaughter statistics.

Then, a few months ago, in January 1943, I learned that he had been posted to a night-fighter squadron, and was now on Bristol Beaufighters. Strangely enough, he did quite well – though some said it was because he could hardly see a thing outside the cockpit and therefore didn't realize he was in any danger. In the meantime, I tried to reassure myself that night-fighting could not be as dangerous as daylight operations, especially now that Hitler was increasingly preoccupied with defending his own territory instead of bombing ours.

Just as I had nearly convinced myself that night-fighting was really quite a cushy job, the attrition wallahs struck. By spring of this year they had decided to vary the defence diet with a spot of night intruder ops. Now, Bart, instead of stooging safely over country pubs and cricket pitches, was being sent, often at very low level, over decidedly hostile territory.

He managed nearly ten nocturnal rhubarbs into France, the Low Countries, and even Germany before his Beaufighter was hit by 88s. The journey home had turned into something of an epic. Calmly informing his navigator/radar man that the flash and bang had done something to his eyes and that he could not even see the glowing red instruments two feet away, Bart had had to fly the badly damaged but still controllable machine by touch alone. His sergeant, who had also been wounded in the explosion, had called out the instrument readings, and when they reached the aerodrome had successfully aligned him with the runway. Despite his blindness, Bart had somehow managed to flare, touch down, and bring the Beaufighter to a safe stop. His oppo had been awarded the DFM for the exploit, though so far, Bart's calm, equally brave achievement had not been officially recognized.

Bart had spent weeks in hospital at Tunbridge Wells, but they had failed to account for his continuing blindness. Finally they had decided to ship him home. So here he was at last, the very first guest in my Ottawa West apartment.

"But how come you decided to come here, instead of taking your furlough in California, or wherever grandaddy is living now?" I asked him as we tucked into the dinner I had cooked. Or at least I tucked in, while he prodded the victuals.

"They would have felt sorry for me."

"But you preferred me?" I asked, feeling warm all over.

"Yes. I knew you wouldn't care."

I swallowed the rest of the cabbage, which had done nothing for our nutrition but a lot for driving the cockroaches out of the apartment.

"No, I guess not," I said.

After a dense pause I said heartily, "Well, this is great. We've got a lot to catch up with, haven't we?"

He didn't answer, though there was indeed a lot to catch up with. He had answered hardly a single letter of mine over the past year and more.

"I don't suppose you feel like talking about any of the jobs you were doing?" I asked, settling down for a good chat.

"No."

"Okay. So let's talk about you."

"Nothing to talk about."

"About your friends, then?"

"Don't have any."

"Not even girl friends?"

"No."

"Good. Now it's my turn. We can talk about me."

"No thanks."

"Uh . . . see any shows in the West End?"

"Saw a review with Hermione Gingold."

"So you did have a girl friend. Who was she, a Waaf?" But B.W. just clicked his tongue and groaned in a long-suffering fashion.

"Hey, I've got a great idea," I said. "Let's just sit here quietly for a while, eh?"

As we sat there quietly for a while I looked at him properly for the first time since picking him up at the reception centre in Montreal. 'Pon my soul, he had changed. And my heart bled several corpuscles.

When I first met him, he had looked like a fresh, unspoiled version of me, poor devil. Owning a face like that, it must have been awful for him in school, especially in California where everybody was supposed to look alike. Much as I hated describing my son as having the lineaments of a horse, his face was definitely equine – if you can imagine a nag with an impertinent mien and

a superior stare. But at least it was a youthful horse, and there was
still innocence in the gaze that had looked out on the world with
no understanding of it whatsoever, but with a determination not
to let anyone know that.

Eighteen months later, his face was weary as Dobbin after too
many rag and bone journeys. He looked thirty years old, rather than
twenty. The tall forehead, formerly smooth and bland as Chinese
ivory, was scored with the stave of tension. It was a forehead that
had anticipated many more flak or cannon hits than the one that
finally came. And lines were forming around a bitter mouth. Lines,
at twenty years of age.

"Well, this is just great," I exclaimed, clapping my hands together
heartily.

Which was a mistake, for it made him start violently. He turned
pale, and breathed quite rapidly for a while.

"Sorry," I said. "Anyway, it really is good to have you here, whatever you think my attitude is. After all, plenty of room in the apartment. And I have this old Plymouth to get us around, maybe,
weekends. Or there's a streetcar stop just fifty yards down the hill
toward the river, down the street from here, if you want to go anywhere without having your dad round your neck all the time."

"I managed without you for twenty years. I guess it won't be too
difficult."

"Er, yes. By the way, I've taken a month's leave from the office
so we can get reacquainted, and I can show you the ropes."

"You needn't have bothered. I'm not staying."

"Oh. Oh, I see. Well, that's . . . When are you leaving?"

"Sometime or other – when I find it convenient," he said, staring
arrogantly.

"Uh, right."

"And like you say, I don't want you hanging around me all the
time."

"Oh. Uh . . . that's kind of difficult, if we're sharing the same
apartment, don't you think?"

"You keep to your half and I'll stick to mine. I don't need anything from you, I don't want anything from you. All I want is time

to decide what to do. But whatever it is, it don't include you — Father."

"*Doesn't* include me," I said, automatically correcting his grammar. "Okay. Well, you're still welcome to, uh . . . still welcome," I said.

He was more hostile than ever. Even though I had been warned to expect this, it was still a bit of a shock.

There was no doubt that he was a very disturbed and unhappy young man. On top of the other problem, he had been made to think that I had been spurning him for two decades. The trouble was that in the flesh I was confusing the picture. The verbal confusion was easily cleared up: he just didn't listen to me. The written confusion could similarly be ignored (though funnily enough he had kept all my letters, as I found out when I came across a bundle of them tied together with a bootlace). Harder to account for was my manner, in which the expected falsity, hypocrisy, selfishness, and indifference were not as abundant as he'd expected. Though that, too, could be explained.

"You were in the movies once, weren't you?" he said. "I guess that's where you learned to put on a good act."

For a while I couldn't understand why he had come to me, given this hostility of his. But after a week or so I realized that it was to give me the opportunity to prove once and for all that I was totally indifferent to his welfare, and, indeed, to his very being and existence. As soon as the old simplicity — my desertion of him and his mother — was re-established to his satisfaction, he could happily revert to hating me unreservedly.

In the meantime, I persisted with my feeble communication. "By the way, what happened to the Armstrong-Siddeley?" I asked one morning. On leaving England, I had made him a present of that beautiful automobile.

"You want it back?" he asked sharply. "Made a mistake, huh, wasting a car like that on me. Well, too bad. I gave it away, one of the guys in the squadron."

"You did?"

"Yes, I did."

"Why?"

"Because it was yours," he said.

After a moment he must have read something or other into my silence, for he started to shuffle in an almost childish way. "Anyway, wouldn't have been much good to me now, would it?" he muttered, with a depth of bitterness.

It wasn't easy, sharing an apartment with a blind man. As the weeks went by, he did everything he could to rile me into revealing myself as an unfeeling parent. Hoping to enrage me into exposing my lifelong hostility toward him, he set about destroying the apartment. He blundered into the furniture and knocked things over on purpose with his cane. There were hardly any knick-knacks left by the end of July.

He would leave his room in a disgraceful state, and when I remonstrated, he took this as proof that I detested him. To the same end he wore my clothes and anointed them with food and drink. Worst of all, he either avoided communicating altogether, hoping to infuriate me with his mulish silence into showing myself up, or started telling damaging lies. These mostly took the form of slander. Like informing our upstairs neighbour, Miss Hemp, that I had been convicted of rape, but that there was nothing to worry about as I had subsequently been castrated.

When Miss Hemp proved to be unfamiliar with the word, he mimed it in such graphic style that she felt quite faint and had to sit on the stairs for a moment – or so he told me.

For the most part I was able to parry the challenges, helped by the fact that I was still awed and thrilled by the miracle of having a son, even an ornery or bad-tempered one.

There were many other causes for friction between us. He hated to be touched, which was sometimes necessary, such as when we were downtown and he was about to step off the sidewalk into the path of a stake truck. He was so sensitive about my help that if, for instance, he was dressing and couldn't find one shoe, I would have to find some way to place the shoe where his angry sweeping hand might contact it without his realizing that I was doing so.

He found fault, whatever I did for him. He had enjoyed reading in bed before going to sleep, so I volunteered to read to him. But after a few sessions he said he would rather listen to the radio. "You got such a whiny voice," he said. "Like somebody doing a lousy imitation of W. C. Fields."

"I do not."

"You do, too, you have a whiny voice. It just don't sound right when you read Gorky."

"*Doesn't* sound right."

"I'm glad you agree. So now can we have 'Big Band Boogie'?"

"Ungrateful child," I said, thoroughly annoyed. "I was only reading Gorky for your sake anyway, you left-wing stooge. I met Gorky, and it's no fun reading him. An apologist for the Marxists, that's all he was."

"You met Gorky?"

"I did – in Moscow in 1919."

The boy's face lit up with excitement. "You really met the great Gorky? Wow!"

"I was even incarcerated in the same cell that he once occupied."

"Hey, that's great!"

"He was put there by the Tsarists. I was put there by the Soviets."

The hostile curtain came down again. "Yeah, well, I don't want to hear any more of your anti-Soviet propaganda," he said. But I was glad to have had a decent quarrel with him at last, instead of the usual sullen exchange.

Actually I had given up trying to overcome the Party line that he had swallowed, complete with hook and sinker. And what made him all the more annoyed was my failing to argue with him when he spouted the usual crimson clichés, or when he attempted to unwind the dialectical convolutions of Marxism and Leninism, as had been demonstrated to him at his Party meetings in California. Once or twice he even ended up putting my point of view so that he could bring his own well-rehearsed arguments into play. Though that seemed to leave him feeling unsatisfied, somehow.

I got pretty fed up with him, sometimes, over his unreasonable demands, his insults, and his rude behaviour. Usually I managed to stifle the annoyance. Until he started missing the toilet.

"Look here, 772 Bandy, I'm getting tired of mopping up after you. Why don't you aim properly?"

"I am blind, you know."

"You can still hear the splashing in the toilet – that should help you aim properly."

"Yes, but it takes time to locate the water and by that time half of it's on your nice clean floor."

"Well, why don't you move the old spout really close, and then slowly pull back until you've got the range and bearing."

"I've observed," he said superciliously, "an increasing vulgarity creeping into your conversation, Father. Kindly remember I was well brought up in a remand school – Grandfather's house – and am not used to crudities of that nature."

This was the first time he had criticised Chaffington, however obliquely. Eagerly, I attempted to deepen the subversion; but I couldn't get him to follow up with any further censure, darn it.

Still, it was a start. I was quite pleased. And there was another hopeful sign. "You're beginning to sound more like me every day, B.W.," I said. Which was true. I used to talk like that when I was his age, much to the annoyance of my fellow students and teachers. He was beginning to expand his vocabulary beyond its basic eighty-five words. Every day, now, he was using new words, and thus threatening his American identity.

In other ways, though, he was very American. In his built-in energy, for instance, now sadly suppressed by the loss of his primary navaids. There was also the American lack of appreciation or understanding of other cultures. Mind you, so far he had only encountered one other culture, and that a pretty bizarre one – the English. He hadn't yet come to appreciate England, especially the mangled vowels or affected speech of the so-called upper classes. He had also been inclined to criticize the habits of the working class, until he remembered that he was supposed to be on the side of the lumpen proletariat.

He wasn't too impressed with Canadians, either. "I don't get it," he said. "They agree with everything you say. When I was here last

I could only tell what they really thought when they started cross-ing the street to avoid me."

He started to fidget. "You're looking at me again," he said. "I can tell."

"In wonderment, Bartholomew, just wonderment. I never thought I'd ever have a son."

"What makes you think I'm your son?" he said. "Hey, listen, I got to tell you the truth at last, sir. Mother confessed one day that you weren't my real dad at all. My real father was Warren G. Cresswell Junior, a banker."

"Shaddup with your lies, you yak-faced sponger, and listen. I love having a son – even if it is you. Truth is, I didn't think I had it in me to have a son."

"So how come you didn't marry Mother, you bastard?"

"Look who's calling who a bastard. Anyway, I've already told you. The Chaffingtons prevented it."

"Oh, sure. Tell me the old, old story."

"Incidentally, how did you manage to get free of their clutches?" I asked.

"It sure wasn't easy," he began ruefully; but then clammed up, and would say no more. And when I persisted, he waved his white stick and shattered another lamp.

"You did that on purpose, you little rat," I said.

"So? Why don't you slug me? Or toss me out on my butt? It's what you want to do, ain't it?"

"Oh, belt up," I said.

There were a million minor problems between us, too, ranging from the problem of how to help him match up his socks without letting him know I was helping, to cutting a loaf of bread. "I like thin slices," I said. "I keep telling you, you cut the bread much too thick."

"I like them thick."

"But four inches?"

"I'm afraid of lopping off a finger."

"Damn it all, B.W., you'd still have four left."

"No, I wouldn't, I'd only have three."

"Four."

"Three."

"Four. Five minus one is four."

"Ah," he said triumphantly, "but one is a thumb."

"Oh, well, if you're going to split hairs," I said huffily; whereupon he threw down the breadknife and stormed out of the kitchen, shouting that I didn't appreciate him, and he wouldn't help in the kitchen no more.

"*Any* more," I shouted back. "You won't help in the kitchen any more, not no more, you ignorant sod!"

The only answer was the shattering of the chamberpot that I had purchased for him out of the goodness of my heart.

SPARKS STREET

"WELL, I'LL BE!"

"What?"

"I'll be hornswoggled, sockdarned, and lapidated!"

"What is it?" B.W. shouted.

"772 Bandy, you remember Guinevere Plumley, don't you?"

"The one with the voice like she's auditioning for the Oily Cart Opera?"

"That's the one. Well, she's at the door, listening to you."

"So what?" he mumbled, whacking his way into the room with his cane.

"Well?" asked Guinevere. "Are you going to keep me on the doorstep like an unwelcome mat?"

"No, no, come in, come in. This is a surprise."

"And what's this about 772 Bandy?"

"He won't let me call him 'son.' I have to call him something. Come in, come in. What are you doing in Ottawa?"

"I just happened to be passing – thought I'd drop in," Guinevere said; and as if to illustrate the expression, stumbled over the threshold. She had obviously not been working on her coordination over the past one and a half years.

As she entered, I gave her splendid breasts a good feel, though of course I did so under the pretence of catching her before she fell. In return she gave me no more than a perfunctory kiss before hurling herself at 772 Bandy and embracing him, displaying the

enthusiasm reserved for someone you don't particularly like. He
staggered, but managed to maintain his balance by tearing down
one of the curtains. He did not look pleased.

He and Guinevere had never got on well in England. It was
evident that the months had not intervened to improve their
relationship.

"Take it easy," he said irritably.

Ignoring his ungracious tone, Guinevere continued to express
pleasure at meeting him again, and said how good he looked; that
he had put on weight, and now looked as sleek as a harp seal.

"Who wouldn't put on weight with the stodge he cooks," he
said, jerking a thumb roughly in my direction.

"Yes, 772 looks pretty good, doesn't he?" I responded. "Specially
with those odd socks. The colours hardly clash at all, do they,
Gwin?"

"You're a liar!" he cried. "There's nothing wrong with my
socks!"

"No, 'course not," I said quickly. "They match quite well."

"You're lying, you're lying!" B.W. shouted, really upset. You'd
have thought I was accusing him of exhibitionism, buggery, or
chewing with his front teeth.

"You're right, 772," I said in tones of surrender. "I'll come clean
– which is more than your socks do. The truth is they don't match
at all."

"They do!" he shouted. He turned toward Guinevere. "They're
not odd, right? Are they? Tell me!"

"Of course they're not odd," she said indignantly. "They look
very nice." And, to me: "Ooooh, you!"

"Are you sure?" B.W. said uncertainly.

"Of course I'm sure, darling. How can you do this to him,
Bartholomew, teasing him like that? It's cruel."

"He's always doing it," B.W. said, "when he's not moving the furniture so I'll fall over it."

"Bartholomew!"

"He does, he moves the furniture," B.W. shouted. "Otherwise
why would I keep falling over it?"

"How could you," Guinevere said, glaring at me as she put an arm round B.W.'s waist. To him she said, "But don't you worry, I'll see he doesn't do any more mean things to you, darling."

I said, "You're staying?"

"Somebody has to, to protect the poor boy," she said. "Officially I'm at the Château Laurier, but I'll be staying here, in order to cheat on expenses. We're expected to do that in our business, of course, to give us useful experience in duplicity."

"I see."

"So be good enough as to take my bags to your room, my good man," Guinevere said, and rolled her eyes lasciviously.

B.W. did not look grateful either for her protection or her domestic proposal. "You're not sleeping in his room, are you?" he asked.

"Of course, dear."

"But, but," he said. He swished his cane around, though this time in a harried fashion rather than as if he were genuinely looking for something to smash.

"Sure," he muttered, shrugging. "It's his joint, he can turn it into an opium den if he wants. It's up to him."

"You don't mind, do you, darling?" Guinevere asked, her boom rattling the cast-iron radiators. "I do rather love him, you know."

"It ain't nothing to do with me," he said, and thwacked his way back to his room and slammed the door.

As soon as the walls had ceased vibrating, she turned to me indignantly, and hissed, "What's going on here? Why are you torturing the poor boy like that? And him without eyes to fight back with!"

"Well, he does it to me."

"Bartholomew! How can you be so childish!"

"I'm trying," I said, "to stop him telling lies about me. The more he does so, the more I tell lies back at him. It's just beginning to work."

That night, after a physical reunion that was frustratingly hushed because we had a Puritan staying next door, she said, "I see what you mean. Do you know what he told me when you were in the kitchen, sobbing over the onions? He said you've been making life miserable for him. Putting ground glass in his sago pudding, and things like that. Sticking pins in his behind, just to see him jump. Is that the sort of thing he's been telling other people?"

"Yes."

"He claims that you sneak into his room when he's asleep, and that you pour warm water onto the sheets, and then accuse him of wetting the bed," she said, snorting with sudden laughter.

"Actually I did that once."

"Bartholomew!"

"In retaliation for when he kept accidentally pouring my whisky down the sink. He's still a teetotalitarian, you know. Anyway, it's beginning to work. He's finding I can cause him almost as much embarrassment as he causes me," I said, while tickling the top part of the cleft between her buttocks. It was one of Gwinny's favourite places.

Gloomily, I added, "What I can't do, though, is make him any the less unfriendly. He does everything possible to make me admit that I didn't want him as a kid, and I don't want him now. Sometimes I think he may be right."

"You don't mean that."

"It's hard not to detest him, sometimes, he's so difficult."

"About the other problem," Guinevere said hesitantly. "Is there no change?"

"They keep saying the same thing. There's no physical injury to the eyes. He just can't see. Dr. Watson calls it Hysteriae Colateral Disneyoptera, I think he said, or Ponsonby's Syndrome."

"Dr. Watson is an eye specialist?"

"No, he's a vet. Friend of mine. But he takes an interest in human beings."

"The point is, do they still think he might regain his sight one day?"

"They're beginning to wonder. Sometimes it's almost as if he wants to stay blind, maybe to pay me back in some way. No, that's psychoanalytical rubbish."

Guinevere was silent for a while, not least because I was gently plugging in, to see if my lamp would still light.

"Maybe not such rubbish," she said shakily. "Or maybe being blind keeps him with you."

"That's even crazier."

"I don't know, darling," she said, in between assorted trills, thrums, and moaning. "He's jealous of me, you know."

"You think so?"

"I think he sees me as a rival," she began. But further discussion was postponed by the resumption of Sports Day, with all sorts of heats and gymnastics, a continued sack race, with long jumps and high jumps and six-inch pole vaults, ending with a hundred-yards dash to the finishing line.

Next morning over breakfast, while B.W. was still in bed, I said, "So. What's the real reason you're over here, Gwinny?"

She treated me to a direct, honest, manly look. "I've been invited to a do by the Governor-General's wife," she said.

"Uhuh. And?"

"What d'you mean, and?"

"You didn't cross the Atlantic in wartime to go to a quilting bee, or whatever it is."

"We went to school together. She's turned sculptor and is showing some of her work."

"Uhuh."

"I have tickets for her exposition. Want to come?"

"Sculpture? Why not? I like sculpture. Rodin, and . . . people like that. Michelangelo."

"Also there's this job in Quebec City."

"Aha. What kind of job?"

"I can't tell you."

"One of those, eh?"

A few nights later, while Guinevere was busy riding sidesaddle, she suddenly reined in. She looked down at me with a concentration somewhat disconcerting considering that she had been in the throes of passion only a few seconds previously.

"Bartholomew?"

"H'm?"

"You're not particulary busy at the moment, are you?"

"No, you're doing all the work."

"I mean, your job here. We could do with an extra body on the team. Would you be interested in helping out for a few days?"

"In Quebec? Doing what?"

"I can't tell you."

"In that case I accept. If I can bring 772 Bandy."

She wasn't keen on the idea, but agreed on the understanding that he would keep out of the way, and not distract me from my duties. Naturally she refused to say what these were, but it was obvious that the job she had in mind for me was an important one.

The business having been completed, she resumed the side-saddle position, and rode off in all directions. She had become terribly keen on sex since "breaking her duck." I was beginning to wish, though, that she wasn't making up quite so much lost time with me. Once or twice wasn't enough for her any more. Now it had to be a continuous performance, like at the movies.

Since her arrival in Ottawa mine had become such a demanding role that by now I was having to fake every second or third ecstasy. Mind you, I was getting quite good at it. As the mercury rose in the tube, I would emit a convincing amount of high-pitched keening, glottal stopping, and whining dyspnea, the aim being to convince her that I was having a good time, but now was the time to stop and have a round of bridge.

Occasionally, though, I made mistakes, like forgetting the penultimate acceleration, the speeding-up part suggesting that you have a train to catch. But generally I became as successful at the subsequent pretence as at the initial reality.

It appeared that my trip to Quebec was not to be. When I approached Mr. Barnes, my superior at Defence, I expected to receive permission on the spot. It was promptly denied. "You've already had a month's leave to look after your son," he said. "I'm afraid we can't spare you, Bandy."

"But I'm not doing anything," I protested. "The last application to join the RCAF was months ago, from that fellow in Utah who wanted to bring along his own hot-air balloon."

"The fact remains that you've already had your leave allocation for the year," he said. "In fact, for the next two or three years, if my records are not in substantial error."

Barnes was a civilian on loan from Bytown Remand School. He had a habit of lining things up on his desk, to ensure that everything was parallel to everything else – except his inkwell, which, being round, could not be laid parallel to anything. He kept it in a rectangular box.

He was not displeased at this opportunity to turn me down. He had not approved of me since receiving my memo recommending that my job be given to a Gestetner. Nor was he too pleased with me on this occasion. While we were discussing the situation, I picked up a ruler that was lined up with the edge of the desk, and used it to alter the position of a similarly oriented box of chisel-point staples, and when, gently but firmly, he took back the ruler, I seized a handful of war utility pencils, tapped them on the desk to align the eraser ends, but then replaced them in a distinctly untidy heap; and while he was busy clucking and restoring them to their original positions, I leaned over when he wasn't looking and pushed the rectangular box slightly out of true – just enough to give him an uneasy feeling that something was wrong on his desktop, but not enough for him to realize what it was.

Generally, it was not one of my best days. When I got home I found that B.W. and Guinevere had been quarrelling again.

Open warfare had broken out on several occasions. This particular battle was over his sleeping habits. After several days when he failed to appear until noon or even later, Guinevere had asked me irritably if B.W. always slept this late. I replied that sleeping in was possibly one of his tests, an attempt to goad me into exposing myself as an authoritarian swine. However, in case it was a symptom of the depression his blindness sometimes plunged him into, I had so far refrained from remonstrating, even when he remained in bed until eight in the evening.

"So you believe that he's just trying to confirm that you're the pretentious, ill-humoured, no-good, treacherous, heartless swine who abandoned him and his mother to their fate?"

"You don't need to list my alleged faults quite so enthusiastically, you know."

"But you think that's the situation, right?"

"I don't know," I said, suddenly feeling depressed myself. I glanced at his bedroom door to make sure it was shut, and lowered my voice. "But I'm wondering how I'll ever be able to prove that I'm glad to have him with me."

"Well, I think it's just sloth, and he needs a good shaking up," said Guinevere, wearing the mean look of the early riser. "And I'm going to do something about it." And she marched over to the bedroom door.

She knocked sharply, and upon receiving a muffled response, opened the door and stepped in, speaking at the same time. "And just how long are you going to keep this up, Bartholomew Wendell Bandy?" she said, standing there with her hands on her hips, but making her voice exaggeratedly censorious, as if to show that she didn't really feel that way.

Unfortunately she did feel that way, so it didn't quite come out as she intended. And B.W. looked highly resentful as he sat up, pushing back his tousled, dark brown hair.

"Your father really loves you, and it wasn't his fault that he was unable to make an honest woman of your mother," Guinevere said.

There was a groaning sound from the next room. She paid no attention to it, but continued, "You've no right to do this to your father," she said, "making him suffer this way. And he is suffering. Come and look at him, see how much he's suffering. I'll have you know he's very proud to have a son. I know for a fact that until you turned up he was convinced that he was totally sterile. So the least you can do is make things a little easier for both of you, instead of behaving in this way, like a child, to see how far you can go before you get a smack. My nanny wouldn't have put up with these shenanigans, I can tell you. So come on, B.W., time to get up. It's after twelve, you should be up and stirring by now."

"I'm surprised you're up this early," he replied after clearing his throat a number of times. "After all your hard work last night."

"Pardon?"

"You like being on top, do you? Gives you a feeling of power, does it?"

"You dirty-minded little beast!"

"At least I don't talk dirty – the way I've heard you begging for more – and not in ladylike language, either."

"Are you going to let him talk to me like that?" she said, turning to me. I was in the doorway by then, wondering which one of them to hit.

She turned back to B.W. without waiting for an answer, and, "I'm not standing here to be insulted like that," she said.

"So grab a seat. I got lots more. Like who the hell are you to come clacking in here in your fancy shoes and hoity-toity voice? I might have been bare naked."

"Barefaced you certainly are. A barefaced, insolent – " She calmed herself with an effort. "But we mustn't quarrel, B.W.," she said, breathing rapidly, which certainly showed off her breasts to advantage. "But I do think you ought to start growing up, you know, and stop feeling sorry for yourself. After all, it's your own fault you're blind."

"It is?"

"Yes. The doctors say it's purely voluntary. You could see if you really wanted to."

"Jeez, I never knew that. There was this explosion right outside the cockpit, and the next thing everything went black. But it was all voluntary. Yes, I see that now."

"Oh, you should just hear yourself, B.W.," she said, so scornfully that even I felt a bit wounded. "You're just dripping with self-pity. Why don't you be a man? Pull yourself together, and get on with it. Get out of this flat, for one thing. Go out and get some fresh air into your lungs."

"Then you'll be able to screw all day as well as all night, huh?" he said. And as she stormed out: "I don't know how you can keep it up, Wing Commander. It must be like snuggling up to a runaway diesel."

But I was in the kitchen by then with the door closed, peeling hundreds of potatoes.

Though the exhibition of his wife's works of art was being held under his auspices, the Governor-General seemed to be trying hard to dissociate himself from the show – presumably in case it received lousy reviews. It was not being held anywhere near the official residence, but at a private gallery on Sparks Street.

There was quite a large turnout for the opening, mostly because there was not much else to do on a Friday evening in Ottawa – or on a Monday through Thursday evening, for that matter. The exhibition provided an opportunity for people to tune into the gossip about who was in favour in the Civil Service, and who was in disfavour and likely to lose one of his windows. It also gave the citizens a chance to catch up on the Prime Minister's latest eccentricity, like his hobby of collecting stone walls and embedding them in the turf near his Kingsmere estate.

It was possible that even the war might be mentioned in passing.

The free food was a further attraction, though in this case the sandwiches turned out to be horrible. Nobody noticed, though, because they were so beautifully arranged on expensive plates. There were also crusty sections of French bread with side dishes of pâté, biscuits with fragments of seafood stuck to them, and dangerous-looking toothpicks embedded in orange cubes of Canadian cheddar.

To drink there was a claret punch with no claret in it, but healthy quantities of fruity juices, the magenta fluid swashing about in vast glass punch bowls, the surface littered with edible flotsam and jetsam.

Nothing alcoholic was being served anywhere in the building. However, as was the Canadian custom, there was an alfresco assembly of males at the emergency exits, where surreptitious flasks glinted in the evening sun.

Guinevere had intended us to be fashionably late, and luckily we were too late. The exhibits were still there but practically all the snacks and beverages had gone. Only pitiful fragments of once beautifully arranged Hollywood Bread sandwiches and other delights remained on the Spode, Limoges, and Wedgewood plates that had been brought from the official residence.

If an impressive entrance was one that caused every eye in the joint to intersect at the gallery entrance, ours was it. Guinevere led the way; and, boy, did the locals have cause to look impressed, not to say stunned. The contrast between the exaggerated perfection of her figure and the face that surmounted it was further heightened by the simplicity of her attire. When I first met her she was inclined to throw on the first thing she found in the clothes cupboard. I think it was to impress me that she had started to make more of an effort. On this occasion she was wearing a short black dress with padded shoulders, slippers in black and silver, and silk stockings only slightly wrinkled. Everybody gazed at her long, Dietrich legs and pouting Grable bust for as long as possible, but sooner or later the assembled art lovers had to look at her face, and that was when the massed intake of breath was heard. In its disdain for such civilized amenities as a standard nose, plucked eyebrows, and a dainty chin capable of a helpless tremor, in its naked rejection of enhancement, camouflage, or distraction, it had an almost barbaric splendour. I felt really proud of her.

Next came B.W. and it was a tribute to his personality that his entrance was not an anti-climax. He had made an effort to appear smart, though in fact he looked naturally elegant in his blue uniform with the simple ring on each sleeve and the lonely wings. But it was his suffering face and noble bearing that extracted the admiration and female longing. The noble bearing was, of course, totally bogus but was forced on him by his blindness, which compelled him to hold his head as if he were playing His Royal Highness the Archduke Francis-Marmalade of Strelsnia-Hertsagoverness.

Next came his genuinely noble father, who, in a fit of untrammelled ostentation was wearing every gong, star, and sash he was entitled to (including some he was not entitled to — a couple of nineteenth-century Imperial Russian medals usually awarded to Trans-Siberian train conductors during the reign of Alexander II, picked up in the Portobello Road for a quid each).

The assembled multitude proceeded to talk about us for the next half hour. But despite the competition from Gwinny's face and my medals, it was B. W. who became the star of the show. I noticed right away that in spite of my son's substantial area of horse face, women regarded him with calculating interest, and even more so when they registered his white stick.

His first sabotaging remark of the evening was to the artist herself. The Governor-General's wife, to whom we were introduced by a naval equerry, was somewhat overdressed for the occasion in a long, ivory gown with a matching cigarette holder. She was a bony woman who wore an expression so worried and vague as to suggest that she was either thinking about her next masterpiece or wondering if she'd left off her knickers. She had a habit of waving her twelve-inch cigarette holder as if conducting a chamber orchestra. Her hands were slender and delicate, surprisingly so, considering that she was a sculptor. Even amateur sculptors would need fairly powerful hands, surely?

There was no sign of her husband, the GG. Perhaps he was with the slackers at the emergency exit.

She was not a particularly tactful lady, as was revealed when she remarked aloud to her naval aide that B. W. was blind.

"Yes, ma'am."

"But how odd," she said. "He won't be able to see my works."

"No, ma'am."

"How very odd," she said languidly. "Still, I suppose we could arrange for a commentator or something. But it's really very odd, you must agree. And this is your father, is it?"

"Yeah," B. W. said. "He's odd, too."

"Oh, dear, is he?"

"For one thing, he has all those medals, and he won't give me any of them."

"Oh, dear," she said, treating me to a look of weary reproach.

"He could easily spare half a dozen medals. But no, he's too mean to let me have a single one," B.W. said.

"That is a shame," said the Governor-General's wife. "But would it be permissible to wear someone else's ribbons?"

"Well, he does."

"Your father wears someone else's ribbons?"

"Sure. If you look closely, you'll see there's several that he couldn't possibly have earned. Like the Medaille Vinaigrette, the Star of Bethlehem Ontario, the Order of Saint Custard, the Exceedingly Cross, and the Award of Dutch Courage, Second Class – that's the yellow one on the end of the sixth row."

"Madam," whispered the naval equerry, discreetly drawing her attention to the line of guests being held up by the smart young officer with the fixed gaze and the white cane. Not that the reception line was showing signs of impatience. There was too much sympathy for that. The moment B.W. had appeared, expressions had melted into puddles of pity, not least because he looked perfect in all other respects – except for his face, but we'll come to that in a minute.

He had grown since I first met him, and was now fully six foot two, with a fine, broad-shouldered figure. His movements were relaxed and unhurried. Only his face gave cause for pause, with its excessive area and length, and its tendency to look supercilious if not kept, as it was being kept now, under firm control.

His fine appearance added class and admiration to the sympathy. Women murmured admiringly, "Oh, look at that poor young man, eh?" And the melting compassion was all the more cloying when it was confirmed that, yes, he had been blinded in the war.

The confirmation that it was the war, you know, was needed in case he turned out to be counterfeit. You couldn't be too careful these days. Only a short time ago a fêted veteran who was thought to have been disabled by the dastardly enemy had turned out to have been laid out by a platoon of venereal chancres.

As he stood near the entrance to the gallery, waves of sympathy

lapped around my boy. I hoped he would not react in his usual
churlish way to the well-meant but rather heavy concern of the
Ottawa matrons, the way they were talking so tactfully to him
about everything except his disability.

To my relief, he remained charm personified. In fact, his behaviour since setting out from the apartment had been impeccable. At
first he had refused to go with us, just as he had consistently refused
to accompany me to any destination where there was the slightest
chance of his meeting someone who might confuse him by report-
ing on me favourably.

On this occasion it was Guinevere who encouraged him to
attend, though in fact it was a miscalculation on her part. She had
not wanted him along. She was apprehensive that he might disgrace
her in some way in the eyes of her friend, the GG's wife. So she had
attempted to repel B.W. by informing him that an art historian of
empathetic proclivity had promised to look after him – stick to him
like glue while he led B.W. round the exhibits and explained the
aesthetic significance of every single item of sculpture. Gwinny
thought that if such a prospect didn't dissuade B.W. from going,
nothing would.

Nothing would. At first he had snorted disdainfully at the idea
of a blind man going to an art show. Then, to my surprise and
Gwinny's mortification, he had suddenly changed his mind. He
would love to go. I was sure it was a breakthrough in our relationship. Fool that I was. I should have marked the timing of his sudden
change of heart. It had come immediately after Gwinny had
described the exhibits.

Now, on this hot August afternoon, he was even being polite to
Gwinny; and for once was making no effort to prick the balloon of
my conceit to see if I burst. Apart, that is, from his exchange with
one young lady, an earnest and sincere student with a fringe and dirt
under her fingernails. And even that did no real harm.

Knowing that I was nearby, he leaned over and said to the girl,
"Did you know that my father is a pederast?"

"Oh, is he?" said the student. "I'm a Bauhaus person myself."

There was certainly no scarcity of people for B.W. to gammon or gull. They kept coming up to tell him about all the wonderful things he was missing because he was blind. He remained polite, and even smiled once. I hadn't realized until then what a good smile he had.

I concluded that he was either making an effort to behave, or making an effort to avoid misbehaving. The problem was that I still didn't understand him, was still not entirely sure whether he was naturally churlish and discontented, or deliberately behaving that way for my benefit. Though either way I was prepared to make excuses for him, considering his behaviour the inevitable result of being brought up by the Chaffingtons with their excessive wealth.

"He's being good today," Guinevere observed.

"Yes, isn't he?"

"It's got me worried. For one thing, why is he using a white cane?"

"It's the usual aid for the blind, n'est ce pas?"

"You know perfectly well that on the few occasions he consents to go out he insists on a plain walking stick, so as not to draw attention to himself. So why all of a sudden is he reconciled to the white one?"

"I'm just glad that he's starting to take after me, and behave in a civilized fashion," I said, wondering how soon I could join the fellows at the emergency exit.

I waited until B.W. had been washed ashore by the latest wave of sympathy, and walked up to him. He was standing at the entrance to the gallery.

"So, how are you making out, 772?"

"Okay."

"I just have to see somebody outside for a moment. Will you be all right?"

"You don't have to pretend with me, Father," he said. And I was pleased to note that there was much less than usual of the sneering emphasis on the form of address. "Go ahead and nip out for a nip. Much more of this and I might be tempted to join you.

"By the way," he added casually, "is it true what Gwinny said? It really is an exhibition of tin cans?"

"Eh?" Actually I hadn't yet looked into the gallery. However, I was clutching a program, so I referred to that. "Well, let's see. I have a program here."

"What does it say?"

"Let me see . . . blah, blah, blah . . . Yes, here we are. It says, 'About the exhibits themselves, the orientating factor is not so much the figurative ultimo, the parallel representation of the, one might say, boundaries of the human syndrome, so much as a votive offering of the material to the immaterial, a leap on behalf of the tenacious imagination to achieve an impregnation in microcosm of the universal void, providing it with the opportunity to reveal itself in all its eristic fecundity.' "

"What does that mean?"

"It means it's an exhibition of tin cans."

Having read all about the exhibition, I now decided it was time to actually visit it. So I wandered into the gallery and discovered that the sculptures were indeed courtesy of Heinz and other manufacturers. The entire gallery had been given over to tin, some of it on shelves specially mounted on the walls, others on 57 varieties of pedestal. Some pedestals supported as many as half a dozen exhibits.

For the most part the sculptures had been created either by twisting together shards, wings, or specially cut sections of tin, or by soldering pieces together. The tins were of many different sizes ranging from the smallest baked bean can to large trade containers for the supply of tomato juice. Some cans had been stripped of their labels, exposing the shiny metal; some had been decorated in bright oil colours; and some had the original wrapping in place, as for instance in *Rumsodden No. 2*, a fine representation of a leaning figure with a large apple juice container for a head, small spaghetti tins for ears, and part of a watering-can nozzle for a nose. Most of the guests were still in the foyer outside, so there weren't many people in the gallery, but those who were there seemed very impressed. "It looks just like a mulberry bush," one lady said, inspecting Exhibit No. 41: *Mulberry Bush*.

"The catalogue says it's meant to represent a mulberry bush

only metaphysically," said her companion. "Actually it's the spirit of incandescent nature made ruminative."

At that point I felt like a drink, and so wandered out again, and sped to the nearest exit.

I had been standing out there in the late evening sun with about fifty other gentlemen, nipping, chatting, and nipping, when for no apparent reason I began to feel uneasy. It was the kind of feeling you get when you've left home and suspect you've forgotten something – to pick up your keys, turn off the gas, let out the cat, or hide the dirty magazines under the cushions in case your mother turned up.

I patted my pockets. No, my money, two dollars in notes, was still there, and the apartment's keys were in my trouser pocket.

"Ah, Mr. Bandy," said Mr. Barnes. "I didn't know you were interested in art."

"I didn't know you were a boozer, Mr. Barnes."

"There's no need to be like that, Bandy, just because I'm the one who has to apply the rules. If I could have sent you to Quebec City I should certainly have done so."

"I'm sorry, Barnes," I said, putting an apologetic hand on his grey serge sleeve. "I'm feeling anxious all of a sudden, for some reason."

"You can be so snotty sometimes, Bandy."

"Sorry," I said. "Are you yourself interested in art?"

"Art, yes. But I'm not all that fond of modern sculpture," he said, gesturing indoors. "Henry Moore and people like . . . whatsisname again?"

"I once owned a painting by Matisse," I said for something to say.

"Lipchitz!"

"Oh, it wasn't so bad."

"No, that was the name of the sculptor I was trying to remember. My taste runs more to painting, personally."

"My brother-in-law sold it for several hundred quid."

"Pardon me?"

"The painting I once had."

"I'm particularly partial to the Pre-Raphaelite school, and the work of such artists as, oh, darn, it's on the tip of my tongue . . ."

"He never gave me the money, either."

"Burne-Jones!"

"Ah? You don't like Jones either?"

"Who?"

"This Mr. Jones you wish to ignite."

"No, no," Barnes said impatiently. "Burne-Jones, the painter."

"Ah."

We continued to nip, swig, and discuss artistic matters; until Guinevere came hurrying out, looking rather pale.

"You'd better come," she said. Her face was like curds and whey.

The moment I entered the foyer of the gallery and heard the tinny clashing, I knew why I had felt so uneasy.

I had heard him asking various people for a description of the exhibits. He had been particularly interested in how they were displayed, arranged, and mounted. There were also the questions he had asked of at least two of my acquaintances which seemed designed to determine just how good my reputation was in Ottawa. The more praise I received the happier he had looked, which wasn't like him at all.

The explanation for his curiosity now became evident. As I hastened into the gallery I was greeted by the sight of tin cans strewn all over the floor, and several exhibits as disabled as the person who was currently disabling them.

B.W. was making his way down the long gallery, feeling his way with one hand outstretched in one direction, and his stick outstretched in the other. He was slicing the cane from side to side, ostensibly to assist him in navigating through the crowded artworks. But somehow he always just managed to strike one or other of the exhibits on either side; with the result that cans of all kinds were being sent flying. Vegetable cans, jam cans, fruit cans, fruit juice cans, soft drink cans, every sort of sliced-up-and-bent-double can, every sort of cut-in-half-and-arranged-in-interesting-shapes can. And as he progressed through the exhibition he was being trailed by the desperate personnel of the gallery, attendants, assistants, and security guards, all of them following in B.W.'s clattering wake, all of them impotently gesturing like lunatics from 999 Queen Street, imploring him, pleading with him to be careful; but with nobody able to bring themselves to actually prevent him from whacking the artworks, partly because of his dangerous cane, but mostly because of his disability. To have restrained him in any way – a blind man who was also a war hero – would have looked like molestation.

And they could not bring themselves to interfere physically also because the scene was so terribly pitiful. For B.W. was crying loudly and plaintively, heartbreakingly, "Where's my father, I must find my father, Bartholomew W. Bandy, his name is, that's W for Wolfe. Please, somebody, won't you tell me, won't somebody tell me where Bartholomew Bandy is? I want my father, he's a wing commander, the one with three rings on his sleeve and all the wonderful medals. Where is he, where is my dad, Wing Commander Bandy, the famous pilot? Won't someone help me, because [a little suppressed sob here] I can't look for Mr. Bandy myself, you see," he concluded. "I can't find my daddy."

Finally somebody grabbed my arm – in a really vicious grip, incidentally – and thrust me forward, saying through his teeth but trying to sound helpful, "Here he is, he's here, this must be your father, this is the only wing commander we have, here's your father, sir!"

"You mean me?" I said.

"Yes, you're his father, aren't you, sir?"

"You think I'm his father?" I said.

"Yes, yes, you must be!"

"No, no, I'm not," I said, "I'm not his father, certainly not. I've never seen this man before in my life," I said.

Just before we left, Mr. Barnes said, "I think I can swing it after all, Bandy, about giving you leave to visit Quebec. In fact, I think we can make that an indefinite leave."

When we got home, I thought I'd start a cheerful conversation. "Well, that was good news, wasn't it, Gwinny? About B.W. and me being able to go to Quebec City with you after all, eh?"

Guinevere had started straight for the bedroom the moment we were over the threshold. But at this, she stopped, and turned – awfully slowly.

"What?" she said flatly.

"My superior says we can both spend as long as we like with you in Quebec City."

She took a deep breath – always an interesting sight to behold. "And that's good news, is it?" she asked, speaking ever so quietly.

"Well, I know how keen you are to have us there."

"She's keen on having you anywhere," said B.W.

Gwinny's cheek throbbed and rippled, but apart from that she was silent for quite a while.

Finally she managed to speak. "Doesn't it bother you," she said, still really slowly and quietly, "that that . . . that son of yours destroyed an entire art exhibition and ruined one of my most trea- sured friendships?"

Even though not a word of criticism of B.W. had escaped her lips on the way home in the car – she hadn't actually uttered a word about anything at all – I began to suspect that she was a little upset. So I crossed the living room and started to comfort her with an encircling arm, saying, "I know, it was awful. I'm seriously think- ing of giving him a really good telling off for behaving that way."

She looked at me. I smiled back. "But you must admit, sweetie," I said, "that it was pretty funny."

She plucked my arm from around her waist and hurled it across the room, where the knuckles rapped painfully against one of our remaining pieces of intact furniture. "Funny?" she bellowed. "Funny?" A saucepan jumped off the stove in the kitchen.

Yes, she was definitely upset. You could tell because she had run into the kitchen where I could hear her rummaging like mad through one of the drawers.

I had a suspicion that it was the one with all the knives. I con- veyed this suspicion to B.W. In reply he suggested that it might be a good idea to hide somewhere. "I can tell from her voice that she's not too pleased," he said. "It sounded so shaky."

We only just managed to get into his room in time. A split second after I had engaged the latch she actually threw herself at the door. You could see it bending inwards from the pressure.

I got quite alarmed, for the door was one of those wartime utility efforts – not much more to it than three-sixteenths of an inch of plywood on each side, with nothing but air in between. And it was Guinevere on the other side. I didn't like the way she was screaming, and kicking the door, and hitting it with something hard. If she took a run at it with her mighty shoulder the door would be gone.

I was also quite shocked at what she was screaming. She was actually saying, "I'll kill you both! I'll fucking well kill you both, you fucking bastards!"

B.W. was just as shocked as I was, as we backed slowly across the bedroom. And then there was one more bang on the door, and the next moment the blade of a knife appeared, neatly surrounded by fibres of plywood. And there the blade remained, sticking through the door by a good two inches, the stainless steel normally used for carving the roast, all gleaming and silvery, and it was also twisting about a bit as she tried to withdraw it. But it had been driven into the woodwork with such force that she was unable to accomplish this, and finally she had to content herself with one more kick that made even the door frame shudder, before retiring into the other bedroom and somehow managing – an amazing achievement – to slam the door despite the pneumatic gadget that was supposed to shut it with a gentle sigh.

"I think perhaps I'll doss down on the sofa tonight," I said.

"That's a good idea, Dad," said B.W. "She'll probably want to be on her own tonight."

"Yes, I think she will."

"And you wouldn't want to disturb her," said B.W.

IN THE CHÂTEAU

WHATEVER THE OCCASION, IT was certainly causing excitement in Quebec City, at least among the astonishingly large parties of officials, politicians, technicians, scientists, soldiers, sailors, airmen, and security people. They had taken over the entire Château Frontenac.

This was the country's most famous hotel, all towers and turrets, each with its condom of steep copper cap, the metal burned green by the atmospheric acid. Adding to the air of secrecy, the hotel entrance, off a secluded courtyard, was suitably furtive, obviously designed to discourage casual traffic from the Dufferin Terrace. This was a 2,200-foot boardwalk providing a splendid view of the original settlement far below, and of the St. Lawrence River, the traditional highway back to Europe.

I had an inkling of what might be happening when I perceived that at least half of the personnel were American, including masses of Secret Service men.

It was frustrating for B.W. (the form of address that my son had finally agreed to). He wanted a share of the spectacular views. He could sense the excitement in the air without any visual clues as to what it was about. Sometimes it drove him almost mad with bitter longing. When he lashed out with his cane, it was out of enraged frustration, now, rather than purely out of goading and mischief.

We were sharing a room high up in the hotel, at the top of a turret – little more than an attic, really, although it had a small balcony. It was the only room available to a pair of latecomers. As B.W. was the sort of American who believed that legs were made for walking only to the nearest transport, he was annoyed at having to negotiate a narrow stairway to the floor below in order to reach the elevator.

"You might at least have gotten us a room with a bath," I complained to Guinevere.

"It was the only room available at short notice," she said shortly.

It was evident by now that Guinevere was deeply involved in the security arrangements. This was a good thing, as it helped her to get over her snit. However, it also meant that she was not as much fun as she used to be. She had become a model of brisk, no-nonsense efficiency. She had even lost interest in my cock-a-doodle-do, refusing to share her own spacious accommodation with me.

"Oh, come on," I wheedled. "You've got lots of room in here."

"I have a job to do," she said. "Incidentally, in connection with it, London have asked me to clear up one or two queries in your file."

"More questions? Haven't they got B.W. and me sorted out yet?"

"They want to know more about your relationship with a man named Strand."

"Who?"

"Heinrich Strand," she said, watching me closely.

"Whatjamean, relationship? I don't have a relationship with him. I met him in India years ago, that's all."

"Under what circumstances, Bartholomew?"

"He saved my life. But I paid him handsomely for it – well over a hundred dollars."

"And you've kept in touch with him?"

"No, haven't seen him since."

"You're sure of that?"

"'Course I'm sure. Look, what is this?"

"Nothing."

"Is that it, then? The confusion as to which B.W. Bandy is the Commie Bastard has finally been cleared up?"

Her only response was to ask me to leave so that she could dress for dinner, presumably in a cloak and dagger. She even failed to treat me to a spot of osculation.

On the very next day, a great grey battleship steamed inch by inch into Quebec harbour. And who should step off the ship, to rounds of applause and cheering from service personnel, and to a crescendo of French-Canadian indifference, but the Former Naval Person. Presumably this time it was the real Winston Churchill. Who was here to confer with Franklin Delano Roosevelt, President of the United States.

From the balcony of our room we were able to obtain a magnificent view of the ceremonial occasion as the Prime Minister stepped ashore to be belaboured by a brass band, soon to be swallowed in acres of banners and ensigns and fields of gold braid, and met by a frockcoated Canadian Prime Minister, my old dog-owning pal, who was also attending the Quebec Conference, and who as host was responsible for supplying the booze and sandwiches.

Or rather, I had a magnificent view, though I was willing to share it with B.W.

"I don't want to hear," he said, trying to look bored. "Formalistic diversionism, that's all it is. Bread and circuses for the masses, to keep them quiescent. But one day their slavery will end in the triumph of international — "

"Oh, belt up. It's just a reception for the greatest man of the century."

"Personally I would nominate Stalin."

"By the way, be careful whenever you step out onto the balcony here," I warned him. And to make sure he understood the dangers, I described it to him: the heavy glass and iron door that led out onto it, and the balcony itself with its ironwork railing.

The railing was high enough, I supposed, and had been painted recently and was in sound condition. But still: the drop beyond was fearful. Just looking over the edge of the balcony made me clutch the railing hard enough to stick a few knuckles through the skin. Even the other balcony twenty or so feet below would not have halted one's progress to perdition, as it was not directly underneath but offset to the left.

"Did they really keep taking you out of the cell and pretending they were going to execute you?" B.W. asked suddenly, resuming an earlier questionnaire. "In Russia, I mean?"

"What? Yes, the GPU, or whatever they called themselves then. Hey, look, they've even organized a fly-past for the old man! How about that – Fairey Battles and Harvards! Here they come! Can you hear them?"

"Huh?"

"I said can you hear the fly-past?"

"What?"

"They've organized a fly-past for the old man!"

"What you say? Look, I can't hear you over the racket from all these planes. What was it you said, Father?" B.W. asked, looking feloniously innocent. The lousy kid was having me on again.

B.W.'s face was raised and his eyes were moving almost as if he could see the receding aircraft. "But why would they do such a thing?" he said, as the blasting roar of the Harvards died away. "I mean, they already had you in jail. What was the point?"

"It was just one of their little games with their prisoners," I said impatiently. "Boy, I wish you could see this, B.W. You get a great view from here of the battleship. I can even read the name on the blunt end. HMS *Repulsive*."

"What? That's not its name."

"Yes, it is. I can see it quite clearly: HMS *Repulsive*."

"I'm damn sure it's not called that," B.W. said angrily. "Why d'you have to say dumb things like that all the time?"

"By the way," I said, "did I mention that there's no toilet on this floor?"

"No, you didn't mention that."

"You'll have to go down to the floor below."

"Oh, great."

"Except that the toilet on the floor below has got a notice on it, Out of Order. It's also in French: Out de Ordure."

"There you go again," B.W. said furiously. "Saying stupid things."

"So I'd better show you where the functioning toilet is," I said, "two floors down."

"Forget it," he snapped. "I'll find it myself."

I had still not been informed as to the role I was to play in the leadership summit; though it was obvious that, given my record and reputation, I would be taking charge of some vital aspect of security.

Meanwhile I was thoroughly enjoying the change from the exhausting routine of doing nothing in Ottawa. Now I was doing nothing in Quebec, but with a fine change of scenery. I spent much of the time showing B.W. the sights, with such informed comments as, "That clopping sound you hear is a horse." Or, "We are now approaching the most cultural tavern in the Lower Town, which should be well worth a visit."

Of course, there is always someone around to spoil the respite from idleness. On the day following Churchill's arrival, we headed down to the Champlain Dining Room – being searched three times en route by three different security organizations – and were then refused admission because our names were not on somebody's list.

"Oh, come on, let us in," I murmured to the silver-haired gentleman who was checking the guest list. With a sly nod and wink, I offered him fifty cents. But he looked a bit affronted at this, and curtly repeated that we would not be allowed in without authorization.

I argued, but he was adamant, and finally I said peevishly, "Oh, very well, if that's how you want it. Anyway, who wants to eat in your old dining room anyway, with all those vulgar chandeliers and all that ostentatious silver. We'd much rather dine at René Arsenault's Hamburger Bar in the Lower Town, wouldn't we, B.W.?"

Just then Guinevere appeared, accompanied by none other than Mr. Slatter, the official I'd met in the PM's residence in Ottawa. "Oh, it's you," he said, without much enthusiasm.

Guinevere, with her slashing eyes and headmistress voice, soon had the situation sorted out. She had the silver-haired gent on his metaphorical knees within seconds. I was quite impressed by her authority. She was obviously a more important member of the Service than I'd thought, or had recently had a promotion. She had also recently taken up smoking. She was puffing now at a cigarette, with quick, nervous, rather amateurish movements, her eyes slitted with determination or cigarette smoke.

I became aware that her companion, Mr. Slatter, was in danger of being struck by a white cane. While his attitude toward Guinevere was one of grovelling respect or outright fear, his behaviour toward my boy was one of pompous condescension. And B.W. was not taking it well. Slatter, whose horn-rimmed spectacles somehow reduced the size of his eyes to those of a recently deceased prawn, was commiserating with B.W. over his misfortune, anointing the lad with the oil of his unction.

"I guess now you'll have to leave the air force," said Mr. Slatter, putting an ever-so-sympathetic hand on B.W.'s arm. "It's such a shame, a fine young fellow like you."

All too obviously, B.W. shook the hand away. "Who are you, anyway?" he asked arrogantly. "Slattern, did you say your name was?"

"I'm with the Government," said Mr. Slatter, "concerned with disabilities, as a matter of fact. I do hope that when you leave the air force they give you a decent pension," he said, in tones suggesting that he anticipated nothing but difficulty in that regard.

"And what d'you mean, leave the air force?" B.W. snarled. "Why should I leave it? I can still . . ." He gestured angrily.

"Of course you can, my dear fellow, of course you'll still be of some use," Mr. Slatter protested, his voice wheezing with sincerity, though his face had gone red with anger over the young man's ungrateful tone. "But you know, just in case, eh?"

Guinevere, who was quite glad to see B.W. in trouble with the authorities, waited a few moments to see if anything further developed. When it didn't she turned to me. "By the way," she said, pointing into the dining room with her cigarette, "you'll find a friend of yours in there."

"Oh? Is Winston dining here tonight?"

She gave me an unamused look and turned away to speak to a security man to let us through.

We entered the dining room. Every eye turned upon us, and there was a hush. Then every eye turned away, and there was a noise.

Churchill was not dining there that night, it seemed. But someone else was.

"Oh, Christ."

"Father," B.W. said severely, "I've told you before about taking the Lord's name in vain."

"He's not a Lord, he's only a Sir."

"Huh?"

"It's bloody Drummond," I said, clicking my tongue in dismay, gazing across the room at Sir Amyas Bloody Drummond. He was tearing with bulging eyes and sweating brow at a steak that wasn't quite as wide as its platter.

His wife was with him. She was eating bananas.

"What's he doing here?" I muttered; though it was easy enough to guess what his duties were at the conference. As on Salisbury Plain, he was ensuring that everything was hunky-dory for his beloved master; or, in other words, he was seizing the opportunity to get away from the wartime austerity.

He had seen me. I nodded, and just barely restrained myself from employing a regal wave, of the kind suggesting that there was an invisible pooch suspended in the air, and one was engaged in stroking its belly. Drummond continued to stare, his face working; filled, I supposed, with passion or sirloin steak.

Finally, having drilled enough holes for the time being, he turned away, and murmured something to his wife. Abruptly he gestured at me – a summons, though, rather than an access of vulgarity.

So having settled B.W. at a table, I walked over, wearing the most perfect Swiss-neutral expression available. With every step I took I reminded myself that I should behave circumspectly, that my days of tangling with VIPs were over. Such confrontations invariably ended in disaster, sometimes for the VIP, but too often for me as well. Well, that had to stop. I was a mature man. I had reformed. I was a dignified, middle-aged officer and gentleman. The frivolities and retaliations were behind me for ever.

Mind you, my tolerance was quickly tested; for though Sir Amyas had invited me to his table, he continued to talk to his wife for quite a while. They were discussing a party they were giving. It was to take place in their hotel suite. The guest list would be very select. Only the most influential and a few choice officials would be invited. They continued to discuss the arrangements for quite a while before finally acknowledging that I was standing by their table, ready to take their orders.

But then to my surprise, Drummond was quite civilized. He seemed to be indicating that he was willing to forgive and forget. He even introduced me to his wife, between bananas.

"How do you dare?" she said, offering me a fish; unless it was her spare icy hand.

"We've had our differences in the past, Bandy, but I hope that's all over now," the Minister said, with a smile that revealed several square feet of yellowing but nevertheless authentic fangs.

After being left standing there for so long, the old me reared its ugly head, and I very nearly responded, as I had responded far too often in the past, with some witless and unnecessarily contumacious comment like, "Golly, Sir Amyas, I never knew they made false teeth in that colour, they look quite authentic." Instead I bowed like the head waiter at the Royal Transport Caff, and replied that I couldn't agree more. "I'm all for letting bygones be sleeping dogs," I simpered.

Meanwhile Lady Drummond, who reminded me of Gwinny's nanny, had been studying me from my boots to my beautifully mantled summit. She interrupted her husband. "Amyas," she asked, "is this gentleman the one you warned me might spread scandalous lies about you?"

"He proved rather more of a gentleman than I expected, dear," Amyas replied, exposing several standby teeth.

His reassurance did not seem to have made much difference to her attitude. "I shouldn't think a gentleman would take such drugs in the first place," she said coldly.

Good Lord, what had he been telling her about me, that I was a drug addict?

"I'm really surprised, Amyas," she continued in what she

probably considered to be an undertone, "that you should insist against all advice on having him at the conference."

"Be quiet," Sir Amyas said, with such ferocity that his wife physically recoiled. And to me he said curtly, "I'm glad we've had this little talk, Bandy. Thank you for coming over." And with a glint in his eyes, he added, "you may return to your handsome young male companion."

"Thank you, sir," I slavered, and was halfway back to our table when it struck me that he had done it again – made a remark that he could built on if necessary, to counter any accusations I might make about his sexual preferences.

I felt my face growing hot with fury at the thought that he had taken me for a homo. Why the hell hadn't I riposted wittily with, "Yes, you must meet my son some time." But it was too late now, I was at the foot of the staircase, as the French say – in French, of course.

It was in her bedroom the following morning that Guinevere told me what my duties were to be. We had disentangled ourselves from the bedclothes and had nearly finished dressing when she spoke up.

I couldn't believe it. "In charge of a wastebasket?" I asked.

"That's right."

"Officer Commanding a bucket of rubbish?"

"It's a very important job, Bartholomew."

"Important job? A wing commander put in charge of waste paper? Not toilet paper by any chance, is it?"

"There's no need to be vulgar, Bartholomew. I thought long and hard before giving you this job."

"Oh, yes, and what were the alternatives? Oiling Roosevelt's wheelchair? Lighting Winston's cigars? Scraping rust off HMS *Repulsive?*"

"Don't be so silly."

"Well, that's great," I said. "I was the fall guy for Lloyd George in the First World War, demoted and sent to a bicycle brigade, abandoned in Russia by the Allies, tricked into giving up my seat in Parliament by our own Prime Minister, accused of treason by the Viceroy of India – and to round it all off, now I've been given the job of emptying wastepaper baskets. That's just great. Now I really feel my life is complete."

"I'll discuss your duties when you're in a better frame of mind," Guinevere said, snapping her garters.

"And after I've emptied it, should I go around polishing a few boots, or scraping the Secret Servicemen's chewing gum from under the tables?"

She came flouncing across. "You know, it was Drummond's idea to give you this job, not mine. I'd've preferred to give it to someone more reliable."

I was so distracted that I failed to follow up the implications of what she had just said. I was determined that for once I wasn't going to let her have the last word. With my usual lightning wit, I yelled, "So I'm incompetent now, am I?"

She stood there like a defensive lineman for the Ottawa Roughriders, flushed and furiously scratching her eyebrows. To make herself more attractive she had tried to pluck them, so now they looked like old boot brushes with missing bristles. "You said it, not me – and I agree," she hollered. "You're unreliable, because you're so beastly odd, and unconventional, and – "

"Unconventional? How dare you?!"

"And you don't seem able to do anything the way a normal person would do it."

"Look who's talking – someone who likes tying people to bedposts!"

"That was a mean, low blow, Bartholomew!" she cried. "That was private business between us – not something to be mentioned in your rotten memoirs! I know you're taking notes, I've seen them! You're nothing but a cad, that's what you are!" And with a sob, she turned and ran out.

A moment later she was back. "What am I doing – this is *my* room," she cried. "You're the one who's supposed to get out!"

As it turned out, the job was not as lowly as it had first seemed. For one thing, it took me close to the leaders themselves, as they discussed the momentous concerns of World War Two.

No, honest, it was actually a vital job. At the end of each meeting I was in sole charge of collecting all the scraps as well as the wastepaper basket and ensuring that the contents were promptly incinerated. It was my job to ensure the disposal of every note, memo, scribble, every word or date or recorded number, every casual sketch or amateurish drawing (and I can report that Roosevelt did some amusing doodles of Stalin) that might even remotely be of use to a garbage-rummaging enemy.

An additional responsibility was the placing of the yellow scrap pads on the conference table before every top-level session; though that, of course, was not a task restricted to people of my ability, but could have been done by anybody with an honours degree.

The job also enabled me to meet Winston at last.

Though the two leaders were lodged at the nearby Citadel, they were holding their meetings at the Frontenac, and that's where I finally met my old friend again.

I met the President, too. He gave me a really nice smile the first time we passed within a few feet of each other. He had already been wheeled into the closely guarded conference room when Churchill arrived one protocol minute later, dictating on the hoof to a frantically scribbling male secretary, and laying wreaths of Cuban tobacco smoke on the graves of non-smokers as he passed.

At the threshold of the conference room he paused, turned, and looked at me again, and said, "I never forget a face. Who are you?"

"Don't you remember, sir?" quoth I, archly. I took a deep breath. "We first met – "

"No, don't tell me – my mind is already cluttered with detail. But I expect you'd appreciate having my signed photograph?" he asked. And before I could answer he snapped his fingers, and another member of his entourage brought out a framed and autographed photograph of the great man and thrust it into my hands.

Mr. Churchill did not actually hand me his autographed photo personally. Nevertheless, the gift struck me as an extraordinary tribute to our friendship. That he should have remembered my modest contribution to his career to the extent that he would personally ensure that I received his picture complete with his very own autograph – well, it left quite a lump in my throat, it really did.

My vital contribution to the war effort also brought me into contact with our very own Prime Minister. Again it was a perambulatory convergence; he was taking his Scotch terrier for a walk along the Dufferin Terrace. We had clashed so often in the past that despite the fidgety *rapprochement* in the Ottawa snow, I expected him to wince as usual. Instead, he actually stopped to talk. His dog stopped as well.

"Ah, Bandy," said William Lyon Mackenzie King in his colourless voice, taking in the glorious view of the St. Lawrence River, while Pat contributed a tributary. "How are you getting on?"

Now I knew why he was being sociable. He wanted something. A moment later I learned what it was. Next time I was in Europe I was to collect a bombed building or two and have them shipped to his garden of ruins up at Kingsmere.

"You understand the sort of thing I want," he said in almost wheedling tones. He even reached out a hand to touch me, though, recollecting some of our previous encounters, he retracted it pretty quickly. "Any sort of ruined material that can be mortared together in my garden to make a wall, or part of a window, or an entranceway. You know the sort of thing?"

I knew the sort of thing: stonework rubble with little historical and no architectural merit whatsoever. But what the hell, every man ought to have a hobby, even a prime minister. And, as it turned out, I did manage to get him a pillar or two and half a dome, and arranged for shipment by an export packer; and, faithful to his instructions, I ensured that the cost was debited to the Canadian government. Unfortunately the whole lot was torpedoed and went straight to the bottom – no doubt to the glee of a U-boat skipper who thought he had seriously damaged the Canadian war effort.

Looking a Bit Hung-over

WHEN I WALKED UP to our hotel room that stiflingly hot August evening, I found B.W. in a blackish mood. It was his day for dreading the future. So he was thinking of facing the past with quiet confidence, and going back to Grandpa and Grandma in California.

I was pretty shagged-out after my important work at the Quebec Conference downstairs, and wanted only to change out of my sweaty uniform and to embalm myself in spirituous liquors. Nevertheless I endeavoured to chaff him out of the Chaffingtons. "That's a good idea," I said, peeling off my blue shirt. Peeling was the right word. It separated from moist skin with a dreadful rasping sound. "I was thinking of throwing you out anyway, and getting a dog."

"At least they got money," he muttered.

"Dogs?"

"Chaffingtons. Which is more than you got."

"That's true."

"What did you do all with your money, anyway?" he asked peevishly. "I thought you came back from India with a shipload of loot."

"I did. Rich as a tea biscuit, I was."

"So where is it? Where's my cut?"

"Lost it all, B.W. Crash of '29."

"Huh. As if having a janitor for a father isn't bad enough, now I find you don't got no money to keep me in the style to which I am accustomed to being in."

"By the way, B.W.," I said confidentially.

"What?"

"I think I'm being watched."

"Watched?"

"Watched. Tailed. Somebody's following me."

"All you do is empty wastebaskets. Who'd be interested in watching that? Anyway, it's me we're talking about. The point is, if I gotta be blind I might as well be it in luxury."

"But B.W.," I said, "I'm counting on you to regain your sight one day, so you can support me in my dotage."

"You've already reached it." He patted his sweating face with a towel. "I mean, why shouldn't I go de luxe?" he said. "I'm no good for anything else. I wasn't even a great pilot, like you."

"Oh, belt up with the self-pity, B.W.," I said, losing patience at last.

"Self-pity? Is that how it seems to you?" he whined.

"Yeah, that's how it seems to me. So snap out of it, or I'll start putting whisky in your Ovaltine. Now I'm going down for a shower, shave, shampoo, and poopoo, okay? I'm hot and tired."

"Yeah, I guess you must be plum-tuckered, after your onerous duties emptying wastebaskets all day," B.W. snapped; and a sweaty silence, as hot and damp as the room, settled between us.

It lasted until I'd returned from the bathroom two floors down. As soon as I walked into the room he said, "What d'you mean, you're being watched?"

"Somebody's following me, I'm sure of it."

"You're imagining it," he said. "You're cracking up, Father. What's that Freudian word when people think they're being persecuted? Para — paracrap something."

"Paracrap? No, I don't think that's one of Freud's half-dozen technical terms. Though it ought to be."

"Anyway, no doubt about it, you're cracking up, Dad," B.W. said cheerfully.

I remained convinced that I was under observation. But by whom, or which? The trouble was, it could be any number of

different security organizations that hadn't yet been informed by
MI5 that I was not a Red in, or under, the bed. Assuming that even
MI5 knew it. This was by no means certain. Efficient communication was not highly regarded in the spy business. Probably they'd
accidentally masticated the message confirming that I was a thoroughly decent and trustworthy sort before they'd even distributed
it around the various departments.

And by gad I was right. The very next afternoon when all the
elevators were busy, I started to trudge up the stairway. And became
aware that somebody was following me.

By leaning dangerously over a banister I managed to catch a
glimpse of him. It was none other than Sam Spade – or someone
who was modelling himself on Dashiel Hammett's downbeat hero.
My shadow even came complete with a trench coat – in midsum-
mer, yet – the collar turned up to expose a pair of regulation eyes,
weary and sardonic.

I turned, and started down the stairs toward him on tiptoe,
intending to surprise him; but he was too quick. He turned and
raced down the stairs ahead of me, and though he tripped over his
coat a couple of times, he was fleeter of foot, or gumshoe. Though
I might still have caught him, had I not run into a glower of waiters
on their way into Sir Amyas Drummond's suite.

The waiters, several thousand of them, were wheeling or carrying all sorts of foodstuffs into the Drummond suite, which was two
floors below my garret. Presumably the gastronomic camel train was
in preparation for Lady Drummond's party. The victuals included
trays of hors d'oeuvres, jars of pâté, meats, and sweetmeats, and
sweetbreads and breads of different makes, and jellies and French
goat cheeses matured in donkey dung, aspects of aspics, crab resting
on beds of marjoram and creamed with a preparation of fenugreek
seed mixed with antelope semen, vanilla beans, cassia buds basted
in crankcase oil heated and refined over a cedar-wood fire, and
monosodium glutamate. I believe there was also an acknowledge-
ment of Canadian cuisine in the form of sirloin of beaver and
roasted marmot.

By the time I had manoeuvred past the waiters, pinching things to eat en route, the spy was too far ahead to catch up with.

I should have guessed who was employing him. I should have known who was closing in on us. But I didn't, with dreadful consequences.

That night, as a relief from the strain and tension of my responsibilities, I went on a toot with a chap I met in a bar, a former bush pilot named Cuthbert. The lucky devil had a job ferrying Hudsons across the Atlantic.

B.W., of course, being a teetotaller, refused to accompany us. "No, you go on your bender, don't mind me," he said. "I'll be quite happy up here alone under the roof. I won't mind having nobody to talk to. Hey, I insist you go out and enjoy yourself, Father, I'll be safe enough cooped up in this tower – "

"Like the Lady of Shalott?" I put in.

"With no friends and nothing to do," he persisted, "I'm hardly likely to get into trouble, am I?"

"I'm glad you feel that way, son," I said. "I wouldn't want you to feel neglected."

For a moment the parentheses of a grin enclosed his wide, thin mouth, though his snarl was as snarly as ever when he snarled, "Go on if you're going. Don't matter about me."

"*Doesn't* matter about you."

"So you admit it at last."

I had a good time that evening with Cuthbert. We visited a representative sample of the ghastly beer halls and utilitarian taverns of the sort that dotted Canada from coast to coast. 'Twas so enjoyable an evening that, upon arriving home, it took me eleven minutes to make the journey from the door of our cramped room to my bed on the far side near the balcony door.

I was anxious not to wake B.W. Normally he did not sleep at all well. When he did he was likely to convulse into consciousness, flailing and frightened. Not immediately recollecting that he was sightless, he would be terrified of the totality of dark. The poor devil had been afraid of the dark even before he was shocked blind.

"So what on earth were you doing in night-fighters?" I asked him once.

"The night isn't dark," he said darkly.

Anyway, this evening, after my night out, I was at pains not to waken him, not least because he hated to smell alcohol on my breath. On this occasion it was beer. Tankfuls of it, my bush pilot pal having an infinite capacity for taking Pains. Pain's Lager, that is. Or maybe it was Payne's – how the hell should I know.

It was a warm evening, as befitted an August night. I could tell it was warm because I kept saying, "Pffff," or, occasionally, "Foooo." I didn't know what time it was, but it could not have been late for I could hear a babble of talk from the balcony below ours. That would be the Drummonds and their friends. Some of their guests must be chatting out there in the Pffff or Foooo heat. Not that I was prepared to step out onto the balcony and confirm it. I had only one goal in life – to reach my beddy-byes.

I finally made it. Before collapsing onto the mattress, I gazed blearily at my son. There was enough light from the balcony to see his face. It looked quite beautiful in repose, and affectingly inno-cent. I leaned over and gave him a kiss, nearly overbalancing onto him in the process.

Whack! My head hit the pillow. The bed immediately took off and climbed at full boost. Fortunately I was in a backward-facing seat, as recommended by the safety-conscious. They said it was safer to face backward in an aircraft because it was safer. Unless, of course, you were the pilot. Facing backward in the cockpit would not be too safe. But what the hell, I wasn't at the controls tonight.

"Pffff," I said.

Unfortunately the ship was flying sideways as well. I sat up again. The bed pulled itself together and flew straight and level. I lay back again. The bed did a hammerhead turn, and headed straight down for several thousand feet.

I must have fallen asleep, because the next thing I knew B.W. was saying, "Shut up! Will you shut up! For crying out loud!"

"What? What?"

"You're in bed two lousy minutes you're already making like a lumber mill."

"In bed two minutes? Two hours, you mean."

"No. Two hours was the time you took tiptoeing across the room – hitting the walls all the way."

"Oh."

"You're back early. Run out of booze, did they?"

"Know something, B.W.?"

"What?"

"Know something? I'm very proud of the way your Grandma and your voclab – vlocaberry – vo-cab-u-larry – are improving every day. That's good, B.W. Everyone should have Grandma and a vocabularrry."

"For God's sake stop breathing – you're stinking the place up with beer."

"Don't go back to them, B.W. I really need you."

"Oh, sure," B.W. said. But then added, "Anyway, after the bust up I had with him, maybe Grandad don't want me back."

"*Doesn't* want you back."

"Right. I ever tell you how Grandad tried to stop me learning to fly?"

"No?"

"He bought up the flying school, and ordered them to tell me I would never be any good."

"Tha's Chaffington, arright."

"They were right, though. I wasn't any good. Don't know why I took it up in the first place. Maybe because I thought it might've pleased Mom, if she'd still been around . . ."

I'm ashamed to say I fell asleep in the middle of his true-life confessions. And slept until B.W. woke me with a series of snores of his own. By which time I was desperate for a pee.

I had been unhappily aware of the need even before I got into bed, but had hoped that the summer weather would somehow evaporate it. Instead it grew more insistent.

The thought of going down two whole floors to find a working toilet was unbearable. On the return journey I would have to tiptoe across the room all over again. By the time I reached the bed I'd need another pee. I had a brainwave. There was a much easier way. After all, by the time it reached the Lower Town, it would be no more than a Scotch mist.

So I went out onto the balcony. There was a warm and gentle breeze blowing across the face of the hotel. It was lovely out there, soft and cool and almost bright as day.

In the brilliant moonlight I did it safely over the edge. Oh, the exquisite pleasure of relief! A prolonged relief, for it seemed to take parsecs of interstellar dawdling to drain the old gravity tank.

Finally I was all done. Smiling all over my face, and even beyond, suffused with warm feelings for humanity, I turned to make my way back to bed. And became woozily aware of cries of various pitches emanating from the night.

I think they'd been going on for quite a while, but so intense was the satisfaction of a job well done that the sounds had not registered until this moment. They seemed to be coming from below. Cautiously I leaned over the metal railing – a lovely railing it was, too, a patriotic affair of intertwined fleurs-de-lys with some very sharp points among them. (I had been very careful of those sharp points whilst engaged in number ones, I can tell you.)

Gripping the rail with knuckles that gleamed phosphorescent in the moonlight – did I mention there was a moon? – I peered over the edge, and soon observed several people cowering back from the edge of the balcony that protruded from the hotel wall quite a few feet below and off to one side.

As I peered down, they were peering up. Whereupon a renewed outcry ensued, and there was much shaking of fists, and some ejaculations. I straightened up and stared out at the night sky, thinking. Then I looked over the edge again. And gradually it dawned on me what had happened.

"Oh, dear."

"What is it?" B.W. called, from the bedroom.

Now the sounds out of the night were being echoed inside the hotel. People were pounding up the stairs. I stood blinking for a moment, then in sudden panic I reeled toward the door. But before I could lock it, Sir Amyas Drummond, followed by his wife and two or three or more guests, burst into the room.

"Oh, hullo," I said, standing there in my guilty jammies, which, I'm ashamed to confess, had a patch of moisture somewhere in the vicinity of the pyjama cord, presumably the result of the warm crosswind or an inefficient ranging operation.

With this evidence staring them in the face, as it were, they started yelling at me, and continued to do so at length, which gave me plenty of time to absorb the fact that many of them were even moister than my damp patch.

For the sake of decorum I will not repeat the vulgar accusations that were bandied about that night. Suffice it to say, as I stood there blinking in the light from the ceiling fixture, that they were most eloquent in describing my habits and ancestry in terms more befitting a meeting of the Socratic Society, well known for its heated and irrational debates, than was appropriate in a civilized environment such as the Château Frontenac. And they concluded on a very unpleasant note indeed, with Sir Amyas pointing to the young man lying wide-eyed in one of the beds, and shouting, "You see? You see what sort of a perverted lowlife vulgarian obscenity we're dealing with? Entertaining young men in his bedroom! There now, you're witness to this," he shouted, turning to the guests who were crowded, steaming, in the doorway. "You see what sort of a decadent human being we're dealing with?"

To which B.W., sitting up in bed, replied, "I don't know who you are, sir, but you're certainly right about one thing, sir. My father — where are you, Dad?"

"Over here."

"Whoever you are, sir, you're right about my father entertaining young men. I'm often quite entertained by him. Dad can be pretty amusing, sometimes, especially when he isn't trying. I guess that's what you meant, is it, sir, about entertaining young men?"

There was rather an awful silence.

"It's his son — that blind boy," whispered one of the guests.

Drummond opened his mouth. Then clopped it shut again, his

face a fiery red above his dinner jacket. Mustering as much dignity as he could about him, he proceeded to mumble, sweat, and moisten his way out of the room.

I was glad of the diversion from my own embarrassment, but in a craven sort of way I felt no satisfaction over Drummond's discomfiture. I had an idea it would make him all the more dangerous; and, being the sort of person I am – accommodating, placatory, and conciliatory to a fault – I was disturbed about that. After all, as everyone knows, I was the sort of person who wanted only a quiet life without strife and conflict, and a pension or two at the end of it.

It was not to be.

"Something strange happened today," I whispered to B.W. when I returned from work the following day.

"Delirium tremens, was it?"

"No, it wasn't that. But don't remind me," I said, putting my hands to my head to see if the sections of cranium that were supposed to be interlocked had finally knitted together after exploding the previous night.

Not quite. But at least my eyes had slowed down a bit.

B.W. felt his way to the balcony door, and fumbled for the catch. A hot wind blew into the room as he stepped out, extending his hands until they came safely in contact with the railing. He gripped the rail confidently, and leaned forward slightly, as if to get a feel of the space ahead and the void below.

Still holding my head together, I moaned.

"Serve you right," B.W. said.

"I haven't had a head like this since Iceland."

"Why Iceland?"

"They're very hospitable there," I said, without further explanation.

"So what strange thing happened today?"

"H'm? Oh, yes. Well, as you know, I wasn't exactly sparkling this morning. God, my stomach can't take quantities of beer like that. Vodka, yes. Scotch, sure. And rye, gin, rum, meths, hair tonic, cleaning fluid, absinthe, yes; but beer ... Anyway, I started work but I had to rush off to the washroom. A fellow can take only so much beer, and my body had taken it. Anyway, I dashed into the nearest cubicle, and groaned in there quite realistically for a while, until I heard somebody come in."

As I told B.W., the newcomer had seemed far too quiet. No clearings of the throat, no belching from either end of the alimentary canal, no hydraulic tumult at a urinal – none of the sound effects associated with a visit to the toilet. So though my head felt too big even to stick down the toilet, I was just curious enough to stick it through the doorway, and saw Drummond.

He was standing with his back to me, not at the urinals, but in front of the washbasins. I could see him in the mirror. He was busy removing a new handkerchief from its cellophane packet.

"Boy, this is dramatic stuff," B.W. said. "Sir Amyas Drummond, about to blow his nose."

Ignoring this, I went on to describe how I had seen Drummond use the handkerchief to remove, very carefully, a sheet of yellow paper from his breast pocket. Presumably the sheet had been torn from one of the foolscap-sized pads I placed around the conference tables so that the various officials and advisers could make notes or doodle to their hearts' content.

"Then as fast as he could, using the handkerchief, he placed the scrap paper in an envelope, and put it away."

"Gee whiz," B.W. said drily, "my heart's thumping like a jack rabbit with the sheer drama of it all."

"Look here, I'm getting pretty damn tired of your wisecracks," I snapped. "Shaddup and listen."

"Yes sir, yes sir," he said, producing an exaggerated salute, if it was possible to exaggerate a quivering, British-type salute.

Losing patience with him had made my head ache again. Rather more quietly, I went on, "The point is, it was the surreptitious way he did it. Kept glancing around, as if fearful that somebody might come in and see him."

In a rather more subdued tone, B.W. leaned against the balcony railing and asked, "You think he'd swiped some stuff from the conference?"

"Eh? I don't know. Anyway, there's nothing to stop any of the officials, advisers, and so on, from taking their own notes away with them, provided they keep them secure. Drummond wouldn't need to swipe anything confidential, he could just collect it and stick it in his briefcase."

"I still don't see what you're getting at," B.W. said.

"Actually, neither do I," I said. "Especially as the paper he was handling so carefully was blank."

"Blank?" said B.W. blankly.

"Yes, blank. Nothing on it whatsoever. I could see it clearly in the mirror," I said, just as someone knocked at the bedroom door.

It was not a loud knock, and out on the balcony, B.W. could not have heard it. I went to the door, hoping it was not another bunch of damp party-goers. I opened the door. And there stood Mrs. Chaffington.

I hadn't seen her for twenty years but she was sufficiently well-preserved as to be instantly recognizable, as superbly dressed as she had always been, thin and stylish, with not a follicle out of place. Behind her stood Sam Spade. So now I knew who had been checking on me, and why: to zero in on Flying Officer Bandy.

At first, Mrs. Chaffington did not see him, and as she was still looking at me, her subtly painted face remained as cold and unforgiving as it had always been.

Until she saw B.W. across the room, out on the balcony. Whereupon she let out a screech of joy, and rushed past in clouds of perfume, crying, "Wendell, sweetheart! Oh, Wendell – it's Grandma – we've found you at last!"

And B.W. started violently, whirled, lurched, overbalanced, and fell off the balcony.

Wire Service Photo,
Aug. 20, 1943

MRS. CHAFFINGTON WAS NOT the pleasantest of women, at least not on the few occasions that I had met her. In some ways she reminded me of the marquis de Sade's mother-in-law. Heaven knows, I would not wish to make excuses for the dreaded marquis, and would certainly not wish to make any other comparisons between de Sade and moi. But Mrs. Chaffington's implacable hostility was, in my opinion, very like that of Madame de Montreuil. The mother of de Sade's wife, Madame de Montreuil had welcomed de Sade into her wealthy but socially inferior family, and at first supported him and helped to hush up the trollops who were accusing him of some very peculiar practices; but as his peccadilloes, like making cuts into the buttocks of harlots and pouring melted wax into the incisions, became better known, she turned against him and interceded with the King to have him put away. The King's lettre de cachet could and did keep de Sade in prison without the tiresome need for a sentence being passed by a court. This spared Madame all sorts of distasteful publicity. She continued to spare herself in this fashion, keeping de Sade under atrocious conditions for years and years, ensuring with ruthless implacability that the marquis was a physical wreck by the time he emerged again into the light of day. He did, actually, as one of the few aristocrats ironically saved by the French Revolution.

All the same, I certainly wouldn't have wished the fright and anguish on her – Mrs. Chaffington, that is – which she quite plainly felt at seeing her grandson plunge to his death. Her screams were quite a contrast to the dissonance of that first acquisitive screech when she burst into the room. When B.W. disappeared into the void, she stood, petrified with horror, staring out at the balcony, her hands embedded in her face. A finger, the little finger of one hand, must have found its way into her mouth and she must have bitten it, for later she would need medical attention to deal with the bite.

As for me, no thoughts of any kind flitted about my skull. My head cleared for the first time that day. I sped across the room, and through the heavy iron-and-glass door onto the balcony, to find that B.W. was still alive. He was hanging in space. Somehow, astoundingly, he had managed to grab part of the stone support below the balcony — though even as I looked over the edge, his hands were losing their grip.

Climbing over the iron railing, I hunkered down, holding onto the top rail by one hand, reaching, stretching, reaching. But he was far out of reach. There was only one alternative: I would have to hang head down and get to him by that means. The decision — no, not a decision, but an act without thought — was hastened, if the distance from one split second to another can be hastened, by the fact that his hands were slowly sliding down the stonework.

Holding backwards onto the railing with both hands, I jammed first one foot and leg through the ornamental work, and then the other. Thus secured — I hoped — I scrabbled down in two frantic seconds, letting go of the railing at the last moment. So now I was hanging upside down by my knees. From this position his hands were now easily within reach.

I had inverted myself only just in time, for as I grabbed hold of one wrist, the strength in his fingers failed. One hand slid entirely off the rough granite.

So I had hold of him by one wrist as he swung wildly over the frightful space. The lurching view below, of boardwalk, old town, vegetation, silver river, seemed thousands of feet down, though it was only scores of feet to the lacerating rock. The view also included B.W.'s face upturned. His mouth was agape and gasping with a terror made all the worse by his sightlessness.

In toppling, he must have struck his nose. It was bleeding. The drops of blood were collecting at his nostrils before being plucked off by the hot wind.

Above, Mrs. Chaffington's private detective was at the railing, shouting incoherently. He was obviously not the sort of person to think sensibly in an emergency. What he decided to do was see whether any help could be arranged from below, from the Drummond balcony, perhaps, though how he thought that could be accomplished I don't know, given that the Drummond balcony was off to one side. He never did elucidate his decisions, or lack of them, but Sam Spade would not have been proud of him.

As for me, my batlike posture was sensible enough in the circumstances. The idea of letting go of the railing so that I could reach B.W. had been the right move. A second's delay would have been fatal. But it was hardly a secure arrangement. One of my legs had already slipped out of the ornamental ironwork, so that I was now suspended by one leg. And even that was losing its hold.

I could feel my leg being dragged painfully through the iron curlicues under the combined weight of two swinging bodies. At the same time I was shouting at B.W. to give me his other hand. I was still gripping him by only one wrist. But he seemed incapable of understanding anything except the void beneath. His free hand was swinging limply.

He was extraordinarily heavy. I could certainly feel it in my shoulder joint. But having my arm wrenched out of its socket was the least of my concerns. My leg was the problem. It was slowly dragging through the ornamental railing.

I looked back up at the railing with the help of quivering neck muscles, hoping that someone would produce an inspired idea. Faces were staring down at me in horror and empathetic anguish, but the sight hardly registered. All I cared about was my grinding leg and the skin that was being peeled off by the fleurs-de-lys ornamentation. I was being skinned despite the protection of blue serge trousers, woollen socks, and stout shoes.

Trying not to kick too wildly so as not to speed up the process of being dislodged, I tried to get my other leg into position to help its mate by jamming it, too, through the railing. It was hopeless. Because of the way I was hanging, my free leg was splayed out sideways, well below the edge of the balcony. Even if I had dared to, no amount of twisting, turning, and kicking could possibly have hooked it into place.

The captured leg continued to slip inch by inch. I reckoned that I had about half a minute to save two swinging bodies from agreeing to obey the law of gravity.

However, help was at hand. At first I thought that the air-force blue material would protect the skin and bone, but the sharp point of one of the fleurs-de-lys was starting to dig into my calf muscle. All too soon, it punctured. It was starting to embed, deep into the muscle. And every pound of our combined weights drove the point deeper.

It hurt. And it hurt more and more with every pendulum swing of our bodies. I suppose I should have been grateful for the spiky ornamentation, for it had now halted the slipping of the leg through the balcony railing, but I was not grateful. All I could feel was . . . well, there was no point in acting the strong, silent, stiff-upper-lip type. Nobody could think the worse of me for hollering. So I hollered.

I hollered. I yelled. I screamed. I was not grateful at all that we were now hooked firmly and safely in place, for the pain blotted out all other considerations, even the desire to live.

Later, reading a history of surgery, I came across a passage describing what it was like to be operated on without anaesthesia. I knew a little of how the patient, Professor Wilson, felt, as his leg was amputated, as he described ". . . the black whirlwind of emotion, the horror of great darkness, and the sense of desertion by God and man, bordering close on despair, which swept through my mind and overwhelmed my heart."

The annoying thing was that help was so long in coming, though there were plenty of people on the balcony up there. They were all either stupidly staring, or shouting encouragingly – to each other. And so the spike had gone deep into my leg by the time the committee decided that the only way to free me was to use a hacksaw on the offending fleur-de-lys. I wouldn't have been surprised if they had forgotten to secure the two swinging bodies before they started sawing. Even then, the best they could manage was to fish for B.W. with looped cords so as to haul him like a fish out of space, bending him upward until he could be gaspingly landed. They didn't seem to care about the additional strain on my hand and shoulder while they were doing this, oh, no. Not that the pain in the shoulder was worth considering, not when there was a sharp iron point being driven ever deeper into the calf muscle by the rescue operation.

It even took them a while to find a hacksaw. They kept bringing the wrong type. "It had to be one that could be inserted through the ornamental work, you see," they explained later, though in a patient and kindly fashion. "They kept bringing the kind of hacksaws that you couldn't work into place, you see," they explained in a patient and kindly way to glowering, muttering, hateful-faced me.

In the hospital grounds

"THERE'S BEEN A GREAT deal of damage to your leg, you know," said the surgeon. He was looking at me as if I had done it on purpose.

"It feels like it, Doctor."

"Treating the gastroenemius and lateral soleus – or as we doctors call them, the calf muscles – treating them in this way is quite unforgivable."

"I'm sorry."

"It is fortunate that the hospital just happened to have a sample of Dr. Fleming's new remedy, penicillin. We were scheduled to demonstrate its remarkable powers before a medical body in Philadelphia. However, the extremely high risk of a lethal infection from your socks prompted its use. Mind you, the medical body will be profoundly disappointed at this premature demonstration. But we took the decision after due deliberation."

"I'm glad you did, Doc," I said.

"All that black paint," he said. "Not to mention your dirty trousers being carried into the wound."

"Are you saying I was wearing dirty pants?"

"All trousers are dirty if they have not been sterilized," he said severely.

He then went on to describe in further detail the awful damage that had been done to my lower extremity.

I kept protesting. "Please, Doctor, I know all this – I was a medical student myself at one time."

"At which school?"

"Toronto."

He sniffed. "Anyway, the point is you will never walk again, Wing Commander."

"I won't?"

"If you do it will be with a permanent limp."

"Oh."

"You will need crutches for the rest of your life."

"Oh, no," said B.W.

"Or a very sound walking stick, for a few weeks at least."

"A few weeks? But I have a job to do," I protested.

"No need to worry about the job, Dad," said B.W., after the surgeon had departed. "The conference ends in a couple of days."

"Good Lord, how long have I been out?"

"Out where?"

"Unconscious?"

"Oh, just a day. Dad?"

"What?"

"Nothing. The nurses say you were in a lot of pain."

"Yes, but I bore it with fortitude."

"That's true – they said you bored them with fortitude. Say, there's one nurse I like the sound of. I was hoping that when I heard her voice again you'd describe her for me."

"Sure."

"But this time," B.W. said, "I want the truth. Not like when you told me the doctor had Bell's palsy, because Bell didn't want it – and a club foot. I listened to him walking, and he certainly wasn't dragging a club foot."

"Did I say club foot? I meant club sandwich. He was dragging a club sandwich."

"Dad?"

"Yes?"

"It must've really hurt."

"M'oh, yes. By the way, how's Mrs. Chaffington?" I asked.

Mrs. Chaffington had ended up in hospital as well, being treated for shock and a bitten finger.

I had thought of visiting her, but upon reflection had decided that she was better off not seeing me until she was feeling stronger.

B.W. sat on the bed; but then got up again and said, gesturing, "Is it okay for me to . . . ?"

"There's a seat just to your left," I wheezed. He wasn't aware that he had sat too close to my leg. Fortunately he couldn't see my bulging eyes.

"Dad?"

"H'm?"

But he remained silent, holding his cane in one hand and caressing the bedclothes with the other.

I knew instinctively what he was trying to say. "No need to thank me," I said, patting his hand.

"Thank you? What for?"

"Why, for saving your life."

"Oh, it was you, was it? Yeah, well, I guess you'd nothing better to do at the time."

"That's true."

After another long silence he said suddenly, "Grandma wants me to go back with her. She has a plane standing by."

"Ah. But you're in the air force."

"I don't think the RCAF would try too hard to get me back."

"Ah. But what about your disability pension?"

"With a billion bucks coming to me I should care?"

"Oh, I see."

"Grandma said if I went back and was sensible, Grandad would reinstate me in his good graces. And I'd be back in his will."

"He had disinherited you, had he?"

"Yes. When I wouldn't quit flying. He seems to hate flyers."

"I wonder why?"

He stood up, though he leaned so heavily on his white stick that it bowed. "So what d'you think I should do?" he asked abruptly, and in a hostile tone.

"Just what I've said all along, B.W.," I said. "It's up to you. It's your life."

He stood there a moment longer; then turned sharply, and stretching his hand out in one direction and poking his stick in another, he tramped off down the long ward.

When I awoke, Guinevere was by the bedside.

With her immediate security job almost at an end you'd have thought she would look a little more relaxed. Instead, she was enquiring about my leg in quite a stilted fashion – very perfunctorily, I thought. Dammit, she should have been showering me with grapes – or better yet, grape juice – properly fermented.

"They told me that if it was absolutely necessary, you could get around on crutches," she said.

"I'm in no hurry to move, Gwinny," quoth I complacently. "I like the rice pudding here."

She turned to a nearby bedpan and addressed it formally. "I have to tell you," she said, "that Sir Amyas Drummond has made some rather serious allegations about you."

"What is it now, I'm an axe murderer?"

"He claims he observed something suspicious in your behaviour."

"Really?"

"He insists on having your room searched."

"What room? You mean the room in the hotel?"

"Yes."

"Oh, hell, now you'll find my book of artistic nudes."

She was evidently not in the mood for my little jokes; which was understandable enough: they were rotten. But after all, I had a good excuse, as I wasn't well.

"I'm sorry to bring it up at such a time, but I'm afraid it won't wait," she said. "The Drummer says he has reason to believe that you've been removing classified information from the conference room."

I sat up, but the movement disturbed my leg, so I lay back again. "That's crazy," I said.

"I know it's not true, Bart," she said, "but he is a Minister. Obviously we have to follow it up.

"The point is, are you well enough to be present – when we search your room?"

B.W. was out when a couple of security men, under Guinevere's supervision, conducted a search of our hotel room as I watched, perched on a pair of crutches. The Parliamentary Under-Secretary was there as well, and soon had cause to make merry.

Nothing in his future would ever exceed the thrill of that moment when they found some conference-room scrap paper. It had not been too cleverly concealed: pinned to the back of the bedside table.

Nothing had been written directly on the paper, which appeared to be part of a scratch pad of the kind I myself had been issuing to the frocks and brass hats. There were indentations in the paper created by a pen or pencil that had pressed words, notes, and scribbles into the previous sheet. The indentations showed up clearly, for someone had brushed a pencil point lightly over the paper to highlight the writing. The words, abbreviations, acronyms, and an idle sketch or two showed up clearly on the yellow paper. One of Guinevere's searchers, an army man, reacted when he saw one of the drawings on the page, a crude representation of a winged dagger. Below the drawing was a single word that the army said would have provided the enemy with a valuable clue, had the paper fallen into their hands.

Nothing else of interest was found in the room, not even a book of nude studies, but it was enough for me. It was obvious that I was a beastly traitor.

The army man and his chum, a squadron leader of the Service Police, who had a habit of making sceptical, percussive sounds such as *Pshaw, Faugh,* and *Fffft,* stood side by side, delicately studying the incriminating sheet, while being careful not to touch it with their fingertips.

Nobody spoke for a while. I looked at Drummond. Drummond looked triumphantly at Guinevere. Guinevere looked dejectedly at her shoes.

Drummond was the first to speak. In calm, reasonable tones and measured phrases, he intimated that he had long suspected me of harbouring treacherous proclivities. He'd had cause to look into my civilian record, my service file, and my security dossier, and all three amply bore out his conviction that I was a thoroughly bad lot, a disloyal subject of His Majesty. My entire career had been one of resistance of those set above me in high office, and often of outright defiance of the law, as when, for instance, I had carried out an illegal and immoral bootlegging operation into the territory of our closest ally, America.

He would not go into detail at this point in the proceedings, he said gravely, not least because my transgressions were so extensive that it could take weeks to elucidate them in a court of law. But in due course he would back up his general allegations with instances of flagrant evasion of the orders of my superiors, which to him, Sir Amyas, suggested at least as much an adherence to anarchist theory as propounded by Kropotkin, as to my services to a foreign power.

Note that Bandy was still sabotaging western democracy, as with his constant submissions to the Air Ministry to the effect that their air policy was beginning to resemble a war of attrition. Worse, he had suggested to his fellow officers and pilots that many of their attacks were not worth risking their lives for –

"That's not true," I said.

"I have written evidence that you did precisely the same thing in the First World War," Drummond said harshly. "Discouraging the men under you from carrying out the orders of what you described as the excessive zeal of the generals."

"There's a certain amount of truth in that," I mused. "I always did try to avoid killing off my men unnecessarily."

Sir Amyas went on as if I had never mused. Plainly reaching the end of his peroration with a dramatic rise in volume, as if already seeing himself on the front benches speaking to a hushed House of Commons, he said that when he happened to mention Bandy's name to Mr. Mackenzie King, the Canadian Prime Minister had needed no urging to credit the possibility, nay, the certainty, that

Bandy had all along been an agent of a foreign power, possibly several of them.

As for Bandy's motive in betraying the Allied cause, he believed he knew what it was. Bandy was known to be paranoid about our glorious ally, the Russians. Drummond suspected that he was in fact working to see Germany win the war in order to avoid the otherwise inevitable triumph of the Soviet Union throughout the world.

That was the reason why I was acting, in effect if not actually in an official capacity, as an agent of the German government. Plenty of proof of that would be forthcoming, not least through Bandy's known contact with a notorious spy, Heinrich Strand, a German national whom I had known and consorted with in India in the 1920s and throughout the 1930s.

"Why, his very appearance is a sham," Drummond cried, very nearly turning to address an invisible Speaker, "a subterfuge, a cover up, making him not what he seems. One instance of that is that he is nearly bald, but conceals the fact, just as he has long concealed his depraved habits and treacherous behaviour, behind a wig, toupee, or the sundry hairpieces in his beaded bag of tricks!"

Later he was heard to express the hope that I would be shot. This was not a completely unlikely eventuality. I understood that a few enemy agents had been disposed of by the British in just such a fashion.

Drummond was quite disappointed when the authorities not only failed to shoot me, but did not even arrest me immediately. However, Gwinny warned me not to stray much further than the hospital grounds to which I now limped back for further treatment.

In due course, the incriminating sheet of paper was tested for fingerprints. Mine were the only prints to be found.

Looking the worse for wear

"HOW DOES IT LOOK?" B.W. asked anxiously. He was standing back from the bed, as the nurse removed the old dressing from the Technicolor production of my leg, which was patterned in vivid hues from ankle to thigh.

"It doesn't look too good," said the surgeon.

"Your leg wouldn't look too good if you'd been fished out of the void by an iron spike," I said testily; then, recollecting the Ottawa art commentary: "out of the androgynous fecundity of the void."

"That doesn't sound very grateful," said the surgeon to the nurse. Turning back to me he snapped, "You should be more grateful. We didn't have to give you the penicillin, you know. We could easily have chosen a rewarding case. There was a man with suppurating testicles in the very same ward as you who would have benefitted from a shot or two." And he turned and walked off in medium-sized dudgeon.

"Our surgeon is still annoyed at having to use up Dr. Fleming's miracle remedy," I said to the nurse, to take my mind off the sight of the wound as she redressed it.

"He has trouble at home," the nurse said. "His daughter has run off with a physician."

B.W. felt his way forward until he ran into the bed. "That's her!" he whispered. "That's the nurse I was talking about. Quick, tell me about her!"

I explained to the nurse that B.W. had liked the sound of her voice, and wanted to know what she looked like.

"Better give him the good news, then," she said brightly.

We looked at each other. She was heavy-featured, middle-aged, and sad.

"She's lovely, B.W.," I said.

The nurse winked, and when she had finished the dressing, walked off with a light tread.

B.W. had gone gloomy again. "Has she gone? She wouldn't be interested in me anyway," he said, feeling around for and sitting on the bedside chair. "I'm not much use to anybody." He rested his chin on the top of his white cane. "Might as well be dead, or back with Grandad."

"You've decided?"

"Well, what else?" he said angrily. "You expect me to give up million of bucks just like that?"

"Well, as I said, B.W."

"Yeah, but you don't goldarn say anything! Why don't you say what you want me to do, for crying out loud!"

"I thought that's what browned you off about Grandad."

"At least I know what he wants. But you, you won't say nothing – anything! You won't argue about Russia, or socialism or anything. You just tell me how they treat people in Russia and get me all confused. Grandma tells me how much they love me but you never say anything – nothin'! You just . . . you just . . ."

His hand encountered a candy bar on the bedside table. Agitatedly he broke off a portion, returning the portion to the table, and started to eat the rest. He looked so smart in his flying officer's uniform, and so unhappy, vulnerable, and confused, that my heart split–arsed.

"B.W.," I said. "If you don't know how I feel about you by now, nothing I say will ever convince you. So cut out the crap, and make up your mind. Do you want me or a billion dollars? I know it's a tough decision, but there you are. Decide."

I was dying to add that if he went back to the Chaffs, they would make sure that he never returned to his dear old dad. But there was no point in telling him what he must already know.

He licked chocolate off his hand, then felt in his trouser pocket for a handkerchief, his fingers splayed so as not to soil his uniform. His temperament was surprisingly mercurial considering he was a product of my loin chops. In a lightning change of mood he leaned over and said warmly, "Hey, I been thinking. This crap about you taking stuff you didn't oughta."

"Yes?"

"It's a mistake, right? I mean, with all those bits of paper you had to deal with, no wonder you brought some of it home by mistake."

"That doesn't sound convincing, B.W."

"Okay," he said promptly, "we'll think of something else. I mean, obviously it was a mistake."

"It was no mistake, B.W. The paper was planted on me."

"Yeah, that's good!" he said excitedly. "That's the line we'll take, right? We'll say you was framed!"

"*Were* framed. Which I were − was."

"Yeah, like I said, it might work."

"B.W., you remember Drummond and the blank sheet of paper? In the washroom, that time?"

"What about it?"

"Why d'you think he handled it so carefully?"

B.W. deliberated for a moment. "The paper was poisoned?" he suggested.

I shifted my leg further away from him. "Anything else you can think of?" I asked.

"He didn't want to soil the paper? I don't know − I'm no good at this kind of thing," he said, making a face.

I felt it was such a simple problem, but it was difficult to concentrate. My leg hurt like billy-oh. "Let's go back a bit," I said. "I'm given the job of handing out the pads of legal-size yellow paper for the big cheeses. And we know now it's shiny enough to take prints."

"Prints?"

"Fingerprints. My fingerprints, B.W."

He stared approximately in my direction.

"Drummond appears in the washroom with a blank sheet of yellow paper. No vulgar remarks, please. Before that, he observes me handling one of the pads. He abstracts the top sheet of the pad. Hey presto, he has my fingerprints."

B.W. rose, his mouth open. "You mean you really were framed?" he said faintly. And: "Yes. That's what it was all about, in the washroom! Making sure he didn't get his own prints on the paper!"

"That's good, B.W."

His excitement faded. He sat on my leg.

"But that's not much help," he said. "You said there wasn't anything written on the paper. Dad? Dad? Why don't you say something?"

"Can't think of anything at the moment."

"Jesus," B.W. said suddenly; and, "Sorry, Lord, didn't mean that. But – Jesus!"

"H'm?"

"No, that can't be it."

"What?"

"No, it's crazy."

"Could you just move a few inches, B.W., while I . . ."

"Oh, sure," he said absently, moving to the edge of the bed, and staring sightlessly at me. "But for it all to make sense, maybe it's Drummond who's the spy."

I lay very still.

"Well, why not?" he went on defensively, taking my silence for scepticism. "If he swiped the paper because it had your prints on it, then he must have transferred the incriminating stuff onto it. And if he did the tracing he must have had the classified stuff to trace – the original." He started to lose confidence. "Or is that screwy?"

"Of course," I said, slowly recovering, "he's not necessarily a spy. He might have taken the material purely in order to frame me. Gwinny said it was he who got me the job in the first place."

I took a deep breath, feeling a lot better in spite of having my leg sat on. "Bartholomew Wendell Bandy, you are a fine, sensitive, intelligent, fairly nice-looking flying officer, whose only fault is this absurd socialist idea that man is altruistic enough to put the good of society ahead of his own selfish interests."

"Well, I still think Lenin and those guys have got it right, and nothing you can say – "

"No, no, I'm not going on about that, B.W. All I wanted to say was, you've got it. That's how Drummond must have done it.

"And all we need to do now," I said, relapsing back into pain and gloom, "is prove that Drummond has the original that he transferred through to my sheet.

"And I can't see there's a hope in hell of proving it," I said, "even assuming he hasn't destroyed the evidence, which could be a pretty stupid assumption."

Just before dawn, after a sleepless night, I fell into a doze and into a nightmare. Once again I was dangling from the hotel balcony at the end of a fishing line. There was nothing but air below, coloured like the sky. I looked down, in spite of a resolve not to look down. I looked down. My brain spun like something mushy in a centrifuge. The walls of the granite cliff swished back and forth at an ever-increasing speed.

In the real situation I had felt little fear, for the actions had been mostly mindless, instinctive, and later the pain had left no room for fear.

I felt it now, gibbering fear, very hard to control. A million thoughts spraying out from a dizzy brain, like, how could I be doing this again, and was it worth doing simply to clear my name and was my name worth clearing, and surely it wasn't worth clearing as it was already so badly regarded by so many people; being accused of espionage or treachery would surprise very few of them. "After all, he's been accused of just about everything else in his life, the same life shows that he despises the governments of men, the Western versions almost as much as the Soviet model. He has no loyalty whatsoever."

The fear was real as I hung, clinging to the rope, swinging, spinning in the hot wind that was making me so cold, holding on with desperate hands, unable, because of the injury, to use my feet for additional support. My hands were close in front of my face, inches away, stark white were the hands, clinging with such pressure they'd surely no need to grip quite so tightly, it was as if they were not merely hanging on but trying to squeeze the very moisture out of the hemp. And then it came to me that this really wasn't a nightmare, it really was happening, once again I was suspended from the balcony, though this time the right way up, and there was the rope to hold onto, lashed onto our balcony, and I was supposed to be swinging across the face of the hotel, supposed to be swinging ever closer to the other balcony, was I never to be rid of these balconies?

The pills, the anxiety, the frantic haste must have had something to do with the confusion between nightmare and reality. I'd had so little time to act, and it had all blurred into a fever of fright. The conference was nearly over, Roosevelt had already left for Hyde Park or Washington or somewhere, and Churchill was getting up steam on his battleship. The captains and the Mackenzie Kings were departing, and with them Sir Amyas, and me stuck in hospital until now.

Desperate and still hot with fever, I insisted on being discharged, and a taxi took me back to the hotel (tailed all the way by somebody in civvies), and an obliging commissionaire helped me and my single crutch into the elevator. Which for once rose as high as the floor below our room, and so, fast and frustrated and clumsy up the stairs to the top – to find B.W. crying.

Lying on his bed, and when I came lurching in, he sat up fast and turned his head away to wipe his face with his blue shirtsleeve, giving up hope. His sight would not be restored, had not been restored even after the shock of the balcony, though some quack had said that a shock or adjustment might do it. And then me, knowing how small was the chance of being able to clear myself. What a pair, him in despair, and me in desperation knowing that once Drummond had departed he would be unassailable, given his power and prestige and position.

I'd talked about the only possible course of action. "Break into his room?" said B.W., unsteady, indifferent. "Why not? Why not?"

We had made our way downstairs, two cripples in search of a
faith healer. On the Drummond fifth floor it was hard enough even
getting near the door to the suite, the corridor outside was busy
with waiters delivering and porters collecting. I thought for a
moment we were too late and the Drummonds had already left.
They were certainly in the process of moving out. When a hotel
employee emerged from the suite, I saw their luggage in there, all
ready, piled up.

The Drummonds were elsewhere, but that was no help. In works
of fiction, getting through a locked door is invariably shown to be
as easy as operating the latch of an outside privy. But neither of us
knew a thing about locks or how to pick them.

We managed, however, to rattle the doorknob.

We retired in disorder, back to our room. And that was when I
put the desperate idea into words, something I'd been hoping not
to hear myself say, the idea of swinging across to the Drummond
balcony. Fate had even supplied the equipment, the rope they had
used to rescue us two days ago, left behind.

And so, one end of the rope lashed to our balcony, and the other
end snaking down the wall of the hotel, I'd gone over the side, over
the top. I was half hoping the rope would not be adequate, but it
was of ample length. So, down the rope in a hurry, so as not to think
about the drop, the fecund void.

What a pair. B.W. whining with a fear of his own, and me trying
to convince us both that it was a simple enough oscillation. Which
in fact it was. The difficult part was mustering the courage needed
to face the possibility that I might not be able to grab hold of the
Drummond balcony with one hand while retaining the grip on the
rope, in which case I would end up swinging in space, perhaps too
enfeebled by fear to make the effort again, or even to climb back
to our balcony.

But down I went, breathless already, using my arms to save my
poor leg. At the knotted end I started the swing, penduluming
wider and wider across the wall. The sleeve of my shirt touched the
wall at one point. Even such a mild contact as that sent me spinning, and it took an entire minute, dangling on the end of the rope,

to get the pendulum action going again in the right direction.
While B.W. gazed sightlessly down, shivering by proxy.

It was not as difficult as I'd imagined, as the bishop said to the
actress. The swing finally took me within reach of the other balcony,
and I managed to grab hold of the ironwork, and after counting stars,
flashes of light, and minor explosions as my heavily protected leg
contacted the stone, I was safe.

Up and over, and down onto the balcony, then secure the rope
for the return journey. With legs trembling like aspen leaves, I tried
the balcony door. It wasn't locked, why would it be? And so I
slipped into the suite.

There was a storm coming. The daylight was fading. It was so
dull in the room I had to turn on the light. Well, if I was going to
be caught, it might as well be in the light. Very conveniently, they
had packed everything together for me. There were four suitcases,
a hatbox, and a steamer trunk, ready for the voyage home.

Not so convenient was that the four suitcases were all securely
locked and only the hatbox and the trunk were unsecured. There
was no way I could get into the suitcases without damaging the
locks, but I could not afford to damage them. It was vital that the
luggage looked untampered-with.

I turned to the remaining two pieces. There was nothing in the
hatbox except hats – didn't think much of her millinery myself. As
for the trunk, it was standing on end near the entrance to the suite.
The halves were partly open, as if eager to snap shut on me the
moment I came too close to the metal jaws. There were only a few
items still to be packed, the things that had been placed on top of
the open trunk, including Churchill's framed photograph.

So he had given Drummond an autographed picture as well. I
was a bit annoyed about that. It appeared that I hadn't been so
favoured by the great man after all, if he was prepared to give a
swine like Drummond a signed photo as well.

I supposed that they were close friends. All the same, it was dis-
appointing. Worse, Churchill had even personalized Drummond's
picture. *For my friend, Amyas Drummond.*

I went through the trunk, drawer by drawer, shelf by shelf,

compartment by compartment, trying my best not to disarrange anything. And, amazingly, I found what I had hoped to find but had not had the least confidence of finding. It was a Ministry cardboard file, containing some official papers, summaries of some conference meetings, memos, guidelines, lists of personnel. And – aha! – a few notes on yellow paper – one of which had the winged dagger on it.

The page of notes was identical, as far as I could remember, to the incriminating material found in my room.

There was no doubt about it, this was the original material. It was easy to tell. Someone had obviously traced over the arrangement of words and lines, including the winged dagger. And Drummond had identified it. Attached to the page by a small piece of white paper were the words: *Churchill's hand*.

I had barely completed the skulduggery that followed when there came the sound of a key scratching at the front door.

Now the door was opening. There was no time to return to the balcony – it was in full view of the entrance to the suite. I would certainly be seen. The only alternative was to dive into the nearest bedroom. Lady Drummond's room. And, oh, grief, her handbag was on the bed. Which meant that she was certain to enter and retrieve it.

One crisis at a time, please. I had only just dealt with the last problem, which involved stealing something from Drummond and simultaneously returning it to him without his knowing. After finding the original paper from which the incriminating material had been forged, I had removed from Drummond's file any other material that looked sensitive from a security point of view, and had hidden the lot in a new location. The winged dagger notes in particular had to be hidden somewhere where Drummond was unlikely to look. If Drummond discovered that any of the material was missing, it was vitally important that he not be able to find it again before I could alert the security people. But the material had to be in his possession without his knowing it, until a search of his luggage was made.

I had hidden the papers in the picture. Knowing how profound was Drummond's love and respect for his master, I thought that the framed photograph was the item most likely to be respected and left undisturbed. So I had taken the portrait apart and inserted the material between the photograph and the cardboard backing, and had then carefully returned the picture to its former location among the few items sitting on top of the trunk – white gloves, a silk scarf, a hotel towel (were they swiping that?), some underwear, and a pigskin travel case – things still to be packed away before the jaws of the trunk snapped shut.

I had only just accomplished this desperate measure when the Drummonds had returned to their hotel room. And now I was trapped in the lady's bedroom.

My heart faltered on hearing their first words. "You left the lights on," came an accusing female voice from the lounge.

"I did no such thing."

"You must have."

"Why would I put the lights on in the first place? It was daylight when we went out."

"I suppose the staff could have left them on. They've been in and out . . ."

Yes, yes, I was urging from the bedroom. It was the staff. Now clear out. Go on, go! Never mind your handbag.

The bitch paid no attention. Through the gap between the door and the jamb I saw her heading straight toward me.

I couldn't see Drummond. Praying that he wasn't in his room, I hobbled fast, wincing all the way, across the carpet to the connecting door between the bedrooms, and swung inside.

Praise be. His bedroom was empty. Without pausing I continued the hobble toward the other door, and peered through.

Sir Amyas Drummond was only a few feet away, straightening his tie in an ornate mirror.

Even as I watched, he turned and made straight toward his bedroom.

I looked around, frantic. There was nowhere to hide except the built-in wardrobe. Though it was empty apart from spare pillows and blankets, the only usable space was packed with wire coathangers. If I went in there they would jangle like the coathangers of hell. So that was out. And the bed was so deep that its belly was dragging on the floor. So I couldn't hide under the bed.

There was no alternative. Just as he was pushing the door open I slipped through the connecting door again, back into madam's room – and she was still there.

She had her back to me. I stood frozen, just inside the room. If she turned a mere few inches she would see me.

She was searching for something in her handbag. Her handbag was a shiny and whiskery model, obviously made from sea lion. Don't turn around, I ordered silently. If she saw me standing there she would almost certainly scream. Drummond would rush in. He was a powerfully built man. I was at an impossible disadvantage, still convalescent after surgery. He would hack me to death and chuck the hunks of gristle that once were Bartholomew Wolfe Bandy over the balcony, down into the Lower Town. I would die in sordid circumstances. There would be no enjoyable obituary. There –

Now she was sitting on the bed, still pawing through the carcass of the sea lion and clicking her tongue irritably. Worse, she was now half-turned toward me. The slightest movement of her head in this direction would bring into view the pitiful figure of B. W. Bandy the First, leaning on his crutch, looking like a soiled diaper.

Then she was rising, and leaving the room. To answer a knock at the door.

She actually left the room without seeing me. She had not turned around. But the peals of rejoicing were soon stilled. It didn't seem possible for the situation to be worse than ever, but it was. Oh, God, no, please no. But, yes. For the knock at the door had come from a member of the hotel staff, come to pick up the luggage.

My heart was thumping so heavily that I could barely hear what was being said out there. Voices discussing the luggage. Lady Drummond saying, "What are you going to do with that?" And a mumbled reply.

Some hours or minutes later, after much fussing and feathering, the door clumped shut and there was silence. Not only had the Drummonds departed. So had their luggage.

I had hoped, somehow, to have the incriminating evidence found right here in their suite. Now it was on its way to the ship. And I couldn't decide whether or not that complicated the situation. I'd had such a scare I couldn't think properly.

With not a single idea in my head I limped to the front entrance. I put my ear to the door for a listless moment, then opened the door – and there, with the SP officer beside her, was Guinevere, who'd had her ear to the door as well.

THE CHÂTEAU AT SUNSET

"LET'S GO OVER IT again," Guinevere said wearily, some hours later.

We were in my hotel room at the top of the tower, our various bodies disposed in various postures, from stiff and watchful to damp and drooping in the heat wave, which had billowed in from Mexico. B.W. was lying on his bed, hands behind his head. The Service Police officer had bagged the only chair and was sitting in it backwards, leaning on the upright, a position recommended in the Service Police training school for use when a casual posture might help to put the accused off his guard. Guinevere, perspiration dripping from her redoubtable chin, hooked nose slicing the air like the bow of HMS *Bellicose*, was pacing back and forth between the door and the balcony. I was leaning against the wall studying the only picture in the room, a reproduction of *The Death of General Wolfe on the Plains of Abraham* by Capt. Smythe-Crippen, RA – Royal Artillery rather than Royal Academy, judging by the artwork, where all the redcoats seemed to have exceptionally long arms.

"Not again," said B.W.

"I want to get it straight," she said.

"You'll never get it straight, it's much too bent," joked the SP officer. He looked around, hoping to see us all rolling about in the aisles, holding our hilarious sides.

The best I could manage was to pluck my blue shirt away from my ribs and blow cool air toward my belly button.

Guinevere said, "You searched Drummond's trunk and found an exact copy of the paper hidden in your room?"

"Not a copy – the original. He reproduced the copy you found by tracing the original onto a blank sheet of paper that he had obtained with my fingerprints on it."

"So it was Drummond and not you who brought up the words and sketches on the paper by running a pencil lightly over the surface?"

"All part of his scheme to frame me, I guess."

"*Faugh*," said the SP squadron leader.

"And you say you replaced the incriminating material you found in Drummond's trunk roughly where you'd found it. Your idea was that you would be able to tell us where it was before we searched the trunk."

"Thus proving that I had been into Drummond's trunk and must have found the material there in the first place before relocating it."

"And you were banking on his not realizing that, before you per-suaded us to search his effects?"

"Right."

The SP man went, "*Chhhh . . .*" and smiled at the ceiling.

"But Bartholomew – how do we know you didn't plant the classified material in the first place?"

"Exactly," said the SP officer. He believed nothing of what I was saying. I could tell by the way he kept going, "*Pshhhh*," or "*Kuh!*", or shaking his head with an indulgent smile.

I half expected him to express his feelings at any moment by pointing to his temple with a forefinger and twirling the finger in a circle.

Even Guinevere, though distressed on my behalf, was finding my story difficult to gulp down.

"It's just not credible," she said.

"Look," I said wearily, "when you find the classified material that I relocated, you will find a page of notes that is obviously the orig-inal of what you found in my room. What's the only conclusion you could come to then?"

The squadron leader said, "Obvious. You planted it on Sir Amyas in the first place."

"If I'd had the original, why would I have gone to the trouble of tracing it onto another piece of paper? Why wouldn't I just use the original?"

Guinevere's forehead went all corrugated. She took out a pack of cigarettes and accepted a light from the SP man.

After a few puffs she was calm again. "Even if we accepted that you had found incriminating stuff on Sir Amyas, you still wouldn't be in the clear," she said.

B.W., who was sitting on his bed with a deeply worried expression, asked why not. "Why wouldn't he be in the clear?" he said.

For a moment she was inclined not to answer the whippersnapper. But seeing that I was also quite interested, she burst out, "It's just not believable, whatever the apparent evidence. A government minister, as close to the Prime Minister as Drummond is, stooping to faking evidence? I know he wants rid of you, Bartholomew, but this is ridiculous!"

"Yeah, right," said B.W., sitting up sharply, his face flushed. "Drummond is part of your old-boy network, so he couldn't possibly be anything but a loyal, decent chap, could he?"

His tone was so arrogantly scornful that even the SP officer's face tightened.

As for Guinevere, the formidable chin canted, and she snapped, "You're not doing your father any good with comments like that."

"So search this guy Drummond's trunk," he shouted back, jumping up. "At least give my dad a chance."

"Sit down and be quiet, sonny," the squadron leader said.

Guinevere picked up a notebook and fanned her shining face. "We couldn't search his luggage even if we wanted to," she said.

"Oh?" I said. "And why not?"

"My dear Wing Commander," said the SP, doing his George Sanders imitation, casually studying the burning end of his cigarette, "didn't you look at the red labels on the trunk?"

"What about them?"

"*Chhhh*," said the SP. "Diplomatic labels, old boy."

There was a silence. B.W. looked around blindly. "What?" he asked. "What about it?"

"Diplomatic baggage, B.W.," I said.

"So?"

"Diplomatic bags can't be searched," I said.

B.W. seemed to contract into himself. "Oh, Christ," he said; and for once failed to apologize for taking the Lord's name in vain.

I had acquired a bottle of Welland Canal rye. I fed myself another two or three ounces – just to make sure that the whisky was up to snuff and hadn't been tampered with.

"Drinking isn't going to help," Guinevere said, lighting another cigarette.

When I didn't answer, she went on, "It's just not like you. I know you're an awful person sometimes, infuriating, vindictive, pretentious, foolish, insubordinate, obsessive – you certainly haven't made friends and influenced people with these stupid submissions to the Air Ministry – "

"They're not stupid."

In a sudden fury, she shouted, "If you go to prison, who's going to look after B.W., tell me that?"

A moment later: "I'm sorry," she said, while the SP man looked at her curiously. "But I just can't see any hope for you. I know Drummond. He'll pursue the matter until you're ruined. And you can't fight back, there's no way we can get into his trunks. Trunk, I mean."

She became aware of the SP's speculative looks. Contradicting her former assertion that Drummond was above suspicion, she turned on him angrily. "It's not as if it's a wholly unlikely story," she cried. "We've had doubts about Drummond for some time."

This was obviously news to the SP officer, judging by the way he let his George Sanders act slip for a second or two. "All the same," he said, "You're not seriously giving any credence to this man's ridiculous story?"

She plonked herself heavily on my bed. Everybody looked at

her bosom for a moment to see if it would bounce again. "One thing I've never understood," she said tiredly, "is why he wanted Bandy here in the first place. It was he who insisted on giving Bandy the job. And then there was Drummond's comment about Bandy's hair."

The SP man seemed to be wondering if she was quite as sane as she looked. "I beg your pardon?" he said.

I was looking equally puzzled. "Hair?" I enquired. "What hair?"

"Exactly," Guinevere said.

"What about Bandy's hair?" the squadron leader asked.

"He wears a wig. Toupee. Hairpiece. Whatever you call it."

"Wig? Toupee? Hairpiece?" I repeated, with an incredulous smile. "My dear Guinevere, what are you talking about?"

"Oh, for heaven's sake, Bart, don't go on pretending."

"Pretending? Pretending about what? I don't understand a thing you're talking about," I said, rising and limping insouciantly around the room.

"Bartholomew," she said, controlling herself with an effort, "I know you wear a hairpiece. You're wearing one right now."

B.W. was also looking alert. "Dad?" he said. "You don't wear false hair, do you?"

"'Course not. The very idea."

"Will you stop that!" Guinevere cried. "I've known about it for years!"

After strolling a mile or so, I sat down again. "How?" I asked — brokenly.

"How? A woman knows these things," she said.

"Oh."

"Anyway, for heaven's sake, let's stick to the point. And the point is that Drummond knew about that funny beaded bag where you keep your spare hair."

"You probably told him about my hair on some other occasion," I said, looking down at my thumbnails and sulking like mad.

"Of course I didn't tell him, don't be so stupid. But he knew. He knew you kept your hair stuff, the adhesive, and everything, in a beaded bag. He made a reference to it, that time we searched your room."

"So what?" I said.

"*So how did he know about it?*" she said, turning to the SP. "When we searched Bandy's room on that occasion, with Drummond present, we didn't find a beaded bag, did we?"

The SP thought about it. Somewhat reluctantly he conceded, "No, not until the more thorough search later on. When I opened the bag I thought at first there was a dead rat in there."

"The point is that Drummond already knew about the beaded bag."

"And the dead rat in it," added the SP, casting me a mean look. "Yes, it's true, Sir Amyas did mention it before we unearthed it . . . You're suggesting he must have been in this room before that."

"Planting the evidence," B.W. put in excitedly.

"He could have seen the hairy equipment on some other occasion."

"Do be serious!" Guinevere cried. "You've seen the way Bandy reacts over his stupid hair. Can you see him allowing anyone even a glimpse of the ghastly evidence? Even I was never shown his beaded bag."

"H'm," said the SP. He thought for a moment, then shook his head. "No, it's so flimsy its knees are buckling. Dammit, it's just not possible, a minister of the Crown taking such a risk merely to get his own back on a . . ." he muttered, gesturing in my direction.

"How about it was a diversion?" said B.W.

We all turned to look at him. He was lying down again, hands behind his head, great damp patches under his arms.

After a moment: "What?" Guinevere asked curtly.

"Supposing it was him who was collecting secret information? Later, if we learned there'd been a leak, would you snoops bother to look any further than my dad?"

Both snoops had at least the decency to look thoughtful. More to herself than to us Guinevere murmured, "Diverting suspicion as well as getting his own back . . . ?" She walked out onto the balcony and looked into space, leaning heavily on the railing.

She didn't look any more hopeful when she returned. "It doesn't really help," she muttered. Then: "As a matter of interest, where did you hide the material?"

"You know very well it's all in the beaded bag," I muttered.

"I'm not talking about your hair. Never mind your hair, I'm talking about the classified material you said Drummond had."

"Never mind my hair, she says. The most closely guarded secret in my whole life, and she says – "

"Listen to him! He seems to care more about his blasted hair than about being accused of treason!"

"I get my priorities right, even if you don't," I said. "I at least am level-headed."

"Is that why you wear a wig, Dad?" asked B.W. "To hide your head because it's so level?"

"You shut up."

"I'd wear a wig, too, if my head was level. I wouldn't want people seeing my head if it was flat."

Guinevere was taking one of her interesting deep breaths. "I think," she said quietly to the SP man, "that I'm going to kill them both right this minute."

"Churchill's portrait," I said sullenly.

"What?"

"Churchill's portrait."

She clenched her eyes. "Yes? And what about Churchill's portrait?" she enquired.

"That's where I put it so he wouldn't find it."

There was a sudden silence.

B.W. sat up and panned his sightless gaze around the room. Even the SP was paying attention.

"You're not," Guinevere began. She had to stop and clear her throat. "You're not referring to Drummond's personal copy of the photograph that Mr. Churchill was handing around, are you?"

She had approached me and was now digging her fingers into my arm quite painfully.

"Are you?"

"I stuck the yellow paper in the back of the photo. I didn't think he would look there. I must say I was a bit disappointed, the way Mr. Churchill had given Drummond a photograph too. I – "

But they weren't listening. Both Guinevere and the SP officer had jumped up and were tearing out of the room. "We'll be back in a jiffy!" Gwinny was shouting. "Don't move! Don't stir! Don't breathe!"

They returned about five minutes later, panting. Guinevere's face was pink and sweaty. Even the SP man was looking a bit excited. She was holding several sheets of yellow paper. "Is this the material you found in Sir Amyas Drummond's trunk?" she asked.

I looked at it blearily. "Yes," I said. "But how . . . ?"

"It seems," she said with a beatific smile, "that Drummond wasn't as enamoured of Churchill as we'd thought.

"He didn't take it with him. He didn't pack it in the trunk. Before he closed up, he threw Winston's picture in the wastepaper basket, frame and all."

SOMEWHERE IN KENT

"I HAD A RUN-IN with an air marshal the other day," I was telling them.

"Oh yes?" Wing Commander Broseley replied in a deadpan voice. "My, I'm so surprised."

"And I wanted to test an idea on you, Bob. And you too, Apples."

"Go ahead, Group Captain."

"The idea is this. That if KRs were completely fair, two or more officers of junior rank should be able to combine their ranks and be superior to any senior officer."

"How d'you mean?"

"Well, take the three of us. Between us we have ten rings, right? Ten rings should be more than enough to outrank some uppity air marshal, who only has five rings."

Joffee was the quickest to respond. "Ah," he said, "but an air marshal has a thick ring on his sleeve. That's equivalent to five ordinary rings."

"All right, but that still gives him only nine ordinary rings against our ten. Ours together should put us in a superior position."

"I see what you mean," Broseley boomed. "So if, say, six flight lieutenants with their twelve rings got together, they could take over the Air Ministry."

"Ah," said Joffee, "but what's to stop two or more air marshals getting together to combine their rings?"

"The tricky part," I conceded, "would be ensuring that they didn't get together. All the same, you're right, Apples," I said. "That's the fly in the ointment."

We all laughed contentedly, as we continued to stroll around the airfield in the spring sunshine. Joffee and I hadn't seen Bob Broseley for about two years, and we were delighted to have him with us again.

"Talking about rank," Broseley said, "I must say that you do look at home, Bandy, in that fine uniform with all the scrambled egg on the hat, and the fruit salad on your manly chest, not to mention the rings on your sleeve. It's a great improvement. As a flight lieutenant you looked ridiculous with all the ribbons and stars below a face that had recently escaped from Shangri-La."

"I particularly like the yawing limp he's developed," Joffee said.

"Yes, that's a good touch, isn't it?" Broseley agreed. "And the way he pauses now and then to lean on that ebony and silver cane in a thoughtful manner, to try and convince us that he really is deep in thought."

And then I removed my cap.

"Oh, my God," cried Broseley, reeling back in horror. "You poor devil!"

He was staring at my naked scalp.

"He was back in Canada," Joffee said. "The Indians, I guess."

"Come on, chaps," I said in the English accent I had been trying without success to perfect since 1917, "there's no shame in being bald, you know."

Gad, it was good to be back. In another Spitfire squadron, too. Unfortunately not as a combat pilot, but as another Mince, a station commander. Still, despite orders that high-up chaps like me should not fly on ops, I had managed a few quick flips over the old ditch. You know, just to get some idea of the enemy defences that, by 1944, were bringing down an excessive quantity of aviators.

Broseley, Apples, and I were strolling, or in my case, limping, about our estate under a mild May sun, graciously receiving the salutations of the lesser breeds within the law. Squadron Leader Daplin was one of the fellows we passed. Even he was forced to salute.

"I bet that hurt," said Apples.

Daplin was about to go back on ops after instructing for three years. He had informed me so earnestly that he was looking forward to flying against the enemy that I was wondering if he should be kept permanently on the ground.

"By the way," I asked, "how's Danny Truelove getting on these days?"

"Bought it over Boulogne," Broseley replied.

"Ah. And his pal whatsisname – Burwash?"

"POW. Lost a leg."

"What about Keith Crumpsall?"

"Bailed out. Lost at sea."

"Burt Hughes?"

"Flamer."

"Buzz Sawyer?"

"Still in plastic surgery."

"Good to hear about the old gang," I said.

As we approached the hangar, Broseley said sombrely, "A lot's changed, Bart, since they got rid of you for the umpteenth time. Rations have been cut again – I don't know how the civvies manage. Half the merchant navy has gone to the bottom. Noël Coward is making patriotic films."

"God, is there no end to the suffering?" said Apples.

"And Yanks everywhere," Broseley boomed, adjusting his moustache so that he could get through the hangar doors. "I had breakfast in an American mess the other day. Do you know, if you order eggs, they actually break the shells and do the eggs the way you want them right in front of your eyes?"

We fell into a reverent silence, thinking about the typical RAF cookhouse, where on the rare occasions when real eggs were available rather than the abominable powdered substitute, the eggs were likely to have been fried the previous evening.

"And the Yanks draw all the best crumpet," Apples said gloomily.

The ground crewmen were having their mid-morning break around the tea wagon as we entered the great, clanging hangar. Broseley had just joined us after his months of desk-flying, and we had something to show him: our very own de Havilland Mosquito.

We stood admiring the sleek, twin-engined machine. It was ours. Apparently the Mossie had caught fire in the air, and been abandoned. But the plane miraculously had reached terra aqua almost unscathed. It had come down in a fluke glide into a nearby reservoir, which had not only put out the fire but ensured very little damage. Learning that it was officially lost, I had claimed it – unofficially – as marine salvage, and had dragged it to this maintenance hangar and had it restored to health.

"We were thinking of selling it to the Americans," said Apples.

The fact that we could even contemplate this fine example of private enterprise showed how well the war was going by May 1944. But at the back of everybody's minds was the fear, once the invasion of the continent began, of another Dieppe disaster.

Corporal Tommy Atkins, who was in charge of the repair work, came wandering up to offer us mugs of NAAFI tea. "Morning, boss," he said.

"Morning, Tommy. Have you found any bumf on the Mossie yet?"

"Still trying, sir."

"Tommy is trying to find us an instruction book for the Mossie so I can fly it," I explained to Broseley.

"Shouldn't think you'd have much trouble. It's just two Merlin engines and some firewood."

After the char and a wad around the NAAFI wagon we walked back into the sunlight and continued our tour of the station, including the bays where the latest versions of the Spitfire crouched. They had been upgrading the magnificent Spitfire for years now, and the performance of the latest mark had astonished me when I compared it with the 1940 version.

It was hard to believe that we had started the war with 180 mph biplanes. Now 400 mph Tempests were reaching the squadrons. And there were tales of 600 mph machines with strange propulsion systems that worked without the use of a propeller, though personally I considered that hogwash. There was no way an engine could work without a propeller.

"I heard you had a spot of bother in Canada," Broseley said as we reached the mess and looked at our watches to see if it was time to start drinking.

"Yes," I said airily. "Nothing much. I was accused of burglary, false witness, dereliction of duty, dumb insolence, conduct unbecoming a gentleman, and high treason. They were talking about shooting me."

"Just par for the course, eh?"

"But it was all cleared up," I said.

Not entirely satisfactorily, as far as I was concerned. True, the Parliamentary Under-Secretary of State had been dropped from the government some time after the Quebec Conference. Poor health had been given as the reason for his resignation. But nothing further appeared to have happened to him. He was still in the Commons, even if he was no longer making pompous speeches, and he was still to be seen about town, acting as if nothing out of the ordinary had happened.

I was never to know whether or not Drummond had intended relaying the classified material in his possession to unfriends. I suspected, however, that we were being treated to another example of the English class system, where people with question marks over their loyalty were often spared public embarrassment or disgrace because they had been to the right schools.

Talking about good connections, I had been seeing Guinevere only very infrequently since she had brought me back for the enquiry that had cleared me. While she seemed prepared to continue our relationship as if nothing had happened, I no longer had the same longing for her. In Quebec she had proved herself so cool, competent, enterprising, decisive, and efficient that I was now more inclined to stand to attention in the parade ground sense rather than in the boudoir manner.

I was also a bit concerned about her interest in some odd sexual variations, some of which were exceedingly risky, the urban excesses including doing it upside down in front of a large window. (I begged off, explaining that the hanging position from the footstraps was too hard on my bad leg.) And once she tried to persuade me to dress up as Nanny and give her a good hiding. (And I was not to spare the other rod, either.)

There was a party in the mess that night to mark Bob Broseley's arrival, and to entertain one of the pilots who had just gained his twentieth victory. Afterwards, reeling back to my spacious quarters – as a groupie I was entitled to no fewer than three rooms, including my very own bathroom – I found that the mail had been delivered: a letter from B.W. A scrawl, rather, with some of the writing falling off the edge of the paper; but a cheerful scrawl, saying that he was being awarded a very good disability pension, and that his separation from the air force was now only days away.

Which ended a perfect day for me. No men lost from either of the squadrons based at the field in Kent; Broseley being posted to us; the fine May weather; and the prospect of flying the Mosquito, the world's speediest production aircraft. And now a friendly letter from my son. Among his other news was that he was sharing my old apartment with a nurse from the Grace Hospital in Ottawa; though he didn't expect the lady to stay long, as her husband was likely to drop in soon from Indo-China.

As for me, to keep myself out of mischief, I was continuing to make submissions to the government based on the relationship between British Commonwealth air force casualties and the results they achieved, as determined by aerial photographs and other sources. Which indicated that we were losing expensive aircraft and even more expensive aircrew at a prodigious rate, especially in Bomber Command, whose losses in the cause of killing civilians were frightful. Air Marshal Harris – who had been picked as bomber chief instead of old Greaves – insisted that the cost was justified. I couldn't help remembering that Field Marshal Haig used to say the same thing in World War I.

None of my friends, however, not even Apples, had much sympathy with my views. Duty was duty. Sacrifices were inevitable. The

Air Ministry hadn't much sympathy, either. I think that was the reason for the OP signal that arrived in the wireless section one morning. Contrary to the general policy discouraging senior officers from taking part in operations, it stated that Group Captain Bandy could, if he wished, fly operationally against the enemy on certain special occasions – such as during any month with an R in it, or an E. However, this signal was soon countermanded, as apparently it was the work of some malicious person at the Air Ministry who had gotten really fed up with my constant barrage of submissions and statistics.

As well as my fine living quarters, I also had a fine office. It was filled with sunshine and Fighter Group sports trophies, and numerous other shiny or valuable awards and mementoes which had been appropriated by the former station commander. And I was in this fine office one morning busily whittling, when Squadron Leader Daplin knocked and entered, smirking all over his face. This expression usually meant that he had bad news and was eager to impart it. This time it was different. He had brought a visitor.

From the outer office came a series of sharp cracks, like office machines or people's heads being rapped with a stick – and a moment later B.W. appeared, waving his white cane with the usual recklessness, his other hand feeling about like a fresh-caught squid in a trawler bucket.

"Oh, my word," says I, rising so abruptly that my gammy leg knocked itself against the desk.

I hobbled over, babbling, and embraced him so enthusiastically that he dropped his white cane. Daplin picked it up and pressed it unctuously into the young man's searching hand.

"Thank you very much, Nick," I said. "That'll be fine, thanks."

Daplin went out slowly, reluctant to miss the opportunity to see the CO turning all slimy and sentimental.

"My dear boy, let me look at you," I said, holding B.W. at arm's length.

There was no change discernible. His smooth, supercilious face was just as expressionless, his blue uniform as impeccable as always.

"What's happened, how come, what gives?" I exclaimed. "Tell me everything that's fit to print!"

He lowered himself carefully into the best chair, the low one usually reserved for AOCs or Waafs with good legs. With a happy and contented expression on his face he announced that he had finally received his discharge from the RCAF.

Massaging my calf and foot, I adjusted my tone up the sympathy scale. "And how do you feel about that?" I asked.

"Just great, Dad. I couldn't feel better about it."

He was so pleased that I was surprised, remembering how hard he had taken the loss of his flying career and great chunks of his future. He told me that as well as a pension, he had been awarded a substantial one-time payment. He would be quite well off, now, he said, provided he didn't eat much, or buy more than one wheelchair.

"That's fantastic," I said, looking at my watch. "Come on, let's get over to the mess." I opened the office door. Daplin was running his fingers lasciviously through the nearby filing cabinet. "One of the good things about being a station commander is that you can open the bar a little earlier than usual," I was saying as I emerged. And, to Daplin: "Just popping over to the mess, Nick."

"Oh, are you, sir?" he said, pointedly studying his watch, the little swine.

"M'oh, yes. Let me know when the boys are due back, eh?" I liked to be there to greet the pilots when they returned from a sweep.

At the bar I received another surprise when B.W. ordered a pint of ale. I had never seen him drink before.

I ordered the same, while asking him about it.

"It was Maggie who got me drinking beer," he said.

"Maggie?"

"The nurse I was sharing the apartment with."

"Oh, yes."

"She moved out, though, couple of weeks ago."

Raising the sympathy even further up the scale, I said, "How do you feel about that?"

He turned grave. Aware of the mess personnel passing back and forth he lowered his voice, and murmured, "Dad?"

"Yes?"

"I need to talk to you privately."

Thoroughly alarmed – don't tell me he had VD? – I said, "What is it, B.W.? Tell me."

"I can't talk in here. Or in your office. Can we go outside?"

I explained that I had to get along to the briefing room, but I could see him afterwards in my quarters.

"With no danger of being overheard?"

"Oh, Lord," I said. "You're in trouble."

B.W. was lying on the bed in my quarters when I finally got through a particularly unhappy debriefing.

"Nice and quiet here, Dad," he said, getting up and making his way into the sitting room. "Throw me the cane, will you?"

I picked up his white cane and tossed it over, busily talking about our latest casualties. We had lost another two pilots to the 88s, though there was a possibility that one of them had bailed out in time.

"I'll have to go with them one of these days, and see for myself," I was saying. "There must be some way to deal with their blasted defences."

"Do a rhubarb yourself?" he asked anxiously.

"Just as an observer. I was thinking of taking the Mossie," I said. I had told him about our unofficial acquisition.

Slowly I realized that he had been grinning from the moment I had walked in.

"What?" I asked.

"You didn't notice?"

"Notice what?"

"Think."

I thought.

"When you threw me the cane."

I thought again; and sank bonelessly onto the sofa, as it finally registered that when I had tossed him the white cane – he had caught it.

"Dad," he said. "I can see."

"Oh . . . Oh, B.W. . . . "

"It was last month."

"And you never said?"

"Not to anyone. I woke up one morning, and that was it. I've been using your old bedroom, did I mention that? Anyway, there were cobwebs in the corner of the ceiling. I remember thinking that I oughta do something about that. And then it hit me."

"Oh, B.W. . . . why didn't you let on?"

He came over and sat close beside me, speaking excitedly but softly. "For a damn good reason," he said. "I had just gotten through the final medicals certifying I was no further use to the air force. And I was in line for that pension."

His voice had turned vehement, though it remained soft. "And I thought to myself, Well, why not, goldarn it? I've done my turn. What am I, Ripley van Daring, pride of the Force, loyally going back to flying fifty feet above the ground in the dark, likely to be picked off any moment by those 88s you were talking about? Maybe that's for you, Dad, you're a brave man, but I'm not you. I know you'll think I'm one lousy yellow quitter. But I reckon I've made the payments. I've got title to my own life, now.

"And another thing," he added, stabbing me almost painfully in the chest with his finger, "I heard too many stories over there about guys getting kicked out of the service without any compensation at all. Some of them, especially instructors, have been treated pretty lousy, I can tell you. And I decided I wasn't going to be suckered like that. Tell them I'd gotten my sight back? No way. No way.

"Jeez, Dad," he whispered excitedly, "I couldn't believe it, it was like a miracle! Sure, I know they said I might get my sight back any time, that it was – they said it was psychic, or some crap. But, oh, man, to actually have it happen – !"

He had moved so close that our arms were pressed together. He started whispering again. "Anyway, I'd already gotten past the final medical board. That civilian buddy of Guinevere's – remember him, Mr. Slatter, was it? – he was on the board and tried to cut the pay-off, but he was overruled, and – anyway, I was on my way out.

What was I going to do? Please sir, I'm all right now, sir, and I want to go back and do my bit? Eff that for a lark!"

He moved away and looked at me hard. "So that's how I feel about it. And now I guess you'll be ashamed of me all over again."

I looked at him, at his piercing brown eyes, the exact same colour as mine, eyes now beautifully focussed, though sparkling with defiance.

"Ashamed of you?" I said softly. "Ashamed? I'd have to be ashamed of myself, B.W."

His face remained expressionless; but underneath it was a seething cauldron of emotion. Or maybe it was just a seething cauldron of curiosity. For the next thing he said was, "I thought maybe you'd be disgusted."

I didn't see why I shouldn't be emotional and sentimental, just this once. I put a hand over his, and said, "My dear son, I love you with all my heart."

He flushed and looked away, terribly embarrassed for me.

"Nothing you could do would ever make any difference to that. And anyway, it would be kind of difficult for me to feel disgusted, because I did the same kind of thing back in 1920." And I related how I had diddled the Canadian government out of a pension that was totally unwarranted.

"You?"

"Moi."

In Russia, I told him, entirely for political reasons, the Allied Military Government at Archangel had raised me to the rank of major-general, in order to sort out a problem involving units of the Russian White, or anti-Bolshevik, army. When I was captured by the Reds on Armistice Day, nobody in Ottawa had caught on to the fact that I should have reverted to my substantive rank of captain. So for two years I remained a brass hat. When I finally got back to Ottawa in 1920, I had claimed all the back pay and allowances due a senior serving Canadian officer, and despite their anguish and prevarication, they had been compelled to pay it, plus a really splendid life pension – which I made over to my parents.

"You keep on amazing me, Dad," he said.

"But hey, listen," I said. "If you're a civvy now, how come you're still in uniform?"

He explained that part of the medical discharge deal was a buckshee fifty-six-day leave, providing him with a fifty-six-day bonus of pay and allowances. But it also meant that technically he was still in the air force.

"Also it's turning out pretty useful," he said, "like for hitching a ride over here with a ferry pilot. And the uniform gets me into places like your base here."

But, he warned me, if the secret came out before the fifty-six days were up, he would truly be paddleless, creekwise. A court martial, maybe, or – at best – a return to operational duty.

So it was necessary for him to keep up the blind act until he was safely free of the air force accountants.

"It sure ain't easy, sometimes," he confided. "Like when I walked into your office and caught you shamelessly exposing yourself – showing everybody your bare scalp. Jeez, that was a shock. I don't know how I kept a straight face.

"Anyway," he concluded, rubbing his hands in glee, "only six days to go, Dad, before I'm a civilian again. But I'm not worried about it any more. I've been goldarn careful, believe me. They can't get me now."

Oh-oh. Oh, dear. He shouldn't have said that.

Lord houghton and friends

A FEW DAYS LATER Guinevere, using the excuse that B.W. was back in Britain, invited us to Walsingham Manor. She was spending more time at home now that her mother was out of the way. Lady Houghton had been knocked down in the blackout by a unicyclist, and was spending a few weeks in her favourite nursing home. The unicyclist, I heard, was killed in the accident.

B.W. was not keen on going. Gwinny's behaviour at the Quebec Conference had not modified his opinion of her. He felt that she had been too ready to condemn me. He claimed that, blind, he had been able to hear the hardness in her more clearly than I ever could, given the distraction of my eyeballs.

Another reason for not wishing to venture past the station guard-room was that he had only thirty-six hours to go before Civvy Street, and he was reluctant to risk his fraudulent cane. Once past the twenty-eighth of May they would not be able to claw back his pension without an act of Parliament. Until then he did not want to run the slightest risk of exposing himself.

In all my life I had never been so happy to be with someone as I was with my son, and I persuaded him to go. I couldn't see that there could be any harm in it. In the end he agreed to accompany me, though only to keep an eye on me, so to speak. "Otherwise," he said, "you'll be getting into another fine mess."

He no longer talked about going back to the Chaffingtons, though I assumed that he was being sensible and keeping his options open. With all that moolah at stake, I found it difficult to understand why he was still sticking around. I mean, most people would have put up even with the Chaffingtons if the pay-off was a billion bucks or so. However, I didn't say so, otherwise his deep-down fears that I wanted rid of him might have scrambled to the surface.

I think he now saw himself as both protégé and guardian. It was my duty as a father, as he saw it, to be available for insults at all times. It was his task as my son to ensure that I didn't do anything foolish, i.e., against his interests. Like, for instance, offering to marry Guinevere. He became indignant at the very thought that I might hook up with her, especially after I had failed to do the decent thing by his mother, an oversight that he still felt keenly. He was acutely conscious of his illegitimacy, no matter how many times I called him a dumb bastard for worrying about it.

At least he was no longer hostile to the extent of continually provoking me. Now, though still rude and prickly on occasion, and still alert to the slightest hint that I wanted rid of him, he had calmed down quite a bit, and sometimes even seemed to enjoy my company.

A disinterested observer might even have said that he was clinging to one who was his only real reference point in life. But who the hell needs disinterested observers? Interested ones are bad enough.

Anyway, to Walsingham Manor and into danger we went. On this occasion we travelled to Buckinghamshire by train. "We should have a car," B.W. grumbled. "You're a senior officer, you oughta have a car."

"We'd have had a car if it hadn't been for you, buster. When I went back to Canada I gave you my beautiful Armstrong-Siddeley, and you promptly got rid of it for a risible sum."

"I had to – it was part of my hate campaign."

Which was why we were now forced to suffer the wartime transport system with its slow, crowded trains, all of which stopped at a junction named Crewe, from which they rarely departed.

At least we managed to obtain first-class accommodation. We

certainly had high-class company in the compartment. It was filled with brass hats: one RAF commodore, three assorted army generals, and one vice-admiral with bushy eyebrows who was complaining about the crush in the corridor outside, which was packed with other ranks.

As the train started off with a neck-spraining jolt: "Dammit, this is a first-class carriage," the vice-admiral boomed. "If people have to stand out there, they ought at least to be junior officers."

Outside, in the corridor beyond the sliding door to our particular compartment, was a struggling mass of servicemen. They and their turd-shaped kit bags were jammed together to an immoral extent. So that when some mischievous or cheesed-off erk surreptitiously slid open the compartment door, one of the men found himself being squeezed into the compartment like toothpaste.

The tall, thin, dishevelled aircraftsman turned around, and finding himself the focus of several pairs of affronted high-ranking eyes, he panicked. Dropping his kit bag, he scrabbled frantically at the door like a cat in a cartoon. But the door had already been slammed shut, and one of his mean friends out there was maliciously keeping it shut.

The aircraftsman, who looked about eighteen years old and resembled an anthropomorphized ostrich, was finally forced to abandon the escape attempt. Once again he faced a compartment ful of yellowish braid, vermilion tabs, and fat gold rings, not to mention magenta countenances.

"Sorry," said the visitor. Nervously he picking up his kit bag and embraced it for comfort or solace, as if it were a turd-shaped teddy bear. Then he placed it on the floor.

The kit bag immediately bent double, as if it had received a blow to the solar plexus. Obviously it had not been packed in the regulation manner.

The AC2 cleared his throat. "Good morning," he said.

Six pairs of eyes gazed at him as if he were covered in chancres.

He cleared his throat again, his Adam's apple bobbing like a fly fisherman's float with several hungry pikes nibbling at it. He lowered his eyes and inspected everybody's feet.

Quite forgetting that I had faced an almost identical situation way back in 1916 I stared at him in as snotty a fashion as the others.

Finally: "Well, sit down, man, if you must!" barked the vice-admiral.

"Ooh, thanksverymuch, sir," the AC2 said, and, spying about four inches of lebensraum between the two generals opposite me, he moved over to them, and with some difficulty, wiggled his buttocks between their beefy thighs until he finally made contact with the upholstery.

"Ah, that's better," he said, "facing the engine. I always like to face the engine when I'm in a train."

The generals, the admiral, and the air commodore all gazed at him stonily. Not too pleased by the way he was letting the air force down, I stared at him even more stonily. Most people looked like one animal or another, and the newcomer was definitely no exception. I, for instance, was said to resemble a horse – thoroughbred, of course. But this one looked like an ostrich with no available sand to bury its head in.

No sooner was the young man settled in place when he realized that his kit bag was lying, gasping, on the floor, in everybody's way. So up he got again, and picking it up, struggled to jam it into the overhead rack between a genuine leather valise and a hamper from Fortnum and Mason's. The fact that a tin helmet was part of his equipage did not much help.

Succeeding at last, he regained his seat. A moment later the rocking motion of the train dislodged his tin helmet. It fell onto the admiral's kneecap. Then it clanged onto the floor and rolled about helplessly for a while.

Everybody except B.W., the admiral, and a general, who had fallen asleep, watched the helmet, and kept watching until it finally settled down with a ringing clunk. Meanwhile the admiral was clutching his kneecap and turning a peculiar shade of puce. Tiny snorts were issuing from his dilated nostrils.

"Sorry," said the aircraftsman. "I suppose it wasn't quite packed properly. The tin hat is supposed to go at the open end of your kit bag, you see," he explained to the air commodore. "You know, like a lid, sort of. Though personally I always think it makes it look as if you're smuggling a small man wearing a helmet inside your kit bag."

The air commodore glared in shame and effrontery. Then he turned his head and looked out of the window as if to show that the passing smoke was of more interest than one dishevelled AC2.

Next, the AC2 removed a railway sandwich from his tunic pocket, and led it toward his mouth.

It halted en route, as its owner realized that everybody but B.W. and one of the generals, who was asleep, was staring at him again with wide-open eyes and fuming expressions.

The young man lowered the sandwich. After a moment he started to pick air-force-blue lint off it. "Got it at the buffet," he said. "This was all they had left."

The air commodore gave up admiring the smoke and grit, and in a suppressed sort of voice asked for the erk's name.

"My name? Oh, it's er, . . . let me see, you're supposed to give your service number as well, aren't you? Mine is . . . let me see, I should know it by now. No, don't prompt me," he said to the air commodore.

The air commodore obviously wasn't the least inclined to prompt him.

As if his tongue had been depressed by a spatula, the AC2 said suddenly, "Ah! I remember the last three numbers, anyway. 671. That's it. 671 Jack Donald – Lamont – sir."

Now he was looking at me. "Excuse me, sir," he said, "but you look familiar. Have we met before?"

"I'm sure we haven't, Lamont," I said coldly.

"It's pronounced Lamont, not La-mont," he said.

"As in lamentable?"

The general who had been dozing woke up with a start. "What's that?" he barked. "Who's lamentable?"

"Jack Donald over there," said the air commodore.

"What, old Jacko? Come to think of it, you're right – Jack McDonald is lamentable!"

"Actually, sir," said the AC2, "it's not Jack Donald or even Jack McDonald, it's Donald Jack."

"Better do something about this PD bloody Q," the general said to the air commodore, "Old Jacko McDonald is due to take over XIV Corps any day now. Coming invasion, you know. If he's lamentable I think perhaps we ought to think twice about it."

"About the invasion?"

"That too."

The admiral was pointing a quivering finger at the erk. "What, him, taking over XIV Corps? Good God, man, he's only an able-bodied seaman, or whatever you air force people call your people."

"Must look into this," said the newly awakened general. "If it's as bad as that, perhaps we should look again at the appointment. Make a note of that, would you, Cecil?" he said to the general next to him, who was only a brigadier-type general. "Jacko McDonald – appointment to XIV Corps. Think again! Got that?"

"Think again about Jack McDonald," Cecil said, scribbling.

The original general nodded, satisfied. He closed his eyes again. They opened them and looked around till they settled on the AC2. "Good man," he said. "What's your name?"

"671 Jack, sir, Donald L."

"Heard that name before. Sounds familiar, what? Anyway, glad you brought it to our attention, Jack. Can't have our commanders gaining a reputation for being lamentable. Good work." And he fell asleep again, while the brigadier also nodded approvingly at the AC2 even though he was of another service. And the AC2 looked around, initially a little mystified, but then in quite a contented way, as he settled back into the upholstery with a sigh, plainly quite pleased to have made at least two friends among all these toffee-nosed gits.

We arrived at Stoppingham Halt, the nearest station to Walsingham Manor. It was more like a garden centre than a railway station. Most of the platform was taken up with violets, pansies, etc., and the waiting room had been turned into a greenhouse for growing tomatoes and a prize marrow. We knew there was a prize marrow in there because the station master told us it was. Learning that our destination was "The Manor" he informed us that they had a fine

Victorian vegetable garden there. Or used to have, until Lord Houghton. He did not actually say what Lord Houghton had done to throw the vegetable garden into doubt.

"M'm," I said, looking around for a taxi. "Is there a cab round here?"

"Yes, indeed, sir, we use the cab of the shunting engine yonder for storing the tulip bulbs, sir."

"No, I meant taxis."

"Yerse, something awful, aren't they, now. Still, got to pay for the war somehow."

As B.W. tried not to stare at the station master, I explained that I was talking about transport. "You know, cars. Cabs, handsome or otherwise – taxis."

"Ah. Understand you now, sir. It was your accent, you see. Neither the one thing nor t'other. But now I got you, sir."

"Good."

"Fine, sir."

"So . . . a taxi?"

"A taxi? Here, sir?" He laughed. "Why, we haven't 'ad a taxi in Stoppingham Halt since Marigold Hornweather went into labour in Cooney's inspection pit. Right howdyedo that was, I can tell you. But don't you worry, sir. The bus will be along in" – He drew a watch from his waistcoat, blew some fertilizer off it   "it will arrive in no time at all. And it will deposit you right at the end of the drive-way to the Manor, sir, if you tell the driver. In fact he'll drive you right to the door, for 'alf a crown."

As we waited for the bus, B.W. said, "And they conquered a quarter of the world?"

I was too peeved to reply. I hadn't minded the train so much, but I did object to arriving at The Manor in a bus. I was worried about what Davis The Butler would think.

My fears were well-grounded. Davis The Butler was not at all impressed when we arrived on foot – the other passengers in the bus having objected to being taken out of their way just to accom-modate a couple of bloody officers.

Guinevere, however, was welcoming enough. She seemed to have regained her former high spirits and aggressively carefree manner, and to be making an effort to rekindle our former relationship with a series of IOUs in the form of fond hugs and the promissory note of a long kiss.

"I'm so happy to see you again, darling," she said in that rich voice of hers that had been grown in thoroughbred manure, Osmunda fern, and special mulches of rock wood, peat moss, Argentine top soil, goose liver pâtés, sherry trifles, and nightcaps of French brandy; the whole warmed by a Patagonian sun and carefully tended by the station master at Stoppingham Halt. "I was hoping we'd have the place more or less to ourselves this weekend, but I'm afraid there's a few visitors, including a friend from your part of the world, and a lady, a friend of Daddy's.

"Still," she said, hugging my arm, "I'm sure we'll find some corner where you and I can be alone. Such as," she added in a booming whisper, "my room from midnight to dawn?"

"If I can have you guarantee that I don't end up in Nanny's boudoir by mistake."

She almost ignored B.W., having given up trying to win him over. Consequently she failed to notice any difference in his behaviour. He was allocated a room on the far side of the house from mine. "So you and her can make as many whoops and hollers as she likes without me hearing," he said sourly when we met on the stairs half an hour later after a wash and brush-up.

He was still grumbling halfway down the tipsy stairway. "Don't know what you see in her," he muttered. "I mean, Jeez, she needs a face transplant."

"She's lively."

"She's only lively to make her boobs bounce up and down. She knows you like that."

A moment later his moodiness evaporated when he remembered that he would be in the clear pensionwise in another day or so. The thought was so stimulating that he was behaving quite childishly as we reached the final flight of stairs, making terrible jokes and prancing like a majorette, twirling his white stick and tossing it in the air and dexterously catching it.

At which point a small, sturdy man with a fussy manner appeared in the hall below. As he entered he was conversing with a shapely blonde woman, who would later be introduced as a Miss Deedes, a friend of Lord Houghton's. Miss Deedes gave the impression of being of the earth, earthy. Normally my eyes would have roller-coasted over her counters quite appreciatively, and inserted them snugly between parts one and two of her deepish cleavage. Later I would ask Guinevere who the lady was.

"Daddy's financial adviser."

"Oh."

But today, it was the man I was interested in. It was the horn-rimmed official I'd met in the PM's residence way back there in 1940, and again at the Quebec Conference last year. Gwinny's civil-ian buddy, Mr. Hinckley Slatter. Who had served on Bart's medical discharge board.

His horn-rimmed spectacles reflected a blaze of yellow from the wall lamps in the oaken hall as he raised his head to stare up at the stairway, open-mouthed with surprise.

"Bandy?" he asked in his margarine voice.

"Oh my goshawks," B.W. whispered, trying to hide behind me.

"Bandy?" Slatter called out again, as Guinevere followed him and Miss Deedes into the hall.

I must admit that, though concerned for B.W.'s welfare, I felt selfishly relieved that for once it was not I who had been caught in an embarrassing situation. It was with a certain detachment as well as relief that I waited to see how my son would handle it.

B.W.'s reaction was not quite up to Whitehall Theatre standards, though certainly up to mine. He fixed a pair of wildly staring eyes a good eighty-five degrees in the wrong direction. "What?" he called back in the hollow tones of a Hamlet or Charlie's Aunt. "Was that a voice I heard?" At the same time he put out a palsied hand, as if the voice, if it existed, was no more than eleven and a half inches from his face.

"It is him," Slatter said, astonished. "It's young Bandy."

"There it is again, Father," said B.W. "Oh, Lord. Now, on top of all my other misfortunes, I'm hearing echoing yet strangely familiar voices. Who is it, Father? I know it can't be Guinevere's voice — it isn't manly enough."

"It could be Davis The Butler," I said, to give him time. "In fact, here he is," I added, seeing that Davis had entered and was conferring with Guinevere. "Maybe the butler did it."

"No, it wasn't him either. Oh, Father, don't tell me I'm going mad."

"I'm afraid you are, son. But don't worry, I heard the voice as well."

"What is this?" Slatter asked confusedly. "He was practically skipping downstairs."

"I certainly wasn't," I said. "I was descending in my usual stately fashion."

"Not you — him — your son. Didn't I see him throwing his cane in the air?"

"Mr. Slatter?" B.W. cried, gazing straight up at the ceiling. "Is that you?"

"You know darn well it's me. And I did see you!"

"Of course you see me, Mr. Slatter. Oh, sir, you're so lucky to still have your eyesight. Whereas I . . ." And B.W. put the back of his free hand to his lofty forehead and turned away, the very picture of despair; though he rather spoiled it when he reached the ground floor and began to lash about with his cane under the pretence of feeling his way — but heading inexorably in Slatter's direction.

Alarmed, Slatter started to retreat, but continued to voice his suspicions as he did so. This conveniently provided B.W. with a fix, so that he could justifiably home in on the disability board member.

By then his stick was positively whooshing through the panelled air, and Slatter was in considerable danger of being severely injured. At the last moment he retreated behind Davis The Butler. This presented B.W. with a problem that had to be solved in less than a second. If he hesitated and ceased to whoosh, it would demonstrate that his blindness was not all it was cracked up to be. If he did not hesitate, an innocent man would go to the gallows, or at least get biffed.

B.W. promptly whacked Davis The Butler on the ear.

"Ow," Davis The Butler said.

B.W. had not lost that battle, but from then on, his weekend was a nightmare. Slatter had seen just enough of the spontaneous clowning on the stairway to rouse his suspicions. His next opportunity to catch out B.W. came the next morning when, over breakfast, he offered B.W. a bread roll. The offer was accompanied by a lighthearted chuckle, as if Slatter was affected by the brightness of the morning, with its silvery rain beating against the Elizabethan glass windows, and its rich grey cloud trailing through the immemorial elms. The chuckle was accompanied by a lighthearted action, the chucking of the bread roll at B.W., whose instinct should have been to catch it as deftly as he had caught the stick I had thrown to him the other day.

B.W.'s control was impressive. Not so much as a twitch disturbed his smooth, bland, and maddening countenance. The playful bread roll pattered against his chest and fell to the plank floor.

"Sorry," Slatter mumbled. Everyone stared at him.

As Guinevere was late coming down to breakfast after her disturbed night – though I was only there until about 3:00 a.m. – she missed this playful test. However, she witnessed Slatter's next attempt to prove that B.W.'s vision was unimpaired. As B.W. was palsying past in the lounge, Slatter stuck out his foot, just far enough ahead of B.W.'s faltering steps to give him time to avoid the obstacle – provided his reflexes had any common sense whatsoever.

It was not an easy challenge to overcome, but once again B.W. was up – or down – to it. He fell over the foot, and as if to save himself, clutched a delicate table with an inlaid top on which sat a crystal vase of flowers which, judging by the colour of the water and the awful smell, hadn't been changed since Dunkirk. As B.W. fell, the table collapsed as well. The vase flew through the air, and this was where I came in. I attempted to catch it before it fell to the polished planks, but the attempt merely propelled it further and faster than ever. Escaping my fingers, it crossed the room and shattered against a portrait of Lord Henry Houghton, a bewigged ancestor who had attained lasting obscurity by exposing himself in public, an exhibitionism that hardly anybody noticed, as it had taken place during a House of Lords debate.

B.W. even turned the incident to his advantage. He landed as heavily as possible and with a most pathetic cry of pain, torn unwillingly from his manly lips. This lost Slatter most of the friendship he had so diligently earned from Gwinny, whom he fancied. It also enabled B.W. to retire to his bed of pain, thus avoiding any further challenges that day. It also made it difficult for Slatter to set any further exams in public. It would be well into Sunday, B.W.'s final day in the RCAF, before Slatter could try again.

That night Gwinny and I had a particularly thirsty encounter. Afterwards as she poured white wine into the glasses on the bedside table, she asked, "What on earth is going on between those two? B.W. hasn't really regained his sight, has he?"

I managed to smother this question with a series of kisses followed by some stimulating activity involving a length of rope, some Siamese silk, a hairbrush, two spatulas, and a Hoover attachment, and by the time we had concluded the experiment she was too tired to pursue the matter.

After the panting had died down and the embrocation had been applied, somehow we got onto the subject of the coming invasion of the continent. It was of considerable interest to Gwinny, who was involved in some very hush-hush intelligence operation connected with it. Whatever it was, she gave the impression that she knew exactly when the landings were to take place.

"When?"

"Good heavens, Bart, I couldn't possibly tell you that."

"Okay."

"Except it'll be in July. I don't think I'm giving anything away by telling you that."

"July, eh? I'd have thought it was sooner than that."

"No. It'll be in one of the weeks of July. And not the last week in July either."

"Or even the second last week in July?"

"Not even then."

"In the first half of the month, then."

"I can't tell you, Bart, I'm sorry. It's cosmically secret."

She was so smug about it that I couldn't help saying, "I know for certain when it'll be. On the fifth of June."

"Oh, really, darling?" she smiled indulgently. "And what makes you think so?"

"Oh, just something I saw," I said. I was thinking about that sheet of scribbles in "Churchill's hand." But all I said was, "Operation D, I think it's to be called. Or something with the letter D in it. Talking about D, are they ever going to do anything about Drummond?"

"I don't think so."

"Why not?"

"Who knows? Anyway, why should you care?" she said in tones that were not entirely admiring. "You've had your revenge."

"How?"

"He's persona non grata, now, in Mayfair, and even parts of Belgravia."

"Good Lord – he'd be better off dead."

"Exactly," she said, yawning sincerely. She reached down, and wrapped her hand round my member and wiggled it about as if conducting the Mississauga Symphony Orchestra in a spirited rendition of *The Ride of the Valkyries*. "I think he really believed that Hitler would have governed the country better than its current rulers. I don't know if it's true, but I heard that when he was reported to the Cabinet, Winston wanted to have him shot. He was really insisting on it – especially after he heard Drummond had thrown his photograph into the wastepaper basket."

"And it was personally autographed, too. Which was more that Winston did for me," I said with a smile – though I was still feeling pretty miffed about that.

By Sunday afternoon, Slatter was desperate enough to attempt a whole series of challenges that tested B.W.'s self-control to the limit. Slatter handed him a hot chafing dish. B.W. unflinchingly grasped it, though he let go fast enough so as to avoid anything worse than a second-degree burn. Later that morning Slatter placed a helmet from a suit of armour in B.W.'s way at the top of the stairs. B.W. tripped, staggered, and would have pitched headlong had not Slatter himself, realizing that B.W. really was in danger of serious injury, reached out and caught him. Though possibly Slatter was ensuring that B.W. didn't have another excuse to retreat to the blessed privacy of his bedroom.

"You're a true stoic," I told B.W. admiringly. "Where the hell did you learn to control yourself so well?"

"Private school."

Naturally, B.W. was doing everything he could to keep out of Slatter's way. He locked himself in the Blue Room, but Guinevere had told Slatter, as she seemed to tell everybody, about the secret passages, and Slatter used the knowledge to leap out from the fireplace in the hope (vain, as it turned out), of catching B.W. reading from Lord Houghton's famous collection of Chinese erotica, or indulging in a game of darts or some similar activity requiring keen eyesight.

The game of hide and seek continued well into the afternoon. B.W. loitered in the shrubbery as soon as the rain let up, but Slatter stalked him through the sodden rhododendrons, and offered him a glass of rotting algae from the goldfish pond under the joshing pretence that it was lemonade. B.W. said he never drank lemonade as it was bad for his complexion.

Finally, six hours before midnight on the Sunday, when B.W. would be beyond the reach of even the most dedicated government bureaucrat, Slatter cracked. We were in the billiard room at the time, breathlessly watching Lord Houghton as he studied the peculiar arrangement of his balls whilst absently dabbing blue chalk onto the wrong end of his cue. In distinctly hysterical terms Slatter brought it all out into the open. He asserted that B.W. was feigning blindness. "He can see as well as anyone," Slatter shouted. "He's not blind at all, he can see, he's cheating the Canadian taxpayer, that's what he's doing!"

Miss Deedes said, "Of course he's blind. He must be – he hasn't once looked down my dress."

"He's not – I'm sure of it," cried Slatter.

"'Course he's blind," said the lady. "He has a white stick."

"If I was covered in grease, would that make me a cross-Channel swimmer?" Slatter cried, his glasses furiously flashing.

"I didn't know that you were a cross-Channel swimmer," the lady said interestedly. She had a London accent, the one without any t's in the sentences. "How long?"

"How long what?" he shouted.

"How long did it take you?"

"How long did what take me?"

"To swim the Channel."

"I haven't swum across the Channel. I was talking – "

"You haven't swum it yet?" I asked. "But you're going to, I take it?"

"'Course not! Why should I?"

"He's not ready to go anyway," I told Miss Deedes, "he's not covered in grease."

"Has he got all his clothes off?" B.W. asked in a pitiful, helpless sort of way.

"What?"

"You have all your clothes off, do you, Mr. Slatter?"

"No, why the hell should I have?"

"Well, you're surely not swimming the Channel in your smart business suit."

Lord Houghton spoke for the first time that weekend. Looking up from a tricky shot with an extended cue he said, "Fellow's not wearing a business suit. Wearing a rather unfashionable sort of jacket."

"But wouldn't that slow him down while he was swimming?" B.W. asked in bewilderment.

Miss Deedes agreed. "That's right. It would act as a drag. If I were you I'd take your jacket off before you cross the Channel, Mr. Slatter."

"I'm not crossing the Channel," he screamed. "I – "

"You prefer the ferry, do you?" B.W. asked.

"Well, yes. I . . ."

"This is all quite irrelevant," I said. "Because swimming the Channel, whether in an unfashionable jacket or not, isn't allowed in wartime."

"Is that right?" said Miss Deedes. "Well, in that case, Mr. Slatter, me old cock sparrow, you'll have to wait until the war is over."

"Though mind you," I said thoughtfully, "it might help the war effort if he did swim the Channel. Seeing him landing on the coast, covered in grease, the Jerries might think it was the prelude to an invasion of excessively lubricated invaders. That would distract them from the real invasion which would come elsewhere – "

"On June the fifth," put in Gwinny, sharing a private little laugh with me.

After that, we all looked at Mr. Slatter, except B.W., who was looking in entirely the wrong direction, and so missed the sight of Mr. Slatter tearing at his hair, which, I must confess with more than a touch of envy, was thick and ample in quantity, or was, before he commenced wrenching at it. He then rushed off to pack his things.

I heard later from Charles Ritchie at the Canadian High Commission that subsequently Slatter attempted to contact the Commission to express doubt as to the authenticity of B.W.'s blindness, and demand that they send a signal to Ottawa to that effect. But it was a Sunday and the High Commission was closed, with most of the staff partying at Alison Grant's flat, and by Monday, of course, it was too late.

So much for the confidentiality of pillow talk. Guinevere must have passed on at least part of our bedside chat to somebody who knew rather more about the coming invasion than she did. Immediately after which she made a frantic call to the airfield to warn them that I was not to move a muscle, not even her favourite muscle, until some of her people got there to ask a few questions. I was not to stir from the airfield until then, and under no circumstances was I to fly anywhere whatsoever, and most certainly not to the continent. If I was ever captured and the enemy found out what I seemed to know, the invasion might very well fail, with unendurable casualties. The very future of the war was at stake.

The call came too late. Nick Daplin answered the telephone, and informed her that I had already left for France.

THE MOSQUITO

WE WERE OVER THE Channel before I finally gave up arguing with
B.W. and concentrated on following the course. Which was not easy
because my radar/navigational skills were rusty, and also because I
was petrified with fear even before we had reached the enemy
defences.

It wasn't so much that B.W. was an inferior pilot. He hadn't been
handling the Mosquito long enough for me to judge. It was the fact
that he was piloting me. I wasn't used to having somebody else at
the controls. On one such inverted occasion I had been emptied
out of the plane, which wasn't conducive to making me confident
about flying with other pilots.

I tried to relax in the navigator/radar position, which was to the
right of the pilot and slightly behind him. As B.W. had refused to
hand over the controls, I had no alternative but to get down to
work; much of which involved staring anxiously out of the window.

A mile or so to the left, a squadron of American light bombers
were hastening low over the choppy sea, on their way, shaky with
apprehension, to the target whose hellish mobile defences they
were already familiar with. They had been there twice before. (I
knew they were apprehensive – I'd talked to their chaplain.) And
somewhere upstairs, but not visible at the moment, were our two
Spitfire squadrons. They were headed for the same target.

The French coast was coming up fast. I stared ahead in yellow-
bellied fear that B.W. would run into a cliff and prang the pair of

us. But somehow the water ended and the narrow beach folded safely under the Mosquito.

Now there was scrubby grassland, deep lanes, and a few scattered farmhouses zipping underneath. In no time at all – well, a minute or two – the town of Caen canted into view. An old town – wasn't the Bayeux Tapestry somewhere down there? – with real live people moving about in its streets, people purchasing baguettes at the local baguetterie, people hanging out the washing in the backyards, people with a real future and everything. I even knew one of the inhabitants. Marguerite Soames. I wondered how she was putting up with the occupation. Defiantly, if I knew her.

My heart took a NAAFI break for a couple of seconds as our sleek, twin-engined aircraft bumbled and rumbled over a rough stretch of sunwarmed aerial highway. I noticed with horror that B.W. was flying lower than ever. The kite was practically combing the Normandy bocage with its propellers. "For God's sake," I shrieked, "do you have to fly so low?"

He turned completely around in his seat to answer. I addressed him again in an even higher voice, pointing a quivering digit through the windscreen at the hill we were now hurtling toward. He turned back and lifted the Mossie casually over the obstruction. Then down he went again to dormouse level. And I decided that it was perhaps best not to distract him with terrified screams from now on, as they might, well, distract him.

I clamped the mouthpiece of oxygen and intercom on again, and in a shaky whine fed him the course changes. I decided not to look out of the windows any more.

But of course I had to. That was why I was here: to watch just what sort of flak the fighters had to face when operating, as they were increasingly being asked to do, at drastically low level.

We continued to head roughly south. At this height we seemed to be travelling at 1,000 mph over the small fields and winding lanes of Normandy, though in fact the Mosquito was practically dawdling so as not to get ahead of the Yank bombers. And changing course repeatedly in an attempt to confuse the defence. Though it was not very likely, despite our being underneath the radar, that the target had not already been warned that thirty-odd bombers and fighters were on the way.

As the Mosquito zipped along, the sun projected geometric patches of light onto the cramped interior, highlighting chipped paintwork, and illuminating enough dust to have made Mrs. Mop cluck like anything if she'd been along. "Can I do you now, sir?" Mrs. Mop's refrain in a popular BBC radio show kept running through my head. "Can I do you now, sir? Can I do you now, sir?"

And then the target appeared ahead. And they were already letting off the fireworks.

When B.W. and I returned from our draining weekend at Walsingham Manor, we were greeted with the news that another attack on the new German airfield south of Caen had been ordered. Which was horrible news.

It had started out as an 8th Air Force show. The Americans had been ordered to hit this dive-bomber base, which had only recently been hacked out of the unsuitable landscape. They had found it bristling like an 88-mm hedgehog. There seemed to be about a million radar-controlled gun barrels pointing at the sky. The Americans had suffered heavy losses.

A week later another strike against the same target was called for, this time the B25s being provided with a cover of Spitfires. Because the weather was bad that day, the squadrons failed to rendezvous. Nevertheless, the Americans pressed home the attack. Sixteen aircraft had reached the target. Seven returned. And two of our Spitfires were lost as well.

Now another strike had been ordered, and we were told that we were expected to do our job properly this time. As if it were our fault that the weather had stymied the escort job. There was much indignation over the wording of the order from Fighter Command, and I got on to the AOC to find out what was so important about this target that it was worth the loss of so many crews. I received only a curt, "Get on with it."

"You're going on the raid?" Corporal Atkins asked. "But we don't have any serviceable kites."

"How about that one?" I said, pointing to the now thoroughly rehabilitated Mosquito.

B.W., who was still cheekily mooching in and out of camp in his redundant uniform, protested. If anyone should fly the Mosquito he should. He had done a conversion course on Mosquitos, while I had no experience of the type.

"My dear boy," I said, "I've driven fifty different kinds of aircraft in my time. Do you think I couldn't handle a little beauty like that? Piece of cake, old son, piece of cake."

"You're crazy, Father," B.W. said. He tended to use the word Father when he wished to be particularly censorious. "For one thing, your leg is so bad you look like you're auditioning for *Treasure Island*. This isn't a nice flight to Whitstable and Hernia Bay, you know. It's a goddamn dangerous operation. Sorry for swearing, God. I'm not letting you kill yourself after all the trouble I took finding you so I could tell you I never wanted to see you again."

"I'm just going along as an observer," I pointed out. "I have to see for myself what the pilots have to face."

It was still my conviction, obsession even, that if the generals in WWI had seen trench warfare for themselves there would have been a million fewer casualties.

Even Wing Commander Broseley was unhappy about the raid. "They're telling us," he said, his ginger moustache quivering like a cornered hamster, "that we're not simply to cover the Yanks against enemy fighters. We're to get right down there and do some shooting up ourselves? Are they crackling, gibbering round the bend, sicking Spits onto a job like that?"

The best I could do in the way of a reply was, "I gather it's especially important that this dive-bomber base gets knocked out, Bob. Maybe it's something to do with the invasion."

Take-off was for 1300 hours, May 29. As the hour approached I began to regret that I'd told everybody that I was going along. I had a premonition of disaster. I'd never had one of those before –

though I could have done with one or two of them in the past. I
tried to think of a reason as to why I couldn't go. I had a genuinely
good excuse – my leg was giving me gyp. Nevertheless, 1305 hours
on der Tag found me hobbling over to the Mosquito in battledress
and flying boots, leaning ostentatiously on my stick.

Already the air was being beaten to death by the bellow of
Merlin engines. The last pair of Spitfires was taking off. I tried to
walk faster. I was late. I'd been held up at the office trying to encourage Daplin to intervene on my behalf. I was hoping he would
suggest that I was too valuable to risk on such a dangerous mission.
But the swine merely pointed out that I was not actually doing
the dangerous bit. All I was doing, he reminded me, was observing from a safe distance.

God, Daplin could be a swine, sometimes.

As I winced up to the Mosquito, I was not particularly pleased to
see that the ground crew had speeded things up for me. Both
engines were already running. Unless it was my crewman showing
off. What was his name again? Forgotten.

One of the erks said something urgently as I ducked down to
climb angrily into the belly of the aircraft. It was too noisy to hear
what he said, and I was in no mood to listen anyway. My bloody
crewman up there must be testing the magnetos at full power. By
God, I was going to tear a strip off him the moment I squeezed into
the cabin. Who did he think he was, trying to do my job?

The fellow trying to do my job turned out to be my son. He was
already comfortably settled in at the controls, wearing battledress
and a white polo-neck sweater.

As the hatch thumped shut behind me: "Hey," I shouted, "get
out of it! Where's my oppo?"

"I signed on in his place," B.W. shouted back over the blasting
roar of the engines. He already had the kite moving, taxiing before
I'd even got to the observer seat. "Hold tight, I'm taking off."

Astonished and confused, I spluttered remonstrances to the effect
that he was crazy, that he wasn't even in the air force any longer,
that he would get us both into trouble, that he had a damn cheek

conning himself aboard my aircraft. But I had to cease gobbling and hastily buckle myself in, for he was lining up for the take-off a machine heavily laden with fuel, bullets, cannon shells, and a downright furious and petrified groupie.

One advantage to being petrified at being flown by somebody else was that there was little terror left over for the actual operation. Naturally the Hun was expecting the onslaught. You couldn't fly this far into France and expect to throw a surprise party. The single runway was ringed by anti-aircraft redoubts capable of throwing up torrents of fire. They even had guns well outside the perimeter, for they were taking potshots at our Mossie even though it was circling well clear of the huts, revetments, bunkers, bays, towers, and the wire-mesh runway.

Part of the reason why the base had not been put out of action was that the rough countryside of scrubby trees, high hedges, and deep-down roads and lanes made even the runway difficult to get at, let alone the Junkers dive-bombers lying snug in their sand-bagged harbours. Even rocket-firing Typhoons would have found it a tricky proposition.

I still couldn't understand why the enemy had gone to such trouble to put in a bomber base this far south. Unless they thought that the Allies might just possibly be landing in Normandy. Which was patently absurd. From the south coast of England all the way to Normandy was much too great a distance for an invasion fleet. Everybody knew that the Pas de Calais was where it was bound to come.

Which made it all the more painful to watch, as the American bombers flew into a sky drenched with curving tracers, balls of red and green fire, puffs of white 88 mm and the bombers' own grey and yellow bursts among the scrubby trees.

Even from a ringside seat, there was so much smoke and fire that it was difficult to tell how many of the light bombers went down.

Then it was the turn of the fighters, which was the moment I most dreaded. They came diving in at maximum speed, cannon firing, trying to get at the Junkers in the bays. We saw one of the

Spitfires blow up, and another go cartwheeling over the ground
before burying itself in the woodland on the far side of the field in
great gouts of yellow flame.

When I saw yet another of my Spitfires trailing glycol smoke and
frantically trying to gain height, I could stand it no longer. "Let's
get in there," I shrieked at B.W., thrashing about in the radar seat
as if I were having a seizure. "Come on, let's go in."

"What, into that?" B.W. asked, indicating the furnace of smoke
and flame, the ferocious tangle of ack-ack bursts, and the slashing
tracers as the Spits completed their run-ins and clawed desperately
for height and cover, or zigzagged frantically at crabgrass level to put
any sort of distance between them and the guns, every zig giving
them another three seconds of life – maybe – every zag another four
seconds of life – perhaps.

"Come on, we can help, we're loaded up!" I yelled.

"No."

"No, what? What're you talking about? Get in there and help!"

"No."

"What're you saying, what're you saying?"

"I'm not going into that, what good would it do?"

"Christ, man, we can help – they're taking a beating – we can
do something!"

"I'm not dying for no reason."

"Then I'll fly," I screamed, and started to unfasten the harness,
unable to stand by any longer and watch the slaughter.

Whether or not I really intended to wrest the controls from him
I've no idea. But B.W. must have thought I was about to do some-
thing along those lines for he took countermeasures. He turned the
Mosquito on its side.

Presumably he had intended keeping me in my seat by doing a
steep banking turn. Well, he achieved an imprisoning centrifugal
force all right, but nothing as simple as a wing-bending change of
direction. Suddenly and incomprehensibly we were being spun
round, round and round like test tubes in a centrifuge, at an impossible rpm. This astounding effect was followed by an equally fantastic series of jolting crashes and flashes of light. Not for the first

time in my life, fast sequences of memory were projected across my mind. In fact there wasn't even time for my whole life to flash before my eyes, for the next thing I knew I was sitting in a pile of wreckage with my leg hurting more than ever.

I guessed that the whole sequence had taken no more than eight or nine or ten seconds out of our lives.

B.W. was thirty feet away. He too was sprawled in the midst of an airframe so pulverized that the largest fragment seemed to be a single propeller boss. He was rubbing his buttocks and wincing. And my leg had been damaged afresh. That was the sum total of our injuries: additional hurt to one leg that didn't seem willing to recover, and one aching bottom.

For quite a while we were unable to believe that we had survived so total a crash, though such miracles do happen in war flying. I personally know of several examples of amazing survival, including that of an American transport that successfully crossed the Atlantic only to hit not just one but two Welsh mountains. The plane landed safely with both wings bent more than ninety degrees so that the wingtips met overhead.

We had the good luck to be one more example, though we wondered for a moment if we were still alive when we looked around at the wreckage, the bits and pieces of the wooden fuselage and wings, the twisted engines, the scattered cannon shells, the shattered Perspex, and the copy of *Lilliput* open at one of Bill Brandt's artistic nudes. We gathered that it was the trees that had braked us to a survivable speed before we smacked into the field and slid to the far side, disintegrating all the way. As the tail section was sitting well ahead of the rest of the debris, we may have hit the dirt backwards.

The engines had failed to catch fire though there was a strong odour of high octane. After determining that my leg was not actually broken, I crawled away across the grass on hands and knees, until I was at a safe distance from the smell.

B.W. did likewise. We met at an anthill.

"What happened?" I asked.

"We crashed."

"Oh, yes?"

"Yep."

"What I was asking was, how did we come to crash? Were we hit?"

"No."

"Did the engines fail?"

"No."

"Perhaps you felt you'd done enough flying for the day and decided to land?"

"Don't be so dumb," he said, rubbing his rump. "Well, if you must know, the wing hit the ground. When I banked, to keep you from making a fool of yourself."

"The wing hit the ground," I said, trying to visualize it. "How? How did it come to hit the ground?"

"I don't know why you're being so nosy."

"Nosy?"

"I mean, we got more important things to think about than crashes, after all."

"No, but I'd like to understand how I came so close to death, B.W. I'm still not entirely convinced I've survived such a crash. But first things first. I guess it's a quirk, but I'm the sort of person who likes to know why he's flying perfectly safely one moment, and the next he's – "

"All right, all right! It was my fault! Now are you satisfied? I was too low when I banked around. The wing hit the trees. All right? You satisfied now?"

I looked at him in a slow, quivering rage. "You . . . you . . ." I said. I took a deep, whistling breath. "You," I said.

"Yeah, well," he mumbled. "We're not all shit-hot pilots like you."

He hung his head. And said, "I mean, what good would it have done?"

Well, of course he was right. What good would it have done? It would have been an utter waste of my life, throwing it into that inferno back there. It had been a crazed impulse, to join a lost battle.

For a moment I had turned into a brainless Carruthers, listening only to the gurgling of my adrenaline.

I was wrong, B.W. had been right. Though I certainly wasn't going to admit it.

"I mean," he muttered, "what kind of fool goes thundering into the valley of death shouting hoo-ray?"

"Yes, well," I muttered back, "we've got more important things to do than talk about that."

"I mean, I thought that was the kind of thing you despised."

"Look, we've got to get out of here before they come looking for us," I said firmly.

"I mean, like those oldtimers of yours who kept going over the top even though they knew it was hopeless, and the brass you hated so much saying, Come on, men, just one more time."

"All right, all right!" I said. "You don't have to go on and on about it."

"I mean, you were thinking just like the sort of brass hat you hated."

"That's a terrible thing to say to your father, B.W.," I said, my voice trembling with emotion.

"Yeah, well. Anyway, no harm done, Pop. I saved your life."

"You what?"

"Sure I did. If I hadn't got the hell out, you'd have got the hell in – and gone for a Burton."

"I would not!"

"You really think you could have gotten through that skyful of hate?"

"Certainly," I said, "and probably got a VC for it!"

"Ha!"

"Ha yourself! And I wanted that VC – it's the only medal I don't have. So on top of everything else you've deprived me of a Victoria Cross."

"You'd have gotten it posthumous."

"Posthumous*ly*. And I would not! Oh, I may have got a scratch or two – which would have earned me another wound stripe, too – if it hadn't been for you."

"You'd have gotten the wound stripe posthumously too."

"Oh, bollocks," I said, and we went on arguing for a while until it suddenly struck us both, that here we were, sitting in a damp field deep in enemy territory, arguing about medals and wound stripes.

"Yes, well . . . I guess we should be making tracks, Pa," B.W. said.

"I guess you're right, B.W.," I said. "Let's get the hell out of here."

MARGUERITE IN CAEN

WELL CLEAR OF THE crash site, we were now patiently waiting for a train.

After hours of anxious travel we had stumbled upon a single-track railway line aligned roughly north and south. Further along the track, beyond a sharp curve, there was a crumbling stone bridge. The bridge had just enough strength to cross the line, possibly because it had not been used for years and had lost heart.

We hid in the long grass close to the bridge, ready to hop aboard if a train ever came along.

The fortunate reader will note that he is being spared the usual harrowing tale of our escape from the crash scene; of how, with pain, agony, suffering, and even discomfort, we made our way across country, lurching for mile after mile through the Normandy bocage, becoming steadily more exhausted in our haste to escape the pursuit.

Actually there was no pursuit. Perhaps the smoke-drenched and fire-streaked sky over the distant airfield had prevented the Jerries from observing our abrupt disappearance into the tangled landscape. All the same, thinking we were being hounded was surely as much a spur to whacked-out flight as actually being chased through the tangled countryside with its dusty fields, scrubby woodland, and deep, deep lanes. A countryside seemingly devoid of inhabitants.

"The French aren't being much help, are they?" I grumbled.

"We haven't seen any yet."

"Exactly. They're never around when you need them."

After a three-hour wait for a train, I was beginning to think this was a disused line.

"It must be in use," B.W. pointed out. "The rails are polished."

"They're rusty, they're only half-polished."

"So maybe we'll get half a train."

In a nearby wood, some brute beast or other made a sound like an unoiled hinge. Insects, loud in the silence, hummed around, looking for a tasty part of us to bite.

"I don't think a train will ever come along," I said sullenly. "The railroad staff probably polish the rails by hand, to fool people into thinking there's a train."

"You're just being silly because your leg hurts," B.W. said.

"Not being silly. And I think we should carry on."

"You're already carrying on."

"I mean, we should continue walking or we'll still be here when the war ends."

"Let's wait a bit longer," B.W. said.

My eyelids drooped in the humming warmth.

"How about a piece of your chocolate?" B.W. said. "I'm hungry."

"I don't have any."

"You must. You always bring a bar of chocolate when you're flying."

"Well, I didn't this time."

"And the result is, we crashed."

"What?"

"I'm pointing out that we crashed because you didn't bring your lucky chocolate bar along."

"Don't be ridiculous. Anyway, you're the one who crashed."

"You crashed as well, didn't you? I mean, it stands to reason, doesn't it, that a chocolate bar was your lucky charm, because the only time you didn't bring one along – "

"Once and for all, it wasn't my lucky charm – it was to eat! It was my foxfurs that was my lucky charm."

"You mean the foxfurs you wore in the First World War?"

"Yes."

The sky was darkening. For a moment I thought it was my eyesight. But it was only the elements. The thought of spending a night out in the open did not make me overjoyed. In a month I would be fifty, assuming I got there. I really was getting too old for this sort of thing.

As we lay there near the bridge, field mice kept rustling out of the deep grass. There seemed to be quite a plague of them around here. They would half-stand for a better look at us, twitching their noses as if we were malodorous, which no doubt we were.

"Was the head still attached?" B.W. asked.

"What?"

"The foxfurs you wore when you were flying. Was the head still attached to the foxfurs?"

"Course. You don't think I'd wear a decapitated fox, do you?"

"You must have looked crazy with a fox round your neck. Were you ever pursued by men with dogs in red coats?"

"Don't be ridiculous. Whoever heard of dogs in red coats."

"I meant the men were in red coats. Dad?"

"What?"

"You don't think we're suffering the after-effects of the crash, do you? Do you think we're delirious?"

"Yes."

"Thank God. I wondered why you were starting to make sense."

I had lost my walking stick in the crash. I took hold of the tree branch that B.W. had cut and trimmed for me with his trusty penknife. I started to gnaw the makeshift cane.

"Your leg hurting, Dad?"

"A bit."

Shyly, he patted my back and muttered something reassuring. A moment later he stiffened. "Listen," he said.

"What?"

"Don't you hear it?"

I listened. It was, at long last, a train.

As it came chuffing round the bend we were relieved to note that
it was not a passenger or troop train, but was all freight, an ancient
steam locomotive drawing mostly flatbeds and enclosed trucks.

By then it was nearly dark, which would make boarding it all the
more hazardous. Nevertheless, we stuck to our plan to hang from
the bridge and drop onto the roof of the train. It was risky but
because I couldn't run it was a less dangerous alternative to being
wrenched up from the track; though we had agreed that if the train
was going too fast we would reconsider the risky procedure.

The speed was not too great. We had anticipated that the train
would slow down a little to negotiate the sharp curve in the track.
So, hanging from the forward side of the bridge so as to avoid being
observed by the engineer, we stiffened the sinews, summoned up
the blood – one, two, three, go! – and dropped onto a truck roof.
Or rather, onto an abrasive tarpaulin, which was covering a load of
freight.

The landing was soft enough, but hard on my starboard extremity. I couldn't help yelling as I landed. Fortunately there were no
guards on the train, and the engineers were far enough ahead that
I could not have been heard over the clattering of the wheels.

"You okay?" B.W. asked as we settled down under the tarpaulin.

My response was a look of reassuring pain.

Now that the sun had gone down, the air was quite chill, so we
were grateful for the tarpaulin cover, and for the softness of the
freight, which was something in bales.

Our luck seemed to be holding. We could hardly have picked a
more comfortable train. "Better than that first-class coach in
England," B.W. said with a contented sigh.

As we sat squinched together between bales, he seemed more
inclined than ever to chat. "You realize we're even now, Pa?" he
said.

"How?"

"You saved my life, now I've saved yours."

"Saved my life how?"

"I got you down in that field safely, didn't I?"

"I don't believe this," I said, shaking my head.

"So now we're quits," he said; and to drown out any protests I might make he started to sing. "Ma momma done told me," he sang, "when ah was in knee pants." And when he finished the refrain he slapped his knee. "Yeh!"

After a moment I managed a laugh – if that's what the hoarse, parched sound was. "You know, B.W.," I said, "you're becoming more like me every day."

He looked alarmed. "How?"

"Never mind."

We fell silent, swaying together, listening to the clatter of the bogies underneath.

"Nobody liked me at school," he said suddenly.

I resisted the impulse to josh him, and remained silent.

"Thanks to you, I had this face that made everybody want to beat me up in the playground. And that was just the teachers."

"That sounds familiar."

"I never really got the feeling Grandpa and Grandma cared two hoots about me, either," he said. "I don't remember ever getting a hug from them like you give me, except when there was company and they were showing what great grandparents they were. It finally got through to me, the day I decided to head into the north woods and join the RCAF. I was just something they owned, along with the paintings, and the private plane, and the mahogany cruiser. Come to think of it, they never showed much feeling for Mom, either," he said, fading.

"No . . . Poor Cissie."

"I guess you really must . . . you know."

"What?"

"You know. On the balcony. To have held onto me like that, when it would have been easy to let go."

The only response I could think of at that moment was to lean against him a little harder.

A moment later he was truculent again. "But don't think I'm going to change what I think," he said. "There's going to be some big changes after the war. And I'll never believe what you said about how the Russians treat their own people. You've been reading too much imperialist propaganda. I'll never believe it."

"You're in good company. All through the Thirties, fashionable leftists and people like Bernard Shaw never wanted to know what was happening, either. And they still don't."

"Shaw? That old fool?" he snorted, before realizing that he was being disrespectful toward an icon of socialism. But then he had taken a dislike to Mr. Shaw because of that mischievous savant's criticism of the United States. B.W. might think he welcomed the revolution, but deep down he still considered that America was number one in God's book.

Only a few seconds seemed to pass before I was roused from a stupor of pain and fatigue by B.W.'s voice and his elbow in my ribs.

"Huh?"

"I said why do you want to get to this place, Kong?" he asked, digging out his penknife and prising open the blade.

"Who are you calling Kong?" I growled.

"I'm talking about the town you want to get to."

"Oh, Caen. I know somebody there."

"You do? Who?" he asked. He was idly slitting open one of the bales.

"She moved there from Paris," was the best I could manage.

"Oh, *she*," he said with a smirk, and, finding that the bale seemed to contain nothing but paper, he disappeared round the corner.

Over the noise of the train I could hear the tearing of sacking. "So how will she help?" he called out.

"Marguerite's the sort of woman who might know somebody in the Resistance movement," I croaked. "Help get us back to England."

I had been trying for hours to remember Marguerite's Caen address, but had so far failed.

"Well, I'll be," B.W. said.

"What?"

"Come and look."

"Couldn't you show me?"

"Oh, sure." A moment later he came crawling back, clutching an armful of used clothing. "I managed to work these out of one of the bales back there," he said.

We examined the items. They included a long black overcoat, a white shirt, a woman's blouse, and one lisle stocking.

"I don't believe it," I said. "We need civilian clothes to get around in – and we catch a train filled with old clothes?"

I was reluctant to move from my present comfy spot on the flat car, so B.W. went back to see what else he could drag out of a tightly packed bale. He returned with an armful of garments, including a smock, a jacket, another shirt, and a complete suit, navy blue, worn, but of good quality.

"What's this?" B.W. asked, indicating the yellow star sewn onto the black overcoat. "What's this mean, d'you think?"

But I didn't know.

The luck that had seen us this far was still doing us good turns. At about ten that night, the freight train steamed slowly onto a double-track main line, through a railway station and onto a siding, where it stopped, presumably to allow more important freight to go by on the main line. In the dark we missed the name of the station, but there was a van parked close to the siding, and in the moonlight we could read the sign on it, and the address was Caen.

"First they outfit us in apparel suitable for two gentlemen of leisure," I said. "And now they deliver us exactly where we want to go. What calamity are they saving us for, I wonder."

By then we were togged out in old clothes, having stuffed our uniforms into the bale. (Somebody was in for a surprise when they found Allied battledress among the cargo.) Thus attired, we dropped off the train and scuttled gladly into the darkness.

Unfortunately I had still not remembered Marguerite's address. But then it was six or seven years since I'd heard from her. As she was the sort of person who would live at the centre – she was definitely not a suburban type – we headed toward the centre of town, ready at any moment to dodge out of sight should a German patrol appear. We were certainly easy to see – the blackout in this town of 50,000 souls was not nearly as total as it was across the Channel.

As we walked/hobbled past the Malherbe lycée, B.W. asked if Caen had an airport.

"There's an airfield at Carpiquet."

"Maybe we could swipe a Hun plane and fly home, like you did in 1918, huh, Dad?"

"That was a fluke, B.W.," I muttered, looking around. I was beginning to wonder if the Germans had wiped out most of the population of Caen, we had seen so few people. But there was at least one citizen of the Republic abroad tonight. He was standing near the barred and shuttered entrance to a cinema. He had stopped to light a cigarette near a torn and faded poster advertising a film starring Jean Gabin. I was keeping a wary eye on him as we passed and so was instantly aware of his reaction. He started violently and uttered an oath.

At first I thought he had burned his fingers on his match. But it was us. He came running over and grabbed B.W. by the arm. "Merde alors," he said, continuing in an emphatic French that even I could understand, "how can you be so stupid? Get out of sight, for God's sake!"

Gesturing feverishly and looking around him in fright, he seized us both by the sleeves, and rushed our protesting, dragging figures along the street, and to a flight of steps leading up the side of a decrepit apartment building. The staircase led to a wooden landing, off which were two entrance doors. With a shaky hand, he took out a bunch of keys, opened one of the doors, and shoved us unceremoniously inside.

With the curtains quickly drawn and the light turned on, he proceeded to upbraid us for attracting attention to the neighbourhood in this stupid fashion. "Is this some sort of suicidal defiance?" he demanded, and actually bunched his fist, as if to give us a good thumping.

His angry words brought a woman of haggard appearance into the room. She was wearing a dressing gown and had the moistly dishevelled appearance of one who had spent most of the day in bed. She looked unwell.

She asked a question. "Look," he said, gesturing at B.W.

Her eyes widened with shock.

"They were walking through the streets as if there was not a thing, not a thing, to worry about. As if an evening stroll rather than extinction was their object. Truly, they must be lunatics from Charenton. And there was a patrol from the Ardenne Abbey in the neighbourhood. I saw it only ten minutes ago. They are crazy, crazy."

B.W., having taken French at school for only a dozen or so years, couldn't understand a word. "Huh?" he asked, a couple of times; and finally turned to me and said, "What's all the fuss about?"

If the couple had been agitated before, it was nothing to their reaction upon hearing these words in English. The man positively gaped. The woman put a hand onto the door jamb for support.

As my eyes adjusted to the poor light of the shabby apartment, I saw that the woman was younger than I'd first thought – in her late twenties, perhaps. With her fair hair and pleasingly arranged features, including a pair of Madonna-like eyes, she would have looked exceedingly pretty had her face not been so heavy with sickness and her movements so effortful.

Whether she was sick or healthy, the man, who was about her age, plainly adored her. The moment she appeared he had skipped over to give her a kiss, and for the rest of the evening he rarely missed an opportunity to demonstrate his affection for her, sometimes in slightly bizarre ways, such as making osculatory attacks from the rear, and gradually working the kisses round from the back of her neck to her throat.

Mostly she accepted the adoration stoically. She was also the one in command. When I claimed that we were downed aviators: "See if they have documents, Alain," she said with quiet authority.

Alain started. "Yes, your papers," he said, retreating a step in the direction of a corner cupboard. His manner, formerly one of anger and incredulity, now exhibited despair over his own stupidity in failing to foresee that we might be part of some Boche trap.

We had, of course, kept our identity cards, and now produced them.

"My God, they really are English," he exclaimed; and, now that we had been established as friendly, he removed a pistol from the corner cupboard and spun it around his forefinger, like a Western gunslinger.

"Let me see." The woman studied the cards. "I suppose they are genuine," she said. Turning to us she asked politely, "You are flyers, you say? You are the people who are bombing us nearly every night?"

"We're fighter pilots," B.W. said with disdainful pride.

We gave a brief account of ourselves, including the details on how we had acquired the civilian clothing, about which Alain and his wife questioned us quite sharply. Shaking their heads, they offered some coarse red wine, and the four of us sat around the kitchen table drinking and talking quietly about the war. Or rather, three of us talked about it, my rusty French coming back to me surprisingly fast, while B.W. gazed around interestedly, as if he were a tourist being shown the birthplace of a famous Frenchman who had been born in abject poverty.

The woman was looking at me in utter despair. "Is our plight so little known in your country that you do not know the meaning of the yellow star?" she asked.

"What's she say? What're you talking about?" B.W. asked.

"I seem to remember it in the newsreels," I said, "about the Jews having to wear yellow stars?"

"To this day, we are not certain what is happening to my people," the woman said. "Though there are dreadful rumours. But you will understand our amazement at seeing you wearing such a star in the streets at such a time. Only a few days since, the police raided this quartier and took away everyone suspected of being a Jew."

As this exchange was in English, it was now Alain's turn to ask what we were talking about. She translated, calmly enough; to which he in his turn explained that though Marie was Jewish, she had survived because nobody among their friends – there was a bitter emphasis on the word "friends" – knew of her origins. Nor, apparently, had the police found out, for they had still not come for her. Not yet, anyway.

"The police?" I asked. "The Germans, you mean?"

"The French police," Alain said. "In this at least they are doing their best to help the occupying forces."

"Now what's he saying?" B.W. asked. But nobody answered.

Marie's father, a Parisian, was an art dealer before he was called up as a reservist and soon taken prisoner by the Germans. Marie did not know whether he was alive or dead. As for her mother, she had not seen her for years. She had not even been aware that Mama was Jewish until she was preparing to flee to America in the late Thirties.

Marie had refused to go with her. She could not take the danger seriously. After all, there was the Maginot Line to keep out the Germans. And Paris was a wonderful place to live when you were twenty-three, and had a good job, helping in Papa's gallery.

"I should have listened to my mother," she said with a rueful smile, as Alain, a sprightly fellow with quick nervous movements, rushed up to her again, slipped his hand into her dressing gown, and gave part of her a reassuring squeeze. Whatever her illness was, he was certainly not afraid of catching it.

Three glasses of wine and some soup, bread, and cheese enabled me to remember Marguerite's address. Alain knew where it was — near the St. Julien Church, he said.

I told our hosts that Marguerite was once the wife of a British general, though they had long since separated. She had fled Paris in 1940 and moved into her parents' house here in Caen. Though of course she might not be living here now.

Suddenly revealing that he could understand some English, Alain said in that language, "If it is possible, we take you to the Maquis — the Resistance."

"That's great."

"Unfortunately it is not possible. We have no contact with the Resistance."

"That's too bad."

Reverting to French he explained that he and Marie were concerned exclusively with helping Jews to hide or to escape.

"No matter," I said. "If I know Madame Soames she will be in touch with the Resistance movement. I'm sure she will help."

"I'm so sorry we cannot do more," Marie said wanly. But then smiled affectionately at her lover. "Alain is not a Jew himself," she said. "But France will regain its glory when there are still people like him to help."

Her reward for this comment was a positive shower of kisses and another quick feel.

She turned her exhausted eyes on me. "You are sure you can trust this Madame Soames, Monsieur?" she asked.

"Oh, sure. We have known each other for twenty years. Whenever I am in the neighbourhood she is always ready to offer me a bed."

"Ah," Marie said, like a good Frenchwoman instantly assuming that the offer was for Margeurite's own bed. I was glad that B.W. could not follow our conversation.

"Tomorrow we will decide what is the best way to get you across town without running into trouble," Marie said. "But now, you must be tired after your experience. And you are hurt. We will look at your leg. You will stay here for the night. But for only one night, I'm afraid. For the sake of others, we cannot take risks, you understand?"

"Of course. Of course, Madame."

Unfortunately, Alain was not as tired as we were, and was inclined to talk. He did so far into the night. He was thrilled to hear about our exploits as fighter pilots. He admired fighter pilots, and was even more thrilled when I mentioned that I had met several French aces during the First World War, and one, Pierre Clostermann, in this one.

Alain was a short, slender, and good-looking man with curly black hair and teeth well cared for. He was originally from Caen but had lived in Paris until the Occupation. He considered himself a sophisticated member of the artistic colony there. He had studied composition, with some harmony and counterpoint thrown in when they could not be avoided – "Truly, they are not really necessary," he said with a shrug. He had also loitered on the fringes of the literary intelligentsia. He announced with evident pride that he had met Merleau-Ponty, Sartre, and Simone de Beauvoir.

"Gosh," I said. I'd never heard of them.

The war, however, had focussed his life a little more sharply. He confessed that he had become somewhat disillusioned with the intellectuals, who seemed more inclined to talk about philosophy than to help the country through its ordeal.

"But when the war is over, I shall go back to Paris and continue with my plans to establish an entirely new art form," he said. "I shall call it Stenmusic."

"Stenmusic."

"Tonality is finished," he said vehemently. "We have seen the end of Beethoven, Bizet, Berlioz, and all the other B's. No doubt," he said contemptuously as he paced the small room, "my friends will regress to the Schönbergian system. But for me it will be Stenmusic."

"How will that work?" I asked, yawning so hugely behind my hand that my eyes watered. I cast an envious glance at B.W. He was sound asleep in the canvas bed in the far corner.

"It is simplicity itself. You create the notes by firing at the manuscript with a Sten gun. Wherever holes appear on the stave, there are the notes," he said triumphantly.

Next morning, with the yellow stars carefully removed from our clothing, Alain escorted us across Caen. Or rather, we followed several yards behind him, in case either party was stopped by the Gendarmes or by the enemy. This morning there were many Germans strolling about in their smart grey uniforms or sunning themselves at outdoor cafés. At one point we thought that four Jerries in a Jeep-type vehicle were taking an unhealthy interest in us. We were mistaken. They drove off without incident.

There seemed to be little sense of urgency or anxiety in the German ranks. Alain had told us that many of the soldiers hereabouts were convalescent. They had been fighting on the Russian front, and after their experiences there they plainly regarded France as a holiday camp.

We arrived at Marguerite's place without incident. It was a large stuccoed building near the University. It badly needed a lick of paint and a gardener. The yellow-ochre stucco was falling off in lumps. The driveway beyond the drunken iron gate was so overgrown that the cobbles were almost invisible.

Alain halted at the gate. "I will wait until I see that you are admitted into the house," he said. "Otherwise, I will not see you again, mon Colonel?"

"I guess not," I said. "Well, thank you very much for your help, Alain. And the best of luck with your rescue work."

"Bye," said B.W.

At the front door I hauled on the old-fashioned bell handle. Nothing happened, so I rapped on the glass part of the door; and started as a voice spoke in my ear.

There was an intercom speaker by the door. It was hanging by two wires, but obviously still working, for it said, "Oui?"

I leaned close. "Margeurite Soames?" I said.

"Yes."

Great. She was still here.

"It's the man with the lost tooth," I said, using the same words as when I had last called on her, in Paris.

There was a long silence. "Margeurite?" I prompted.

"Just a moment, chéri, I am on the telephone. Just a moment."

A couple of minutes later the door opened and there she stood, fifty-five years old, but still a Fragonard model, exploding into delighted little cries of welcome.

"But my God," she said, clutching her bright yellow peignoir to her, "here are two Bandys! My God, as if one is not enough!"

"This," I said, "is my – "

"You don't have to tell me," she said at the top of her voice, and waving a lighted cigarette. "There could not possibly be another like you unless he was from your very loins."

B.W. winced. He was not excessively pleased, either, when she embraced him as warmly as she had greeted me, and gave him only one kiss less than I had received. In the process she almost set fire to her peignoir with the cigarette, but brushed a shower of sparks off herself as casually as if this sort of thing happened every day. "But come in, come in," she cried, and once inside, looked again admiringly at B.W.: "But he is even taller than you. And he is so . . . so . . . ?"

"Handsome?" B.W. suggested.

"But of course," she cried, and continued to praise his appearance the more enthusiastically for having so obviously hesitated, flatterywise. "Charming, charming," she said, and patted his cheek.

"But please, mount, mount," she said, and led the way toward the staircase, turning to gesture so enthusiastically that her scorched peignoir fell open and gave us a treat.

The rear view, too, was pretty nice, as we followed her to the stairs. Her hips swayed as if on gimbals. Despite my foot, which was hurting even more than the balance of the limb, I felt quite a few tingles at the sight of her figure and her creamy skin, without a pucker, tuck, or wrinkle in sight.

"I am living upstairs, you see," she explained, and added vaguely, "there was trouble with the furniture."

There was trouble with the furniture all right. There wasn't any. The whole of the ground floor was deserted. Light patches covered the walls where paintings had hung.

Upstairs, her sitting room more than made up for the scarcity downstairs. It was crowded with furniture and knick-knacks, quite overcome with tables of various sizes, chairs, sofas, sideboards, ottomans, curtains, pelmets, swags, ornaments, photographs, small watercolours, albums of phonograph records, and a morose parrot in a bright green cage whose only contribution to the conversation was the occasional earsplitting screech.

Taking both my hands and drawing me onto a sofa, Marguerite trilled to the effect that it was wonderful to see me again, though one could hardly fail to notice that it was B.W. she was looking at appreciatively — or was it regretfully? — as she spoke. Which reminded me that once or twice I had wondered if she was quite as enamoured of me as I should have liked. I could not blame her

for having doubts, for I had not behaved very gracefully during our
first encounter. This was way back in 1918 when she was the wife
of my air force brigade commander, Arthur Soames, or "Arser" as
she called him – a name that we chaps in the squadrons had happily
adopted. On my first trip to Paris, as described in Volume III of my
memoirs, she had invited me to her apartment in Montmartre
while her husband was away bungling. I'd just had a tooth extracted
and was so woozy with nitrous oxide that I kept telling her I loved
her. "Let's not go to a party. Let's go to stead in bed – bed instead,"
I amended, amazed at the things I was amending. "Oh, Marguerite,
if you only knew how difficult it is, since I first tasted the joys of
connubial bliss. I can hardly think of anything else but sex, except
for flying, administration, maintenance, parachutes, things like that."
But when I got to her place I found she had taken the gibberings
of a gas-besotted birdman seriously. "On the way here you said
some lovely things to me, Bart'olomew," she was murmuring in
memory. "And I meant every one of them," I replied, trying to
remember what they were. Then I was making verbal love to her,
quite amazed at how chick and swave I was being, and thinking, By
Jove, I ought to take a whiff of N2O more often. But, "I have no
intention of going to bed with you," she had said, leaning over to
extinguish her butt in an ashtray. In doing so, her starboard breast
had rested for a moment on my thigh, which immediately started
quivering like mad. "I have always been faithful to Arser," she murmured, "even though we have been married for more than a year."
But then, tasting of smoke and lipstick, she had kissed me – and her
tongue had darted straight into the dentist's excavation.

I jumped, and clutched at her frantically in an effort to extract
her tongue from the crater, which agitation convinced her of my
passion, whereupon hot with eagerness herself she took me by the
hand, saying, "Come," and started to lead me in the direction of a
room that I sincerely hoped was the bathroom, as I feared I was going to be sick at any moment. We had not been intimate, as I was in
no mood for further excitement. I had felt guilty about it ever since,
and so had kept in touch down the years as if visits were apologies.
Besides, that day her husband had arrived home unexpectedly,

forcing me to flee through his study window. I had been having enough trouble with the brigadier without rousing any further suspicions in him.

Long divorced from Arser, she had continued to live in Paris until 1940. Like thousands of others she had fled the capital ahead of the Blitzkrieg, and had taken shelter in her parents' house in Caen. Soon bored with provincial life, she found that she would not be allowed to return to Paris. "So I am here ever since," she said with a sad little pout.

She was still holding my hands, while B.W. wandered about, looking at things. "But it is so good to see you again, Bart'olomew. And you are still flying, hein? You are truly formidable – at your age, still intruding into France in your magnificent RAF aeroplanes. But tell me everything. How is that charming Icelandic girl you introduced me to? She is well?"

"She died a few years ago."

"Ah." Her face turned tragic. "So beautiful and so full of life. You were so happy. Ah – but you are wounded!"

"It's just an unbearably agonizing scratch, that's all."

"But let me see! So, you are bandaged from the knee. It is a clean bandage. You have already received help, hein?"

I started to reply, but B.W. said quickly, "A pharmacy. We got some bandages from a pharmacy, Madame."

"Please, darling, call me Marguerite," she cried, and started to fuss nervously with her appearance. B.W. seemed to be making her nervous with his appraising regard.

She turned quickly to me, sounding so girlish with her quick enthusiasms. "But you are not telling me anything," she exclaimed reproachfully. "Tell. Admit. Confess everything!"

"We've come to you for help, Marguerite."

She pressed my hand between hers. "And you have come to the right person, darling," she said.

"The Resistance – do you know anyone?"

"Do not worry," she said. "I will see that you are delivered into the right hands."

When I started to reply, she put a soft, warm, and scented hand gently to my mouth. "I have a friend, Pierre, who will help us," she said. "But first we must catch up with our lives. It is a wonderful moment for me, you know, to meet such an interesting friend from the past. Life has been so unutterably dull for the last three or four years. I left all my good friends behind, and I have made so few friends here. Papa and Mama are both dead. Ach, the people here are dull as ditchwater. Shopkeepers! There are no galleries to speak of, no smart shops, no music, no little affairs." She uttered a sigh so comprehensive that her bright yellow gown parted, as it had a habit of doing, to reveal even more of her chest, which was as formidable as ever, though perhaps not quite so jaunty as of old.

"Who's Pierre?" I asked, as B.W. continued to pick his way round the sitting room.

"Pardon?"

"You said Pierre will help us."

"Of course! My friend Pierre, he will help." She lowered her voice confidentially. "He has much to do with the Maquis, I think. Though of course," she winked, "in his position he cannot talk about it. Security and so forth, hein?"

"Of course. That's great, Marguerite. In the circumstances the sooner we get in touch with the Resistance the better."

"What circumstances are those, Bart'olomew?"

"Well, you must know that – "

"Dad," said B.W.

"The invasion – "

"Dad?"

"What?" I asked, just as a bell rang rustily.

We froze. The parrot screamed. I looked at Margeurite.

"Ah," she exclaimed. "What luck, hein? That must be Pierre."

She ran to the window. "But yes, it is him," she cried excitedly. She waved lustily, but then turned, putting her hands to her face in dismay. "My God, here I am in the company of two men so early in the morning, and I am not even dressed! And he is so jealous!"

Her expression changed again. Now it was cool, one might almost say cold, though a smile went with it. "My God, it is just like the first time we met, eh, Bart'olomew? But this time it will not be necessary for you to jump out of the window, no?"

She became aware that B.W. was making for the window. She hurried over to him. "All the same," she said, "it is better if he doesn't see you at the window before I have a chance to explain, you understand? With me in this so flimsy robe, hein?" And as B.W. obediently moved away, she bustled over to her intercom and spoke into it. "Allo?"

"It's Pierre, chérie."

"Come up, darling," she replied; and with bright eyes and flushed cheeks, she turned to us and said, "There, did I not say?"

I was still trying to work out why it would be any worse for Pierre to see a strange man at the upstairs window than when he entered this room to see two strange men attendant upon his scanty mistress – presumably she was his mistress as he had a front-door key – when Pierre entered, and proved to be the subject of the photograph that B.W. had been frowning over, a handsome middle-aged man with short greying hair, a man with an air of relaxed authority, attired in the beautiful grey Wehrmacht uniform decorated with officer's insignia, and with the red, ivory, and black Knight's Cross round his pillarlike neck. He entered, swiftly but confidently, with a Luger pistol at the ready.

"Here he is," Margeurite said gaily. "Here is my friend, Pierre Wassermann. He is from Alsace, aren't you, darling?"

When she turned back to me, her face was no longer welcoming. "So," she said, closing her peignoir with an air of finality, "you see how it is? I called him the moment you came to the door, chéri."

"Ciao, bébé," said the parrot.

ARDENNE ABBEY

I WAS BEGINNING TO see that my son had a quality about him, an inherent sceptical alertness that compensated to quite a large extent for his lack of life experience. He had tried to put me on my guard by waving one of Marguerite's nicely framed photographs at me. It was a picture of Pierre Wassermann, and though he was in civilian clothes he, as B.W. put it, looked like a kraut. B.W. had also attempted to discourage me from discoursing too frankly with the lady. I should have listened to my son. For now we were both buried in Ardenne Abbey.

This was the headquarters of a substantial army unit on the northwestern edge of the city, judging by the defensive arrangements and the plethora of army signs and abbreviations that were planted all along the driveway and at the side of the abbey. I managed to observe quite a bit of the defensive arrangements and to note the appearance of a Wehrmacht general before we were marched inside and into a guard room.

After being searched for the third time, we were placed in separate rooms in the cellar, presumably very temporarily, for the cells were not all that secure. In my few square feet there was a window, though the view was not very impressive, as it looked onto sloping brickwork, with a narrow band of daylight at the top.

So far we had been handled efficiently and unemotionally. This was mostly, I think, because Wassermann and his men were veterans. True fighting men have a comradely sympathy for enemy front-line soldiers, and treat them quite well when they're not actually trying to kill them. It is often the scum in the rear or inexperienced soldiers or, worse, patriotic civilians who maltreat their prisoners.

I had the impression, too, that we were not being taken too seriously as captives. I felt a bit miffed about that. After all, I'd owned up to my name, rank, and number. I'd informed them with utter frankness and sincerity that I was the equivalent of a full colonel. They ought to have been really pleased to have me. Instead they seemed in no hurry at all to interrogate either of us. Nor were they the least interested in our request that we be passed us on to the Luftwaffe where we hoped to be entertained in a Staffel mess before making our escape. Really, you'd have thought we were more of a nuisance than a good find.

Another impression was more satisfying: the absence of tension among the soldiers. The men seemed as laconic as it was possible for Germans to be, the officers relaxed as sunbathers. In fact, quite a few of them were literally sunbathing, on a south-facing lawn. This was a pleasing sight. Not the sunbathers as such. Nearly naked men were not my idea of tourist attractions. It was pleasing because it indicated that this major enemy HQ was not keyed up for an invasion.

My! What would they have given to know the actual date of the invasion, eh?

I was getting quite peckish by the time I heard the chinking of cutlery and the clash of dishes from the abbey kitchens. A while later they brought in a tray of bread and soup, and a mug containing a brown liquid that not only smelled of wood but actually had splinters in it. I had barely time to wolf the victuals before they came for me. The door banged open and a large gentleman with NCO's stripes ordered me to *raus!* And he and two soldiers marched me upstairs to a much nicer part of the abbey.

I kept an eye open, especially when I was led through a room that was furnished with tables on which maps of various sizes were spread. I slowed down, and craned my neck to study one of the maps, but there was a thump in the back from the NCO to remind me that a little learning is a dangerous thing.

I was marched onward along a stone corridor. Actually, it was my escorts who were marching; I was keeping resolutely out of step. Which discomfited them. Soldiers can get terribly upset if you don't keep in step. But I had a good excuse: my foot, which had started swelling and was dashed uncomfortable to walk on. And walk on it I had to, as they had confiscated my homemade stick.

We finally arrived in what must surely have been the best room in the abbey. It was a spacious lounge, done up in white and gold, with amazingly tall windows.

"Very nice," I said. But in spite of the compliment I received another thump in the back and a series of German barks from the NCO, presumably an order to be a good boy and to be seen and not heard.

Apart from the escort there were just three others in the splendid room. Wassermann was one of them. He invited me to sit at one side of a very large and ornate table, so bright with gold paint that I had to slit my eyes. I recognized the antique table right away, of course. It was a Louis XX bureau de crat, otherwise known as a Louis d'or.

Wassermann sat beside me with his pistol casually to hand.

"Say, that's a nice Lager," I said.

"It is a Luger."

"Could I just look at it a moment?"

"Do not be foolish."

"By the way, Pierre, are you related in any way to the Wassermann test?"

"Be quiet."

Receiving no encouragement on this side of the table, I turned my attention to the far side at which sat an officer and a person in civilian clothes.

The officer introduced himself as Captain — but I missed the name. He looked like the Hollywood actor Conrad Veidt, the one who usually played sinister parts. He proved to be quite decent. He offered me a cigarette. I took one, in case it came in useful, say for bribing a field marshal.

The civilian beside him was not quite so nice. He failed to offer me anything but a fixed stare. He was wearing a leather overcoat, though the room was decidedly warm.

The captain opened the proceedings by screwing his cigarette into an ivory holder and taking a few puffs. And it was soon evident that I was wrong in thinking that they were not interested in yours untruly. "Well," he said pleasantly, "we keep learning more and more about you, Group Captain Bandy."

"A most interesting catch," said the civilian, boring fresh holes in me with his pointed eyes.

I barely glanced at him, as I was more interested in Conrad Veidt, or rather, in his extremely long cigarette holder. He kept dragging at it, but the smoke was taking a long time to reach him. Most of it trickled out only after he had removed the mouthpiece from his lips. I wondered if this was his way of giving up smoking.

"Yes," Conrad continued airily, "Berlin has promised to send us a most remarkable dossier on your past activities, military, civilian – political. It seems, for example, that you and Mr. Churchill are close friends."

"Gosh, I don't know who could have said that."

"You said it, Group Captain."

"Ah, that explains it."

"Explains what?"

"I do tend to exaggerate slightly, now and then," I confessed. "Actually I hardly know Mr. . . . what was the name again?"

"You have said many times that you and he are like this," Conrad said, holding up his forefinger and middle finger and twisting them together.

"I don't think either of us resembles a finger," I replied stiffly, to show how offended I was.

He held up his fingers again, and frowned, puzzled. "Is this not an English gesture? Do not the fingers represent the close relations between you and Mr. Churchill?"

"Well, that depends. Which finger is me?"

"Please?"

"Am I the forefinger or the middle finger?"

"What does this matter?"

"I think I must be the middle finger. The nicotine-stained one can't be me – I gave up smoking a long time ago."

Wassermann murmured at the captain. The captain flushed and glared at me.

Quickly, to placate him, I said respectfully, "Excuse me, Captain, but can you tell me what is to happen to my – to the flying officer who was with me?"

"Your son?" The captain relaxed again and even smiled to himself. He shook his head. "Most remarkable – a father and son flying together in the war." He continued to muse amusedly on this for a while. Then: "But don't worry, Herr Bandy, he is of no interest to us. He will be sent to a prisoner-of-war camp in due course."

But then the civilian spoke. He did so in what he probably considered to be a Dangerously Quiet Voice. "Let us not too hasty be," he said with a slight lisp.

He tilted over onto one buttock to murmur to the captain; but then, recollecting his manners, he turned to me and said politely – they were all being so nice, today – "you vill not be insulted if vee visper to each osser now and zen, vill you, Group Captain?"

"Please. Make yourself at home."

"Sank you, Group Captain."

The two of them conferred in whispers. It gave me an opportunity to study the civilian, who, in spite of being reasonably nice, made me a bit uneasy.

It wasn't just his eyes, though they had a disconcerting fixity. I tried to overcome their impact by telling myself that he had trained his eyes to obviate the blinks. Unlike the two army officers who looked clean and uncomplicated, the civvy had an unhealthy aura. Of an age somewhere between thirty and seventy, he had a pale, pudgy face, in the middle of which was a small, square black moustache. Maybe that was what was making me fidget. Maybe this was Hitler himself taking an interest in me, concerning himself with (relatively) minor matters, instead of concentrating on the important aspects of the war, such as the development of the secret weapons he was always boasting about. Or he should get busy and do something about improving his Nazi salute. Seeing him in the newsreels, it had often struck me how irritable, self-conscious, and perfunctory his Nazi salute had become, as if he were pretending he didn't mind that six million Germans were doing it so much better than him.

Bailing out of these thoughts, I became aware that a hissing argument had broken out between the two men opposite. Conrad Veidt seemed to be expressing some distaste, and was apparently refusing to oblige Herr Hitler. But obviously Hitler outranked him, and after a while Conrad gestured as if to say, All right then, do what you want, you swine, you have the seniority.

"My colleague in zuh all-conquering German Army," said Hitler, speaking in a sarcastic tone that brought a flush of anger to the cheeks of the captain, "sinks zat zuh var is still being fought by gentlemen – an ettitude zet vill not survive a dose of General Patton, I sink," he said, almost humorously; though his staring eyes still looked like they belonged in a coffin. "Oh, dear, zet means I a gentleman am not. I vish to point out, Group Captain, zet your beloved son" – he actually blinked at this point as he worked out the English grammar – "may not necessarily in a stalag luft arrive, but may be useful as a, a key foolishly stubborn individuals to unlock." He paused to nod approvingly to himself, plainly pleased by his conquest of English phraseology.

I cleared my throat. "As long as you understand that I really and truly don't know anything that will be of much interest to you, Mr. . . . ?" I replied, raising my eyebrows at him. "Mr. . . . ?"

"I am of zuh Geheim Staats Polizei, Mr. Bendy. Zet is all you need to know."

"Oh-oh," I said.

"Ah. I see zet you know who ve are, and vat to come is, if you do not cooperate."

"You're going to torture me?"

"If you must be so crude as such a vord to use."

"But surely the torture has already started?"

"Vot torture?"

"Your Music Hall accent."

He looked blank. "I do not understand."

"Never mind."

"Oh, it is not I who vill not mind, Mr. Bendy," he said, shivering as if he were frightening even himself.

But wait. It seemed that the policeman really was feeling chilly even in that hot room, for he pulled his leather coat more closely around him before continuing. "But there is no need to vorry. I am sure you are right, that you nothing except paltry matters know." He leaned forward. "But it is zuh paltry matters that often of most interest to us prove to be. Like vot on pieces of yellow crap paper is written."

I stared at him, trying to keep my face straight.

"Oh, sorry," he amended. "That should be yellow scrap paper, not so?"

Behind my brave façade a storm of frightful proportions raged. He knew about the Quebec Conference, did he, and my part in it?

The shock of his words had brought up the image of the paper to which Drummond had attached the note *Churchill's hand* – and the date scrawled on it. The date on which I had based my remark to Guinevere about the invasion coming on June 5.

I had been joking. Suddenly I knew – I was certain – that June 5 really was the day that the landings would take place.

The Allies would be storming ashore in the Pas de Calais in four days' time. And I who knew the exact date was in the hands of the Gestapo.

AT THE SEASIDE

THEY HAD THEIR NEW headquarters in a grey stone mill on the out-skirts of Caen near Authie. It was at the head of a small, scruffy valley, and was quite isolated, presumably so as not to disturb the neighbours with the screaming from the top floor of the building.

Before direct experience intervened I hoped that the cries might just be a recording. They had all been so nice up to now, surely they weren't going to descend to Gestapo clichés? No, it was just a record, or a special chorus chosen from the nearest SS unit for their skill in simulating aural torment effects, to soften us up.

Which they were doing very effectively. I knew that I, for one, felt very soft. Presumably B.W., ensconced in another part of the cellar, was feeling soft as well.

The cellar, stone flags underfoot, rough and grimy walls press-ing from the sides, had once stored quantities of wine, judging by the smell. You could still smell the wine, mixed with other odours to produce an impertinent but not overly excremental bouquet. The wine cellars, split up by concrete blocks into separate win-dowless compartments, had certainly come in handy for the new owners.

I was not left to languish for too long in the cell before I was taken to the top floor and along to another windowless space. It was furnished with one chair and one medical gurney. Over the next few hours it was established that my hollerings at least were not a recording.

Thankfully I was never laid out on their notorious table with its securing straps and stains, as I believe some prisoners were. Perhaps in my case they didn't have time.

The chair was bad enough, and it was my own fault that they were now taking me seriously. Initially they were not certain that I knew anything worthwhile. But my reactions, including a labial rigidity, seemed to have persuaded them that at least I *thought* I knew something of interest. And after all, I had attended the top-level Quebec Conference, at which the Allied invasion of the continent must have been discussed. So almost anything I could tell them might be worth probing for.

Their certainty was also clouded by their mystification that an officer of my rank could have been given such an apparently menial task as that of wastepaper basket emptier. No German officer of any rank would have lowered himself to that extent. It made the interrogators wonder if they were beating up the hierarchical equivalent of a file clerk through some farcical error. Not that that greatly restrained the people in the black and silver uniforms from all the nastiness. Which in my case involved stepping on my foot.

Hitler-in-the-overcoat, apparently quite senior in the black ranks, had taken a particular interest in our case, and was often to be found wincing sympathetically as the burly troops trod on my leg in jackbooted relays.

"I am only doing mine job, ja?" said Hitler. "Including zuh use of a Music Hall accent?"

Belatedly, he had understood my jibe.

An hour or so into the second day of my interrogation they brought B.W. into the room. I was glad to see that at worst he had been roughed up. On the other hand, he was about to graduate to some senior ordeal.

Before Hitler went to work on B.W. he was good enough to explain that at the Quebec Conference a firm decision had been made as to the date of the invasion.

"Invasion?" said B.W., looking amazed. "What invasion?"

"The invasion of the Continent."

"Oh, that invasion."

"Ja, that invasion. About vich any scrap of information ve obtain can useful vill be."

"I don't know anything."

"Ve know that you don't know anything."

"And I know that you know that I don't know anything."

"But ve suspect that your father knows."

"That's why you're torturing him, is it?"

"It is also vy ve now you put to some discomfort must," said Hitler sorrowfully.

B.W. could not take his eyes off me. I had been stripped and my leg was all too visible. It looked like a special treat for a starving Alsatian.

"What have you done to his leg?" B.W. asked, in an extremely high-pitched and emotional way. "Oh, God, look what you've done."

He swore dreadfully at our captors, ending, "Leave him alone, he doesn't know anything, he's just an adventurer."

Just an adventurer? *Well.* After all the trouble I'd gone to, to convince him that he had a dad that he and history could be proud of.

"How can you do that to a human being?" he asked in agonized tones.

The question seemed to annoy the Gestapo officer. He placed his white, pudgy face close to B.W., breathing all over him. "I am afraid you human beings for the moment are not," he said softly. "You are only a source of information. Information vich ve vill have. That is the only reason ve you hurt must. Understand? It is purely a matter of research until your father us vot ve must know tells."

"You swine," said B.W. He actually said it. I thought perhaps he was adding the words to the swill of clichés deliberately, for satirical effect. But no, he was serious.

"Even a little information vill help, you know," Hitler said, turning to me, "before ve on your son start. Any little thing you can remember. So little to ask, yes?"

After half a mo, he turned back to B.W. His hand, seemingly of its own accord, strayed down, and he caressed the lad between the legs. "It will be a shame to damage such a strong, youthful body unnecessarily."

B.W. stared at him, first in shock, then in a highly affronted way. In fact there was enough outrage there to cause him to lower his head sharply and butt the Gestapo officer on the nose.

When the fuss had finally died down – Hitler had felt quite faint when he saw his own blood – they started in on B.W. I had a ring-side seat, as he was directly across the room from where I was lashed to the chair. While they had used mostly their boots on me, in his case they used rubber truncheons on his knees. Quite light taps on the knees from a rubber truncheon can be surprisingly painful. With B.W., they were not at all lighthanded.

When the truncheon produced no results other than expressions of extreme pain, they resorted to a very much nastier method that cannot be described in a family history. And after a while B.W. called out, "Tell them what they want to know, Dad, you can't know much, make them stop, make them stop."

Now that really was a bad moment. They would certainly have stopped hurting the boy if I had told them even a little of the little I knew.

I was tempted to do so. I very nearly convinced myself that I could hold back the one really important detail. I very nearly convinced myself that the detail was not really important. But I could not overcome the memory of my Soviet incarceration. I knew from experience that once you start talking it is impossible to avoid saying too much.

So I was forced to remain silent while B.W. suffered, but not in silence, imploring me over and over again to tell them what I knew. He thought I knew almost nothing. He kept asking me to make them stop; and finally came the worst moment of all when he screamed at me that he had been right about me all along, that I didn't care about him, and he would never forgive me, never, and from now on we were through, through.

All my efforts to build up his faith, trust, and confidence in me were being undone. How desperate I was to rationalize. Surely I was mistaken about that date, June 5. I knew nothing. I'd gotten it all wrong. It was absurd that a date of such vital importance would be committed to a scrap pad. It could not possibly be the real date. Mr. Churchill had merely been doodling his daughter's birth date or something equally unclassified.

Except that it might just possibly be the date, and the lives of tens of thousands of sons and fathers, career soldiers and rough patriots, poltroons and geniuses, could be the prize for the enemy. For even now, on the third day of June, 1944, there was still time for the Wehrmacht to alert their defences and their reserve divisions.

And it was in the flash of that moment that I realized I had already done wrong, by speaking out rather than remaining stoic and steadfast. I had assailed important individuals who had better things to think about than my measly concerns. I had pestered the Air Ministry for two years over my concern for aircrew casualties, out of fear that we were repeating the terrible strategy of attrition that in the First World War had wasted so very many lives. And affected so many survivors like me, who had, even now, not entirely recovered from the dreadful insensitivity of 1914. It was only now, here in this room where the very walls seemed to have absorbed and to be radiating back the agony of patriots, that I saw that the aggression of the chiefs of the fighters and bombers was the expression of a determination, as ruthless as it was vital, to win the war regardless of the cost in lives and treasure, in order to save the world from people like this man here.

In the middle of the night there came a series of explosions, above which I could hear the unmistakable, glorious sound of Merlins, later confirmed as the engines of Mosquito fighter-bombers armed with rockets.

In that very first pass over the grey mill it blew half the building to bits, including the corner containing the stairway from the cellars to the upper floors. Two other Mosquitos failed to hit the building. Nevertheless it was a magnificent achievement to cause such destruction to a stout building huddled in a valley – even if half the prisoners in the cells were killed or injured in the process. Somebody must have had a very strong motive for biffing the Gestapo headquarters in Authie that morning of June 4.

Little did I know that it was not the Gestapo but their victims who were the target of the RAF attack. Or, to be precise, one particular victim.

The crump and clatter of falling masonry had scarcely died down when it was succeeded by small-arms fire and the bark of grenades. Some minutes after that the gunfire sounded very loud in the passageway. There was a warning cry, and the door to my quarters sagged on its hinges, admitting a cloud of dust and smoke and a chap with a blackened face.

He crouched just inside the cell, sweeping the room with a Sten gun. And then aimed the weapon straight at me.

I was certain he was going to shoot. I lay there and looked at him.

His hesitation was fatal to his mission. He seemed to struggle with himself. Then abruptly he gestured for me to precede him out of the cell.

I was unable to do so. My reluctant rescuer called for assistance, and another member of the team entered, and helped me to my feet, or in this case, foot.

"My son – he's somewhere down here – "

"We have him – he is safe," said Alain.

I saw B.W. briefly before we were separated. He was groggy. I don't think he really knew who I was. In blowing the door of his cell they had knocked him silly. Though, apart from the disorientation and the rubbery state of his knees, he was unharmed.

We were kept separated, for some reason. He was whisked away to some other destination. Supported by a couple of Alain's men, I was taken through the smoking, cordite-reeking darkness to a clapped-out Citröen van. Complaints about being separated from my son were either ignored or were unheard over the rattle of small-arms fire that was still puncturing the dark. I was bundled into the van and hidden under a heap of laundry. Fortunately it was fresh laundry. I was glad about that. I was feeling bad enough without being buried under heaps of work clothes, dirty underwear, and hardening socks.

We seemed to bump and grind through the night for hours. The weather, after being reasonably good for days, was deteriorating fast. The van was being rocked and buffeted by the wind whenever it crossed higher ground. It grew so cold that I was now grateful for the weight and warmth of the laundry.

Half an hour – two hours? – later we lurched to a halt, and the unsteady engine died. Emerging from the heap like a dung beetle, I found myself in a cobbled yard. A moon was dashing through the gaps in the sky, pursued by violent clouds. As if to revive me, the elements threw blustering, ill-tempered rain in my face.

I was half-lifted across the yard and into a whitewashed farmhouse, where I was installed in the kitchen. Mugs of coffee, a loaf of bread, and a pot of pâté were placed on the table by the oldest member of the team. He appeared to be the owner of the house.

"My son?"

"He is safe. He is not far from here."

"Why aren't we together?"

Alain didn't seem to know how to answer. In fact, considering that the operation, which I assumed was to rescue the prisoners from the Gestapo, had been an outstanding success, he seemed angry and disappointed. "You must be very important for London to have set up this operation at such short notice," he said, almost as if he resented it.

"You mean, this operation was to rescue me? Me personally?"

Alain seemed unable to meet my gaze. "It was not easy," he muttered, "when we have to rely on a complicated system of code words on the radio."

The older man didn't seem to like me, either. He said accusingly, "After this attack, the Boche will make things very difficult for us."

"Well, merde alors," I said. "Would you like me to go back?"

"What is it you know that is so important?" Alain asked, drawing the curtains more securely across the kitchen window. The rain outside was lashing the panes.

Assuming I had the date right, June 5 and the invasion of the Pas de Calais were only a few hours away, and out of gratitude for being rescued I was inclined to tell him.

But caution prevailed. After all, Alain had already proved that he was not what he seemed to be.

When I failed to answer he said roughly, "You must move to the cellar."

"What?"

"You must stay in the cellar," he said, fiddling with a skeleton key. "They will be looking everywhere for you."

Yet he hesitated, and instead of leading the way down the stone steps, he poured glasses of cognac. His hand was shaking. Reaction after the battle, I supposed.

"Thanks. I could do with a doctor as well, Alain."

He looked at my filthy bandage, which was seeping. "I suppose it is worthwhile," he said grumpily.

Which seemed an odd thing to say.

As much to distract myself from the discomfort, I tried to engage him in conversation. After all, there was plenty to talk about. But he burst out angrily with, "I do not want to talk." And he stalked out, shouting to one of his men to fetch old Simeon.

That was another thing – the way they were watching me. As if they didn't trust me to remain under the protection I was so grateful to have acquired.

And why had they separated us? Ach, the cognac was making me stupid! I ought to have been able to work it out, but couldn't. Of course I was pretty feverish by then. The leg, which was more mush than leg, did not exactly encourage clarity of thought.

The doctor, or at least a silent person with some medical experience, arrived at last. He examined my leg, shook his head, applied dressings to calf and foot, and wrapped it in a mile of bandage. He produced an assortment of pills, and selected some big round ones that I'm sure were for horses. Perhaps it was my face.

I slept, restless as a geyser, far into the evening, in an upstairs bedroom, this despite what Alain had said about hiding in the cellar. I guess they thought I was too sick to remain down there.

It was dark before I groaned down to the kitchen. Alain was there with a bottle of cognac much diminished. I asked him what was going on.

"What do you mean?" he asked, pouring me a prodigious amount of cognac. His own glass looked as if it had been in use for quite some time.

"Just that. What's going on? Why are you all behaving as if I'm the enemy?"

"I don't know what you're talking about. I was just coming up to fetch you." He gestured feebly at the cellar door. "Really, you should hide. There are German patrols everywhere. You can take your drink with you."

His free hand, near the pistol in his belt, was moving, working, twitching. And he was polishing off the cognac at a rate of knots.

"You've had orders from London, haven't you?" I said.

"What?"

"You've had orders to kill me."

He sat down, so abruptly that the pistol banged sharply against the chair. The curtain at the kitchen window billowed as the wet wind tried to get in.

"It was supposed to have been done already," Alain said. Dark patches stained the skin under his eyes. "They didn't say why. Just that it was vitally important.

"If only," he said, throwing up his arms in despair, "I had not already met you, it would not be so difficult. I would have done it already. I have done worse."

"I can see their point of view," I mused. "London, I mean. Without necessarily agreeing with them," I added.

He was supposed to shoot me in the cellar. And I could not even explain that it was no longer necessary; that in a few hours the invasion would be underway and his orders would be redundant.

He was thoughtfully chewing the chequered tablecloth. "If I merely keep you prisoner," he said at length, "surely that will achieve the same end, namely your silence."

"I couldn't agree more."

But he shook his head. "No," he said. "There are too many

informers in the Resistance. One of us might find out what is to be found out, and warn the Boches."

"Well, that's easy," I said. "I just won't say anything."

"But every moment you are alive increases the risk."

"I don't mind taking the risk."

"It is up to us to take the risk, not you," he said, plainly feeling that I was being unreasonable.

"You're right," I said. "It's up to you to take the risk."

"We will," he said, opening another bottle of cognac.

"Good. That's settled then. You won't risk shooting me, because if you don't shoot me, I won't talk."

"But if we do shoot you, you won't talk either. That is certain."

"You have a point there, Alain," I said, nodding seriously. "Not a very good point, but a point nevertheless."

"And besides, we have gone to great lengths to rescue you from the Gestapo in order to dispose of you. It seems only logical to complete the mission, Bart'olomew."

"Surely rescuing me in order to dispose of me cannot appeal to the orderly French mind."

"No," he replied gloomily, "I admit there is a certain illogicality in the sequence."

He poured another two glasses of cognac, thinking deeply. His face lit up. "Wait!" he cried.

"I am more than willing to wait, Alain."

"Perhaps it should be stated the other way round. It is not a case of rescuing you in order to shoot you. It is a case of shooting you in order to rescue you."

"Rescuing me what from?"

"Among other things, from your failure to become bombed."

"I haven't failed," I said. "I'm thoroughly bombed."

"You should have been killed in the bombing. You have ruined the entire operation by surviving," he said indignantly.

"Let's stick to the point, Alain, shall we? And the point is – what is the point, Alain?"

"The point, Bart'olomew, is that we have to kill you in order to save your life."

"That's darn good of you, Alain," I said emotionally. "Being so concerned to save my life."

"I wouldn't do it for just anybody, Bart'olomew. It is only because I like you."

"I don't suppose you could grow to dislike me, could you, Alain? And then you wouldn't have to shoot me."

"If you refuse to agree to be shot, I could very easily come to dislike you, Bart'olomew. It is making things very difficult for me."

"Tell you what. While we're thinking about it, let's have some more of that fine medicinal brandy."

"An idea magnificent," said Alain, replenishing our glasses without spilling a drop – though it took about five minutes.

"All the same," I said, "there seems to be something very contradictory about saving somebody's life in order to kill him."

"It is undoubtedly a contradiction, Bart'olomew."

"Almost as absurd as saying that a Frenchman is an Englishman."

"Truly absurd," Alain said, shuddering at the very thought.

"Or that an order to advance means that you are to retreat. Or that retreat means advance."

A great revelation came up on Alain's face. He upended the cognac bottle, forgetting to place a glass under it, and looked truly enlightened as he mopped his shirt with a corner of the tablecloth and wrung it out with his bare hands. He leaned over and looked very thoughtful and sincere. "You have hit the veal calf on the head, Bart'olomew," he said gravely. "As we soldiers know, an order to advance may or may not mean an order to advance. For example, it might not be in our personal interests, Bart'olomew, to carry out such an order. We might prefer to prevaricate, or even to move a little further away from danger. In which case, advance could in fact mean retreat.

"However," he went on, with the light of battle in his eye – or the light of prevarication – "there can be no doubt whatsoever – and this is something of great importance for us soldiers, Bart'olomew – that an order to retreat would never be taken as an order to advance." He struck the table with his fist. "Never! It would not be in our personal interests. And therefore, you are right,

Bart'olomew, when you say that an order to rescue somebody means to rescue them. And to rescue them means to rescue them. It does not mean anything else."

"That's it, Alain. You've got it. That's just what I was saying."

"Except, of course," he said, suddenly filled with doubt, "that – "

But I interrupted quickly before he could reach the exception. "You have settled the argument beyond . . . beyond question, Alain. I am filled with admiration for your fine French intellectually lucid mind."

"And you are so splendidly discerning, Bart'olomew."

"Thank you, Alain. So now we do not have to go into the cellar. We can have a drink instead." And we shooks hands on it, very warmly indeed. In fact we even gave each other a kiss on the cheek.

And after all that, it seemed that I was wrong. The whole of June 5 went by, and the invasion did not come.

It seemed that the date scribbled on the yellow paper had had nothing to do with the landing. Churchill had gotten it wrong again. Of course, it was just as well, considering the awful weather along the coast. Nevertheless, I was left with the thought that I had put B.W. through all that suffering for nothing.

It had all been for nothing. I could have squealed after all.

The thought plunged me into depression; or it would have done had my hangover left any room for a depression.

And then early on the following morning, Alain came into my sleepless bedroom and said solemnly, "It has commenced."

He was looking calm as custard, and speaking as casually as if introducing a chamber music concert. "There are a thousand planes in the air. There are thousands of parachutists all around us."

"In the Pas de Calais, you mean?"

"Here. In Normandy."

And then he screamed, and danced around the room, and embraced me. "The Allies have landed," he shouted at the top of his voice. "The liberation has begun."

So the landing was to be here in Normandy instead of the Calais

area. How about that? The Allied Command had completely bamboozled me.

As the paratroops came down in their thousands, and the black and
white striped fighters, bombers, and fighter-bombers blasted along
at treetop level, rocketing every military target in the area, and the
naval guns, far out to sea, flung shells the size of bungalows at the
seashore, into the coastal defences, and as harbours miraculously
sprang up where no harbours had been before, I told B.W. that this
was why I had been a bit reluctant to cooperate with the Gestapo.
Slowly the hurt over my failing to save him from their tortures subsided, as he understood that I really had had something to keep
quiet about; and he was reconciled at last.

We determined to make for the coast, which was not far, Caen
being only a short length of Orne canal from the sea. But we could
hardly go for a country stroll through enemy territory, even though
Alain claimed that apart from the Caen garrison there was little in
the way of a German presence in the immediate area – if you
didn't count the forces manning the "Atlantic Wall." There was a
further problem. I couldn't walk. B.W. solved it by trundling me,
his very own father and senior officer, in a wheelbarrow. Armed
with hoes we set off at five in the morning, with me protesting all
the way about the smell from the wheelbarrow. It had been sitting
in the farmyard for months half filled with a particularly noxious
gallic manure, and even though it had been washed out it still stank.
I thought B.W. was very mean in suggesting the smelly wheelbarrow as a mode of transport; in fact, I'm sure he did it on purpose
as he was still a bit miffed at me for not saving his life. He claimed
that the smell was necessary to keep at bay any Kraut patrol that
might otherwise have taken an interest in a pair of rather uncon-
vincing French peasants, one of them highly annoyed and wounded,
the other looking about as French as a hot dog. As it turned out, the
greatest danger we faced was from the Typhoons that were raging
overhead, seemingly firing their rockets at anything that moved.
As for the Germans, the protection of the pong was quite unnecessary as they were too busy being rounded up or beaten up in their

pillboxes by the Canadian troops who had landed near a place
called Bernières-sur-mer. When we were finally challenged it was
by our own fellows, when, on the beach, we met a party of them
headed by Matthew Halton of the CBC, who said, "And perhaps for
a reaction from the native population, we have here two typical
French peasants, one of whom appears to have been wounded, poor
devil. Pardonnez-moi, Monsewer, but do . . . you . . . speak . . .
English?"

"Yes."

"That's great! So could you give us your reaction to the invasion of the Continent of Europe by the Allied Forces; to this return
to Europe after four long years of war?" Halton asked, holding out
his microphone.

"Well," I said, "first of all, my name's Bandy, and this is my son.
His name is Bandy as well. We're from Ottawa, Ontario, or at least,
that's where we were living, through originally I'm from
Beamington, Ontario. Bandy here, however, was born in California,
I believe it was, wasn't it, son? And – " By that time the CBC cor-
respondent, watched by a crowd of soldiers with leaves stuck in
their helmets, was attempting to retrieve his microphone; but I had
too firm a grip on it. "And we'd both like to welcome you guys to
France," I continued, "and I must say it's just great, meeting all you
Canadians here, even though you are a bit late, you know – you
were supposed to be here on the fifth of June, you know, not the
sixth of June. But never mind. For one thing, I guess the weather
wasn't too good yesterday, and anyway, we didn't mind waiting, did
we, Bartholomew?" I asked, passing the microphone to B.W.

"No, we didn't mind at all," he said, "because here they are, and
I'd just like to join my father in welcoming you to French soil, and
remember, when you come up against those Germans, they put
their pants on one leg at a time, too, so you just got to give your
best shot . . ."

There was a brief struggle as Mr. Halton attempted again to
wrest the microphone from us. Soon he would be planting his foot
in B.W.'s chest for purchase, so great was his eagerness to retrieve
his equipment. But B.W. held on until the last moment saying,

"And I'd just like to say hello to the folks back home. Hi, Aunt Ruth! Hi, Mr. Antonioni – he was the principal of my old school – and hi, Grandad, you old buzzard. And I'd just like to say – " But he didn't get to say it, for Mr. Halton had finally recovered the microphone, though only after he had gritted his teeth and under his breath threatened to punch B.W. in a vulnerable location where the Gestapo had already done some damage. "Well, all I can say," B.W. said in an affronted sort of way, and sounding remarkably like yours *vraiment*, "if that's the way you're going to behave, we French peasants would just as soon not have you land here, if you don't mind. That's all I can say." And he looked at me with his wonderfully disdainful, his splendidly supercilious face, and I looked back at him ever so proudly, thinking to myself that he was getting more like me every day, and what a good thing that was for the future of civilization as we know it.